The Eagle's Vengeance

By the same author in the *Empire* series

The Eagle's Vengeance

Empire: Volume Six

ANTHONY RICHES

HODDER &
STOUGHTON

First published in 2013 by Hodder & Stoughton
An Hachette UK company

1

A CIP catalogue record for this title
is available from the British Library

Hardback ISBN 978 1 444 71190 5
Trade Paperback ISBN 978 1 444 71191 2
E-book ISBN 978 1 444 71194 3

Typeset in Plantin Light by Palimpsest Book Production Limited,
Falkirk, Stirlingshire

Printed and bound by Clays Ltd, St Ives plc

Hodder & Stoughton policy is to use papers that are natural, renewable
and recyclable products and made from wood grown in sustainable forests.
The logging and manufacturing processes are expected to conform to the
environmental regulations of the country of origin.

Hodder & Stoughton Ltd
338 Euston Road
London NW1 3BH

www.hodder.co.uk

For Julie and Julian Dear

ACKNOWLEDGEMENTS

Before we get down to the action it behoves me to admit that without the input and support of a large number of people this book wouldn't be in your hands or on your reading device. Whilst I am certain to forget someone as I write this grateful acknowledgement of their help, I really am suitably mindful of everyone's assistance with what is frequently misunderstood as a solitary trade. If I forget to write your name here then I promise to buy you a drink and salute you the very next time we meet!

My wife (for I am strictly forbidden to call her 'partner') Helen and children John, Katie and Nick tolerate the inevitable intro-spection and occasional moods that result from the process of dragging a novel from the depths of my imagination. I'm sure those long drives to wherever we're going, with me multi-tasking (driving, biting my nails and plotting, and only sometimes in that order), can be more than a little irritating. For that, and many other acts of tolerance, my love and thanks.

My agent Robin continues to dispense good advice and alco-holic lunches, and my editor Carolyn never ceases to impress with her patience and deft guidance, while the team at Hodder are always helpful, supportive and encouraging. Thank you, publishing professionals: you make the job of writing about as easy as it's ever going to get.

My pre-readers – Viv, David and John – always provide honest and insightful feedback at that 'nearly done but not quite right' stage, helping me to see the wood from the trees.

And you, reader, since you keep on reading the stories that I am compelled to write, giving life to their characters (and purpose to their creator), you play as much of a part as anyone else on this page. And, if I may be permitted a small advertisement while I'm at it, there's still a lot of the empire we haven't seen yet, and a lot of history for the Tungrians to fight their way through in the next twenty-five years of Rome's travails. Stay with me, and we'll witness the fall of a dynasty, a savage empire-spanning civil war and the iron hand of a despotic tyrant from the perspective of the soldiers who shape those bloody events.

Thank you.

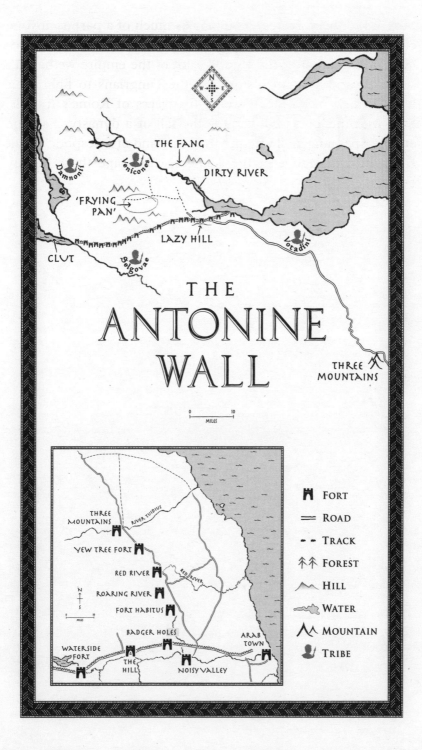

THE
ANTONINE
WALL

THE FANG

DIRTY RIVER

Damnonii

Venicones

'FRYING PAN'

LAZY HILL

CLUT

Selgovae

Votadini

THREE
MOUNTAINS

0   10
   MILES

THREE
MOUNTAINS

RIVER TUIDIUS

YEW TREE FORT

RED RIVER

RED RIVER

ROARING RIVER

FORT HABITUS

BADGER HOLES

ARAB
TOWN

WATERSIDE
FORT

THE
HILL

NOISY VALLEY

N
S
MILES

Symbol	Legend
FORT
ROAD
TRACK
FOREST
HILL
WATER
MOUNTAIN
TRIBE

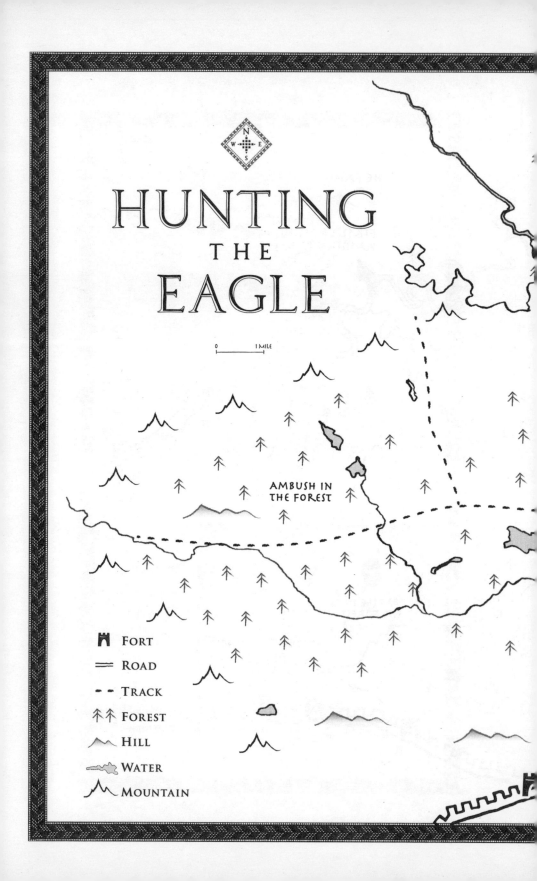

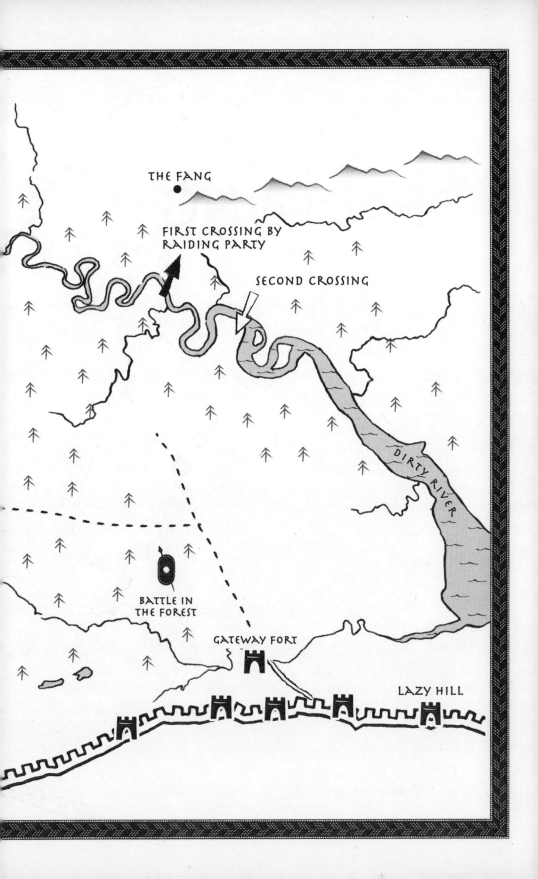

Prologue

'*Silence!* Silence for the king!'

King Naradoc of the Venicones smiled thinly at the ritual command, more usually issued to the noisy crowds of warriors who thronged the tribe's royal hall when he held audiences with his people. On those days when the tribe's elite gathered to pay homage to their ruler the hall would be filled with the noise of men competing to be seen and heard, each of them accompanied by half a dozen of the biggest and most fearsome members of his household, every one of them covered in the swirling blue tattoos that were the tribe's distinguishing feature, their weapons surrendered at the massive arched doorway under the watchful eyes of the king's guard. Each clan's heavily tattooed champions would rub shoulders as they waited for the king's entrance, friendships and enmities playing out in jocular exchanges that all parties knew would end in swift punishment if they were to escalate beyond mere words, no matter how barbed they might be. With the hammering of an iron-shod staff, wielded against the thick wooden floorboards by Naradoc's shaven-headed and hard-faced uncle Brem in his appointed role as the enforcer of the royal will, the gathered clan heads would swiftly fall silent. Turning as one man they would bow towards the throne into which Naradoc would already have settled, and he would gesture regally to them, displaying his acceptance of their obeisance.

But not today. While the hall was as thickly wreathed with smoke from the fires that warmed its air as ever, the wide open space before the king's throne was all but empty. It had been cleared for this audience at Brem's suggestion, the older man's expression inscrutable as he had delivered his opinion on the matter of exactly how their unwanted guest should die.

'It would be better not to shed this man's blood publicly, my lord King. The Selgovae will not take his murder lightly, whether he be disgraced and banished or not.'

Naradoc had nodded sagely at the wisdom of the proposal, and had thereby consented to have no presence in The Fang's hall beyond that required to ensure their security, a handful of his guards whose loyalty was beyond question. Behind him he could hear the sounds of four men taking their seats in smaller versions of the throne arrayed in an arc: his uncle, brother, cousin and nephew, the remnants of a royal family grievously reduced by the tribe's losses in battle with Rome two years before. Glancing round he saw Brem's hideously disfigured huntsman who now went by the name of Scar, so horribly wounded in the battle that had taken Naradoc's brother that for a time it had seemed unlikely that his wounds would ever heal. The Romans had left him for dead on the battlefield given the slim chance that he would ever make a saleable slave. The cicatrice that covered half his face, part bone-white and the remainder a gruesome ruddy shade of red, gave him such a fearsome aspect that the king found himself perpetually amazed that he had managed to gather about him a score and more of the tribe's young women. Over the last year he had honed them into a sisterhood of hunters, their single-minded ferocity in capturing and torturing Romans from the wall forts reducing most warriors who fought alongside them to an uneasy combination of unrequited lust – for the Vixens were renowned for their chastity and, some men muttered, their fond-ness for each other – and unease at being around women who took pleasure in hacking off their captives' sexual organs and stitching the dried remnants to their belts. When the scrapings and rustlings had died away to silence, the king waited a moment longer before tossing a question over his shoulder, consciously copying the style his brother Drust had been wont to employ during the years that had preceded his ill-fated decision to go to war alongside the Selgovae people.

'Who's first, Chamberlain?'

The decision to go to war, Naradoc mused, that had resulted in Drust's death in battle, a warrior's death celebrated in song, a glorious death with a dozen Roman soldiers dead around him, but death nonetheless, leaving his brother to mount the throne to which Drust had been so well suited, and in which he still felt so ill at ease. Brem replied to the question, and to Naradoc's ear his uncle's voice was gruff, his disapproval of their visitor's presence apparent in both tone and inflection.

'A visitor from beyond our tribal lands, my lord King, a Selgovae nobleman who has come to seek our assistance. Come forward, Calgus!'

They waited in silence while the gaunt figure came shuffling forward across the empty hall, flanked either side by hard-bitten tribesmen who were the only remaining men loyal to the former Selgovae king. The tendons in his ankles had been cut by a vengeful Roman officer two years previously, if the stories were to be believed, wounds which had long since healed, but which left him unable to walk any faster than a painfully slow flat-footed shuffle. A half-dozen of the household guard walked behind them with hands on the hilts of their swords, veterans of the war with Rome who, Brem had told him more than once, would sell their lives in his defence in an instant. When Calgus reached the edge of the royal dais he bowed as deeply as he could, holding on to his companions for support. His voice was thinner than the last time he had spoken in the great hall, but Naradoc could sense the steel in its reedy tones, and he suppressed an involuntary shiver at the deceit and guile of which the former Selgovae king had once been capable.

'King Naradoc, I thank you for receiving me in your royal hall. I come to you as king of the Selgovae, seeking your help as one ruler to another. In return I offer—'

'*King* of the Selgovae, you say?' Naradoc poured scorn into the question, shaking his head to provide his own answer. 'A half-crippled beggar and his last two retainers, more like. A once mighty ruler and the man who shook the Roman army's grip on this land you may be, but Rome still rules south of their north-ernmost wall and here you are, reduced to the status of supplicant to the Venicone people.'

Having silenced the Selgovae with his interjection, the Venicone king leaned back against the carved wooden backrest of his throne with a mischievous smile, turning in his chair to share his amusement with his family.

'You still have balls, I'll give you that, Calgus, *former* king of the Selgovae. I hear that your younger brother now rules your tribe, and that he has sued for peace with the Romans in order to relieve your people of the vicious abuse dealt out to them by the legions since they lost their ill-fated war against the empire. I hear you are forbidden to return to your former kingdom on pain of death, for the crime of starting a war you could never hope to win on the Romans' own ground. And yet you come here . . .' He shook his head in amazement at the Selgovae's sheer nerve. '*Here*, to the heart of the Venicone tribe's power, heedless of the defeat to which you led my brother Drust with your enticements, and your mistaken confidence in your own ability to defeat Rome's legions in battle. That, I am forced to admit, shows great bravery on your part.'

He paused for a moment to study the man standing before him between the warriors who had carried him to The Fang's gates.

'Well, either great bravery or equally great stupidity.' He gestured to the warriors. 'Put him on his knees.'

Sharp iron flashed in the firelight as his carefully positioned guards took Calgus's supporters unawares, stabbing their stealthily drawn long knives into the Selgovae warriors' backs and throats in a flurry of violence that made the king start despite the fact that he'd ordered it. In a blur of bright iron the two men died without even baring their own blades, their bleeding corpses pushed forward onto the floor in front of the exiled Selgovae king who closed his eyes and shook his head, putting a hand to the bridge of his nose. A rough push in his back was enough to send him full length onto the hall's cold stone floor, his hands smearing the pools of blood spilling from his men's corpses. Naradoc nodded down at him, a half-smile expressing his approval of the other man's helpless prostration before him.

'That's better. Now we see the real Calgus, stripped of any pretence to nobility or power. There you lie, crawling in the blood of your last two friends in the entire world, a helpless shadow of the man you once claimed to be. So tell me, once king and present beggar, what is it that you believed you might gain by coming here? What strange process of thought was it that gave you the expectation of any greeting other than sharp iron, given your part in the disaster that befell my kingdom two years ago?'

Calgus pushed himself laboriously up off the floor and into a kneeling position, wiping his hands clean of his companions' blood on the worn cloak that was wrapped about him. His long red hair had faded in hue since his crippling, and was shot through with streaks of grey, but any man who had known him at the height of his powers, in the days when his bloody uprising had tested the Roman army's grip on northern Britannia to its limits, would have immediately recognised the glint in his eye.

'And greetings to you, Naradoc, King of the Venicones. My thanks for your most generous welcome –' he waved his hands at the corpses before him '– and for ridding me of the burden of these two. In truth, their wit and charm had long since started to wear a little thin, although I might have wished for a gentler way to find relief from their presence. As to why I come to you now, the answer is simple enough. I possess something from which I believe your tribe can profit, a symbol of Roman power upon which few men ever get to lay their hands. I still have the Sixth Legion's imperial eagle, torn from their ranks in battle as we overwhelmed them early in the war. The loss of such a thing is a disaster for them, and its possession by a man such as *you* would be salt to rub in their wounds, now that they have realised that their encampment on the wall built by their emperor Antoninus is not likely to last beyond the end of the summer. The legions, I hear, are in a state of revolt at being sent so far north and forced to risk the ire of your warriors, the righteous anger that has already led them to abandon this more northerly wall twice before. Your open possession of their eagle will be the final straw upon that particular horse's back, I suspect.'

He stopped talking and sat back upon the haunches of his wasted legs, the muscles withered from lack of meaningful exercise. Naradoc shifted slightly under his calculating gaze, shaking his head slowly from side to side.

'I found myself wondering, Calgus, as you were speaking, why is it that I feel a distinct lack of comfort around you? And then the answer came to me. You are a snake, pure and simple, a devious, treacherous reptile in whom I would repose any trust only at the greatest risk to myself. You offer me a Roman eagle?' The king waved a dismissive hand. 'You can keep it. The Romans are a single-minded people, a vindictive people, and I know full well that they will not cease hunting for this lost icon of their power until it is recovered, at whatever cost to them in blood. I also know that they will visit their revenge upon whoever is left holding the eagle a dozen times whatever they calculate their own loss to have been. They would send forth a legion's strength to punish us, if they believed we held this symbol of their power. And if our fortress here is impregnable against any attack they might make, there are dozens of our settlements that would be unable to resist them. No, Calgus, you can keep your eagle, as I wish you had withheld the invitation to my brother Drust to join the uprising that not only cost him his life but also robbed my tribe of thousands of warriors. I recall only too well your words in this very hall as he sat where I sit now, promising him both plunder and freedom from the Roman threat for ever. And what rewards did your war bring to my people? Only disaster, and evil tidings that thrust me onto a throne that Drust should have occupied for years to come.'

He snorted derision, shaking his head angrily at the Selgovae.

'And now, given that you're a sad, broken shell of the man you once were, I dismiss you from my presence. Go now, or risk my implacable anger . . .' His hard expression slowly turned to a grim smile, as Calgus looked about himself helplessly. 'But of course, you've nowhere to go, have you, with your people turned against you and your last supporters dead on the floor before you? And I'm sure you'll be unsurprised that I intend to keep your horses, which I suspect were probably stolen from my tribe in any case. So, what alternatives do you have now, eh Calgus? How shall we deal with this uncomfortable situation into which you have thrust yourself? I could have my men help you to the gates, but what then? Nobody in my kingdom will feed you out of pity, I can assure you of that. Your name is not much loved around these parts. Perhaps the best thing I can do is offer you the relief of a swift death, rather than the protracted discomfort of starvation, or even being pulled to pieces by the wolves when you are too weak to resist? It's your choice, Calgus. Take all the time you want in making it . . .'

The Selgovae looked up at him with a gentle smile, and Naradoc narrowed his eyes in suspicion.

'Faced with the options of a slow death and quick one, it's in a man's nature to look for the third choice, wouldn't you agree?' The cripple raised a hand to forestall any reply, still smiling up into the king's abrupt discomfiture. 'Knowing that I was likely to face just such a hostile response to my reasoned approach, I took the precaution of carefully preparing the ground for my arrival over several months of careful negotiations with the men upon whose power you depend. You would have been disappointed at the ease with which my servants were able to come and go with my messages to the nobles arrayed behind you, Naradoc, and further distressed by the readiness with which *they* have agreed with my suggestions as to how your tribe might be *better* ruled.'

The king leapt to his feet, pointing a trembling finger at the kneeling figure before him.

'*Behead him!*' He stepped forward, clenching his hand into a fist. 'I'll nail your ears to my roof beams, you rotting cocked spawn of a deformed whore! I'll throw your guts to my dogs to play with! I'll . . .'

He stopped in mid-sentence, shocked to feel the sudden unnerving prick of cold iron on the back of his neck. Calgus

raised an eyebrow at him, tipping his head to one side in a deliberate caricature of the king's posture a moment before.

'As is so often the case, the single most terrifying moment of
your life can come just when you least expect it, eh Naradoc? I
experienced mine alongside your brother, when I realised that the
Roman camp we were storming was nothing more than bait to
lure us into a trap, bait your *revered* brother was no more able
to resist taking than a dog with the scent of a bitch in heat. He
was a headstrong, foolish man, Naradoc, and if he had been just
a *little* more calculating he might still be wearing that crown, with
you sat behind him in a position rather better suited to your
limited abilities. Instead of that you're now experiencing the
bowel-loosening sensation of a sword-point in your back where
there should be stout noblemen lined up behind you, if you'd had
the intelligence and ruthlessness to keep them there. I would call
you *King* Naradoc, if it wasn't so obvious to both of us that you're
no longer the king of anything more substantial than the shit that's
trying to burst its way out of your backside. '

Naradoc stared helplessly down into Calgus's eyes, realising
with a further, sickening lurch of his stomach that the crippled
Selgovae was shaking his head at him with a look that was more
pity than contempt.

'Do take a look around you, your *majesty*, and see what remains
of your kingdom.'

Naradoc turned his head to meet his family's eyes with a
sidelong gaze, only to find their return stares expressionless for
the most part. His brother had the good grace to look vaguely
embarrassed, but his uncle, cousin and nephew all wore faces that
might as well have been crafted from stone. The man whose sword
was prickling the back of his neck, the hunt master Scar who, he
realised with a defeated sag of his shoulders, had been his uncle's
sworn man since Brem had rescued him from the battlefield and
nursed him back to health, stared back without any expression
capable of moving the mask of scar tissue that clung lopsidedly
to his face. The king tried to speak, but the words came out as
no more than a whispered croak.

'You *bastards* . . .'

Calgus laughed at his bitterness.

'They're just realists, Naradoc. Your younger brother gets the crown, that's obvious enough. Your mother's brother Brem gets your wife, for whom he tells me he has long harboured urges hardly fitting in a man when expressed towards his queen. He tells me that he plans to spread her legs in your bed quickly enough though, so the status will hardly matter. His son, your cousin, gets your oldest daughter, who I'm sure you will be the first to admit is of the age to be bedded. I'm sure she'll give him a fine crop of sons with hips like those. And your brother's son gets your younger girl child. She may be a little young for the marital bed, but he's only a boy himself. I'm sure they'll work it out together, eh? And you . . .'

He paused for a moment, waving a hand at the men behind the king.

'My lords, whilst I am comfortable enough in this position of supplication, it might be more fitting if I were to continue my employment as the *new* king's adviser on my feet?'

A pair of men stepped forward at a signal from Naradoc's brother, helping the Selgovae back into a standing position. He bowed his head to the new king, all the time keeping his eyes locked on Naradoc's furious gaze.

'You made the fatal mistake, my lord was-king, of failing to safeguard your own position once you were obliged to put on your crown. Those first few years on the throne are never easy, are they? There's always such a fine balance to be trod between being too harsh and seeming too soft. In hindsight I'd say you should have found a way to quietly dispose of your younger brother. I believe that hunting accidents are a favourite means of both avoiding future conflict in the family and showing your teeth to the surviving members to put them in their place, but then that's not really your style, is it? Such a shame, when a judiciously timed murder or two can often avert a great deal of inconvenience . . .'

He glanced across at the king's younger brother, smiling at the predatory look with which he was staring at Naradoc's back. 'It's just as well your sibling doesn't seem overly troubled by the morality of arranging for *your* disposal, now that your situations are reversed.'

Finding his tongue with the sudden realisation that his death was imminent, Naradoc roared his defiance at the brother who had so comprehensively betrayed him.

'You bloody fools! This man will have you at each other's throats in days! And you, brother, how long before you too have just such a *hunting accident*, leaving the way clear for our uncle to take the throne!'

Even as the feeling that he might have been duped sank into his brother's eyes, Calgus spoke again, his tone warm in contrast to the words that spelled out the would-be usurper's fate.

'You know he's right, my lord. You really are quite exceptionally stupid not to have had the good sense to side with your brother the king, but that's just a lesson you've learned too late. And now that I consider it, I suspect that an accident is somewhat less likely to convince given that we'll have two victims to mourn . . .' He paused, his gaze alighting on the man's white-faced son, barely into his teens. 'No, my mistake, of course that will have to be *three* victims, won't it?'

He turned to the two men's uncle, opening his hands in question.

'Perhaps a family squabble under the influence of an excess of your excellent beer might have more credibility as the regrettable cause of your being forced to take the throne, obviously with the greatest of reluctance? What do *you* think, my lord, King Brem?'

I

'*Mercurius?* Mercurius is the winged messenger, right?' The First Tungrian Cohort's senior centurion shook his head in weary disbelief, rubbing a hand through his thick black hair. 'We've marched all the way from Dacia to the edge of the German Sea, over a thousand miles in every weather from burning sunshine to freezing rain, and now the only thing between my boots and home soil is a mile or two of foggy water . . .' He sighed, shaking his head as he stared out into the thick fog. 'So you'd think a ship called the fucking *Mercurius* with over a hundred big strong lads at the oars would be moving a little bit quicker than the slow march. This is a bloody warship after all, so surely all the man in charge has to do is say the word to have us skipping across the waves.'

Tribune Scaurus turned to look at his colleague Julius with an indulgent smile, while the three centurions standing behind him exchanged wry glances.

'Still feeling unwell are you, First Spear?'

Julius shook his head dourly.

'I've puked up everything in my guts, puked once more for good fortune, and then last of all I chewed the round pink thing and swallowed. I've nothing left to give, Tribune, and so my body has settled in a state of discontented resentment rather than open rebellion. Now I'm just bored with this snail's pace that seems to be the best this tub can do.'

'Aphrodite's tits and hairy muff, don't let the captain hear you calling his pride and joy a *tub*! I caught him stroking the ship's side yesterday, and when he saw I was watching he just gave me one of those looks that said "I know, but what's a man to do?"'

Scaurus turned and nodded at the second largest of the four centurions standing about him, a heavily muscled and bearded man in his late twenties.

'Quite so, Centurion Dubnus. The man's as proud of his command as a legion eagle bearer, and just as likely to reach for the polish from the look of it. Did you not see the way he frowned when the goat they sacrificed before we sailed sprayed blood all over the deck?'

The tribune turned back to face Julius, the first spear just as heavily set and with the same thick beard as Dubnus, sharing his brooding demeanour and predisposition to dispensing casual violence to malcontents and laggards, although where the younger man's thick mane and beard were jet black, the senior centurion's hair was visibly starting to turn grey.

'And as for your urgency to get your feet on dry land, First Spear, I'd imagine that the *Mercurius*'s captain is probably equally keen not to run his command ashore in the fog. Apparently we'll know we're getting closer when we can hear the Arab Town trumpets, if his navigation's up to the job. And remember if you will, that for our colleague here a return to Britannia raises fresh questions as to just *who* might be waiting for us when we arrive.'

He tipped his head at the least heavily muscled of the centurions, a lean, hawk-faced young man who had sought refuge with the Tungrian cohort two years previously and who was now listening to their conversation with a look of imperturbability, then turned back to his senior centurion.

'News of our return to the province will have gone before us, Julius; you can be assured that the return of two full cohorts of auxiliaries will be of great interest to the governor's staff. You know as well as I do that there are never enough soldiers to go around. For all we know there might well be senior officers waiting for us when we dock, backed up by a century or two of legionaries fresh from battering the Brigantes back into an appropriate state of subservience. We have to face the possibility that the imperial arrest warrant in the name of Marcus Valerius Aquila, formerly of the praetorian guard, might by now also mention that the fugitive senator's son is going under the alias of Centurion Marcus Tribulus Corvus of the First Tungrian Cohort. After all, there's been more than enough time for the authorities to make the connection between those two names, especially when you stop to consider the fact that it's been over a year since we allowed that blasted corn officer Excingus to escape with the knowledge of our colleague's true identity.'

The light of realisation dawned on Julius's face.

'And that's why we're travelling on this warship, rather than wallowing around on the sea with the rest of the men in those bloody awful troop ships? And why we've shipped four tent parties of the biggest, nastiest men in the cohort along with their distinctively unpleasant centurion.'

The last of the officers grinned jovially down at him, his voice a bass growl.

'Well spotted, little brother.'

Scaurus nodded, his face an impassive mask despite the urge to laugh at the effortless way in which Titus, commander of the Tungrians' pioneer century, got away with treating his first spear like an uppity younger sibling.

'Indeed it is, First Spear. *If* we face a welcoming committee, then it may be small enough to be faced down by my rank and your men's muscle long enough to see Centurion *Corvus* here safely away into the hills. And if, in the worst case, we're greeted by too many men to bluff or bully into submission, then our young colleague here can at least surrender with his dignity intact, and without his wife watching or his soldiers indulging in any noble but doomed heroics.'

He turned sharply to his bodyguard who was lurking a few feet away with a look of inscrutability, although long experience told him that the German would have heard every word.

'That goes for you too, Arminius.'

The tribune's German bodyguard grunted tersely, staring morosely out into the fog.

'You will forgive me if I do not promise to follow your command absolutely in this matter, Rutilius Scaurus? You know that I owe the centurion—'

'A life? How could I forget? Every time I turn around to look for you you're either teaching the boy Lupus how to throw sharp iron about or away watching the centurion's back as he wades into yet another unequal fight. I sometimes wonder if you're still actually *my* slave . . .'

A trumpet note sounded far out in the fog that wreathed the silent sea's black surface, muffled to near inaudibility by the clinging vapour, followed by another, higher in pitch, and the warship's captain stepped forward with a terse nod.

'That's the Arab Town horn. Seems we're making landfall just as planned, Tribune. Your feet will soon be back on solid ground, eh gentlemen?'

Titus put a spade-like hand on Marcus's shoulder.

'Never fear, little brother, whether there's one man or a thousand of them waiting for you, you'll not be taken while my men and I have wind in our lungs.'

His friend shook his head, and shrugged without any change of expression.

'No, Bear, not this time. If there are men waiting for me then I'll surrender to them meekly enough, rather than adding more innocent blood to my bill. And besides, the dreams still tell me that my destiny awaits me in Rome, whether I like it or not.'

Dubnus nodded, his voice taking on a helpful tone.

'It's true. He was rolling around in his scratcher for half the night and muttering on about something or other to do with revenge. I put it down to the amount of the captain's Iberian that he'd consumed earlier in the evening, while I was cursing him for a noisy bastard and trying to get to sleep myself . . .'

Marcus nodded with a sad smile.

'It's a rare night when my father doesn't rise from the underworld in order to remind me that I am yet to pay Praetorian Prefect Perennis out for the deaths of my family, while our departed colleague Carius Sigilis fingerpaints the same accusatory words in his own blood across whatever flat surface he finds in the dream.'

Julius and Dubnus rolled their eyes at each other.

'Those words being *"The Emperor's Knives"*, right?'

Marcus nodded at Dubnus's question. Sigilis, a legionary tribune who had served alongside the Tungrians as they had fought at the sharp end of the struggle to beat off a Sarmatae incursion into Dacia, had named the men who he believed had murdered Senator Aquila and slaughtered his family in the days before he himself had died bloodily at the hands of tribal infiltrators. He had told the young centurion that he had heard the story from the mouth of an informer hired by his own father, a distinguished member of the senatorial order whose disquiet at the increasing frequency of financially motivated judicial assassinations under the new emperor, Commodus, had led him to commission a discreet investigation into the matter.

'Yes Julius, it's still the same message after all the months that we spent making our way back down the Danubius and the Rhenus. The shades of the departed still harass me night after night, hungry for blood to repay their own, and for revenge which can only be taken in Rome, it seems. I'll admit that I grow weary of their persistence on the subject, when it seems unlikely I will ever see the city of my birth again in this lifetime.'

The Arab Town port's foghorn blew again, the mournful notes distant in the clinging mist, and Marcus turned to stare out at the seemingly impenetrable grey veil.

'So if my time for capture and repatriation has come, I will accept that fate without a fight. It seems to me that I've been running long enough.'

'Only in Britannia, eh Tribune?'

'Quite so, Prefect Castus. Quite so . . .'

The younger of the two men standing on the Arab Town dockside hunched deeper into his cloak, pulling the garment's thick woollen hood over his head with a despairing look up into the fog that wreathed the port's buildings. His companion, a shorter and stockier man who seemed comfortable enough in the wind's chill, shot him an amused look and then glanced around at the three centuries of hard-bitten legionaries waiting in a long double line behind them. Apparently satisfied with what he saw, he resumed his vigil across the harbour's almost invisible waters, waiting until the foghorns had been blown again before speaking again.

'Yes, Fulvius Sorex, only in Britannia could the fog be quite this impenetrable. Thirty years of service to Rome has taught me that every province has its endearing little characteristics, those features a man never forgets once he's experienced them. In Syria it was the flies that would crawl onto the meat in your mouth while you were chewing, given half a chance. In Judea it was the Jews, and their bloody-minded resentment of our boots on their land almost a century after Vespasian finally crushed their resistance into the dust. In Pannonia it was the cold in winter, harsh enough to freeze a river solid all the way down to its bed, and in Dacia . . .'

He fell silent, and after a moment the younger man glanced round to find his companion staring out into the fog with an unfathomable expression.

'And in Dacia?'

Castus shook his head, a slow smile spreading across his face.

'Ah, the rest of the morning wouldn't be long enough to do Dacia justice. But, and this is my point, this misty, swamp-ridden, rain-soaked nest of evil-tempered, blue-painted madmen gives Dacia some bloody stiff competition. Let's just say that . . .' His expression hardened. 'There! There they are!'

He thrust out an arm to point at a dark spot in the murk, and his companion narrowed his eyes to gaze in the indicated direction, nodding slowly.

'You know I do believe you're right, Prefect Castus. I can hear the oars.'

As they watched, huddling into their cloaks for warmth, the indistinct shape gradually coalesced out of the fog and hardened into the predatory lines of a warship being propelled slowly across the harbour's dark-green water by slow, careful strokes of its banked oars.

'That will be what we've been waiting for, I presume?'

Sorex nodded in reply to the older man's question.

'I expect so. That, and the First Tungrian Cohort, or so the despatch said, with the Second Cohort to follow in a few days' time. Bloody auxiliaries . . .'

The prefect's smile became wry, and he turned to raise an eyebrow at his superior, a man a good twenty years younger than him and no more than a year into his military career.

'I'd be careful not to take that tone with their commanding officer if I were you, Tribune. As I recall the man, he's not the type to receive a slur of any nature without turning it around and ramming it straight back down your throat. He always was a headstrong type even in the days when he was little more than a boy in a man's tunic, and he's gained more than enough experience of battle since then to have worn his patience with *less* experienced men as thin as my third best pair of boots.'

Sorex pouted, not deigning to make any response as the crew shipped their oars neatly and allowed the vessel to coast gently up to the dock under the helmsman's skilled control. Fully resolved out of the fog's murk, the ship was revealed as a swift and deadly engine of maritime destruction, with bolt throwers mounted fore and aft and a crew of thirty marines standing to attention on the main deck. Men leapt smartly down onto the dock's wooden planks and swiftly moored their vessel against the quay before reaching to grasp the gangplank being thrust out from the ship's side. The captain was the first man down the narrow bridge, a hard-faced bearded man who threw Sorex a perfunctory salute and nodded to Castus as he waved a hand back at the docked warship.

'Yes, Tribune Sorex, your cargo's safe. There's an imperial official who's not taken his eyes off the chests all the way across from Germania, Procurator Avus, as dry and humourless a functionary as it's ever been my misfortune to welcome aboard the *Mercurius*. The bloody fool even insisted on sleeping on the deck beside them, despite the fact that I had half a dozen of my marines standing guard on them at all times.' He turned back to the ship and barked an order at his second in command. 'Get those chests brought on deck and ready to unload, and make sure the marines stay with 'em to keep the soldiers at arm's length until they're off the ship and properly signed over to the army! Those thieving fuckers could be up one of Vesta's virgins without the bitch knowing that she was no longer in possession of her cherry until the bulge started to show.'

A party of men was making their way down the plank behind him, led by a tall, angular man clad in the sculpted bronze armour of a senior officer, and Prefect Castus stepped forward to meet him as his feet touched the quayside, his hand thrust out in greeting.

'Rutilius Scaurus! Few sights could give me more pleasure than to see *you* returning to this revolting excuse for a province!'

The newcomer stared down at him for a moment before a smile of recognition creased his face. Taking the older man's hand he nodded slowly.

'Artorius Castus! I've not seen you for the best part of ten years, when you were first spear of Twelfth Thunderbolt and I was a fresh-faced junior tribune, good for nothing more than running messages and annoying the senior centurions with my enthusiasm and ignorance. I thought you would long since have retired to enjoy the fruits of your service.'

Castus grinned back at him fondly.

'Retirement's not for me, young man. They made me Provost of the fleet at Misenum as a reward for long service, but you know as well as I do that all the Rome fleet's sailors really do is stage mock sea battles in the Flavian arena and raise the awnings over the audience when the sun gets too hot to bear. That's no life for a soldier, now is it?' Scaurus shot him a knowing glance. 'So, I used what little influence I had to get appointed as Sixth Victorius's camp prefect, and here I am up to my arse in unfriendly natives once again. But I'm forgetting my manners . . .'

He waved a hand at his companion who was waiting with a look of barely restrained impatience.

'This is my current commanding officer, Tribune Gnaeus Fulvius Sorex. Fulvius Sorex, allow me to introduce Tribune Gaius Rutilius Scaurus, the officer commanding the First and Second Tungrian cohorts.'

Scaurus turned to the legion tribune and bowed formally, although his expression was wary as he looked the other man up and down.

'Tribune Sorex, I must confess myself slightly confused. When we left the province the Sixth Legion was under the command of Legatus Equitius, and the tribal rebellion was well on the way to being contained. Perhaps you could—'

Castus raised a hand to forestall any further discussion.

'Indeed, we *could* elucidate on what has happened since then, but not here. Perhaps we might repair to the transit barracks for a more private discussion?'

He peered past Scaurus at the five men behind him, and the tribune turned and raised a hand to invite them forward.

'My apologies, I was distracted by being greeted off the ship by a colleague of such distinction. Allow me to introduce the First Tungrian Cohort's first spear, Julius, and my aide, Centurion Corvus. Julius is my intended temporary replacement in the event of any mishap, and Corvus would in turn step up into his boots as senior centurion should the need arise, which is why I tend to take them everywhere and make sure that they know everything I know. As to the others, this is Centurion Dubnus, the long-haired gentleman is my slave and bodyguard, Arminius, and the centurion bowing the gangplank under his weight is Titus, the commander of my pioneer century.' He turned back to the mist-covered waters. 'And since I'm guessing it will take several hours for my command to straggle into port, I'll leave the last three here to make sure that our men are handled appropriately when they stagger off the transports. As you suggest, let us decamp to somewhere both private and a little warmer?'

Turning away from the dockside he shot a hard glance at the German, raising an eyebrow and staring significantly at the heavy chests that were being craned over the warship's side with ostentatious care by the crew. As each one touched the quayside a party of six heavily built men attached thick ropes to its carrying rings and hauled it over to where another half-dozen marines were guarding those that had gone before it, their demeanour that of men who knew how painful life could get were they to fail in their duty, and all conducted under the watchful eye of the close-lipped official who had accompanied them across the ocean. The camp prefect led them across the dock and into the fortress that loomed over it, walking swiftly to a transit barrack from whose chimneys lines of grey smoke were rising. Once they had taken off their cloaks and gone through the usual ritual of warming their hands at the glowing stove while the camp prefect thrust another log into its cherry-red belly and bid them to take their seats, Scaurus addressed the subject that had been raised at the quayside with the same note of concern in his voice.

'So tell me, gentlemen, now that we have our privacy, is your news bad? Legatus Equitius was both a colleague and a friend to all three of us, and a good man besides.'

Prefect Castus looked to his colleague, who merely shook his head and beckoned him to continue with the tale.

'You're wondering if the legatus has been killed? It's nothing that simple . . .' He took a seat before continuing, gesturing to the other men to make themselves comfortable. 'This will take some telling. You've been away in Germania for what, a year or so?'

Scaurus nodded.

'Fifteen months. My cohorts' initial mission to Tungrorum in Germania Inferior resulted in our being sent halfway across the empire to Dacia in defence of an imperial goldmine. It's taken us half a year to make it back here, mainly due to the Danubius freezing solid for the best part of two months.'

Castus smiled knowingly, winking at Sorex.

'Ah, there it is, just as I told you, Fulvius Sorex, Pannonia in the winter. Did you lose any men to the cold?'

Julius nodded, his face hard with the memory.

'A few, until we learned not to put sentries out after dark during the worst of it.'

'Yes indeed. Anyone foolish enough to make a move on you under such conditions would be stiff as a plank themselves long before they were in position to attack. But I digress. Suffice to say that a lot has happened in Britannia while you've been away. The Brigantes' rebellion south of the wall was suppressed easily enough, given that the tribes to the north had been put down so hard before it started. I believe you played some part in that?'

'We had a hand in it. Do continue, Prefect.'

Castus smiled indulgently at Scaurus.

'I see you retain the same impatience you had as a younger man, Rutilius Scaurus, but I take your point. With the Selgovae, the Carvetii and the Votadini tribes all safely back in their boxes it was easy enough for Governor Marcellus to march his legions back south and rip through the Brigantes, and indeed he did so with such gusto that I expect they'll be keeping their heads down for a good long time. Two men of military age crucified for every soldier that we lost, villages burned out for any hint of collaboration with the rebels, well, you know how it goes. The revolt collapsed almost overnight once the tribesmen realised that we were deadly serious about ending it, and that, we presumed, was that. I'd joined the Sixth Victorious by that time, and I was more than happy with what I found, a well-trained and aggressive legion whose commander was more than capable even if he did lack a thick stripe on his tunic.'

He shot a quick smile at the tribune, whose senatorial status was clear enough to the other men, and Sorex shrugged easily.

'You know my views on the subject, Prefect Castus, a man doesn't need to be of the senatorial class to have the ability to command a legion. Indeed Praetorian Prefect Perennis seems bent on removing the requirement, to judge from what I hear in my correspondence from Rome.'

Castus inclined his head in recognition of the point, flicking a glance across the Tungrian officers to find the young man who had been introduced as Centurion Corvus staring at Sorex with narrowed eyes, an expression which softened in an instant as he sensed the prefect's gaze upon him.

'So, all tribal uprisings in the legion's operational area were defeated, and that, I assumed, would be that. The men were looking forward to the resumption of garrison duties and the chance to see the inside of a bathhouse again, while the centurions were planning some nice, hard patrolling to keep their troops in shape, and the occasional raid to make sure the natives knew who was on top. And, I have to say, I was in full agreement that this was the only sensible course of action given that the men had been at war for the best part of two years and were desperate for a rest and the chance to see the inside of their home fortresses again.' Castus paused significantly for a moment. 'And of course I was almost immediately proven to have it all wrong. Governor Marcellus had complete victory for the taking, but in that moment of triumph he over-reached himself. He decided to go one better than just restoring order to the north of the Emperor Hadrian's wall and enforcing the peace from our existing line of forts. He decided instead to re-establish control of the northern tribes' lands with boots on the ground, rather than simply following the decision that was made twenty years ago to simply leave them outside of the empire.'

Scaurus shook his head in disbelief.

'Surely he didn't . . . not the *northern* wall?'

'He won't get any closer to those chests than the rest of us managed. Those boys look every bit as keen as the marines were. And your lads aren't going to make them any friendlier behaving like that, are they?'

Titus nodded his smug agreement with Dubnus's bluntly stated opinion, and the two men watched pensively as Arminius strolled away from them up the quayside with his hands behind his back, ignoring the thirty-odd pioneers who were amusing themselves by sneering over at the legionaries and laughing with each other in the manner of men who were sharing a private joke. Their centurion took a deep breath of the sea-tinged air, inflating his barrel chest and rolling his massive head around his shoulders before replying.

'And why send a barbarian to do a job that needs treading softly, eh? That boy's never really happy without a sword in his hand and someone to fight.'

Predictably, the German got no closer to the chests than the nearest of the legionaries, who simply shook his head discouragingly and pointed wordlessly back at the watching Tungrian centurions. Arminius shrugged and turned away, pulling his cloak tighter about him as a wind from the sea swirled the mist that still hung in the air.

'Told you so.' Titus hooked a thumb over his shoulder at his men waiting patiently behind them. 'The only way to get to see what's in them would be to let my boys loose on those children . . .'

Dubnus shook his head in apparent disgust.

'Bugger me, Bear, do you ever give it a rest? My boys this, my boys that . . .' He spat over the quayside into the dark water swirling around the jetty's thick wooden pilings. 'I'll tell you what, let's swap. You can have a play with my century, and find out what it's like commanding men with a little more in their favour than big muscles and loud voices, and I'll give your boys a taste of real discipline, rather than all that warrior brotherhood rubbish you spoil them with.'

Titus smirked at his colleague in return, drawing himself up to his full height and looking down his nose at the irritated Dubnus.

'Discipline? With a bunch of girly men you stole from a legion? Men their centurion was happy to see the back of given their habit of running away whenever a fight was at hand? Any of my boys could run your century, little brother, so why would I lower myself to such a thing?' A crafty smile crept onto his face. 'And besides, it takes a big man to control a herd of bulls like the Tenth, I'm not sure you'd be our sort of centurion, *Your Highness.*'

Castus nodded grimly at the Tungrian tribune.

'Oh yes, he *did*. He ordered all three legions north again, minus a couple of cohorts apiece to keep control of the Brigantes, and he ordered all three of the legions' legati to re-establish Roman control over the northern tribes in the only way he believed possible, by putting their lands inside the empire. He re-garrisoned the wall that the Emperor Antoninus built a hundred miles to the north of the wall raised by his predecessor Hadrian . . .' The camp prefect sighed, shaking his head. 'The idiot sent the legions north to re-occupy a defensive line that has been found to be untenable on the two previous occasions it has been manned. Even I, brand new to the province, could see that it was a mistake, and the gods know that the legati did their best to dissuade him from the idea, but you know what a stubborn old bastard he is once he has the bit between his teeth. The worst of it is that he did it without any reference to Rome, whose permission for such a rash move we can be sure would never have been forthcoming.'

Scaurus stared in disbelief at the older man.

'Ulpius Marcellus took it upon his own head to set imperial frontier policy? Had he gone utterly *mad*?'

'Apparently not, but he might as well have. Once it became clear to the legions that they were going to be occupying the new line of defence for the foreseeable future, well, they revolted, and pretty much to a man. The legionaries of the Twentieth went as far as to offer their legatus Priscus the purple, which was the one thing guaranteed to get the attention of Rome even if he did display the remarkably good sense to refuse their generous offer of the throne. Once the praetorian prefect got to hear about the whole sorry mess he started throwing orders around like the bride's mother on the wedding day, understandably given that he's effectively running the empire, and none of it was ever going to be pretty. The governor's already gone, of course, recalled to Rome by a fast courier for an interview without wine with some fairly serious characters, I'd imagine, and with his career in tatters around him.'

He shook his head again.

'He'll be lucky to keep his head on his shoulders. The legion commanders were next on the list, naturally enough, although the orders were for them to hand over command to their senior tribunes and step down to await replacements from the capital. The rumour, as the despatch rider told me once I had him appropriately well oiled, is that Prefect Perennis intends to put equestrian officers in command of all three legions in order to teach the senate a sharp lesson as to the realities of power, promoting men who learned their trade in command of auxiliary cohorts like yours . . .'

'And so there you have it, gentlemen.' Tribune Sorex's voice rode over his colleague's with the ease of a man born and raised to rule those around him. 'Legatus Equitius is confined to the fortress at Yew Grove, with all of the respect due to his rank of course, and I am empowered to keep the legion in hand. Soon enough now I expect a new legatus to take command of Sixth Victorious, and a new governor to deliver the orders which I expect will have us marching south again.'

Julius looked at him with a questioning expression.

'You're still occupying the northern wall, Tribune?'

Sorex shrugged.

'Of course we are, Centurion. We were ordered to do so by the previous governor and we've received no orders to withdraw since then, only the despatch which called Ulpius Marcellus home and relieved the three legions' legati of their commands. An uncontrolled withdrawal could quickly turn into an undisciplined rush south, or worse, trigger another mutiny. So, for the time being we hold all twenty-six of the northern wall's forts, and we will continue to do so until ordered to withdraw by the replacement legion commanders.'

Tribune Scaurus stroked his chin, his eyes narrowed in thought.

'All of which is very interesting, and I greatly appreciate the time taken by two august personages such as yourselves to come all the way out to the end of the wall to brief me, although I doubt it needed both, or even either of you to pass a message that could just as easily have been delivered, albeit without quite such sensitivity, by a centurion.' He stood up, turning his back to the stove and luxuriating in its heat before looking down at the two men with a look that combined curiosity with an edge of irritation.

'So, am I right, gentlemen?'

Dubnus shook his head in mock amazement.

'*Our* sort of centurion? There's the problem, right there! You've let them get soft, *big* brother, unused to the touch of proper discipline. I pity whoever gets them when you stop a bluenose spear, or finish your twenty-five and go to live out your days with some pig-ugly giant of a woman who'll be able to suffer you on top of her without bursting. That poor bastard will have to use a tree trunk for a vine stick, won't he! And you can shove that "your highness" crap right up your big fat arse, the days when my father ruled in the lands south of Hadrian's Wall are dead and gone.'

Titus laughed aloud, well used to their habitual arguments about the way he led his men and delighted to have drawn blood with his jibe.

'I shouldn't worry your pretty head on the subject, *Prince* Dubnus, you'll never have command of my boys. I plan on outliving you, given your habit of throwing yourself into the thick of the fight at the first opportunity. You'll be the one who ends up as a pincushion, not me!'

The two men grinned at each other, ignoring Arminius who was shaking his head in disgust at their argument.

'Two grown men arguing as to who's got the biggest prick? If your first spear was here, he'd be telling you both to get a grip.'

The two centurions turned to look at him with hard smiles, and Dubnus smirked in amusement.

'And this from a long-haired slave whose main duty is to test the heat of his master's bath!'

The German raised a sardonic eyebrow.

'Serving Rutilius Scaurus has many benefits that you may not have considered, Dubnus. Remember all those dinner parties he was invited to at every fort we camped outside on our march back up the Rhenus? While you were taking your pick of the rather thin selection of overpriced and underwhelming whores on offer, I was taking *my* pick of the female servants in a nice warm kitchen, once I'd eaten my fill. And, I'll remind you, I get to know where we're going long before it filters down to your level.'

He paused, looking at the chests in their orderly line along the quayside.

'So I'll tell you this for nothing: from my experience of senior officers, the way those two invited our boy for a private chat, there's no way we're going to be strolling back to whatever dunghill it is you're keen to get back to any time soon.'

Prefect Castus looked at his colleague with an expression which very clearly communicated that his part of the briefing was at an end.

'As I told you, Fulvius Sorex, Rutilius Scaurus has lost neither his perceptive abilities nor his direct manner in the last ten years. I suggest you enlighten him as to our purpose in coming here.'

Sorex nodded, stepping forward.

'Yes, that's astute of you, Rutilius Scaurus. We could indeed have sent a junior officer to bring you the latest news, which means, as you have already surmised, that your presence here presents us with something of an opportunity.'

Marcus spoke, his voice suitably respectful despite the question's sharp edge.

'It's more than that, isn't it, Tribune? We present you with the only means possible to get something done, something you judge to be vital?'

Scaurus stared at the young centurion for a moment before turning back to Sorex with a disarming smile.

'Forgive my aide his temerity, colleague, he does have the tendency to speak out of turn when something occurs to him, although on this occasion I suspect he's cut to the heart of the matter. Do continue, Centurion Corvus.'

The young centurion spoke again, his voice clear and hard in the barrack's silence.

'From what you've said, Tribune, every other military unit in the whole northern military zone is under orders to hold position, orders with all the weight of the throne behind them. The sort of orders that a man disregards at the risk of his career, his life and even his family's lives, if he miscalculates badly enough. And here we are, as if sent by our Lord Mithras himself, the answer to your prayers for a force of men big enough to do whatever it is you think needs doing, and not subject to the restrictions placed upon your freedom of action by Prefect Perennis.'

In the young centurion's mouth the praetorian prefect's name become something akin to an expression of hatred, spat from between bared teeth with the vehemence of a man ridding his mouth of venom sucked from a snake bite. Scaurus spoke quickly, taking back the focus of attention, his voice deliberately breezy.

'My man Corvus has the measure of it, I suspect. So what is it that needs doing so badly that you've both come all this way to meet a pair of travel-weary auxiliary cohorts off the boat from Germania Inferior?'

Sorex leaned forward, lowering his voice in spite of their privacy in the barrack.

'Sixth Victorious is a legion with unfinished business, Tribune Scaurus. We lost an eagle in the first days of the northern tribes' rebellion, and with it the head of Legatus Equitius's predecessor Sollemnis, both lost in an ambush sprung north of the wall by a tribal leader called Calgus—'

Scaurus waved a dismissive hand.

'Don't trouble yourself with the history lesson, colleague. The centurions here both fought in that battle, and witnessed your legion's betrayal by one of your predecessors, although I expect his part of the disaster has been quietly forgotten since then, given who his father was.' He paused and waited for Sorex to acknowledge the open secret that it was the praetorian prefect's son who had orchestrated the Sixth Legion's disastrous losses for his own ends. 'Centurion Corvus was part of the fruitless hunt for the legion's lost eagle, and all three of us subsequently took revenge upon Calgus and his tribe for their actions.'

Sorex took a moment to master his irritation at being cut off.

'I see. Well then, you may find my news on the subject of the eagle, the legatus's head and this fellow Calgus of interest. We have intelligence that all three are gathered in the same place, ripe for capture.'

Marcus shook his head with an expression of disbelief.

'That's impossible, Tribune. I killed Calgus before we left the province.'

Sorex raised a patrician eyebrow.

'You *killed* him, Centurion? You actually saw him *die*? Because the way I've heard it, he was crippled and left for dead by a Roman officer, in the expectation that the wolves would find him and exact an unpleasantly slow death. Except, it seems, by means which I neither understand nor particularly care about, he managed to avoid such a gruesome end. And more to the point, Centurion Corvus, he apparently still has possession of my legion's eagle. An eagle whose loss, as you all well know, puts the Sixth on borrowed time and at constant risk of being cashiered and broken up to reinforce the other legions. In its place another legion will be raised, and the Sixth's officers will either be sent to serve elsewhere under the cloud of their shame or simply dismissed from imperial service in disgrace, with their careers at a premature and ignominious end. All of which means that it will come as no surprise to you that before formally relinquishing his command to me, Legatus Equitius charged me with achieving just one task before his replacement arrives. He ordered me to spare no effort in finding and retrieving the Sixth Legion's eagle, and I gave him my word that I would do so. And let me assure you, gentlemen, whatever else I may or may not be, I am certainly a man of my word.'

Prefect Castus leaned forward again, his gaze locked on Scaurus.

'So here we are, Rutilius Scaurus, in possession of detailed knowledge of where the legion's eagle waits impatiently to be retrieved, but without a single man we can task to its rescue without putting them at risk of dreadful retribution if their disobedience is discovered. Not to mention the strong potential for our own execution. But you and your men are subject to no such restriction. You can be away into the frontier zone in hours, and have the Sixth's eagle safely back in friendly hands within days, not to mention the dead legatus's head. It's time the poor man was made whole, and allowed to sleep in peace with his reputation restored, and you're just the men to bring that about, I'd say.'

When Scaurus and his officers returned to the dock in the company of the legion officers they were greeted by the sight of the first of the Tungrian cohort's transports sidling up to the quayside. The ship had a round-bottomed hull, having been constructed for carrying capacity rather than for speed, and, with its sails for the most part lowered and only enough canvas spread to allow it to crawl carefully into port, it was wallowing on the incoming tide in a way that Marcus knew from grim experience would be making the men on board queasy and eager to disembark.

'That's your century, isn't it, Dubnus?'

The big man stared hard at the ship for a moment before nodding his agreement.

'Yes. There's my miserable sod of a standard bearer busy heaving his breakfast over the side. A shame to have got so close to dry land and still not manage to keep your biscuits down.' He winked at Titus and Marcus before snapping to attention and throwing tribune and first spear a vigorous salute, his facial expression the epitome of determination. 'I'll go and get them disembarked and off into the transit barracks, with your permission First Spear?'

Julius nodded, and Titus waved him away with a dirty look, leaning close to Marcus and muttering a comment in a rumbling tone so that only his colleague would hear it.

'Someone needs to tell that boy that sucking up isn't going to get him anywhere. Look at the smirk on the camp prefect's face.'

The two centurions stared at the scene before them on the quay's worn planks. The warship *Mercurius* had undocked and was backing away from the quay, the oarsmen pulling its heavy hull away from the land with slow, rhythmic strokes while the marines on deck stared impassively down at the legion centuries standing guard over the ten chests they had delivered from

Germania. Julius looked over at the legionaries, then back at the warship's slowly receding bulk.

'They'll anchor in the channel to make room for another transport, so you can bet that Tribune Sorex is going to want to get those chests away before another century of our lads is dumped into his lap, *if* they contain what we're all thinking.'

The legion tribune was engaged in brisk discussion with the procurator who had accompanied the cargo across the German Sea, consulting a writing tablet that the other man had produced for his perusal. As the Tungrian officers watched, Avus pulled a purse from his belt and tipped out a handful of coins for the tribune to examine, waiting while Sorex picked one and raised it for closer examination. Titus's eyes narrowed as he watched the two men discussing the chests' contents, and at length he growled a single word.

'Gold.'

Marcus nodded his agreement with his friend's opinion.

'Indeed. And if each of those chests is filled with coins like that one then we're looking at enough money to pay all three Britannia legions for a year or more.'

Sorex placed the coin back in the official's hand and nodded, gesturing to the nearest of the chests. He waited while the heavy lock was opened, waving the closest soldiers away before raising the lid and peering at the contents for a moment. Julius snorted, sharing a moment of amusement with his tribune.

'Now there's a man with temptation put before him.'

'I doubt it.' Marcus and Julius turned to look at Prefect Castus who had moved silently to stand alongside the first spear. 'The tribune's father is an extremely rich man. I doubt that the sight of even that much gold is going to excite him when his father's property in Rome is probably easily worth two or three times as much. He'll make very sure that the chests are carefully watched though, set guards upon the guards so to speak.'

Marcus frowned at the sight of the tribune moving on to the next chest and waving a hand to order the procurator to open it for his perusal.

'What's it all for, Camp Prefect? Why bring so much money into the country in one shipment and risk losing the lot in the event of a storm?'

Castus shrugged.

'That sort of information is beyond my need to know, I'm relieved to say. My job is simply to make sure that it all gets to Yew Grove without any of it going missing, after which I shall bury it nice and safely in the treasury next to the chapel of the standards and then start praying for that gaping empty space in the chapel where there should be an eagle to be filled before the empire finally runs out of patience with the Sixth.'

He looked out into the mist, tipping his head to a dark spot which was slowly coalescing into the shape of another transport creeping into port to take the place vacated by the now invisible warship.

'And here's another one of your ships. I'd better go and get that gold moving, before Fulvius Sorex starts getting nervous at the thought of your soldiers dribbling on his precious cargo. He already looks about as twitchy as a stores officer presented with a century of new recruits to equip.'

The Tungrian Fifth Century disembarked from their transport with the look of men who were profoundly relieved to have their boots back on solid ground for good after a week spent hugging the coast of Germania, Gaul & Britannia. Several men bent wearily to kiss the quay's wooden planks, while others touched amulets or simply muttered prayers of thanks for their safe delivery to land. Their chosen man Quintus, responsible for the century when Marcus was elsewhere, busied his soldiers with the routine of parading in their usual marching formation alongside the cohort's other centuries, inspecting each man's equipment to ensure that none of them had managed to leave anything aboard the transport in their relief at reaching dry land. Discovering that one of the younger soldiers had managed to mislay both his dagger and the iron butt-spike from one of his spears, his voice was once again raised in a tirade of abuse as the mortified soldier scrambled back up the gangplank and onto the ship in the forlorn hope of recovering his equipment from the acquisitive hands of the transport's crew. The century's standard bearer, a stocky man whose lined and weather-beaten face gave him the look of a man comfortably past the age of retirement from imperial service, chuckled happily and muttered an aside to one of the men behind him.

'There's another, which makes four. One more and I win the wager.'

The veteran to whom he was speaking shook his head with a grin, looking down the quay at the figure walking towards them.

'I doubt it, Morban old mate. I'd say you're out of time . . .'

The standard bearer shook his head in disgust, saluting tiredly as his centurion stopped a few paces away and received Quintus's salute, formally assuming command of the Fifth once more.

'Oh yes, here he comes now, looking as fresh as any man that's enjoyed a good night's sleep. Bloody typical, we get to lurch across the sea in that leaky puke bucket while the favoured few are entertained on a racing hound of a warship. They were probably here hours ago, with time for a few beakers of wine while they waited for us to roll into harbour . . .'

Marcus ignored his standard bearer's usual monologue of discontent for a moment, looking up and down the ranks of his century with an eye on his men's physical state after the best part of a week afloat and finding their faces on the whole considerably more cheerful than he would have expected. Turning back to the grumbling veteran he put out a hand for the century's standard, smiling grimly at the reluctance with which Morban handed it over.

'It seems that the sea air has disagreed with more than your temper, eh Standard Bearer?'

Frowning in apparent non-comprehension, the burly soldier looked up at his officer questioningly.

'Centurion?'

Marcus lowered the standard until its metal laurel-wreath-encircled hand was inches from Morban's nose.

'Unless my eyes deceive me, Standard Bearer, this once faultless symbol of our century's pride is showing signs of rusting. I suggest that you improve its appearance considerably before we parade again, or my disappointment will be both vocal and prolonged.'

He turned back to the ranks of soldiers, raising his voice to be heard.

'How many of you were sick during the voyage, I wonder? One hand in the air if you managed to avoid vomiting the whole way from Germania.'

Thirty or so hands went up, and the young centurion turned back to Morban with a smile.

'And you were giving odds on how many men being sick, Morban? Forty?'

A voice sounded from the front rank, the gravelly rasp of a soldier called Sanga who was one of the century's stalwarts.

'It was forty-five, Centurion.'

'I see. Oh dear . . .' Marcus made a show of reaching for his writing tablet and checking the numbers inscribed upon it before speaking again. 'So if there are sixty-eight men in the century, of whom nearly half managed to hold on to the contents of their stomachs . . .' Shaking his head in mock pity, Marcus turned back to Morban. 'You've a long memory when it comes to odds, haven't you, Standard Bearer? Doubtless you recalled the voyage over to Germania last year, and how we were tossed mercilessly by waves the whole way there. As I recall it, hardly any of us survived without throwing up on that voyage, myself included. Unlike the one we've just completed, with hardly a swell to bother us. So, what odds were you offering?'

'One as per man under or over the target, Centurion.'

Marcus smiled again at Sanga's confirmation of what he had suspected.

'I see. A rusty standard *and* a purse made considerably lighter than you might have wished. Isn't life just a valley of tears some days?' He leaned to speak quietly into Morban's ear, his lowered voice hard in tone. 'Polish that standard, Morban, polish it to within an inch of its life. Make it shine as if it were solid gold fresh from the jeweller's workbench, or you'll find yourself watching another man carrying it, *and* adopting your status as an immune while you forge a new and exciting career in waste disposal. Latrine detail beckons *you*, Standard Bearer, if I don't find that proud symbol of *my* century's pride in the condition I expect at my next inspection.'

He turned back to the troops, looking up and down their line as his brother officers and their chosen men chivvied their soldiers into order. Julius's trumpeter blew the signal for the cohort to come to attention, the call promptly repeated by each century's signaller, and Tribune Scaurus walked out in front of his men with a slow, deliberate gait, stopping a dozen paces from their ranks and looking up and down the long line of weary faces. The soldier who had been sent to search for his equipment bolted back down the gangplank with a look of terror at the scowl on Quintus's face, throwing himself into the century's formation just as the tribune drew breath to address them. Tribune Sorex and Camp Prefect Castus stood off to one side, and Marcus noticed a group of four men gathered behind them, each of them wearing a black cloak over his thick brown tunic.

'Soldiers of the First Tungrian Cohort! In the time that it has been my honour to command you, we have performed deeds that I would have considered unlikely, perhaps even impossible, only two years ago! We have faced the tribes that inhabit the north of this province on the battlefield half a dozen times! In Germania Inferior we put paid to the schemes of the bandit leader Obduro, and in Dacia we not only took part in a successful defence of the province, but we also saved enough gold from the traitor Gerwulf to pay every soldier in a legion for three years!'

He paused, looking across his seven hundred men with a proud smile.

'Gentlemen, at every opportunity for any man here to have folded under the pressure of the odds against us, not one of you has ever failed to stay faithful and loyal to the emperor, to your cohort and to each other!' He paused again, looking across the silent ranks. 'Soldiers of the First Tungrian Cohort, I salute you for it.'

Drawing himself up, he saluted to the left and right, and Marcus heard a hoarse voice whisper loudly enough for him to hear.

'Fuck me, but this ain't lookin' good. What odds you offering we're straight back into the fuckin' shit again, eh Morban?'

A second later he heard the loud crack of brass on iron as Quintus stabbed out from behind the century with the shining brass-bound end of the six-foot-long pole that was his badge of office, snapping Sanga's helmet forward with a sharp blow. Up and down the cohort's length hard-bitten non-commissioned officers were administering similar summary justice to these men whose amazement at the tribune's gesture had got the better of their discipline, and Scaurus regarded them with a knowing smile on his face.

'And so, Tungrians, I have news for you!' A sudden and profound hush fell over the parade, as the usual fidgeting and whispering died away to utter and complete silence. The tribune paused for a moment before continuing as if weighing his words before speaking, smiling into the face of his men's eager anticipation. 'You are doubtless all very keen to return to your barracks on The Hill – and in due course, I am sure that you will! For now, however, we will be based at another fort a little more distant . . .' He paused for a moment, and the entire parade seemed to hold its breath. 'We will be marching north, to take up a position on the wall built by Antoninus Pius!'

The silence was gone in an instant, chased away by the muttered comments and curses of hundreds of men as this news sank in, and Scaurus looked around again with the same knowing smile while his centurions swung and faced their men with hard faces, more than one of them striding forward to wield his vine stick at a hand or a knee in swift punishment. Silence fell again, the front rank's faces now mostly set in lines of sullen disappointment and, in a few cases, pure anguish.

'I realise that this news is unlikely to delight you gentlemen, that much is obvious! But we *will* do our duty as ordered!'

He stepped back with a nod to Julius, and the first spear advanced until he was only a few yards from the grim faces of the cohort's front rank.

'Like the Tribune said, we *will* do our duty as ordered! If any of you cunt hunters entertain fond ideas of slipping away after darkness, now that you're so close to the pleasures of home, think again! Firstly, the local fornication opportunities are limited to a few worried-looking cattle . . .' He paused for effect. 'And no, the nearest brothel is not close enough for you to ride to it on an ox. And secondly, if any man here is missing at tomorrow morning's roll call then not only is he under an immediate death sentence when he's recaptured, but I'll have his tent mates flogged until their backs are raw meat.' He paused again, smiling at the soldiers arrayed before him. 'And just so we're clear, if an entire tent party decides to go missing together then I'll have the rest of their century punished, so don't any of you try to get clever. Centurions, fall your centuries out into the transit barracks and send your men to the fort's stores in numerical order for rations and urgent equipment replacements, starting with the Tenth Century and counting down. We march north at first light tomorrow.'

'The little that we know as to the whereabouts of the Sixth Legion's eagle is the product of only a very little hard information, and rather more supposition than I like if I'm completely honest, now that Fulvius Sorex isn't here to put the optimistic side of the story. If ever a man was destined for high office . . .'

Camp Prefect Castus leaned forward and tapped a finger at the map he had unrolled across the table between himself and Scaurus, watched intently by Julius and Marcus. Tribune Sorex had ridden west once the Tungrian cohort's tribune had agreed to undertake the proposed mission, leaving his colleague to impart what little they knew as to what had happened to the Sixth Legion's standard after its capture. The four black-cloaked men that Marcus had seen standing behind him on the parade ground were arrayed across the room's rear wall, their faces closed to his scrutiny by expressions of boredom and disinterest.

'This is the place where I believe the eagle is to be found. And given the location, its retrieval will be no simple task.'

The Tungrian officers leaned over the map to see where his finger was planted. Scaurus inhaled sharply, shooting a hard glance at Castus before looking back to the map with a calculating expression.

'Gods below, Artorius Castus, I might have been a little slower to accept your challenge had I known where it would send us!' He turned to his first spear and shook his head. 'How much do you fancy that then, eh Julius? It seems that this missing eagle has chosen to roost a day's march north of the Antonine Wall, and deep enough into Venicone territory that we could find ourselves facing more of those tattooed maniacs than we can handle. Not to mention the fact that one or two of them might well recall the day we left the Red River clogged with their dead.'

The Tungrian first spear looked down at the map with obvious disgust.

'Can we rely on any support from the legions based on the wall?'

Castus shook his head with an expression of regret.

'To be blunt, First Spear, I'm afraid not. The legions' detachment commanders are all very clear that the first man to stir from his given position without clear orders to do so will be taking a risk with his rank, and that such a loss of status might well be the very least of his problems. There's not a man among them who will send out anything more aggressive than a party to gather firewood.' Castus shrugged at them with an apologetic expression. 'Sorry, but there it is. There's no point trying to polish this particular turd . . .'

Marcus cleared his throat as he stepped forward, drawing curious glances from the men around the table.

'But you do have some assistance to offer us, don't you, Prefect? Why else would those men standing behind you be privy to the preparations for a mission which needs to be planned with as much secrecy as possible?'

Castus nodded, clearly suppressing a smile.

'All in good time, Centurion. First we'll be clear as to exactly what it is that you'll be faced with.' He waved a hand at the land around the eagle's presumed location. 'The Antonine Wall was built along the line of two rivers, the Clut to the west and the

Dirty River to the east. The ground to the north is open, in the main, but there is a range of hills that runs away from the wall to the north-east, and that's where we think the eagle has come to rest. The range is split in two by the valley of the Dirty River, and where the hills rise again to the north of the stream there's a particularly steep peak on which the Venicones have built themselves a fortress so strong, and indeed so difficult to even access, that it has never been attacked by our forces, not even during the glory days when Gnaeus Julius Agricola briefly conquered the far north. He was wise enough to leave a pair of cohorts to stop anyone getting in or out of the place, and the tribesmen eventually staggered out half dead from hunger, after which the commander on the spot tore out the fortress's gates and knocked some good-sized holes in the walls to make it indefensible. While the wall was manned it was kept under close watch, but the Venicones rebuilt it pretty much straightaway once we'd pulled back to the southern wall and left them to their own devices twenty years ago.'

He looked about the gathered officers with a wry smile, tapping at the Venicone fortress's place on the map.

'Imagine, a fortress built from stone atop a five-hundred-foot-high hill, a hill with a southern slope so steep that an armoured man would struggle to climb it even if he weren't being showered with rocks and arrows. It looms over the valley of the Dirty River like a tooth poking out of the hilltop, and the Venicones have long since called it "The Fang" as yet another way to intimidate their enemies. One of their tribesmen we captured a fortnight ago coughed up the news that your old enemy Calgus has taken up residence there, bringing the Sixth's eagle with him, and has managed by some devious means to install a new king, a man who is therefore well disposed towards him. So, far from lying dead where you left him with his bones scattered by the wolves, the man that sparked this bloody mess of a rebellion is now the controlling influence behind the deadliest of the northern tribes. And the Venicones, should I need to remind you, were never completely smashed. Unlike the Damnonii and the Selgovae they retain much of their strength, and all of their threat. So your task is simple enough, gentlemen. You must cross the valley of the Dirty River, an unmapped morass of swamps and sinkholes that will swallow an armoured man whole in an instant, never to be seen again. That done you must enter The Fang, by means either overt or covert, recover the eagle and, if at all possible, finish the job with Calgus while you're at it. That man will continue to plague us until his head decorates the legate's desk in Yew Grove.'

Scaurus turned to his centurions.

'Well now gentlemen, you heard the choices on offer. Will our approach to this task be overt or covert?'

Julius shared a momentary exchange of glances with Marcus before replying.

'An open approach will bring the Venicones down upon us like a hammer falling on a clutch of eggs. We only escaped their wrath the last time we met because the gods sent us a storm to make the river between us impossible to cross, and I'm pretty sure that they'll remember the design on our shields well enough, given how many of them we killed that day. The merest sight of us with our boots on their turf will be enough to bring them out to confront us in force. But if we send a scouting party to infiltrate this fortress in the sky unsupported they will almost certainly be run down and captured before they can return to the wall, if the Venicones' strength is mustered around their fortress. We must find some way to lure these tribesmen away from The Fang, and allow whoever makes the silent approach a fighting chance of escaping with the eagle. Will you allow me to think on it for a while and to consult with my centurions?'

Scaurus nodded and turned back to the camp prefect.

'And now, Castus Artorius, perhaps the time is right for you to introduce us to these silent assassins who lurk behind you?'

Castus frowned back at him with an apparent expression of consternation.

'Assassins, Tribune? Whoever mentioned such a term?'

The younger man smiled wryly at him, shaking his head in amusement.

'Nobody. And nobody needed to mention it for my mind to go back ten years to the German Wars. I seem to recall that you gathered a similarly nondescript group to you then as well, men whose natural demeanour was to fade into the background and leave the posturing to the soldiers while they quietly got on with doing whatever unpleasant but necessary task was required. So tell me, Prefect, what skills have you assembled to do your dirty work this time?'

The prefect gestured to the tallest of the four.

'I'll allow their leader to explain what his men are capable of. Drest here is that rare commodity, a Thracian possessed of both patience and subtlety, and I have learned to trust his judgement implicitly. And now, since my tired old feet are sorely in need of a dip in some hot water, I'll leave you to it. Drest?'

He closed the barrack door behind him, leaving the two groups of men eyeing each other. The man to whom he had signalled stepped forward and bowed fractionally, extending a hand to his comrades.

'Tribune, Centurions, allow me to introduce my colleagues.' His voice was soft, but when Marcus stared at him he found the return gaze hard and uncompromising. 'These two young men are Ram and Radu, twin brothers raised on the plans of Pannonia in worship of the sword . . .'

'They worship the sword? They're *Sarmatae*?'

Julius's voice was cold, but both Drest's expression and his voice remained level.

'They *were* Sarmatae, First Spear, before their tribe, the Iazyge, rose against Rome and they were taken captive and enslaved. Prefect Castus found them in a slave market, and outbid a dozen other would-be buyers at my suggestion to secure their ownership.'

'At *your* suggestion?'

Drest turned back to Marcus.

'Indeed, Centurion. It is my pleasure to serve Prefect Castus, and to provide him with the benefit of my experience in the procurement of men with certain rare skills, men whose services will enhance his ability to discharge his responsibilities to the empire. In this case, since I see the question in your eyes, I suspected that these men's origins might have endowed them with certain abilities with bladed weapons. Their tribe are famed for their skills with spear and sword, and those expectations proved to have been well founded.' He studied the Roman with a curious expression. 'Speaking of skill at arms, I believe that you, Centurion, have some reputation with your swords? Your men call you "Two Knives", after the Dimachieri, the gladiators who fight with two swords, I hear?'

The young Roman smiled thinly.

'You hear a lot, it seems. Is that the skill that you bring to the Prefect's service?'

The answering smile was equally uncompromising, the small group's leader clearly untroubled by the status of the soldiers before him.

'An ability to listen is indeed one of the abilities I bring to my master's service, Centurion. As to Ram and Radu, I suggest that you might like to train with them when the opportunity arises, and take your own gauge of their prowess. I find their speed quite breathtaking on occasion, especially when they meet opponents with sufficient skill to push them to their limits. *Perhaps* you might have sufficient skill to bring out their best . . .'

Julius snorted a quiet laugh into his hand and Marcus smiled again, his eyebrows arching in genuine amusement.

'And there's another of those skills for which the Prefect selected you, I imagine? The ability to probe at a man's defences with nothing deadlier than words, seeking to pique his pride and thereby betray his weakness?'

Drest bowed again, his expression equally amused.

'And I see that I have met my match in you, Centurion.'

Marcus shook his head.

'And I doubt you've even really tried yet, have you? But when the appeal to pride fails, perhaps there's an ego that can be massaged?'

The Thracian raised his hands in a gesture of surrender.

'In which case, enough! I'll deploy more of my verbal lock picks later, when I can see more clearly which one to use. It is my experience that there is no man alive whose personality will not open to me if I only find the right tool. Speaking of which, allow me to introduce the other member of our small but efficiently constructed band. This is Tarion, an Illyrian from Virunum, in the province of Noricum.'

He waved the last man forward, and as Tarion bowed to the officers, his face carefully neutral, Julius shook his head in confusion, waving a hand at the knife hanging from his belt.

'I see no sword on this man's belt, only that toothpick. How can he fight when he lacks any proper weapon?'

Drest nodded to his colleague, who put a hand into his tunic and then flicked it forward with the fingers opening as if he were performing a magic trick. A slim sliver of polished iron hissed across the room between Marcus and Julius and buried itself in the wooden wall behind them.

'Check the point of impact, if you would Centurion?'

Marcus smiled to himself again at the peremptory tone of command in Drest's voice, staring back at him for a moment to make the point that this fresh verbal trick had not gone unnoticed before turning on his heel and examining the spot where the blade protruded from the wood, still quivering from its impact with its point neatly bisecting a small knot in the thick plank.

'Not only can Tarion throw a blade to hit a target the size of a man's eye, but the "toothpick" he carries on his belt is quite the most deadly weapon I have ever seen when used at close quarters. While a man armed with a sword is still struggling to bring his weapon to bear, Tarion will have stepped in close, opened his throat and then moved on to his next victim. But I can assure you that he was not selected for his abilities with knives; they were a happy discovery once his service had been secured from the magistrate in Virunum.'

Julius's face darkened in disapproval.

'He was a bandit?'

Drest shrugged.

'It would be more appropriate to use the term "thief". Tarion here was before the magistrate having been caught with his hand upon another man's purse, a crime compounded by his then committing the worst possible error for a man in his line of work, namely failing to run fast enough when the fingers were pointed.'

'So he's not only a thief, but not even a good one? What use would we have for a dishonest incompetent?'

Drest shrugged in the face of Julius's scorn.

'That's hardly for me to say, I have such a small basis for comparison. Perhaps the man himself might venture an opinion?'

He gestured to the thief, whose face was set in what Marcus assumed was professional neutrality.

'I was caught because I broke my own rules and attempted to rob more than a single mark in the same place. The man was a merchant from the looks of him, and possessed of a purse so heavy that to have left it there unplucked seemed improper.' He shrugged. 'That was my mistake. He had the purse doubly secured to his belt by a hidden chain, having been robbed before. As to whether I am an effective thief, I'd say that you, First Spear, might be the best judge. I found this in your belt pouch as we were coming through the door . . .'

He held out his closed fist and opened the fingers to reveal Julius's brass whistle resting on his palm. Dubnus sniggered behind his colleague, trying and failing to muffle his uncontrollable amusement behind a hand, and even Marcus was forced to smile at his brother officer's discomfiture.

'I'd say that's sufficient evidence for us to accept that your man here has some ability in his chosen profession. But what good will it serve us? Our task is one of infiltration and murder, not the picking of merchants' purses.'

Drest spoke up, stepping forward and taking the whistle from his comrade's outstretched hand.

'He's a good deal more than a simple thief, Centurion. He has silent feet to complement his swift fingers, and an uncanny ability with a lock. If I were going to attempt to get into The Fang unnoticed, then he would be my first man over the wall.'

Scaurus spoke, having stood in silence while the introductions were made.

'"If" being the operative word, as you so correctly identify. It is clear that Artorius Castus hopes that we will accept your services in this matter, and equally obvious that he reposes a good deal of trust in you, but you can be sure that I do not yet share his views as to your suitability.' Drest stood in silence and waited for the tribune to continue, his expression untroubled, while Scaurus played a calculating look across his comrades. 'Some proof of these abilities is called for.'

Drest shot the tribune an amused glance, clearly unabashed by the tribune's status.

'And you have a fairly specific idea as to how we might provide you with that proof, don't you, Tribune?'

The Roman smiled grimly at him.

'Indeed I do. But be very careful in considering whether or not you can accept this challenge. I'd imagine that the punishment for being caught attempting what I have in mind will involve a vigorous session on the sharp end of a scourge, rapidly followed by the enthusiastic application of a hammer and three big nails.'

2

The next morning was clear and bright, overnight mist burning off in less than an hour as the Tungrians prepared to march north. Marcus stood with his helmet under one arm and watched as the Sixth Legion's three centuries readied themselves to escort Tribune Sorex's gold chests back to their fortress at Yew Grove. He nodded in wry recognition as their centurions undertook the ritual final preparations, inspecting the waiting soldiers alongside scowling chosen men who had already scrutinised their troops' readiness with sharp and unforgiving eyes. Camp Prefect Castus stood and watched beside Marcus with a look of satisfaction at the scene before him.

'Is there any better sight in the entire world than a few centuries of battle-hardened infantry commanded by men at the peak of their powers? I've trodden parade grounds across the length of the empire, from the burning sand of Syria to the ice and snow of Dacia, and nothing has ever put a lump in my throat like the sight of good soldiers ready for whatever the day might throw at them.'

He paused for a moment, and Marcus sneaked a sideways glance that found the older man gazing misty-eyed at the ordered lines of men before him.

'This is my last posting, young man, and I had to beg the powers that be for this chance to be a fighting man one last time, even if I am only supposed to be the officer who organises the legion's food and pay. Take a lesson from where I find myself, Centurion, suddenly clinging on to the arse end of my career and wondering where all those years went. Make the most of each and every day you have under the eagle.' He laughed, shaking his head to dispel his melancholy. 'Well at least Procurator Avus should be happy that his precious cargo will be travelling under suitable protection. Doubtless he'll be expected to report to some exalted person or other as to the state of affairs he discovered here . . .'

Marcus followed his gaze to find the imperial official standing a short distance away with a look of approval at the soldiers' ranks. Looking back at the column his eyes found his wife Felicia and her assistant Annia, an island of femininity in the column's sea of iron. The young centurion stared wistfully as his wife handed their infant son up to the now heavily pregnant Annia, who had already taken her place in the cart that had been procured for them at Castus's order. The camp prefect had readily agreed to take his wife, his baby son Appius and the doctor's assistant with him to the Sixth Legion's fortress at Yew Grove, as part of the well-protected convoy of wagons that would deliver Tribune Sorex's gold to the buried strongroom safe behind its heavy stone walls. The final member of the women's small party was his standard bearer's grandson Lupus, whose furious protests at being made to accompany the women had fallen on deaf ears. Marcus had taken him aside once his initial anger at the decision had burned out and the boy had been reduced to tearful silence, squatting down on his haunches to look up into the child's resentful eyes.

'We don't always get what we want, young man, and nor should we. What use is a life that doesn't contain the occasional disappointment to remind us just how pleasant success tastes, eh? This time you have to go with Felicia and Annia, and that's all there is to it.'

Lupus had shaken his head, his reply petulant even though he knew that when the centurion spoke so firmly his will was not to be questioned.

'But I came with you last time you marched to fight.'

Marcus had smiled, conceding the point.

'And we were lucky enough not to get you killed. But this time I need you to go with the women. Besides, I'll feel happier with one of us close to them.'

The boy had nodded solemnly at him, his eyes widening at the centurion's words, and put his hand to the hilt of the half-sized sword strapped to his waist, much to the amusement of the soldiers. Catching the direction of his companion's stare, the Prefect nudged him with an elbow and nodded towards the two women.

'Don't worry, Centurion, I'll make sure they're not bothered by the soldiery. Indeed it will be a pleasure to escort two such agreeable ladies to a place of safety. I believe that your woman is a doctor with some experience of treating battlefield wounds?'

Marcus smiled wryly.

'She has saved the lives of several men I would have said were fit for nothing more than a quick and merciful release from their suffering, but she has experience at inflicting damage as well as repairing it, if the need presents itself. And I suggest that you approach her assistant with care. Annia is, as you can see, somewhat heavy with child and she is not, I can assure you from recent experience, particularly happy with that condition. I think the father of her child is looking forward to facing off with the Venicones as a relief from her vividly expressed disappointment that his manhood hasn't yet dropped off as the price for putting her through such discomfort.'

The older man snorted a laugh.

'Your first spear is keen to jump out of the skillet, is he? In that case we'll just have to hope that the fire isn't too hot!' His expression softened as he watched Felicia climb up into the cart and take the child from her friend. 'As for your woman, you needn't worry yourself as to her safety while you're away pulling barbarian beards. I have a woman in the vicus at Yew Grove who's well accustomed to the life of a soldier's wife, and she'll make sure that they're both looked after.'

Marcus nodded his thanks, tensing slightly as he saw that Julius was beckoning to him.

'Excuse me, Prefect, my presence is being requested by my superior officer.'

The prefect nodded, his face creasing into a smile.

'It's time then, is it? Have fun . . .'

The young centurion saluted Castus and turned away, walking towards the parade ground across which the First Tungrian Cohort was arrayed. As he made his way between two of the convoy's gold carts he found his path blocked by the Sarmatae, Ram and Radu, who stood waiting for him with their hands on the hilts of their swords. He paused for a moment, waiting for them to step aside, but neither man showed any intention of moving.

'Gentlemen?'

Ram stepped forward, a broad grin on his face as he closed to within a foot of the Roman.

'We fight. Now.'

Marcus shook his head.

'No. We *march* now. There'll be plenty of time to fight later, and besides, we have no practice weapons to hand.'

The answer was instant, and delivered in a tone of voice which raised the hairs on the back of Marcus's neck.

'*Now!* We practise like we fight, not with wood, but with iron! We fight like men! We promise not to cut your pretty face, Centurion . . .' Ram looked back at his brother with a smirk, missing Marcus's quick pace backwards, and the sudden narrowing of his eyes as he readied himself to fight. 'But perhaps he not a man, perhaps he a—'

Whatever insult the Sarmatae had intended to throw at Marcus was lost in the sudden woosh of air from his lungs as the centurion stepped forward swiftly and put a hobnailed boot into his groin, sending him reeling away from the wagons, clutching at his abused testicles and fighting for breath. Regaining his balance to toss his helmet aside and unsheathe his swords in a flicker of polished metal, the Roman barely had time to raise his defence before Radu was upon him, his swords a whirling torrent of sharp iron, and for the next dozen heartbeats it was all he could do to parry the other man's cuts and lunges.

Only distantly aware of an uproar of noise from the gathered soldiers, and wondering what his wife was making of the unexpected display, he bared his teeth in a snarl of naked aggression and sprang forward at the Dacian with a ferocity born of the anger that had swiftly replaced his initial surprise at the nature of the twins' challenge. Matching his opponent blow for blow he began to force the pace, his retaliatory cuts and lunges delivered so fast that the Sarmatae's eyes widened as he found himself unexpectedly on the back foot in the face of the Roman's speed and power. Parrying a thrust of the long spatha's evilly sharp patterned blade, Radu spun away to his right, escaping from Marcus's incessant attacks for a moment and shouting to Ram in a tone laced with urgency.

Flicking a glance at Ram, Marcus realised that while he was bent over with his hands on his knees and his chest heaving, still struggling to breathe, he was clearly already over the worst of the kick's physical impact. Looking back to Radu just in time to steer a vicious stab aside with his gladius, he realised that his opponent would simply seek to hold him at bay until his brother regained his wind and returned to the fight, at which point the two men would clearly overwhelm him with their combined pace and ferocity. Realising that he needed to overcome the man facing him in the next few strokes or face inevitable defeat, the Roman stepped into the next attack and pushed Radu's swords wide before snapping a vicious butt into his face, the crushing impact sending the Sarmatae reeling away with blood streaming down his face from his broken nose.

Grasping at the fleeting opportunity he had created, the Roman took two quick strides to Ram, tossing his own weapons aside and smashing the stooped tribesman's head back with a vicious uppercut before grasping his tunic and spinning him round, wrapping one arm across his face. Whipping out his dagger he put the weapon's point under his captive's jaw, pressing its point on the spot where a simple thrust would open the blood vessel beneath the skin. The Sarmatae reacted instinctively, biting down hard on the tunic-covered arm that was holding his head back, stiffening with a squeal of pain as Marcus quickly moved the knife's point to the soft flesh beneath his ear and pushed it into the gap between cartilage and skull to send a thin runnel of blood down his captive's neck.

'If you bite me again I will make a gift to you of this ear, as a memento of our fight today. That, and your brother's head.'

Radu shook his head and advanced towards the two men, ignoring the blood that masked his lips and chin, crabbing sideways in search of an angle at which he could renew his attack on the Roman only to be frustrated as Marcus manhandled his brother round to negate the threat.

'You've lost. I could cut his throat and take his swords in less time than it takes to tell, and you wouldn't be much of a challenge now that I understand your rather crude style. Stand down.'

Before the younger twin had time to reply a commanding voice rapped out from behind him.

'Leave it!'

Marcus craned his neck over Ram's shoulder, jerking the dagger's blade fractionally to ensure that the Sarmatae stayed quiet. Drest was approaching them across the parade ground with a hard grin, and as he passed Radu he patted his man on the shoulder.

'You lost to a man with more battlefield experience. Learn from that, eh? And next time, you might want to give him a little more warning. It seems that the centurion here has something of a temper once he's roused.'

Radu shook his head dourly, re-sheathing his swords as he spoke to Marcus with a dismissive tone to his voice.

'If this fight were real I would have killed you by putting my iron through my brother. *We* take no prisoners!'

Marcus pushed Ram away, bending to wipe the dagger's point on the grass before dropping it back into its sheath and reaching for his swords.

'I will remember that. And perhaps next time we spar you can give me a little more warning, so that I won't have to resort to such ungentlemanly conduct to fight the pair of you off.' He turned to Drest. 'That was a little more intense than I was expecting, not to mention somewhat sooner than I *thought* we'd planned it?'

The Scythian shrugged.

'This way it looked somewhat more convincing than would otherwise have been the case. And this way we had an audience of men all baying for blood, and one man in particular who was sufficiently distracted for Tarion to perform his magic.'

The Roman resisted the temptation to look around at the spot where Procurator Avus had been standing a moment before.

'And it worked?'

Drest shrugged again.

'I have no idea. But I hear no cries of *"thief"*, which is always a good sign . . .'

The Thracian tipped his head towards the waiting cohort, and Marcus turned just in time to see the thief pass something to Tribune Scaurus and slip away between two centuries, a wink of gold catching his eye as whatever it was changed hands. He glanced at Drest before walking away towards his place in the cohort's line, shaking his head at the cheers that were now echoing off the Arab Town transit barracks as the Tungrian soldiers roared their approval of his victory. His Fifth Century greeted his return by beating their spear shafts against the brass rims of their shields until Quintus called for silence, and the Roman settled into position next to Morban with a sidelong glance at the standard gleaming atop its pole.

'How much did you pay to have it polished up that well?'

The standard bearer opened his mouth to protest, but a familiar voice from behind him pre-empted his complaint.

'Two denarii, Centurion.'

The young centurion shook his head in bemusement at Sanga's interruption.

'Which you doubtless recouped handsomely with a wager on that unexpected display of extemporisation?'

'Extemp . . . ?'

Marcus spoke over his shoulder, an acerbic note in his voice.

'Extemporisation, Soldier Sanga. It means making it up under pressure, an ability to which I believe you're no stranger given some of the legendary excuses you've offered up for your misdemeanours during the short time I've been your centurion.'

Morban shook his head, stiffening his back as Julius called the cohort to attention and speaking out of the side of his mouth.

'Didn't make as much as a sestertius. None of these cowards would gamble on the outcome.'

Marcus shrugged.

'You can't blame them, there were two of them against one of me.'

Sanga's voice grated out again.

'It weren't that, Two Knives—'

'Call the fucking Centurion *"Centurion"* Sanga, or I'll put another fucking dent in your helmet!'

Marcus heard the soldier mutter an obscenity under his breath before shouting out the answer that he knew Quintus was waiting to hear.

'Yes, Chosen Man!'

'That's better! Carry on with your little story . . .'

'Morban was trying to get us to bet against you, and none of us was having any.'

Marcus frowned, unsure whether to be flattered or annoyed.

'Really?'

'Yes sir. No bugger here's going to bet against you in a sword fight, not given what a mad bastard you are once your temper's lit, beggin' your pard—'

A sharp rap of brass on iron silenced the soldier in mid-sentence, and a moment later the command was given for the cohort's seven hundred men to turn to their right. Lifting spears and shields from their resting places the soldiers swivelled into the line of march, ignoring the sniggers of the Votadini warriors who had accompanied them all the way to Dacia and back. Morban scowled at them, shaking his head in disgust.

'I don't know what that lot are laughing at, they look like a right bunch of mongrels.'

The Votadini warriors were clad in and equipped with a widely varied assortment of Roman and Sarmatae armour and weapons, equipment taken from dead friend and foe according to need and circumstance. 'Legion plate armour, barbarian dog caps, and of course they're all wearing our hobnailed boots. Poor old Uncle Sextus would have been ripping his hair out, if he'd had any . . .'

Marcus frowned down at him.

'They do have a rather informal appearance, I'll give you that, and yes, perhaps our last First Spear, the gods grant ease to his departed spirit, would have found their mixture of kit a little challenging. Should I point out that harsh truth to Martos on your behalf, do you think?'

A warrior of fearsome countenance who had lost an eye in the liberation of his tribe's fortress city from Calgus's men two years before, the Votadini prince had long since settled into a state of contentment with his place in the cohort as an ally, but still kept his men apart from the centuries and guarded both their independence and their reputation jealously. Morban recoiled visibly, shaking his head vigorously.

'There's no need for that Centurion, I was just saying . . .'

Marcus ignored the standard bearer's grumbling and raised his hand in salute to Martos.

'You're whining because they get to go home while we have to march north.'

If the Roman had expected that stating the obvious would silence Morban's complaints, he was to be disappointed.

'It don't seem all that fair, now that you raise the matter, sir. How come they get to wander off to enjoy themselves while we're straight off to the north without even the chance to put our noses round the door at the Hill?'

'Because, Standard Bearer, as you might be reminded by the prince's missing eye, their home was ravaged by Calgus's Selgovae and left under Roman control once we recaptured it. He's going to make sure that none of the tribal elders have had any clever ideas about taking the throne from his nephew, and to make an offering at the shrine to his wife and son. And besides, it's not your *nose* you want to put round the door at our old fort, is it?'

'You're right, Centurion, it ain't his nose! Not that his old chap would reach round a door! It can barely poke its head out of his bush unless he gives it a good old tugging!'

Sanga's gruff voice and the answering laughs of the soldiers around them were lost in a sudden bray of trumpets as Julius decided that the cohort was ready to march. Knowing that the soldiers would be quietly seething at having their return home snatched away from them so suddenly, the first spear only waited long enough for the last century to be clear of the fort before ordering his trumpeter to sound the signal for the double march. The ferocious pace soon quelled the unhappy mutterings of his troops as they threw back their heads to gulp down the cold morning air. After an hour or so the harsh pace started to tell on men whose previous few days had been characterised by the forced inactivity of waiting around in barracks for the transport convoy to assemble, followed by the cramped circumstances of the crossing itself. Marcus and Morban, marching at the Fifth Century's head, exchanged knowing glances as the Fourth Century's chosen man stalked down the line of his men looking for strugglers, pouncing on one soldier who was marching with a slight limp.

The hard-faced chosen man had been deliberately selected by Julius to pair up with his centurion, Caelius, as a means of counterbalancing the officer's quiet and reasonable demeanour in any other circumstance than the chaos of battle, where he was transformed into a warrior leader of legendary ferocity. His chosen man's reputation for driving his men along with an assortment of well-used jibes and threats was widely known and well founded, and the panting soldiers in the Fifth Century's front rank cocked their ears expectantly as he bellowed a challenge at the labouring man, his face inches from the hapless struggler's ear.

'Having a hard time of it, are you sonny?!'

Whatever it was that the soldier said was inaudible to the men marching behind, but his inquisitor quickly satisfied their curiosity.

'Blister?! A fucking *blister*?! You'll just have to march through it, won't you boy?! I don't care if your boots fill up with blood until they squelch like a whore's cunt on pay day, you'll keep marching until the tribune decides it's time to stop!'

Marcus shared a glance with Morban.

'That's come depressingly early in the day. This is clearly going to be a long and painful march . . .'

With the usual turf-walled marching fort constructed, nestled beneath the walls of Fort Habitus on the road that speared north from the wall built at the command of the Emperor Hadrian sixty years before, Marcus turned away from his supervisory duties to find two of his soldiers standing to attention, both men saluting neatly and waiting for their centurion to speak.

'Ah yes, Sanga, and Saratos isn't it? Chosen Man Quintus told me the pair of you had requested permission to see me. What can I do for the pair of you?'

Sanga spoke for both men, his voice nervous at dealing directly with the centurion.

'This is the settlement where my mate Scarface was born and raised, Centurion sir. Me and Saratos here thought it might be nice to pay the local mason to carve him an altar, and when we come back this way we can make an offering to his memory. He was a daft sod, begging your pardon, sir, but the lads in our tent party wanted to find a way of remembering him.'

He shut up and waited for Marcus to speak.

'Scarface . . .' The Roman put a hand over his eyes and shook his head slowly before lowering his arm and nodding at the men standing before him. 'May Mithras above us forgive me, but to my great shame I must admit that I've not thought of him lately. Thank you for the reminder, Soldier Sanga.'

Sanga smiled.

'I can still hear his voice in my head, when it's quiet in the tent and the rest of the lads are all snoring and farting. "Are you still keeping an eye on that young gentleman like you said you would, Sanga?" or "Don't you forget our agreement, Sanga. If he won't look after himself we'll just have to be there to stop him getting hurt, won't we?"'

Marcus nodded soberly.

'He always did seem to believe it was some sort of sacred duty he had to keep me from harm. There was a time when I couldn't turn around without finding him lurking about close at hand, looking in another direction and trying to avoid my eye. Which is how he got himself killed, of course.' He fished in his purse, pulling out a handful of silver coins. 'Whatever Morban's spared you from the burial club for the altar, add this to it, and make sure there's a good carving at the top of the stone. Morban *has* given you some money?'

Sanga grinned back at his officer, raising one hand to display his scarred knuckles.

'Yes sir, and there was never a danger that he wouldn't come up with the coin. Morban knows when to take liberties and when he's safer just putting his toes on the line rather than risking getting them stamped flat.'

The gold convoy halted for the night some twenty miles down the road south from Arab Town, in a spot that had clearly been the point which the day's march had been intended to reach. Leaving the road at the leading centurion's pointing signal, eschewing the blare of horns that usually accompanied tactical manoeuvres in favour of a more stealthy approach, the column moved up a rough track that sloped away from the cobbled surface and wound around the base of the hill that overlooked the route south, gradually climbing until it opened out onto the flat summit.

'Another night, another turf wall.'

Felicia nodded at Annia's words, pulling on the horse's reins to halt the cart, as the three centuries' officers issued a flurry of orders to their men. The orderly ranks dissolved into what at first glance seemed like barely organised chaos, although the two women, long used to the routines of marching camps, watched with experienced eyes as some of the soldiers dug turfs and quickly built a four-foot-high wall around the clustered tents that were being erected by their fellows, while others stood guard with purposeful stares at the landscape around them. Work details were heading away from the camp to fetch water and firewood, the foragers all still fully armed and armoured, and the men working to build the camp all had their spears and shields close to hand in what both women knew was the prescribed routine for camping in hostile territory. Lupus popped up from the place in the cart's bed where he had been sulking for most of the day, his eyes bright as he watched the legionaries go about their duties to build a defensible camp out of a bare hilltop, one hand on the hilt of the sword that hung at his side. Prefect Castus strolled down the line of carts, his eyes roaming along the line of armoured men set to stand guard on the gold wagons, before coming to a halt alongside the women's cart.

'Good evening ladies. I trust that your day's ride was pleasant, or at least not too unpleasant . . .' Finding Annia's eyes upon him in a cold stare he coughed and turned away, gesturing to the camp with a raised arm. 'Please don't be alarmed by the fact that the men are all still in their hard kit, it's just routine given recent circumstances. Once the tents are raised the wagons in front of you will be driven into the open space that's been left in the middle, so that we can put three centuries' worth of spears between them and any unfriendly natives. Just follow them in and we'll have your equally valuable cargo just as safe as the emperor's gold, eh?'

Felicia watched as he marched briskly back down the line of wagons, turning to look at Annia.

'I'd say that the Prefect is one man we ought to be cultivating, wouldn't you?'

Her heavily pregnant companion snorted, shaking her head in disagreement.

'It's thanks to the Prefect that I'll more than likely be giving birth to this child in a legion fortress while my man is freed to go adventuring without a care in the world.'

Felicia smiled gently, putting a hand on her friend's arm.

'You must have seen a fair few babies being born over the years, given that you ran an establishment that catered to the entertainment of men?' Annia nodded. 'And tell me, in all those deliveries of helpless little scraps of humanity, when your women were puffing and groaning to push their children out into the world, did you *ever* see a man add any value to the proceedings?'

The other woman nodded reluctantly, and Felicia reached behind them to rub the boy's head affectionately.

'And besides, we have all the male assistance we need right here with us, don't we, Lupus?' She turned back to the camp before them, pointing a finger at the first of the gold wagons as it started to roll forward behind the paired horses that were straining to shift its dead weight. 'Let's go and take our place in the camp and then work out what we're going to eat tonight. Perhaps the Prefect will detail us an escort and allow us to pick herbs for a stew?'

'That was cruel, having to lead the cohort far enough to the west that they could practically smell home, then turning them north at The Rock and thrashing them up the road for another ten miles.'

Dubnus raised a jaundiced eyebrow at his friend, looking around at the roughly finished surroundings of the hastily rebuilt Fort Habitus officers' mess in which they were sitting.

'Not as cruel as camping here for the night. Of all the places that we could have pitched up it had to be this one, the place where I told my half century of former legionaries the story that turned them from cowards into men. Now they're walking round like they own the place, bumping fists and muttering "Habitus" to each other as if they're some sort of secret society. If they find out that I made up the whole thing about this place being named for a centurion who died in defence of his men then I'll have some excitement to deal with, that's for certain. And after all, I only did it as a way to wake up their sense of pride when they were hanging from their chinstraps.' Dubnus took a deep swig at his beaker, wiping the excess from his moustache. 'Ah, proper beer. That wine you lot are always sipping is all very well, but it's not a drink for a man, is it?'

Marcus smiled and raised his wine cup in salute.

'I thought you might appreciate it, although I don't think I'll ever really get a taste for the stuff.'

His friend emptied the beaker, slamming it down onto the table before him exuberantly and grinning happily at his friend.

'Appreciate it? You have no idea how good that tastes after a year of that sour German muck.'

Marcus stared off into space, his expression wistful.

'I think you'll find I can do a fairly good job of imagining just how good it feels. Probably about as good as a cup of my father's best Falernian would taste to me if I were sipping it in his garden after having spent a couple of hours bathing away dust and the smell of horses.'

'Yes . . .' The big Briton raised his refilled beaker, tapping it to the Roman's cup. 'I'm sorry, that was—'

Marcus shook his head.

'Tactless? Not at all. Why shouldn't you enjoy being home?' He raised his cup in return. 'I'll drink a toast with you. To home . . .' They drank. 'And we'll drink it again, on the day that my boots tread the Forum's flagstones again. And here's Julius. Pour him a beer, he'll probably be in need of a drink.'

The first spear dropped his helmet down onto the table with a heavy thud, drawing a dirty look from the mess servant who was promptly treated to a swift rebuttal.

'Don't be giving me the eyes boy, fetch another jug unless you want your arse tattooing with the lace holes of my boots. We're fighting soldiers, not the weak-kneed half-wits you've been used to dealing with. I came through here two years ago when this fort was nothing more than a burned-out shell, on my way to give the Selgovae a good reaming as repayment for their having it away with *your* fucking eagle.'

Shaking his head in disgust he turned back to his comrades, ignoring the stares his outburst had drawn from a trio of legion centurions at a table in the far corner.

'And yes, young Corvus, you're bloody right. I do need a beer, if only to wash away the memory of an hour of my life I'll never get back, spent listening to a spotty nineteen-year-old trying to tell us he's got the local area under control while his three centuries hide in their barracks sharpening their military skills by a combination of wanking and playing knuckle bones. One word from Rome to pull back and this lot will be off down the road to the south like Greek athletes racing for the last bottle of oil.'

He tipped the beaker back and drained it in a single swallow, reaching forward and pouring out the last of the jug's contents as Dubnus watched disapprovingly. One of the men in the corner got to his feet and advanced across the room towards them with a determined expression, his comrades looking after him with a mixture of curiosity and concern. Planting himself in the first spear's field of view he waited for Julius to become aware of his presence, his eyes fixed on the big man until the Tungrian turned his head to look at him.

'What?' Julius looked up at the newcomer with a curled lip, sliding down in his chair a little to make himself comfortable and folding his arms to push out his massive biceps. 'I'd be very careful, sonny, standing there with a face on you like you've got a pair. If you've come looking for a set of lumps you'll find me ready and willing to oblige you, given the deep joy I've been forced to inflict on my men today.'

The legion centurion shook his head, saluting punctiliously as he spoke.

'Nothing of the sort, First Spear. But I couldn't help overhearing your comments about my cohort, and I just wanted to explain a few things to you.'

Julius raised an eyebrow at his brother officers with a bored expression.

'You want to hear this tale of woe?'

To Marcus's surprise Dubnus nodded, his face suddenly serious.

'Why not? There's been a lot happened since we were here last, and given that we're marching north to put our cocks well and truly on the block I'd like to hear what the centurion here has to tell us. If you don't like what he's got to say you can do your usual "fuck off and die quietly" act once he's done telling it.' He turned to the legion centurion with a wink. 'Take a seat brother, and have a beaker of this most excellent beer, if the idiot behind the counter ever bothers his arse to bring us a refill.'

The other man smiled wryly.

'I can help with that much, at least.' He clicked his fingers to get the mess steward's attention, raising his voice in a peremptory tone. 'Two jugs of beer, and make it quick or I'll have a chat with your chosen man and have you put to work moving shit from one place to another and then back again with the smallest and heaviest shovel you've ever seen!'

With the beer swiftly delivered and poured he took a sip and then leaned forward, his voice pitched low to avoid the words carrying to his comrades.

'I'm Tullo, Third Century. And yes, First Spear, our tribune is no more than a boy, but even if he wanted to do anything more than keep the locals' heads down his orders leave no room for doubt. If we stir from this fort without orders from the new legatus, then he'll find himself so deep in the shit he'll be breathing through a reed. And as for the men . . .'

He sighed, shaking his head, then raised his eyebrows in question at Dubnus.

'You know that nightmare we all have, given we command centuries made up mostly of local boys, the one where we have to order them to start killing their own people? Well it's not a nightmare for me any more, because my lads have been through it. When the Brigantes revolted, we were part of a three-cohort force that was sent south to make sure the cheeky bastards didn't get any smart ideas about burning out the Yew Grove fortress, while the rest of the legion got stuck in to making sure the wall forts weren't overrun. Three cohorts wasn't enough, of course, we needed a full legion to do the job properly, but given that we were all that could be spared the legatus told us to do our best, and put the most experienced of his tribunes in command, a man with experience from the German Wars and a right hard case.'

Tullo took another sip of beer, aware that he had the Tungrians' full attention.

'It was all a bit half-hearted at first. The Brigantes were scared shitless once they realised the full implications of what they'd done, which meant they kept well out of our way for the most part, and our lads were all a bit stunned by the turn of events that had their own people burning out farms, but it wasn't until we reached Sailors' Town that we realised just how serious it really was. We knew the auxiliaries who were based in the fort there pretty well, given that we'd marched up and down the road from Yew Grove a good few times over the years, so when we got within a mile or so of the place the men started to look pretty unhappy.'

He drank again, his eyes meeting the Tungrians' over the rim of his beaker.

'It was the smell that gave it away, you see, the stench of rotting meat. Putrid it was, like the smell you get on the farm when an ox dies in the summer and you don't find its carcass for a week. I could hear the flies before we even got inside the fort, and when we saw what the bastards had done . . .' He stopped, shaking his head with moist eyes. 'You'll think I've gone soft, but none of you could have witnessed what we saw without it hitting you like a kick in the balls. They'd killed everyone, not just the soldiers but every single person in the fort's vicus as well, and then they'd piled them up on the parade ground and left them to rot. Soldiers, old men, women, children, all butchered and left for the crows, their bellies distended with the gases and their eyes pecked out. Half of the men were choking their guts up while the rest were crying like babies at the sight of the bodies of little kids with their throats cut. Once we'd burned what was left of them the tribune got us centurions together with a face like thunder and told us that it was time to teach the Brigantes what happens when they go too far. He was right, of course, and there wasn't one of us that ever considered disobeying his orders, but . . .'

'But what?'

Julius was leaning forward now, his eyes fixed on Tullo's face.

'We were ordered to conduct an offensive sweep of every village within ten miles of the fort.' The legion centurion's face was stony, his eyes fixed on the mess's wooden wall. 'And just what *do* the words "offensive sweep" mean, you might ask? The orders were made very clear, and read out to the cohorts on parade to make sure that not one of the men was in any doubt as to what would be expected of them. We were to surround each village in turn with overwhelming force, allowing no escape routes, then subdue the population and pull out every man of fighting age to be sold into slavery, without exception. Every item of any value was to be confiscated, every roof to be burned, and anyone offering any resistance was to be killed without any warning. And that's just what we did . . .'

He looked around at their uncomprehending faces with the ghost of a wry smile.

'You can't see it, can you? The Sixth recruits its men from the area to the north and the south of Yew Grove, smart local lads who want to better themselves and see a brighter future serving under the eagle than hunting or farming the land they were born on. A good number of them were recruited from the very villages they were being ordered to ransack and torch.'

Tullo fell silent, taking a long drink from his beer, and Julius voiced the question that every one of them was thinking.

'How did they respond?'

The legion man shrugged.

'Well enough, I suppose, given the circumstances. A few men decided to run rather than face their own people with a drawn sword, and inevitably most of them were captured and brought back to face military justice.'

'The usual?'

He nodded again at Marcus's question.

'The usual. We beat each of them to death at dawn the day after they were dragged back into camp. I say "we", because it was clear to the officers that we'd have a mutiny on our hands if the condemned men's tent parties were ordered to carry out the sentence, so we did it for them. Some of them hated us for it even more than they'd hated us before, and some gave us a grudging respect for sparing them the choice between mutiny and murdering their friends for doing something they'd all considered.'

He drank again, and Julius pursed his lips in appreciation of the stark nature of the war the legionaries had been required to fight against their own people.

'So you finished pacifying the area round Sailors' Town and then marched up here?'

Tullo lowered his beaker, nodding gratefully as Dubnus refilled it to the brim with a sympathetic grimace.

'Yes, and we were lucky in not being posted to the Antonine Wall. We've heard stories from the messengers stopping here overnight on their way south as to just what it was that the cohorts up there had to cope with. What they found themselves faced with was having to live alongside forts burned out and left to rot the last time they were abandoned twenty years ago, while the Venicones raided from the north at every opportunity and ambushed the work parties sent out to cut wood for the reconstruction work. A couple of centuries were torn up so badly that the legatus had to ban any detachment of less than a half a cohort from going north of the wall. There are some nasty rumours doing the rounds as well, about men who can change themselves into wolves at night and a pack of female warriors who hunt down any man left alive after an ambush and cut off his manhood before torturing him to death. All bullshit of course, but you put men under that sort of strain and the stories are going to fly thick and fast. It wasn't much of a surprise when the Twentieth Legion mutinied and offered Legatus Priscus the throne, if only he'd get them back south to the old wall. They were bloody fools though . . .'

Julius nodded his agreement.

'If he'd taken the offer seriously he would have led you all off to fight for the empire in Gaul or Germany, with your three legions against double the number in all likelihood, and if you'd lost that battle you'd probably never have seen Yew Grove again even if you'd lived. So what stopped this Priscus from taking them up on the offer?'

Tullo sank the rest of his beer before speaking again, wiping his mouth with the back of his hand.

'Simple common sense, I expect. He came through here a

month or so ago, headed south to Yew Grove with our legatus after they were both relieved of command, and he looked like a man with a calm head on his shoulders, a proper Roman general. Not like that fool Governor Marcellus, it was all his fault for sending us north in the first place. And now he's been recalled to the hardships of his estate in Rome while the rest of us poor bastards pay the price for his stubbornness in blood and terror . . .'

'Look out for some ligusticum, Lupus, that's the herb we need to bring a bit of life back to lamb that's been dead for longer than might be ideal. You know what to look for, those broad three bladed leaves?'

The child nodded at Felicia, answering without conscious thought, his eyes bright as he searched the ground before them for any sign of its presence.

'Yes, Mother.'

The doctor stared fondly at the child for a moment before returning to her own search, shaking her head at the speed with which he had adopted her and Marcus as his de facto parents. Behind them a tent party of soldiers were searching the trees clustered around them with hard eyes, having been warned of the dire consequences that would befall them if they were to allow any mishap to befall the woman and child.

Lupus was the first to smell it, wrinkling his nose at the faint but still unmistakable aroma of burned wood, and as he turned to Felicia with a questioning look she nodded her head.

'I smell it too.' They advanced down the hill's slope, finding a faint path through the wild vegetation, but before the child could investigate any further, the tent party's leader, a tall soldier with a fresh pink scar across the bridge of his nose, put a hard-fingered hand on his shoulder.

'Not quite so fast, young 'un.' He turned to Felicia with an apologetic expression. 'I'm sorry, Domina, but we'll lead from here. There may be things down there best not seen by the likes of you and the boy.'

The doctor smiled up at him wryly.

'We've both seen rather more "things" than you might think possible, soldier, but I appreciate your concern for our safety. After you, by all means.'

The soldier nodded his thanks to her and ordered his men to form a skirmish line, advancing down the slope to either side of the path with their spears held ready to fight. Behind them Lupus drew his short sword, drawing amused smiles from the soldiers closest to him which he ignored with a face set hard in concentration. A hundred paces further down the hill the canopy of trees opened to reveal the late evening's pink glow, and the soldiers stopped their advance to stare down into the ruins of what had clearly been a prosperous village until quite recently. Thirty or so burned-out dwellings were arrayed before them, their remaining timbers black with soot, previously straight beams that had been gnawed by fire until they had been left twisted and notched. The inferno that had been visited upon the settlement had reduced it to a ghost town, with only the skeletal remains of its once comfortable existence to bear witness to what had been there before. The tall soldier grimaced at the village's wreckage, shaking his head.

'Offensive sweep. Everyone in the village either killed or enslaved, anything of value confiscated and the houses and crops put to the torch. We did a few of these, back when the rebellion was getting nasty, just to show them who was in control . . .' His voice tailed off, and he looked about him hollow-eyed. 'Just like my own village, I expect. You'll find what you're looking for easily enough, every house had its own little patch of herbs.'

He led his men forward, putting his spear over his shoulder and shrugging at Lupus who was still holding his sword out in front of him.

'Nice strong wrists you've got there, sonny, but you've no need for the blade. There's no one round here to offer you a fight, that's for certain.' He stepped into what had been the vegetable garden of a half-collapsed house, reaching down to grasp a knee-high plant and pull it up by the roots. 'Here you are ma'am, ligusticum.'

Felicia looked down at the herb garden, plants growing uncontrolled in the absence of their previous owner.

'And not just ligusticum either. I see thymus and feniculum as well. Gather it all please, especially the ligusticum. That which we don't use for cooking can be boiled up to make a very effective means of cleaning wounds and preventing infection. Oh, and I'll have as much of *that* as you men can carry . . .' Directing the soldiers' attention to a plant that had grown up in the shadow of the destroyed structure's remaining beams, she laughed at their mystified stares. 'That bush isn't just good for producing raspberries in the autumn, the leaves are wonderfully powerful sources of goodness. And we'll have a strong need of that particular remedy before very long, I expect.'

She turned to see Lupus stretching up to pick a dark-purple berry from an overhanging bush.

'Leave that, Lupus dear, it's quite the most poisonous fruit known to man.' She turned to the soldier. 'I'll have a helmet full of those berries though, if you could pick them for me without breaking them please? After every battle there are men whose injuries are too terrible for them to live, and who nevertheless cling on to life for hours or even days of suffering. Even a few drops of the juice of that berry are usually enough to send them on their way without further suffering.'

Tullo sat back and sipped at his beer again, looking with what Marcus took for calculation at the three men facing him.

'So now you know what we've been through perhaps you'll find it in you to recognise that in our shoes you might be looking just as shagged out and pathetic as we do now.'

Dubnus held out his beaker and tapped brims with the legion centurion.

'Here's to you. I don't reckon our men would have reacted any better if we'd ordered them to sack the villages around our fort on the wall.'

Julius nodded reluctantly, and Tullo leaned forward again, slipping a wooden tablet out of his tunic and putting it on the table next to his beaker. When he spoke, his words were pitched so low that the Tungrians had to strain to hear them.

'The rumours have it that you're marching north to get our eagle back.'

He sat in silence, staring intently at Julius and waiting for the first spear to reply. After a long pause the burly centurion sat forward and narrowed his eyes in question.

'That's supposed to be a secret. Who the *fuck* told you?'

Tullo smiled tightly back at him.

'My first spear. And don't worry, I know how to keep my mouth shut.' He pointed to the tablet with a meaningful expression. 'As it happens I'd say he had good reason for letting me in on that little secret, since he knows what's written in here.'

The first spear's face set in sceptical lines and he shook his head.

'I'll be the judge of that, if it's all the same to you.'

Tullo shrugged, picking up the tablet.

'Suit yourself. Hear me out for just a little longer and then tell me to "fuck off and die quietly" if you like.' He leaned close again. 'It wasn't *just* me that joined up, all those years ago. My brother Harus came to present himself to the recruiting centurion alongside me, two years younger than me and about twice as good at soldiering as ever I managed. He could've done the job of centurion without breaking a sweat, and I reckon he'd have made a bloody good cohort first spear, perhaps even got the big man's job at the head of the legion's first century with a little bit of luck. But all of that command stuff wasn't for him . . .' He paused for a moment and looked up at the roof, shaking his head with a smile. 'No, all Harus ever wanted to be was the man carrying the emperor's eagle round, the daft sod, and bugger me if he didn't manage to get himself the job not soon after I made centurion. He was the senior officers' golden boy you see, as honest as the day is long, deadly with a sword, the sort of strong-jawed man they take out into the villages to impress the young lads on recruiting tours, and did he love that eagle? He must have spent an hour a day polishing the bastard, and I swear he used to take it to the latrine with him to make sure nobody got the chance to put their dirty fingerprints on it.'

'This is all very touching, but I'm starting to lose the will to live here. What's your point?'

Tullo raised an eyebrow at the frowning first spear.

'See this?' He pointed to a dark stain in the tablet's wooden casing. 'It's his *blood*. He stopped an arrow in the throat at the battle of the Lost Eagle and choked to death. I found him later that afternoon, after we'd pulled your knackers out of the fire . . .' His smile hardened momentarily as he leaned across the table. 'Oh yes, I remember that all right, how you lot had been left to fight the barbarians to the death, and how that crusty old cavalry tribune Licinius led what was left of the Sixth down that forest path to save your arses. Anyway, I knew where to go and look for him, right in the middle of the circles of dead legionaries that were all that was left of the six cohorts that Legatus Sollemnis led into that ambush. There was a sword hidden beneath his body, with a beautifully made pommel that looked just like an eagle's head. A lot like that one, as it happens . . .'

He pointed at the swords resting against the wall where Marcus had left them.

'When I saw you unfastening them earlier I wondered if that weapon looked familiar, and now I see it up close it's clearly the same sword. And why, I wonder, does a centurion end up wearing a sword that I was told had probably belonged to Legatus Sollemnis, hidden under Harus's body to keep it from the barbarians? None of my business, I suppose . . .'

'Bloody right it's not.'

He ignored Julius and continued.

'So why did I go and find my brother, when there were barbarians to be taking revenge upon? Partly to be sure that he was dead, and that he'd not been taken captive by the bluenoses, and partly to see what I could salvage from his body to remember him by. The blue-nosed bastards hadn't had the time to strip him clean, else you wouldn't be wearing that pretty sword, Centurion, but they had taken his bearskin which was the only thing he was

carrying that wasn't standard legion issue. And they left this . . .'
He raised the tablet again. 'None of them could read, I suppose.
And even if they could, who could ever make sense of it?'

He opened the slim wooden box, presenting the Tungrian
officers with the wax writing surface. Dubnus peered at the tightly
packed words, struggling to make sense of them.

'Not me. It's impossible to read.'

Tullo smiled at him, tapping his nose.

'Not if you know what you're looking at. Allow me to explain . . .'

'I'm done for the day. Come back tomorrow.'

The stone mason turned away from the two soldiers, closing
the door to his workshop and fishing in his purse for the key with
which to lock it firmly shut. Sanga and Saratos exchanged glances,
the former reaching into his own purse to fish out an impressive
handful of coins. Jingling them noisily he shrugged, speaking
loudly as he turned away.

'Come on then, Saratos, let's go and find a mason who's bright
enough not to turn away customers who want to pay extra for
excellent fast work. We'll just take all this silver to a man who
doesn't turn good money away . . .'

The mason shot out an arm and grabbed the soldier's sleeve,
quickly releasing the hold when he saw the look on Sanga's face.

'Not so hasty, sir, I only meant to say that my normal business
hours are at an end. For customers such as your good selves I'm
always available to discuss commissions for fine stonework.
Statues, gravestones—'

'An altar. A nice big one with a carving of a soldier.'

The mason smiled broadly.

'Altars are my speciality, gentlemen. What wording were you
thinking of having inscribed onto the stone?'

Sanga nodded to Saratos, who passed over a tablet in which
Morban had painstakingly written out the words that Sanga and
his tent mates had agreed.

'For the ghost gods . . .'

The mason beamed at the two men.

'A nice traditional start, if I might say so, gentlemen. So many men seem to omit it these days just to save money, and I've always thought it's a false economy not to give the appropriate reverence to the shades of the departed. I . . .'

He saw a look of impatience creeping onto Sanga's face and returned his attention to the tablet.

'. . . *dedicated to the memory of the soldier Scarface . . .*'

He looked up at Sanga with a look of confusion.

'Did he not have a *proper* name?'

Saratos snorted.

'Yes, have *proper* name, but he call *Scarface* by men he fight and die with. So *Scarface* is he name for altar.'

Sanga nodded, his eyes misty.

'Couldn't have put it better myself.'

The mason shrugged.

'As you wish, gentlemen. So . . . *a man whose scars were all in his front.* A noble sentiment for a soldier, I'm sure. How soon would you like this to be completed, and where shall I place it?'

Sanga weighed the handful of coins with a meaningful clink of metal.

'Here's how it is. We're marching on tomorrow, as far as the northern wall and then some more, and we'll be back inside a week or two. When we march back we want to see a nice, crisp new altar, with a carving of a soldier fighting, in the front rank mind you, and that wording, installed on the roadside as close to the fort as you're allowed to put it. Think you can manage that?'

The mason drew himself up, holding up his splayed hands to display the broad, scarred fingers that were the tools of his trade.

'With these two hands, gentlemen. I'll put my other commissions on hold until this task is completed.'

He spat on his palm and offered it to Sanga, who took it in a powerful grip.

'Done.'

He handed over the coins, nodding as the mason slipped them into his purse.

'Just don't let me down, eh? Old Scarface meant a lot to me.

If I find myself disappointed, then mark me well, you'll be wearing your danglers for earrings.'

The mason bowed obsequiously as the soldiers turned away, weighing the purse in his palm with a smile as he watched the two men disappear down the hill into their camp.

Calgus shuffled flat-footed into the eagle's shrine, pausing for a moment to look around the room's smoke-blackened walls. The dead-eyed gazes of several dozen men returned his scrutiny, their stares unblinking in the dim light of the shrine's lamps, part of the mystique that the tribe's holy man had woven around the legion standard since the crippled Selgovae leader had surrendered it to the new king as the price of his safety among the Venicones. Pride of place among the severed heads that lined the shrine's walls was given to that of the legatus his own champion had killed on the same afternoon that his once powerful tribe had overrun the Sixth Legion early in the revolt two years before and captured their precious eagle standard. Stored for many months in a jar of cedar oil to prevent it rotting, the head had then been dried in a smokehouse until the skin was taut around the dead Roman's skull, and its features shrunk in size to those of a child, albeit still recognisable as the defeated legion's commander.

'You have come to worship the eagle, perhaps?'

The former Selgovae king frowned momentarily, then smiled as his eyes found the priest in the room's half-darkness.

'I come to refresh my memories of the glory I won in taking the eagle from the Romans. You will recall that my tribe were at war with the invaders long before your people deigned to join us in our fight?'

The holy man stepped out from beside the wooden case in which he kept the eagle with a forbidding look on his face.

'I recall that your leading us to war resulted in the death of my king, and the loss of enough men to force the Venicones back onto our own land. Were the Romans to attack us now, rather than huddle behind their wall, then I doubt that we would have the strength to resist. It is fortunate for all of us, but especially for *you*, that they seem to lack any further appetite to come north.'

Calgus nodded his reluctant acceptance of the sentiment.

'It seems that everyone is tired of war, Priest, except for me. I still dream of one more battle, and another defeated legion to send the Romans south with their tails between their legs. We only have to tempt them over the wall and onto your tribe's ground, and we could yet have them by the balls.'

The priest grimaced.

'One more battle, Calgus? One more chance for my people to bleed for your ambitions? You may not be king here, but it's clear that you still harbour ambitions that will either result in the destruction of Roman power over the north of their province or the Venicone tribe being crushed beneath their boots, if you were ever to get your own way on the matter.'

He stepped closer to Calgus, pulling a dagger from his robes to show the Selgovae the blade's bright line, and the former king recoiled involuntarily before regaining his equilibrium.

'You *threaten* me, Priest?'

The holy man laughed hollowly.

'No, Calgus, I do not. If I wanted you dead I would simply whisper in the ear of King Brem's master of the hunt, and have him send one of his Vixens to deal with you. Imagine the shame of that, Selgovae, dying at the hands of a woman.' He leaned closer to the deposed king, lowering his voice. 'They are vicious bitches, Calgus, more likely to hack your balls off and leave you to bleed to death than to give you the mercy of a clean death, and I would set them upon you without a second thought to spare my tribe the risk of your leading us to yet more disaster, if I did not already know that your death is close to hand.' He lifted the blade again. 'No, I show you this sacred knife, with which I perform my rites of sacrifice and augury, to make clear the means by which I have predicted your doom.'

Calgus smiled broadly, shaking his head in disbelief.

'Your bloody-handed "augury" may deceive the simpletons of your tribe, Priest, but you have no more chance of predicting what is to come from examining the guts of a dead sheep than I have of ever running again. You can take your predictions and put them where the sun—'

The priest laughed again, turning the knife's blade to catch the lamplight and sending flickers of illumination across Calgus's face.

'The sun? Or perhaps you meant to say "the son", the child of a man who suffered a sad reversal of fortune at the end of his life. The son returns, Calgus. The *son*.'

The priest smiled at him without any hint of warmth, and the Selgovae's eyes slitted as the meaning of his words sank in.

'What?'

The amusement had fled from his face in an instant, replaced by a snarl of anger, but if the priest was discomfited by the change it wasn't apparent.

'I read your fate in the liver of a blameless lamb, Calgus, and from your reaction it's clear enough that you know all too well of what I speak. I sacrificed the animal in order to see your fate, Calgus, and when I laid its liver on the altar I saw three things in your future.'

Gritting his teeth at having to stoop to entertaining the priest's tale, Calgus put his face inches from the other man's.

'And?'

The priest shook his head in dark amusement.

'What, you wish to know my "bloody-handed prediction", do you? I thought that they were only for simple—'

'Tell me what you saw, Priest!'

The holy man opened his hands.

'Very well, Calgus, since you insist. There were three things in your future, as revealed to me by the gods through my ability to read the sacrifice. I saw the son, still strong with the urge for revenge. Doubtless you have ordered the deaths of enough men that one of their sons has survived to dream of revenge upon you. I saw a prince, a man apart from those around him. Might he be the same person as the son? I cannot say. And I saw death, Calgus, unmistakable and implacable. Death.'

The Selgovae shook his head in bafflement.

'The son . . . I know of such a man. But I know of no prince, nor of any king I killed whose son remains alive to seek revenge.' He frowned. 'And death? Whose death, Priest?'

The holy man shook his head again.

'I am not blessed with such powers that I can predict the future to such a degree of accuracy. All I know is that there is death in your future. Perhaps it beckons the son, perhaps it will take the prince. Most likely this death is your own, since I named you in the sacred words I said before sacrificing the lamb. But there will be death, Calgus. And *soon*.'

3

The Tungrians paraded to march north again at first light the next day, Tullo's tablet safely tucked away in a corner of Tribune Scaurus's campaign chest. Drest and his companions were never far from Marcus's place at the head on his Fifth Century, and as the Roman marched his men onto the parade ground he felt the eyes of the Sarmatae twins on his back. Julius and Scaurus stood in conversation for a few moments, the tribune emphasising his words with several chopping gestures into his empty palm, after which the muscular first spear stalked down the line of his centuries followed by a pair of men the soldiers had learned to give careful respect over the previous year. Going face-to-face with Castus's mercenaries with the barbarian giant Lugos looming over one shoulder and Scaurus's muscular servant Arminius at the other, the first spear stood for a moment in silence, allowing time for their threat to become apparent with his hard stare fixed on the Sarmatae twins' bruised faces. Both of the men arrayed behind him were carrying their usual weapons, in Lugos's case a war hammer so heavy that few other men could lift it without grunting and straining at the effort required, let alone wield it with the giant's terrifying speed and power, one side of the weapon shaped into a pointed iron beak while the other sported a viciously hooked axe blade. Julius pointed to the twins, his face hard with purpose.

'You pair of maniacs are a little bit too quick to start throwing sharp iron around for my tribune's liking, so he's instructed me to make it very clear to you that the use of swords for training bouts is specifically forbidden.' Ram and Radu stared back with what Marcus, standing nearby, had strongly suspected was a deliberate failure to understand, and the first spear crooked a broad finger at

Drest. 'You, come here and translate this so there's no chance of misunderstanding. You two, listen to me and *don't* fucking interrupt unless you want a bloody good hiding.'

He waited for Drest to translate, smiling grimly as the threat of violence sank into the twins' expressions.

'These two men . . .' He hooked a thumb back over his shoulder at the barbarians behind him. '. . . are the two nastiest bastards you're ever likely to encounter, and they both seem to have a soft spot for Centurion Corvus for reasons I struggle to understand. So, in the event that either of you takes a blade to *my* centurion without *my* permission, they are both ordered to take their iron to *you* with equal vigour. And that, gentlemen, will mean that you will be fighting for your lives. Do. You. Understand?'

Both men listened to the translation with glum faces, nodding at its completion. Julius nodded dourly, speaking over his shoulder as he turned away to get the column moving.

'Good. You two, watch them. And don't wait for an order to deal with them if they get uppity, just put them out of the fight in any way you choose, and we'll worry about the niceties afterwards.'

'Niceties?'

Arminius smiled knowingly at Lugos's frown. The hulking Selgovae tribesman's grasp of Latin had improved over the months since his capture early in the campaign against Calgus, but many words still eluded his understanding.

'Yes. Niceties. You know the sort of thing, finding a small coin to put in the dead man's mouth for the ferryman. Gathering wood for a pyre.'

Lugos nodded solemnly.

'Niceties. A good word. I would remember it.'

'I *will* remember it.'

The big man turned to stare down at the Fifth Century soldier who had reflexively corrected him without any invitation to do so, his expression quizzical.

'This is . . . wait, I remember . . . yes, this is . . . *piss taking*?'

'*No!*'

The Tungrian's eyes widened, and he raised his hands in disavowal of any idea that he might have been making fun of the Selgovae warrior looming over him. Lugos stooped his neck until his face was close to the soldier's, who was prevented from shrinking away by the unhelpful refusal to budge of the men behind him, and patted his hammer's roughly shaped iron beak.

'Yes. *Will*. Is another good word. I *will* teach you not take piss. I *will* give you tickle with hammer. You *will* need "niceties".'

Arminius peered around the big man at the terrified soldier, raising an eyebrow.

'What he needs is a change of leggings, I'd say. Leave him alone you big horrible bastard, you've made your point.'

The Tungrians marched north again that morning at a fast pace, alternating the double march with the standard pace all day to cover the best part of thirty miles, their hobnailed boots rapping onto the parade ground at Three Mountains an hour before sunset. Julius watched his men stagger wearily onto the flat surface with an appraising stare, grateful that he'd not been carrying a shield, spears or a pack for the day's march.

'The men are just about shattered, Tribune, so I propose that just this once we might break the first commandment and allow them to use the marching camp that was left here last year when the Petriana wing cornered the Venicones in the ruins of the fort.'

The burned-out shell of the large fort that had guarded the road north before the northern tribes' revolt stood before them, its soot-stained stone walls looming over the parade ground in mute testimony to the ferocity of the storm of iron that had washed over the empire's northernmost defence under Calgus's leadership. Tribune Scaurus nodded slowly, scanning the fort with hard eyes.

'That looks like a punishment frame up there.'

Julius turned back to face him with a grim smile.

'It is, and it was used to torture and kill one of our own not too long ago. One of the Petriana's decurions told our own tame cavalry decurion the story, and Silus told it to me in turn one night after a few beers. It seems one of the Petriana's officers had a hard-on for treasure, and used to go looting whenever he got the chance. Silus knew the man of course, and he told me that he kept his stolen gold in an oak chest that was always locked, with no one brave enough to try to rob him on account of how fierce he was. Anyway, although they never found out quite how it happened, the same night that our old friend Tribune Licinius managed to bottle up the Venicones in there –' he tipped his head at the fort's blackened walls '– while he was chasing them north after we beat Calgus at the Battle of the Forest, the ink monkeys crept out in the dark and lured this gold-struck idiot into some sort of trap. They dragged him off into the fort, strapped him up there on that frame and went to work on him with their knives right in front of the cavalry lads, cut him a hundred times and then stuck a spear through each thigh and slit his belly wide open, but he never gave out as much as a squeak. Which, fool though he was, is not something I could have hoped to match under the same circumstances. In the end their king got bored of the whole thing and cut his throat, leaving him hanging up there as a lesson for the horse boys to keep their distance. Apparently when the tribune ordered his campaign chest to be opened there was enough gold in there to retire a legion century and still have enough left over for them to get pissed and laid every night for a month.'

Scaurus smiled wryly at the first spear.

'The moral being not to get too greedy, eh?'

Julius barked out a laugh.

'The moral being not to be so stupid as to wander away from your unit at night when there's barbarians about, I'd say. Anyway, the fort's unusable without a few days' putting new gates up and the men are just about beaten for the day, so . . .'

The tribune nodded.

'Agreed. It's not as if there's a barbarian army in the field. We'll use the existing marching camp, but let's not relax too much. We'll do without listening patrols, since there won't be anything to listen to out here, but let's keep the guard routine nice and tight, shall we?'

⋆   ⋆   ⋆

'I never thought I'd be so grateful to see another bloody legion fortress.'

Felicia glanced across at Annia with a look of concern, realising from her assistant's pale face and look of discomfort that she was badly in need of a rest from the wagon's constant rattling over the road's cobbles. The high stone walls of Yew Grove had come into sight as the road had crested the last hill that lay between the gold convoy and its destination in the softening light of late afternoon, and the soldiers marching at the convoy's front and rear had promptly started belting out a marching song at the tops of their voices.

'They sound rather grateful too.'

Annia managed a strained smile at her friend's straight-faced statement.

'I'd imagine they're sending a message to the vicus whorehouses, given that we're less than a mile away from hot baths and free time.'

Felicia laughed.

'You're probably right. When did a man ever think with anything other than his stomach and what hangs from the end of it?'

She passed across the leather bottle which she had filled with tea brewed from the leaves of the raspberry bush the previous evening.

'Another drink of this might help to ease the cramp?'

Annia waved it away with a disgusted expression.

'I've already had enough of that for one lifetime. The midwives may well swear by it, but all I know is that it tastes like horse piss. Save it to offer your new suitor, one mouthful of that might shrivel his prick up for a day or two and stop him sniffing round you like a dog after a bitch.'

Felicia's expression darkened. Tribune Sorex had met the convoy just after midday, escorted by several centuries of legionaries heading north under the command of a hard-faced centurion with a thick black beard and a long scar that bisected one eye and ran to his jaw.

'On you march, Centurion Gynax, I'll escort the gold back into the fortress. Good luck with your quest for the eagle!'

Gynax had saluted with what had looked to Felicia like a knowing look, and Sorex had sent his men on to the north with a lazy wave of one hand before reining his horse in alongside that of the camp prefect and chatting to his more experienced subordinate for a while. Once satisfied that no harm had befallen his precious cargo, he had dropped down the convoy's line until the medical wagon had passed, falling in alongside the doctor with a broad smile.

'Well now, ladies, how are you? I swear you both look more radiant then you did yesterday, if that's possible!'

Annia, slumped heavily in her place on the wagon's bench seat in a position intended to protect her from the road's potholes, had regarded him with a disbelieving glare, and Felicia, sharing her discomfort at his insincerity, had answered with care.

'And you, Tribune, you truly look as if you don't have a care in the world. How do you keep such equanimity under such trying circumstances?'

Sorex had smiled back at her, allowing his hard gaze to linger on her body for longer than might have been polite.

'Equanimity, madam? It's simple enough. My gold is about to roll into the strong stone walls of a legion fortress, where it will be carried down into the chapel of the standards and placed under twenty-four hour guard . . .'

'*Your* gold?'

He'd affected not to have heard Annia's muttered response.

'Apart from that, I have several centuries heading north to investigate a fresh piece of information as to the whereabouts of my legion's missing eagle—'

Annia's response was louder than before, and she'd leaned forward awkwardly with a questioning look.

'You sent our men north yesterday to chase your eagle, following "unmistakable intelligence" as to the eagle's whereabouts, as I heard it. So what news do you have now?'

Clearly taken aback at being questioned by a mere doctor's orderly, he'd frowned at her for a moment before deciding to dignify the question with a response.

'As it happens, madam, we have information that the lost eagle, far from residing in the Venicone fortress to the far north, may well have been sent south to dwell among the Brigantes. A sort of double bluff, if you like, hiding the thing where we are least likely to look for it. Of course the tip may be false, but I would be failing in my duty were I not to investigate the report, wouldn't you say?'

Felicia had nodded, tapping her assistant's ankle with her toe in warning.

'Quite so, Tribune. I'm sure that you will be leaving no stone unturned in your search for such an emotive symbol of your legion's pride.'

Sorex had bowed his head in recognition of her words, the predatory smile returning to his face.

'*Emotive!* Just the term I would have used myself! You really are quite a lady, Doctor, both erudite and possessed of looks that would put Aphrodite to shame were a comparison ever possible. I look forward to seeing more of you!'

And with that he had spurred his horse back up the column, leaving the women staring after him in a combination of bemusement and disbelief. Annia shook her head in disgust, leaning back in the wagon's uncomfortable bench seat.

'Best beware that one, I'd say. I ran a whorehouse for long enough that I've seen thousands of men looking for sex, but only a very few with the look that one has about him. He's a taker, and a cruel-looking bastard at that, and if you let him get you alone he'll be buried up to his balls in you before you know it, and you without much choice in the matter I'd guess.'

Felicia had stared at the tribune's receding back with a troubled expression.

'Yes, I've seen that look before. It's the one my first husband used to give to the women he regarded as being there solely for the purpose of conquest, once he had me safely married. As you say, I may have my work cut out to avoid the tribune's attentions until our men return from the north.'

★   ★   ★

'It just don't feel right to me. It's like going to a whorehouse without getting a few beers down your neck first.'

Spared the usual labour of throwing up a turf-walled marching camp, the Tungrians found themselves bemused at the opportunity to do nothing more than sit around their tents and talk, waiting for their rations to be prepared by those men deemed suitably skilled in the use of the big iron cook pots that each century dragged into their section of the camp from the mule carts that carried their tents.

Sanga grinned lopsidedly at the speaker, a soldier from the adjoining tent party by the name of Horta who was known to fancy himself as the big man whilst never quite finding the courage to square up to the party's de facto leader and press his claim.

'From what I've heard you're more one for getting a few too many beers down your neck first, and then presenting your chosen lady of the evening with a length of saggy meat that's no use to either of you!'

His mates guffawed quietly, used to his acerbic way and well-practised in giving him a taste of his own repartee if he persisted with levity at their expense, but Horta, it seemed, was less able to enter into the cut and thrust of the continuous jockeying for position that was part and parcel of life in the cohort.

'Fuck you, Sanga, I can make any women squeal with delight!'

The men about him shook their heads in dismay, more than one of them wincing visibly. This, as they well knew, was not how the game was played. Sanga grinned at him again, his eyes slitting with calculation as he selected his response.

'I *have* heard that from the ladies, to be fair.' Heads lifted again, as the men around the pair waited for the follow up, knowing that the rough soldier was silently counting in his head as Horta nodded sagely, accepting the apparent compliment. 'More than one of the whores we've both had has told me how happy she was to take your money in return for nothing worse than a peck on the cheek and a few reassuring words. So one or two of them must have squealed at the prospect of an hour off!'

The two tent parties collapsed in mirth, only Horta and his mate Sliga remaining stony faced.

'Fuck you, Sanga!'

The veteran shook his head in bemusement, altering the tone of his voice to match that of the other soldier, albeit pitched two octaves higher.

'*"Fuck you, Sanga!"* Is that it? Is that the best you can do, Sliga my old mate? No witty put down? Nothing better than *"Fuck you, Sanga!"*?' He got up, brushing the grass's damp from his tunic. 'There's no sport to be had here, I'm going to offer my services to Quintus for fetching water. Make sure there's some dinner left for me if it arrives while I'm away, or I'll be roasting a slice of one of your arses for my evening meal. You coming, Saratos, you barbarian bumboy?'

The Sarmatae got to his feet with a hard smile, flexing his biceps at the veteran soldier.

'Yes, I come carry water for you. Can carry two bucket more than you, since you tired from fucking animals.'

Sanga nodded appreciatively.

'There you go, Horta, that's the way to do it. Take the insult and give it back with interest. And don't be trying to stare me out, you pussy, not unless you want to lose that little battle as well.' Horta blinked, and his tormentor raised his eyes to the sky in wry amusement. 'See? Come on, Saratos. See you later, losers, we're off to spend some time with real men.'

Felicia looked about their new quarters in the Yew Grove fortress's vicus with an expression of relief, absent-mindedly stroking at the downy hairs on the head of the infant lolling slackly in her arms. The richly dressed woman who had led them from the gate to her house caught her stare and nodded apologetically, gesturing at the spare bedroom's lamplit space, a pair of beds standing on a plain tiled floor, its walls simple white-washed plaster.

'I'm sorry that I've nothing better to offer you. I know it's not up to much.'

Annia spun round to face her, the movement made ponderous by her swollen belly.

'You're *joking*! We're used to taking up residence in the fort's medical quarters, with wounded soldiers watching our every move like hungry dogs waiting for a bone, or in a tent surrounded by a sea of iron and leather. Have you ever lived in the middle of a cohort in the field after a few days on campaign?' The slightly built woman shook her head quickly, nervously fingering the collar of her rich wool stola that was the mark of a wealthy man's companion, the garment somehow slightly incongruous on her elegantly spare frame. 'You should try it, Domina, there's nothing quite like the smell of eight hundred men rank with days of dried sweat, all of them reeking of badly wiped arses and the stale cum left on their tunics from furtive nighttime wanking.'

The woman had introduced herself as Desidra at the fortress's gate, and had seemed nervous in the presence of the tribune and his men, keen to gather the women about her and be away from under their hungry eyes, and Felicia saw the same uncertainty in her as she raised her eyebrows, clearly taken aback by Annia's words. She took their hostess's hand in a warm two-handed grip.

'Ignore her, Domina, she's just tired and grumpy from carrying that baby for the best part of nine months, not to mention a two-day cart ride from the coast with legionaries making crude gestures at her at every turn.'

Annia nodded with a hint of a smile.

'Cheeky bastards. And me the scourge of every soldier within fifty miles of my old establishment. In my prime I only had to look at one of those mules with the merest hint of discouragement and they'd be falling over themselves to get back in my graces. If there was no smile from Annia then there'd be no pussy for him from any of my girls that night.'

The mistress of the house's painstakingly plucked eyebrows arched again, this time more in amazement than distaste.

'You were . . .'

'Oh yes, I was the madam of a brothel in Germania, and rather a good one too. I . . .'

Felicia smiled wanly at their new friend, waving a hand to silence her assistant.

'I suspect there are better ways that we might have got to know each other than swapping such revelations within a few minutes of meeting each other. But, since we're here, perhaps I ought to explain just who we are? Or did your . . . husband explain that already?'

Desidra shook her head.

'There was no opportunity. He banged on our door, told me to take care of you all and then hurried off shouting something about gold. I barely had time to get to the fortress's main gate before your cart arrived.'

Felicia smiled.

'In which case this must all be a little disconcerting. Perhaps we might take a seat on these highly inviting beds? I'm willing to risk the chance that either one of us might pass out from the simple joy of touching a clean sheet!'

She eased the sleeping Appius down onto the nearest bed's softly yielding surface while Annia sat down with a sigh of pleasure, then slumped back onto her back with her pregnant belly uppermost.

'Any time spent not carting this little monster around is a minute well spent.'

Desidra conceded the point.

'I have never carried a child myself, and the time when that is possible may have passed me by, but I can see that you carry a heavy burden. Now, if I am to understand what you have said, you –' she looked at Felicia with more than a hint of disbelief '– are a *doctor*? And you, madam, from your statements a moment ago, are a retired . . .'

She struggled for a polite way to continue the sentence, and Annia, her good temper returned with the bed's soothing embrace, smiled serenely at the ceiling in response.

'Prostitute, yes. Although the term we usually went under was "whore". And, let me tell you, you're looking at the best doctor and the best whore in the whole of this shitty, fucked-up country.'

Felicia waited in trepidation for Desidra's response, raising an eyebrow as the older woman smiled back at Annia and replied with a hint of mischief in her voice.

'Well you were clearly an industrious whore, my dear, to judge from your current condition!'

The Tungrian woman gaped for a moment then laughed uproariously, struggling into a sitting position.

'You're not quite as strait-laced as you might seem, are you?'

Desidra shrugged, the line of her jaw hardening as she raised her head defiantly.

'I had a life before Artorius Castus plucked me from a slave market to take care of his material needs, taking pity on my emaciated frame and never for a moment seeing the woman within. My father and brothers were killed in the German Wars, and I was washed up on the empire's border in a slave convoy, more dead than living, barely hanging on to my humanity through rape and degradation all the four months it took me to travel from my village to the marketplace. A woman doesn't survive being enslaved in the middle of a frontier war without learning to deal with the harshest aspects of life, no matter how soft the clothes I wear now that Artorius and I have become man and woman.' She looked about the room, shrugging at the bare plastered walls. 'And yes, you are stuck with these somewhat disappointing surroundings, at least for the time being. Once Legatus Equitius has returned from his visit to Fortress Deva, I'm sure Artorius will ask him to take you into his residence, but until then it'll be the five of us, a former slave, a former whore, the doctor and her infant son and . . . what do you call the child playing outside?'

Felicia smiled again, leaning back to look out of the room's window to where Lupus was regaling a group of wide-eyed vicus children with a story from his adventures with the Tungrian cohort.

'Lupus? Oh now, there's a complex story for you, Domina, but if ever there was a child born to be raised to manhood by soldiers, Lupus is that boy. Every day he trains to kill with a German who cares for him as if he were the father the boy lost in the barbarian revolt, while he provides my husband with a replacement for the younger brother he lost to Rome's murderers. And as for his grandfather . . .'

She frowned at Desidra's sudden inattention to her words, realising that the mistress of the house's face had suddenly turned to Annia, whose beatific expression at the bed's comfort had abruptly vanished as she stared in horror at the wide, wet stain on the sheets beneath her.

The next day's march north wound through a low mountain range, and the Tungrians hunched into their cloaks as curtains of misty rain advanced down the valley on a bitterly cold north wind. Trickles of water insinuated their way down necks and into socks, eventually soaking the soldiers through almost as thoroughly as a heavy deluge might have done. Wet, cold and exhausted from a third day marching at the double pace for much of the time, the cohort marched wearily across the bridge over the Wet River and found themselves facing the ruins of the fort that had for a time guarded the crossing.

'Silus!'

The grizzled decurion rode up the column at Julius's call, the riders of his squadron following in a long string, their progress punctuated by the barrage of insults and crude humour that was their customary accompaniment. Silus reined his horse in and jumped down to salute the first spear.

'You want me to go and find you a marching camp?'

Julius nodded, glancing round at their grim surroundings and pointing at the shattered ruins of the Wet River fort on the hillside to their north like a set of broken teeth.

'Well I'm not going anywhere near that. Not only will it be of absolutely no value defensively, but it'll scare the living shit out of the weaker sisters among the men. Besides which, before we know it we'll have Morban taking bets with the more easily led among us that the souls of dead soldiers are roaming the ruins and then paying someone to wander about groaning and rattling their mail once the sun's down.'

The horsemen quickly located the site of an old marching camp, the once proud turf walls sunken and gapped by decades of neglect, but the Tungrians set to with the urgency of men keen to be done with labour for the day and soon had it patched up to the first spear's satisfaction. Julius toured the four-foot-high enclosure in the day's last fading light and nodded his satisfaction to his officers.

'Very good. Construction teams dismissed, and we'll have double guards tonight this far north, supposedly friendly territory or not. And if you want a little ray of sunshine for your men, you can tell them that today was the last day we'll need to march quite that hard. Tomorrow morning we'll be approaching the eastern end of the wall and I think a gentler pace might be a wise way to approach, given how jumpy we're likely to find the occupying forces.'

Annia lay asleep on the wider of the guest room's two beds, her new-born daughter dozing contentedly in the crook of her arm after her second feed of the evening. The room was lit by a pair of oil lamps either side of the bed, and in their pale golden light Felicia and Desidra stood and watched fondly as the baby's tiny hands clenched and unclenched in her sleep.

'Your friend may have a hard face for the world, but she melted quickly enough once that tiny life was placed in her arms.'

Felicia nodded at the whispered comment, recalling the moment she'd held Appius for the first time.

'She wears the face that life thrust upon her when circumstances forced her to offer her body to an unending succession of men for whom she felt no emotion other than loathing. But when you scratch the surface of that hard mask you find all the same vulnerabilities and hopes that the rest of us entertain.'

Castus's woman was silent for a moment, staring down at mother and child with an expression of longing.

'I must confess myself more affected by the presence of this baby than I thought would be the case . . .'

Felicia nodded.

'It's a common reaction among the childless. Before I had my son I only had to see a child under five to desperately want to become a mother.'

'And now?'

'And now, Domina, whenever I see a baby I see years of dirty napkins to boil clean, food to mash and sleepless nights.'

The older woman looked up at her with a disbelieving smile.

'I realise that the nature of your calling compels you to seek to lighten my mood, and I thank you for trying, Doctor, but we both know that you worship that little man just as much as you love his father. And doubtless I would love my child no less, were Artorius and I to succeed in conceiving.'

'Your husband entertains hopes of a child?'

Desidra laughed softly.

'Of course! What man doesn't? He longs for a son to pass his blood down to future generations.' Desidra looked down at the sleeping baby for another long moment. 'Tell me, how will this one's father react to the delivery of a little girl? If I am to believe Annia, he is a man with a fearsome reputation?'

Felicia nodded, drawing the older woman away.

'And well deserved. He rescued her from her brothel and the owner sought to punish him by means of her humiliation and murder. When Julius brought her to safety he was painted from head to toe with the blood of the men he had caught raping her. Annia later told me that he hacked off one of her attackers' manhood before leaving him to bleed to death with the ruined meat on the floor in front of him.'

Desidra's face hardened with the image, her eyes narrowing at the prospect of such bloody revenge.

'There is more than one man upon whom I would have wished *exactly* such a death, given the chance. But seriously, how will such a man react to a female child?'

Felicia shrugged.

'I cannot tell you, but be assured, that little girl lies in the arms of a woman more than capable of putting Julius in his place should he react badly. In that partnership I'd have to say that she wields the longer sword.'

Rising from their damp blankets in the next day's dawn, a cloud-less sky having coated every surface with frost, the soldiers were for once grateful to receive the order to march. The cohort headed north-west in windless conditions towards Broad Land fort, the point where the road north would meet the Antonine Wall, trails of steam rising from each man's gear as it dried under the heat of his exertions, and conversation was limited to the occasional collective groan of complaint as individual soldiers broke wind.

'You don't fancy a ride today then, eh Centurion? The tribune has asked me to scout as far north as Broad Land, and I have permission for you to accompany us if you're game.'

Marcus looked up at Silus as the grinning decurion ranged up alongside him with a pair of riders following behind, looking down at the labouring troops with a sardonic smile.

'No thank you, Silus. The first spear did mention the possibility at this morning's officers' meeting, but you know how it is for us centurions. We share our men's hardships with the same pleasure that we take in their victories. And besides, where else would I hear the broad range of marching songs that we use to pass the time?'

The men in the century's front rank behind him took his words as a cue for song, dragging in lungfuls of air before roaring out the first verse of a ditty they had been working on for several days.

> *'We are the emperor's finest,*
> *We're marching to the front,*
> *We're going to kill the Venicones,*
> *'Cause they're all fucking cunts!'*

Silus pursed his lips approvingly.

'It has a certain poetic ring to it. And not a word about the cavalry either, which makes for a pleasant ch—.'

His words were drowned out by the next verse.

> *'Our cavalry's brave when on parade,*
> *With lots of shiny kit,*

But they piss off quick when the fighting starts,
And leave us in the shit!'

Silus looked down at his friend with a wry smile.

'We're never going to live down that battle on the frozen lake, are we? Come on my lads, let's leave these mules to fester in their own stink, shall we?'

The horsemen cantered away up the column's line, pursued by the words of the song's next verse.

'Our cavalry ride fine horses,
Of white and brown and black,
But each noble horse is deformed of course . . .'

The marching men took a collective gulp of breath to bellow out the last line at the horsemen's receding backs.

'By the arsehole on its back!'

The riders returned two hours later with news for the tribune.

'The wall's still manned sir, although the centurion I spoke to at Broad Land wasn't all that helpful. Seems to me like they're all just waiting for the command to head south as fast as their feet will carry them. When I asked him the best way to get a party of men into Venicone territory he pointed to the west and told me I needed the next fort along, Lazy Hill.'

The impression was reinforced by the state of affairs that they found when the cohort marched up to the Lazy Hill fort late that afternoon and were directed into a waiting marching camp. Julius left his centurions supervising its renovation to the standard he expected and took Marcus and Dubnus off for a good look around. His report back to Scaurus was delivered in a tone bordering on disbelief.

'It's not good, Tribune, not good at all. The fort's been rebuilt neatly enough, but the wall's in a bit of a state. It happens with turf structures if they're not maintained, but it's never a good sign when there are trees growing out of the rampart. They've got guards posted, but none of them seem to have any apparent interest in doing anything other than stand their watches and get off duty. There's enough rusty armour and dirty tunics here to have made dear old Uncle Sextus shit a cow if he'd lived to witness the state of them, may Cocidius watch over him, and none of the weapons that were on display looked like they had much of an edge. All of which tells me that the man at the top of this particular cohort has stopped caring what state his men are in. I had a chat with the duty centurion, since he seemed a bit more aggressively minded than the rest of them, and he confirmed it for me. The senior centurion has orders to do absolutely nothing to provoke the locals, orders which he seems to have embraced happily enough. The rest of the officers are variously bored, frustrated, and just pissed off with life, and their men are in a state of perpetual fear that the Venicones are going to come over the wall for them. I can understand it well enough, these boys are survivors of the battle of Lost Eagle, so they've been fighting without much respite for two years, but honestly, Tribune, this place is a disaster ready to happen.'

Scaurus nodded at his first spear's description of the fort's garrison, shrugging resignedly.

'Nothing we can do or say is going to change the state of things here though, is it? The army's grip on the north has been over-extended, and these men know only too well what that might mean if the tribesmen decide to come knocking on their door. I think the best thing we can do is ignore them and get on with doing the job we came for. And for what it's worth, I tend to share their viewpoint in one thing at least – the sooner we're back on this side of the wall and heading south the better. Let's go and see what the senior man can tell us about the state of affairs on the other side, shall we?'

They found the cohort's first spear in the fort's headquarters, and while his salute for the newly arrived tribune was smart enough, Marcus could sense just how demoralised he was beneath the surface. His chin was neither bearded nor clean-shaven, and there was a whiff of alcohol in the air that had Julius's nostrils flaring as he sniffed ostentatiously. The legion officer smiled sheepishly, offering them seats with a wave of his hand and reaching out to grasp the back of the chair he intended to sit down in once the senior officer was seated.

'When the guards reported you coming up the road, I dared to hope that you might be carrying orders to head south or that you might be our replacement.'

Scaurus laughed curtly, ignoring the seating and dropping his written orders onto the room's large wooden table.

'I'm afraid not, First Spear. We've been sent here by your Tribune Sorex to mount a raid into enemy territory. Our objective is a Venicone fortress that is known as "The Fang", I believe . . .'

The centurion gaped, shaking his head vigorously.

'But you can't—' He saw the look on the tribune's face and regained his composure. 'By which I mean to say that the locals are quiet at the moment and that's just the way we'd like them to stay. They've enough warriors to knock over any of the forts along the wall, and you can be sure that none of the other garrisons would come to our rescue, given the general order to hold position. Not to mention the fact that the local madmen would still have us outnumbered even if half a dozen forts tipped out their men and came to the rescue.'

Julius stepped forward with his face set hard, his notoriously thin patience evidently exhausted.

'In which case you'd better set your men to making sure that your walls are fit to repel them and your spears are nice and sharp, because we're under orders from the commanding officer of *your* legion to go and rescue *your* eagle from those tattooed lunatics. Once the order's given for you lot to pull back to the Emperor Hadrian's wall the chance will be lost for ever. The days of glorious campaigns into the north are gone, and your standard will vanish into the deepest forests never to be seen again other than by the tribal priests who'll be wiping their arses on it as part of their ritual.'

He paused for a moment to allow the thought to sink in.

'Worse still, Sixth *"Victorious"* –' he snorted in dark amusement '– will more than likely be removed from the records with the notation *"Eagle Lost – Disbanded"*. It'll be a sad end for a proud legion, and one that'll most likely leave *you* holding the shitty end of the stick. No one's going to do any favours for a centurion from one of the four cohorts that survived the massacre at Lost Eagle, are they? Once the emperor loses his patience with your failure to restore your honour by getting the bird back that'll be it for you. The cohorts that were sent to reinforce you from Germania will be detached, since they had nothing to do with the original foul up, and the rest of you will be split up to fill the ranks of the other Britannia legions while the men in the shiny armour get on with forming a new legion with an unspoiled name. I can see it now . . .' He paused and stroked his chin reflectively. 'Yes, First Imperial Legion Commodus, that'll be it. A legion that can be trusted to look after their eagle, unsullied by the presence of so much as a single man who participated in the loss of the last one. The new eagle's probably already been made and shipped to the province ready for the order to be given for you lot to be disbanded.' He paused again, fixing the first spear with an acerbic glare. 'So, all in all, if I were you I'd be trying to work out just what I could do to help us recover the bloody thing. Have you got a map of the area?'

The legion officer pulled a curtain away from a large map with a sick expression, Julius's words clearly sinking in as he pointed with his vine stick.

'That's us, here at Lazy Hill. You can see the line of the wall to the east and west, and then here are the High Mountains running away to the north-east.' He pointed to a black cross painted onto the map. 'There's The Fang.' He turned to Scaurus with a hint of desperation in his voice. 'But Tribune, as Mithras is my witness, if you try to break into that place you'll not be seen again. We've only one man that ever got over those walls and even he doesn't quite understand how he managed to escape.'

Scaurus's eyes narrowed.

'One of your men has been *inside* The Fang?'

The centurion smiled tightly.

'He's a bit of a celebrity, Tribune, but to be honest with you I'd say his door's flapping on its hinges, so I'd advise that you take anything he tells you with a large pinch of salt. He was captured by the Venicones about three months ago, the only man left alive out of a forage party of thirty men we sent out in the days before we were ordered not to allow any detachment of less than three centuries north of the wall. We found them slaughtered, with their heads and pricks cut off for trophies, and given that several men's corpses were nowhere to be found we reckoned they'd been taken to be stretched out on a stone altar and sacrificed to the Venicones' gods. The general assumption was that the ink monkeys would torture the shit out of the captured lads for long enough to drive them out of their minds before killing them, and certainly nobody ever expected to see any of them in one piece again. Verus pitched up three weeks ago, stark naked apart from a fur cloak he'd taken from some woman he'd killed and covered in mud, babbling about having been on the run for eight days. And he weighed thirty pounds less than when he was taken.'

The tribune nodded decisively.

'I'll see him now. Alone.' The legion man nodded, turning for the door. 'Oh, and centurion, this man's instability . . .'

'Yes, Tribune?'

'How does it manifest itself? Does he perhaps take drink in the morning, to soothe his nerves?'

The centurion's face crumpled as if he'd been punched, and his eyes closed as he answered, his voice little more than a whisper.

'*No . . .*'

'That's something to be said in his favour then, isn't it?' Scaurus stepped close to the abashed centurion, lowering his voice so as not to be heard outside of the office. 'I suggest you get a grip of yourself man, and look to your command before it falls to pieces around you. You know how it goes – you can lead, you can follow, or you can just get out of the way. If you don't think you've got it in you to provide your men with leadership, then I suggest you nominate your successor as First Spear and make way for someone that can.'

After a long silence the other man opened his eyes again, straightening his back.

'Thank you, sir. For not just demoting me, I mean. I'll get things straightened up round here soon enough . . .'

Scaurus nodded and turned away to look at the map.

'Demoting you might be a little beyond my authority, First Spear, even if I were tempted to do so. And besides, my men and I are believers in more direct ways of dealing with officers who fail to meet the required standards. If you let me down in this then I promise you that you'll have nowhere to hide from whichever of us survives this apparent suicide mission.'

After a few minutes' wait the door opened and a single soldier stepped into the room, snapping to attention and saluting smartly, staring at the wall behind Scaurus. His bare forearms were covered in the marks of what appeared to be recently healed burns, and his eyes were bright and hard beneath a full head of white hair.

'Soldier Verus reporting as ordered, Tribune!'

The Tungrians took a moment to assess his state, and Marcus realised that he was looking at the best turned out legionary he'd seen since their arrival. Scaurus stepped forward extending an arm to invite the soldier into the room.

'Take a seat please, Verus. Be seated gentlemen, let's not stand on ceremony.' He waited until everyone was seated before continuing. 'Without intending any disrespect to your comrades, legionary, you are by some distance the most well presented of the legion's soldiers I've seen all day. Why would that be, do you think?'

Verus smiled darkly.

'That's an easy one to answer, Tribune. I've seen the Venicones at close quarters, and I expect to see them again before very long. When they come over that wall there's at least one man who'll be ready to meet his gods with clean armour, and with blood on his spear blade.'

'I see. Your first spear tells me that you've recently achieved the notable status of being captured by the locals and then managing to escape?'

The soldier nodded, his face perfectly composed.

'That's correct, Tribune. I spent fifty-seven days as their prisoner before the gods saw fit to show me a way to escape from their fortress.'

Scaurus leaned forward, intent on the legionary's answers.

'Let's make sure that I have this right. You were taken to the fortress that they call The Fang?' Verus nodded again. 'Your first spear told us that he believed you had been taken captive for the purpose of sacrifice, rather than being killed on the spot.'

'So did I, sir. And I still believe that the Venicones intended to offer my blood to their gods, once they had achieved their initial purpose of breaking my spirit.'

The words hung heavily in the air, and Julius leaned forward to speak.

'They tortured you?'

Verus returned his stare with an unflinching gaze.

'Yes, First Spear. They tortured me for all of these fifty-seven days. They left me locked in a cell too small for a man to lie down in for much of the time, crouching in my own shit and sleeping so little that I lost all track of time. They used hot irons to burn my skin in their ritual patterns, inflicting enough pain on me to keep me in constant agony, but never enough to kill me. And they abused me in other ways, degraded me in a manner intended to reduce me from a man to a slave, lower than a slave . . .'

'But you held firm?'

The soldier stared back at Scaurus with a look of triumph.

'I held firm. Yes, I screamed in agony, I howled in my degradation and I cried like a baby at the shame of their using me like a woman, but I never lost my hold of who I was.'

'And who are you, legionary?'

Scaurus's question was gentle, but the reaction to it was anything but. Leaping to his feet and sending the chair flying, the soldier sprang to attention and roared out his answer.

'*Legionary Verus, Fifth Century, Eighth Cohort, Sixth Imperial Legion Victorious, Tribune sir!*'

Once Verus had retrieved his seat and sat down again at the tribune's gentle direction, Julius had asked him the question that Marcus had been burning to hear answered.

'So, soldier, tell me, just how did you escape from The Fang?'

The legionary looked up at the ceiling for a moment, smiling dreamily at the memory.

'My torturers became careless. They took my silence, and my downcast appearance for those of a man they had broken, as I gathered they had done with other men before me. They became ill disciplined with their tools, and there inevitably came a fleeting moment when one of them allowed a small knife to fall to the floor without realising the slip. I put my foot over the weapon, and when he turned away to tend to the fire in which his branding iron was heating up I stooped without making a noise and picked it up, tucking it between my buttocks beneath the filthy leggings I was wearing. When they returned me to my cell I knew that I only had a matter of hours in which to act, before the blade's absence was noted. To understand what I did next, you have to understand the fortress's construction.'

He raised an eyebrow at Julius, who nodded and gestured for him to continue.

'The Fang is built on a hilltop. It looks to me to be the sort of place that has been fortified since the beginning of time, and the fortress's walls are built on top of an old earth rampart. They put up a ten-foot tall wall of stone based on a wooden framework and set with mortar, and over the years the wood and mortar have rotted and aged to leave it quite unstable. I had already realised that the mortar holding a large stone in my cell's outer wall was crumbling, and I had guessed that it was an external wall from the way it became so cold at night. And besides, I was uncertain as to how much more of their torture I could tolerate, or how long it might be before they would tire of my resistance and sacrifice me to their gods without waiting any longer for me to surrender my sanity to their degradation. The priest who had branded me that day had seemed particularly satisfied with his work, standing back to look at me from various angles in the manner of a man surveying a completed piece of craftsmanship. He seemed proud of his work, and I assumed that with the ritual pattern complete I might be murdered at any time.'

'You dug your way out of the cell?'

Verus nodded in response to Marcus's question.

'As I said, the mortar was rotten. My job with the legion is that of builder, so I know just how far gone mortar can be without the rot being obvious. This stuff was like powder, and the knife's blade was the perfect tool for raking it out. I had the stone more or less free of those around it by the middle of the night, and then the small size of my cell became an advantage. I put my back against the inner wall and my feet to the wall then bore down on it with all the strength I had left. I managed to push the rock from its place, leaving a gaping hole out into the darkness. Of course I had no idea whether I would emerge over a sheer drop, but a quick death would have been preferable to the way I expected the priests would kill me, and so I wriggled through the hole and found myself tumbling out onto the grass slope at the fortress's foot.' He looked at the men around him, his face shining with sincerity. 'Fortuna was with me that night. I slithered away down the hill as quietly as I could, and given the absence of any moon I must have been invisible to the men on the walls. I was almost at the slope's foot before they realised that my cell was empty, but the noise they kicked up when they did so was enough to make my blood run cold.'

'They pursued you?'

Verus nodded at the question, shivering despite the room's warmth.

'Yes, they sent out a hunting party of the tribe's young women, the bloodthirsty bitches they call their Vixens. They came down the hill behind me with their horns blaring at the stars, and their dogs bayed and howled once they caught my scent, but they were too late. The land to either side of the Dirty River is a swamp, you see, covered with a thick clinging moss which conceals deep pools of watery, rotting vegetation. I crawled into the morass and submerged myself in one of these pits, holding onto a trailing bush to avoid being pulled down and drowned. I stripped off my leggings and washed away the filthy smell of my cell and became part of the landscape, making it impossible for the dogs to find my scent.'

Marcus frowned.

'The first spear told us that it took you eight days to return here, and yet it can't be more than a dozen miles.'

Verus nodded with tightly pursed lips.

'The dogs weren't able to find me, but those evil bitches hunted for me day and night, their wild cries and curses echoing across the marsh. They never once gave up on the chase, sleeping out in the open and slinking around in the mists, and they had sufficient cunning that I was nearly taken by them more than once . . .'

He shivered, lowering his head into his hands with an expression of such dread that Scaurus stood with an apologetic expression, patting the emotionally exhausted soldier on the back.

'I'm sorry, Legionary Verus. We've kept you talking for long enough.'

When the soldier had left the room he turned to Julius and Marcus with an enquiring expression.

'So, First Spear, what do you think?'

Julius shook his head.

'He's like an overwound bolt thrower. The way he jumped up like a madman when you asked who he was is a clear enough giveaway. And when you overstress a bolt thrower it's a toss-up as to who'll get hurt worst when you finally loose the missile, the enemy or the men around it.'

The tribune nodded sagely at his first spear's opinion.

'I completely agree. On the other hand, if he really spent eight days avoiding capture, and presumably living off the land wearing no more than a coat of mud, he must know the ground between here and The Fang quite intimately.'

Julius pursed his lips and nodded reluctantly.

'Like I said, it's a toss-up.'

Scaurus agreed.

'I don't see how we can ignore the opportunity he presents. Whoever's going to lead the raiding party will just have to keep a good close eye on him, and act quickly if he looks like doing something rash.'

'Act quickly? Are you proposing that we take the poor bastard back out into Venicone territory and then put iron through his spine if it looks like he's about to throw a wobbler as a result?'

Scaurus turned an imperturbable glance on his senior centurion, raising an eyebrow in silent question. Julius returned the gaze for a moment before shaking his head and turning away.

'And they call *me* the nastiest bastard in this cohort?'

Evening came to the Yew Grove fortress in its usual ordered manner, the distant sounds of shouted commands and stamping boots as the guard was changed at the nearby gate reaching the ear of the sleeping baby, making the infant stir in her sleep. Annia woke, her maternal instincts alerting her to the child's minute movements, but Felicia shook her head from the chair facing her, and the still weary new mother slumped back onto her bed and was asleep again. A smile of contentment touched her friend's face at the sight of mother and baby dozing together, and she closed her own eyes to luxuriate in a rare moment of peace, allowing a long, slow breath to escape from between her lips.

A knock at the door snapped the doctor out of her reverie, and the sound of voices in the house's hall furrowed her brow as she recognised the sound of Tribune Sorex's voice. He appeared in the room's doorway a moment later with Desidra behind him, a nervous smile on the older woman's face clearly signalling her unease at the senior officer's presence. When Sorex spoke his voice was lowered to a whisper, pitched low enough not to awaken the sleepers.

'I heard that your assistant had been delivered of her child, and so I thought I ought to come and pay my respects to the new arrival. Here, a gift for the little one.'

He handed Felicia a gold aureus, and she nodded her thanks.

'I'm sure that Annia will be most touched, Tribune. Allow me to thank you on her behalf when she wakes.'

Sorex bowed his head graciously.

'Indeed, madam, but there is a way that you can render me some small service by way of thanks, if I might elicit your professional opinion on a personal matter?'

'With pleasure, Tribune. Perhaps in another room?'

They moved into the hall and Felicia looked to Desidra, waiting for the mistress of the house to indicate which room they should use, but Sorex simply pointed to the front door, turning to the prefect's woman with a knowing smile.

'This is a personal matter which on this occasion does not require your presence, Domina. You will favour me with your absence, if you know what's good for you and your husband?'

To Felicia's consternation the older woman shot her an apologetic glance and scuttled for the door, leaving the two of them alone. Taking her hand, Sorex bent to whisper in her face.

'Desidra does know what's good for her, you see. She knows that if it weren't for your presence I'd have her legs spread wide on the bed she shares with Prefect Castus at this very moment, since she's long since realised that allowing me to fuck her every now and then is infinitely preferable to the indignity I could heap on the prefect without very much effort. But now you're here, Doctor, and you're an altogether more enticing prospect for a little enforced enjoyment, aren't you?'

Felicia's eyes widened at the revelation, and she moved to back away from his leering grin, but the grip on her hand tightened, and she started as he put a hand under her stola's hem, his questing fingers cupping her crotch.

'So here's what we are and are not going to do, my dear. You *are* going to submit to my attentions in an accommodating manner, make encouraging noises and generally do whatever it takes to give me the impression that you're enjoying it just as much as I undoubtedly will. You are *not* going to call out for help, not that it'll bring anyone other than a woman who gave birth only a day ago and whom I will have no compunction in knocking senseless given her clearly expressed attitude towards me. And in return for your complicity your friend and her child will be safe from the dangers that so often frequent places like this. After all, there are hundreds of soldiers cooped up in that fortress with nothing better than a selection of saggy, over-used whores to service their needs. It wouldn't be a surprise to anyone, least of all me, if half a dozen of them were to abduct your friend and she was never be seen again. Or at least not alive. I can make that happen with a few words in the right ear you know, I have a tame centurion who does whatever I tell him to, not that he takes much encouragement. So, do we have a deal, Doctor?'

He tugged at the knot in her loincloth, pulling the garment loose and tossing it aside, pushing her back against the wall and probing vigorously between her legs.

'There we are! A little dry, but a few minutes of vigorous fingering will soon change that.'

Felicia grimaced at the intrusion, closing her eyes to block out the sight of his triumphant grin.

'You know that my husband will kill you for this, when he returns from wherever it is that you've sent him.'

Sorex lifted the hand that was massaging her vagina and slapped her face.

'Eyes open, madam. Please don't think that I'm going to be satisfied with you scowling and crying your way through this. I want to see the signs that you're loving every little bit of it, or I won't be able to keep my side of the bargain and leave your friend unharmed. As for your husband's return, let's just say that I've sent his cohort into the jaws of the nastiest, most dangerous tribe on this entire disgusting island. The centurion and his cohort are going to vanish without trace in the bogs and mists north of the Antonine Wall, and you will be left here as a widow. I foresee a long and entertaining relationship between the two of us, at least until I am recalled to Rome to enjoy the fruits of having delivered the right results to the right people. But enough about me, I think it's time to introduce the star of this evening's performance.'

Smiling happily in the face of her horror he raised his tunic to reveal a bobbing erection.

'Ah yes, here he is, and looking rather keen as well, if I might say so. Doubtless he's keen to be hidden deep inside you, my dear, and I see no reason not to indulge his every whim, do you? I think you're about as ready for him as you're ever going to be . . .'

Turning Felicia to face the wall he gripped her hair and bent her forward, pushing her face up against the painted plaster and spreading her legs wide with his feet.

'*Stop it!*'

Sorex turned his head to find the child Lupus standing in the door of the house's dining room where he had been playing on his own, his half-sized sword drawn and a pale expression of fury on his face. Sorex tightened his grip on Felicia's hair and turned her to face the boy. A draught of cold air raised gooseflesh on her buttocks.

'Tell him to leave us, woman, or I'll be forced to take that toy from him and make him eat it!'

'Will you now, Tribune?'

Sorex released Felicia, turning with a look of fury to find a tall, dark-skinned man standing in the house's open doorway, Desidra peering round him with a look of terror on her face. After a moment's silence the newcomer stepped forward into the room, unpinning his cloak and dropping it onto a chair.

'I believe it's customary, Fulvius Sorex, for a tribune to stand to attention in the presence of a senior officer. I'll remind you that while I am no longer in command of this legion, nothing in my orders to relinquish operational control of the Sixth to you made any mention of demotion. A legatus I was and a legatus I remain, to be accorded every right, privilege and every little bit of respect I've earned in ten years of soldiering for the empire. And that's before we get onto the fact that I have four very ugly and easily provoked soldiers of my personal bodyguard who I have little doubt would take the greatest pleasure in subduing you, were I to give them the command to do so.'

He gave the tribune's exposed and wilting erection a wry glance.

'And *that* doesn't count as standing to attention, Tribune, although I see you're having trouble on that front too . . .' He strolled across to Felicia, who had straightened up and rearranged her clothing. 'Doctor, it's a pleasure to meet you again although we might both have preferred the circumstances to be a little more auspicious. I do hope that your dignity isn't too bruised, it looked to me as if this man was struggling to make much of an impression upon you.'

She nodded, looking at the child who was still standing in the dining room's doorway with his sword raised and a look of murderous anger on his young face.

'Ah, if I remember rightly, this young man's name is Lupus?' The boy nodded, his gaze fixed on Sorex. The legatus walked slowly across the hall and squatted in front of him, his face a bare six inches from the short sword's point. 'I am Legatus Septimius Equitius, young man, and I have known your guardian Centurion Corvus for long enough to have heard your story from his lips. I recall him telling me that you train in swordsmanship with your tribune's German servant most days?' Lupus nodded again, his lips pulled back to show his teeth and his eyes still locked on the tribune. 'And so if you decided to punish this man for hurting my friend the doctor, you could probably hurt him very badly indeed.' He reached out slowly with a gentle smile and pushed the sword's point aside. 'Sheathe your sword, young soldier, the time for you to use it in anger is not yet upon you, and there are other ways to achieve the same result, even if they are less immediately satisfying.'

He stood and turned back to Sorex, shaking his head in disgust.

'It was fortunate for everyone that I happened to spot Prefect Castus's woman lurking in the entrance of her own house as I rode up to the fortress gates. She was initially reluctant to explain why she might be shut out of her own house, but I thank the Lightbringer that I persisted with my questions for long enough to discover that you intended raping the doctor here. While she has not spoken of it, something is telling me that the centurion's wife is unlikely to have been your first victim. You can thank the gods that I came along in time to save you from the child.'

Sorex scoffed, his confidence starting to reassert itself.

'The child? I'd have broken his neck like an unwanted puppy.'

Equitius raised an eyebrow.

'Perhaps you would. Or perhaps he'd have opened an artery with that deceptively harmless-looking sword. It has the look to me of a weapon whose acquaintanceship with the polishing stone is a very close one. And now, I'd suggest that you make your exit, and resolve not to trouble any of these ladies again for fear that you have a good deal more than a vengeful child to worry about. I suspect that Prefect Castus, whilst being at the end of his military career, would take the most grave and fatal objection were he to discover your forced relations with his woman. Get out.'

Sorex turned on his heel and left with a scowl of fury at the legatus.

'And there goes a man who will now stop at nothing to see me either dead or disgraced. Not that he'll have too long to wait for the latter, I suspect, once the new legatus arrives with whatever orders he has from Rome for me.' A movement at the bedroom's door caught his eye. 'Ah, madam, you must be the proud mother that Desidra here was telling me about.'

Annia stared about her at the crowded hallway with a look of puzzlement.

'I seem to have missed something. Who's the stranger, and why has Lupus got a face on him like the one my man wears when he's about to tear someone's head off?'

4

'We've been here long enough for the Venicones to have got wind of our presence, and for them to have gathered a good-sized war band as a precaution against any incursion we might be planning. It's highly likely that any move we make north of the wall will result in an immediate response, and in sufficient strength to destroy one cohort without any problems whatsoever . . .'

Scaurus paused and played an appraising gaze across his officers' faces.

' . . . and so I therefore plan for us to make so much noise leaving camp that they won't fail to hear that we're on the march up the Dirty River. By the time we're within striking distance of The Fang they'll have gathered every able-bodied man for thirty miles ready to come after us, all of them dreaming of the chance to tear a Roman cohort limb from limb. And that, gentlemen, will be a *lot* of angry barbarians. They will come over the river like a pack of starving wolves hoping to catch us on the march, too fast for us to outrun them and too strong for us to face in a stand-up fight.'

After two days of enforced rest while the cohort waited for the moon to enter its darkest phase of the month, and recovered from the rigours of the march north, the centurions had gathered for an evening briefing from their tribune. Each man held the customary cup of wine that had become a hallmark of the relaxed ease with which Scaurus managed his officers, their attention locked on the senior officer as he outlined his intentions.

'At the point that the tribe comes after us in strength, Silus and his cavalrymen are going to help us pull off a neat little trick I have in mind to prevent those tattooed maniacs from running us to ground and overwhelming us. And while we dance with the Venicone war band by way of distraction, Centurion Corvus and his men are going to slip quietly into their fortress and take back the Sixth Legion's eagle. With a nod and a wink from Fortuna we'll regroup here in a few days with the legion's standard rescued and the bluenoses well and truly discomforted, after which we'll make our exit down the road to the south at the double. It is to be hoped that the barbarians don't go on the rampage against the wall forts, but even if they do, our duty is to get the Sixth's eagle to safety however much we might want to stand and fight.'

Julius raised his cup.

'I'll drink to that. And if the goddess Fortuna doesn't hear our prayers, here's to the next best thing, the strong sword arm and bloody blade of Cocidius the warrior!'

The gathered officers echoed his sentiment and tipped the wine down their throats, holding cups out for a refill as Arminius came forward with the jar. Dubnus winked at Marcus.

'So tell me brother, who will you be taking with you on this suicide mission?'

The Roman made a momentary show of pondering before replying.

'Well obviously my scout, Arabus, since he's the perfect man to send ahead of us to look out for the enemy. Lugos won't hear of being left behind, of course, and the legionary Verus will show us the best approach to the fortress, given his knowledge of the Dirty River's plain and its marshes. Aside from us four, Drest and his men will get the chance to show us just how good their professed expertise at fighting and stealing really is. That's eight, and more than enough, I'd have thought.'

Arminius spoke without turning away from his duties with the wine jar.

'Nine, Centurion. I still owe you a life.'

Dubnus grinned at his friend.

'It seems that you will be taking this insubordinate slave with you whether you like it or not.'

He held out his empty cup, pulling a mock apologetic face as Arminius scornfully poured a half-measure into it.

'I take it all back! You're the greatest warrior that ever drew breath, and without you to watch his back our friend there would be at the mercy of all comers. Just fill me up properly, eh?'

The muscular German simply raised an eyebrow at him before moving on to the next man, much to the delight of the gathered centurions. Arminius spoke over his shoulder as he progressed down their line, his attention fixed on the wine he was pouring.

'A half-cup's all you're getting, Centurion. Tomorrow you march out to give the Venicones' beards a mighty tug for the second time in two years, but this time there'll be no river in flood to hide behind. I'd say you're going to need your wits about you.'

The Tungrian cohort marched north-west from the fort with great fanfare the next morning, each century's trumpeter striving to outdo the others in the gusto with which they signalled their centurions' orders. Marcus took Prefect Castus's man Drest up onto the fort's wall, and the two men watched as the long column of soldiers headed out down the road towards the High Mountains. As the cohort's last century exited the fort's northern gate and marched away into the wilderness Marcus shook his head, his lips pursed in grim amusement.

'You know Drest, when you're part of it a cohort on the march seems a mighty thing, a never-ending column of well-drilled fighting men, all armour, weapons and hard faces, and yet when I stand here and look out at them from this vantage point . . .'

The Thracian nodded his head in agreement.

'Indeed. A column of seven hundred men suddenly looks like not very much at all.' He turned his gaze from the distant marching column to the Roman standing next to him. 'I presume that illustrating the insignificance of your cohort when taken in the context of the threat that awaits them was not your only purpose in inviting me to join you here?'

The Roman nodded.

'I would have been disappointed had you failed to see through my intention.' The two men huddled deeper into their cloaks as a cold wind made the legion cohort's detachment flag snap and dance above them, and Marcus raised his hand to point out across the Dirty River's valley to the line of hills on the horizon, a tiny speck on the skyline betraying the Venicone fortress's position.

'Let us be very clear with each other. I mean to find that eagle, if it still abides in The Fang, and I also intend to retrieve the head of the man who was betrayed in its taking as well. This will be the last chance anyone has to attempt their rescue for many years, possibly for ever, and I do *not* intend to fail. So, if you entertain thoughts of merely making a gesture at its recovery, and if the prospect of attempting to gain access to such a daunting fortress is giving you pause for thought, it would be as well to say so now. Disappointing me once we're north of this wall might prove a lot more hazardous than gracefully backing out of our enterprise before it enters hostile territory.'

He fell silent having never taken his eyes off the distant skyline, and Drest looked out at the receding backs of the cohort's last century, the morning sun glinting off the pioneers' axes, answering Marcus's question in a matter-of-fact tone of voice.

'I was born in Debeltum, Centurion, in Thracia, and I was the son of a shopkeeper. Debeltum is a veterans' colony that was established by the Emperor Vespasian, and as a result the tradition of service runs deep in the community. For years I entertained the notion of joining the legions and seeing the empire, much to my father's dismay since all he wanted was for me to take over the running of his shop and keep him in his old age. Six months before I would have been eligible to join up he was suddenly and unexpectedly bankrupted by a creditor from whom he had borrowed money in an ill-advised manner, a man he discovered bore a grudge against him only at the moment the bastard appeared at our door with a gang of toughs and put us out onto the street. My father was utterly broken by the shame and shock of having his respectable trade destroyed before his eyes, and I was forced to take work as an unskilled manual labourer, earning next to nothing for breaking my back from sunrise to sunset simply to earn sufficient money for us both to eat. After two years of this precarious existence I took the bold step of entering a gladiatorial ludus as a trainee, hoping to win my freedom in the arena along with enough money to see him live in comfort once again.'

He paused, raising an eyebrow at Marcus.

'When I knew that I was to go north from here in your company, I spoke to your men to find out what sort of person you are. They told me that you were trained to fight by retired gladiators?'

The Roman answered without taking his eyes off the horizon.

'By one retired gladiator and a soldier recently paid off from his service.'

Drest smiled.

'Which explains your ready ability to resort to dirty tricks when you sense a need to level the odds in a fight?'

Marcus shrugged.

'The teaching of dirty tricks was shared between them, but it was the soldier who taught me how to lose the veneer of civilisation and fight like an animal when the need arises. He'd seen battle in the German Wars, and understood just how thin the margin between victory and death can be.'

'Yes, your men told me about your wilder side too.' The Thracian waited for a moment, and when Marcus failed to respond he started talking again. 'Unlike you, I wasn't cut out for the arena, and I realised as much within a few weeks of signing my life away. There's a very simple hierarchy in any ludus, and most instructors can see where a man will fit within that pecking order within a few hours of their arrival. Firstly there are the idiots who simply shouldn't have been allowed entry, men who will be defeated and quite probably killed in their first bouts simply because they are too dull-witted or physically soft, included purely to make the numbers up and provide the crowd with a splash of blood on the sand nice and early in the day. Perhaps one or two men in ten fits that description, poor bastards. Then there are the workaday fighters, men with the muscles needed to sustain the pace of the fight and who can be trained to wield a sword or throw a net with sufficient dexterity to have a decent chance of surviving, if they also have the resolve to put another man down when the opportunity presents itself. Seven or eight men in every ten fit into that category in some way or other, the competent fighters who will never be champions but whose careers might last long enough to see them survive, as long as they have some measure of luck. And then there are the remainder, perhaps one man in every ten. The predators, Centurion, the born killers whose circumstances and upbringing have sharpened the advantage that nature gave them to a razor edge, and hardened them to maiming and killing their opponents in the arena. Just how deadly they are depends upon their abilities with a sword, but the very best of them, those with the speed or the cunning to take down whatever the life of a professional fighter throws at them, they are the men who retire with a wooden sword and an income for life.'

He paused again, looking at Marcus.

'And in which of these categories would you say that I fit, Centurion?'

The Roman turned to face him, looking him up and down.

'You clearly had the muscles after two years of manual labour, and your sword work seemed competent enough from what I saw when you were sparring with your Sarmatae, but I see one thing lacking for you to have been in that last group of killers.' Drest waited, a slight smile creasing his face. 'You talk too much, even when you're sparring. You're a man better suited to calculation and intrigue than to the cut and thrust of combat.'

The Thracian nodded.

'Perceptive enough, Centurion. I was clearly doomed to live a precarious existence as a fighter, never quite dangerous enough in combat to stand out from my fellows, and always at risk of being singled out by one of the predators and maimed or killed just for getting in his way.'

'So what happened? You clearly survived.'

Drest shrugged.

'I never fought. Prefect Castus toured the ludus one evening as part of his official duties as first spear of Twelfth Thunderbolt, looking for gladiators to put on a show for the legion, and happened to observe me giving after-hours instruction to one of the poor fools who was destined to die in his first bout, unless the gods took a rather more generous view of things than he was likely to get from his fellow competitors. His interest was piqued, and so he had the ludus's owner call me over to enquire as to why I was still working with the man when I could have been resting in my cell. When I told him of my fears for my comrade he turned to the owner and purchased me on the spot. When I asked him why, my thoughts still reeling as he led me away to his quarters and wondering if I would be expected to warm his bed for the privilege of my rescue, he told me that decent men were rare enough to merit saving. In truth he had chosen better than he knew, for though I do not have that killer instinct of which I spoke, I do have both my letters and my numbers, and I have learned the art of commanding the other men in his service. And now, Centurion, you would doubtless like to know why I have told you all this?'

Marcus stared at him flatly, his tone mildly acid.

'It had crossed my mind.'

'It's clear to me now that Prefect Castus rescued me from either death or being maimed in the arena, and in return I have enjoyed a decade of life in his service, with the promise of my freedom when he retires. And so Centurion, if he tells me that I must swim the River Styx with a knife in my mouth and rob Charon of his accumulated coinage, then you can rest assured that I will do so to the best of my abilities, as repayment of the debt I owe him.'

The Roman looked at him for a moment longer, his expression thoughtful.

'And I believe you in that. But what about your companions?'

'We all owe the prefect our lives in one way or another.'

Marcus shook his head.

'I know that. My question has more of a bearing on their characters than their histories.'

Drest shrugged.

'Every man makes his own choices in life, but I've never seen any of the three of them refuse to obey an instruction given to them by either the prefect or by myself in his place. I believe that they will do as instructed when the time comes.'

The young centurion raised a hand to point at the hills on the northern horizon once more.

'I hope you're right. I expect that where we're going will be an unforgiving place to discover that such faith is ill founded. Tell your men that we leave the fort an hour after sunset, and send your thief to me. I have a task for him.'

The Tungrians marched to the north-west from Lazy Hill for less than an hour, passing the ruins of a long abandoned outpost fort and following the weed-riven remnants of the paved road that skirted the edge of the Dirty River's swamps, when Julius called a halt in a narrow valley that hid them from any observation. The bemused soldiers stood in their column and talked quietly as their centurions hurried forward to the column's head at the insistent summons of a trumpet. Sanga rested his shield on his booted foot to keep the brass rim from unnecessary scratching and looked at Saratos with a wry smile.

'Now we'll find out what it is that the tribune's got in mind for us, eh? Let's hope he's got a trick or two in mind or we'll be up to our arses in hairy bastards like you before we know it, eh?'

Tribune Scaurus launched into his briefing without preamble, his tone laced with urgency to be back on the march.

'As far as the hangers-on and probable spies at Lazy Hill are concerned, we've marched north to attack The Fang. I expect that at least one of the natives that have clustered around the legion cohort there like flies on shit will be over the wall and away across the river, once the sun sets tonight, taking the news of our departure to whoever it is that rules the Venicones. And they in turn will be baffled, gentlemen, baffled and not a little worried given that we're not going to make the expected appearance outside their walls tomorrow. They will be nervous at our non-appearance, given that it's only ten miles from the wall to their fortress, and they will wonder just what it is that we're doing out here if it's not to attack them directly. Their chief won't take kindly to having our boots on his land, and not knowing where we might be heading, so he'll be pretty keen to know where we've got to. Scouts will be sent out to find us, which of course they will, given the trail that we're going to leave behind us as we march, and it's when they find that trail that the real fun will start. Don't forget, gentlemen, I spent months getting to know this landscape before Calgus managed to whip the tribes up into rebellion, and I have a few choice pieces of ground in mind.'

He smiled around at the gathered officers.

'And the first of those is very near to here, less than a mile up this road. The road forks there, gentlemen, one track heading north along the Dirty River and so close to The Fang that the more sharp-eyed Venicone sentries would be able to count the number of teeth our colleague Otho has left in his mouth . . .'

He paused to allow the centurion to bare his gap-toothed grin in a face long since battered during his days as the cohort's boxing champion, smiling to himself as the officers grinned and sniggered despite themselves.

'But the path that we shall take heads up into the forest to the west, and then dips back into a ring of hills that the soldiers who served here when the northern wall was first manned used to call the "Frying Pan". The ground inside the hills is more or less flat you see, and once inside we'll be out of view from the fortress, which I expect will have Calgus and whichever king it is he's manipulating more than a little worried. Hopefully they'll take the bait and come after us in force, leaving our raiding party with a clear run to The Fang. So, let's start the guessing games, shall we gentlemen?'

Marcus gathered his party in the fort's headquarters building as torches were being lit in the narrow streets and along the length of the rampart that marked the empire's northernmost boundary. He spent the next hour explaining to them what it was that he intended for their night's work and checking that none of them would make any noise as they moved, waiting for Tarion to return from the task he had been set. The first spear escorted the thief into the room, watching as Tarion huddled close to the stove for a short time before he would speak, his face white and pinched from the sudden dip in temperature as the sun had set in a cloudless sky.

'I waited at the foot of the wall, wrapped in my cloak against the cold. The weaselly little bastard almost fell over me, he was so close to the fort, but my cloak blended with the shadows and protected me from being seen.'

'Did you see his face?'

The thief nodded at the senior centurion.

'Just for a second. It was that red-headed lad that runs errands for the landlord of the beer house in the vicus.'

Marcus and Drest exchanged glances. The fort's vicus was a thin affair of half a dozen buildings set up to accommodate the few whores with sufficient avarice and insufficient caution to ignore the risks and follow the cohort to the very edge of the empire.

'Right, I'll have that fool flogged for bringing a spy into the vicus, and then I'll put him up on a . . . What?'

Marcus had raised a hand, his comment couched in a throwaway tone so as to make it easier for the first spear to ignore if he chose to do so.

'It's only a thought sir, but you might want to keep the whole thing to yourself for the time being, just in case the boy's brave enough to return. There could well be more than one of them in the vicus, and I doubt the landlord's any part of it given he was shipped in here by the army from the south less than a year ago, which means that the only way to be sure you get them all is to wait to see if the boy comes back.'

The first spear mused for a moment, nodding slowly.

'You're right Centurion, we'll wait for him to return and then lock the entire vicus down while we beat the name of his conspirators out of him.'

Marcus winced inwardly before speaking again.

'In which case, First Spear, I think it's time we made as quiet as possible an exit from the fort and went on our way.'

The senior officer nodded.

'You'd best make your way along the rear of the wall down to the next mile castle to the east, and then out through their gate. Are you sure you don't want an escort to take you part of the way? We got to know the ground out there reasonably well before the orders came to stop any operations over the wall, and I've got a couple of decent scouts.'

Marcus shook his head.

'I'm grateful sir, but the more men we take the more likely we'll be detected. Besides which, my man Arabus has spent long enough with your scouts to have the ground pretty well laid out in his head, and your soldier Verus will know more than any of them, I expect. We'll keep our numbers to nine, I think, and pray to Our Lord Mithras that the Venicones aren't out hunting tonight.'

'There it is. That's The Fang all right. I stood here one evening before the rebellion started, when the forts on the Antonine Wall were no more than a succession of burned-out shells that had been abandoned twenty years before. Arminius and I had dismissed our cavalry escort and ridden up here alone, to reduce the risk of our being discovered by the Venicones and hunted down like the intruders we obviously were. They carried a fearsome reputation even then, long before we faced them on the banks of the Red River.'

Tribune Scaurus pointed out across the valley from the vantage point of the slope up which he and Julius had climbed as the day's last light had ebbed from the western sky. The ring of hills circled about them was a line of darkness on the horizon beneath the cloudless night's blaze of stars, but to the north-east of their place on the hillside one flickering light was perched above the shadow's rim where the Venicone fortress stood high above the valley's floor ten miles distant. The Tungrians had marched into the heart of the feature that Scaurus had told his centurions was called the Frying Pan, a ten-mile-wide bowl surrounded on all sides by hills, marching two abreast down tracks that were little more than hunters' paths with their footsteps muffled by the carpet of pine needles underfoot and the dense forest on all sides. At the onset of night they had camped in the shadow of the hill at its centre, their tents raised in one corner of a long abandoned legion marching fort that had been carved into the forest twenty years before.

'We can presume that they know we're out here, so tomorrow we need to get their attention before they have time to wonder if there might be more to this than one auxiliary cohort chancing its arm against the only remaining tribe still intact, now that the revolt has run its course.'

Julius frowned in the darkness, remembering a hillside scattered with barbarian dead two years before.

'You don't believe that we broke them at the battle near the Fortress of Spears?'

'I hoped so, at the time, but now?' Scaurus shook his head, the gesture barely visible in the absence of a moon to illuminate the landscape. 'No First Spear, I believe we destroyed a large part of their strength, and killed their king, but I'd wager good money they still retain enough warriors to make short work of seven hundred infantrymen. Given that our old friend Calgus now seems to be in a position of some influence over there –' he gestured out across the valley again '– and his apparent determination to claw his way back from the grave's edge, the very word "Tungrian" should be enough to have him foaming at the mouth with the urge to see us hunted down and destroyed. After all, it was our very own Centurion Corvus who maimed him not so very long ago.'

Julius stared at the spark of light that glowed on the distant hilltop, crowning the brooding black mass that lurked above the river's valley, grimly wondering what opposition the raiding party might encounter if they managed to make their way over the fortress's battlements. Turning back to look down the slope he waved a hand at the cooking fires that had been lit in the hill's shadow, safely concealed from the eyes that would be searching for any sign of their presence from the barbarian fortress's position high above the Dirty River's wide valley.

'You want us to light cooking fires again tomorrow morning then?'

'Yes. And this time I want a little more smoke, just enough to make sure that the barbarians have a good enough idea where

we are to bring them at the gallop. We'll let the fires burn
until we're ready to march, then follow standard routine and put
them out. Let's not risk our ruse becoming too apparent. And
now I suggest we go and see if Titus and his men managed to
finish off that job we left them working on before it got properly
dark. We'll need Silus's horsemen to put on a convincing show
tomorrow, if we're to duck under the punch that Calgus will throw
at us as soon as he thinks he knows where we are.'

Summoned to the king's presence, Calgus found Brem waiting
for him in the great hall among a half-dozen of the tribe's clan
leaders, the disfigured master of the hunt Scar standing away to
one side with the woman Morrig, the leader of his pack of hunt-
resses, one pace behind him. Even the grizzled family leaders
were shooting occasional glances at the Vixen, and the Selgovae
could discern the same mixture of curiosity and caution in their
stares that were his own uncontrollable reaction to the huntress
every time he encountered her. A boy barely out of his teens was
kneeling before the king, and the Selgovae recognised him as one
of those who had been recruited at his suggestion to cross the
river's wide swamp and insinuate themselves into the Roman forts
astride their wall. On seeing Calgus shuffle into the hall Brem
nodded impatiently, waving him towards the throne.

'Here he is! Now that my *esteemed* adviser is here perhaps we
can hear the news that our spies among the Romans have brought
across the river!'

Calgus took his place at the king's side, as painfully aware as
ever that he was the only unarmed man in a gathering of warriors
whose bodies bristled with sharp iron. Trusted members of Brem's
inner circle, every man present wore at least two weapons on his
belt, and several of them habitually carried up to another half-dozen
knives about their person, whereas he had decided never to ask for
the permission to carry as much as an eating knife in the certain
knowledge that such permission would never be granted.

'News, King Brem? Are the Romans finally preparing for their
great retreat back to the south?'

Brem turned and grinned at him without very much humour.

'Far from it, Calgus. Despite your repeated reassurances that they will turn tail and slink away they continue to hide behind their wall like frightened children. I have restrained my natural urge to send my warriors against them for too long, it seems to me, and now we have news of new arrivals at the fortress they call Lazy Hill. You may recognise these men by their tribal name, and I certainly do. They call themselves *Tungrians*.' Calgus started at the name, and Brem grinned at him with fresh amusement. 'Yes. The same men who defeated my nephew and then tore the beating heart out of my tribe. And the same men who took away your ability to walk at any better pace than that of a withered ancient. Now they have marched north again, fouling my land with the touch of their boots.'

Calgus nodded slowly.

'Who brought this news?'

Brem pointed to the boy kneeling before him.

'The lad here has braved the swamp after dark to bring us these tidings . . .'

The king was still speaking, but Calgus was suddenly unaware of his words, locking his gaze with that of the child.

'How many men marched north, boy?'

The answer was prompt.

'All of them, my lord King. I counted their standards as I was taught, and I saw the same nine centuries leave through the fort's north gate as I saw arrive three days before.'

Calgus thought for a moment, then turned back to Brem who was regarding him with an expression halfway between irritation and anger at being disregarded.

'Three days? It is not what it seems Brem. Their foray onto your land is nothing but a distraction, a ruse to draw away your strength and leave this fortress bare. They seek to rescue the eagle!'

Brem shook his head with an expression of disbelief.

'Eagle?' He held Calgus's eye before speaking again, his voice louder this time. *'Eagle?'* He stood and shouted up at the tower's roof high above him. 'I expect you to advise me, to share whatever wisdom you have left in you, and yet all I seem to hear from you is eagle, eagle, *eagle*! Enough! I *know* that you captured a Roman standard! I *know* how dearly they hold this statue of a bird! You do not need to wave the memory of your victory over the Romans at me with every opportunity!'

Calgus shuffled forward, his arms spread wide to implore the king to listen.

'But my lord King, why else would they wait three days until the darkest night of the month? While these Tungrians act the part of the worm on the hook, a few of them will be moving silently across the Dirty River's swamp and preparing to infiltrate this stronghold, hoping to—'

Brem waved an impatient hand.

'No more, Calgus! I have already decided. We march at first light, every warrior that has answered the call to arms by that time and the remainder with orders to follow our trail. We will track these Tungrians down and then, with Cocidius's blessing we will have their heads! Your eagle will have seven hundred pairs of Roman eyes to watch it, an entire cohort, and its shrine will become a place of dread, lined from floor to ceiling with the heads of the invaders and dedicated in my name to our god, and he will grace us with great favour as a reward for such honour being devoted to his name. And you, *adviser*, you will advise no more. Now is the time for you to fight! Since you can walk no faster than a child at the best of times you will be mounted on one of my horses, and you will ride with me into whatever battle awaits us. When the time comes I will put a sword in your hand, and you will fight our enemy alongside me, earning the respect of the people who suffer your presence with revenge for my brother seething in their hearts.'

Calgus bowed as deeply as he could.

'Of course, King Brem. Your command is my duty. Might I enquire as to the defence that will remain about this place?'

Brem nodded sagely.

'I am hardly as stupid as you imply, Calgus. Fifty men will be left to guard The Fang under the command of my son, more than enough to safeguard it against any raiding party, and my master of the hunt and his Vixens will be set to patrol the swamp as a precaution against any attempt to approach from the river. I have yet to meet the Roman who could cross that fetid desert of mud without betraying himself to their hunting skills, eh Scar?'

Once through the mile castle's gate Marcus's raiding party went forward slowly into the darkness, allowing their eyes to adapt to the absence of any light stronger than that cast by the countless pinprick stars wheeling majestically above them. Making their way stealthily down the long slope of the hill atop which Lazy Hill's silhouette rose over the wall's long straight line without any sound louder than the rustle of the long grass that covered the plain, they gathered around Marcus as he whispered the command to halt. Lugos uncoiled a rope that he had carried looped around his body, handing it to the Roman who in turn passed one end to the waiting legionary.

'From here we follow Verus's lead. Keep hold of the rope at all times, and move slowly and cautiously. If you hear a sound that you don't like, tug the rope sharply twice and we will all stop and go to ground. If that happens, nobody moves again without my permission. Any man that loses the party will be left behind. And believe me when I tell you that I wouldn't want to be out here alone. Arabus, stay close to Verus's shoulder, we may have need of your instincts out there.'

The Tungrian scout nodded solemnly, taking his place behind the legionary. He had scouted the Dirty River valley's floor the previous night, after a day spent in discussion with Verus and the Lazy Hill garrison's scouts on the subject of how to safely pass through the river valley's swamps. Slipping over the wall shortly after sunset, his exit had been accomplished with such stealth that the sentries set to stare into the night's darkness had not recognised the tiny sounds of his departure as anything other than the usual nighttime noises to which they had quickly become accustomed. Marcus had warned the duty centurion to expect his return in the hour before dawn, smiling at the man's incredulity that anyone could have left the fort without his men's knowledge.

'My scout learned his art in the dark forest of Arduenna, in Germania Inferior. In this darkness he could get close enough to any one of your sentries to cut the man's throat without ever being detected.'

Shrugging at the officer's continued disbelief, he had taken the man with him to stand on the wall, warning the legionaries on guard to be ready for the scout's reappearance so that they could abandon their usual bored pacing of the rampart and stand staring out into the dark landscape. At length the scout had stepped out from the wall's bulk directly beneath them, walking into the light of their torches to a collective gasp from the waiting soldiers, having approached the rampart some hundreds of paces from the fort and edged painstakingly down its length in the shadows until he was directly beneath the officers. Once through the wall gate he had briefed Marcus as to what he had found out on the Dirty River's flood plain.

'It is a dark and friendly place to the silent walker, Centurion, *if* you know where the paths through the swamp are to be trusted. Long ago, when this wall was your empire's first line of defence against the northern tribes, the legions built causeways out into the Dirty River's swamp. They built wooden walkways on the firmer ground, and dumped tons of gravel into the softer mud to make safe footpaths along which to send men out on patrol without losing them in the morass, but over the years much of this work has simply sunk into the swamp. I followed the direction that Verus gave me and crossed the river, and beyond it I found a place that he had told me about, a copse of trees close to the foot of the hill on which The Fang is built where we can wait during the day without being seen. I stayed within the trees in silence for long enough that I became accustomed to the noises of the night.' He looked up at Marcus with warning in his eyes. 'The valley teems with life, most of it quiet and furtive in its movements, but I also heard sounds which were not made by any animal. There are hunters roaming the swamps on the river's northern bank I believe, quick and for the most part as quiet as I am myself, but I heard something as I was preparing to leave the shelter of the corpse, the sound of something moving through the long grass, and so I froze where I was and waited for whatever was making the noises to appear. It was a hunter, with a spear that glinted in the starlight as it probed the vegetation, searching, I presume for me. Something had alerted this hunter to my presence, my different smell, perhaps, or a small noise I made while I was crossing the valley.'

He fell silent, and Marcus looked at his man for a moment, taking the measure of his temperament and finding no fear in his eyes but rather a look of slight bafflement.

'How many of them were there, Arabus? How many men were hunting for you?'

The tracker had held his gaze steadily even as he'd shaken his head slowly from side to side.

'They weren't men, Centurion. As Verus told us, the swamps are haunted by women who use dogs to hunt for infiltrators. I believe that the Dirty River's mud masked my smell, and so when we cross the stream we must all coat ourselves with it as our main defence against detection.'

The raiding party followed the abandoned road north-west away from Lazy Hill in silence, treading carefully on the track's gapped cobbles as they moved cautiously through the darkened landscape. Marcus found the road's presence unexpectedly reassuring, despite its state of weed-infested disrepair and the vegetation pressing in on both sides where normally the verges would have been cleared back for twenty paces or more as a precaution against ambush. After a mile or so the ruins of a fort rose out of the forest's black mass to their left, and Verus halted, whispering to Marcus.

'That is Gateway Fort. It used to serve as a customs post for the frontier, a place where the tribes to the north of the wall came to gain admittance to the empire. If a local turned up at Lazy Hill without the appropriate clearance stamped on his hand in purple dye then he would have been turned around and sent away with a boot up his arse just to make the point. Now it's just a burned-out and rotting shell, haunted by the ghosts of the men who gave their lives to take and hold this ground, the spirits of the departed indignant that we have betrayed their sacrifice by abandoning the wall. I've heard men coming back in from night patrols say they've heard noises from inside the ruins . . .'

Marcus nodded, looking up at the abandoned fort's silhouette. *We over-reached ourselves to satisfy the pride of an emperor,* he mused, *and when Antoninus Pius no longer had need of the fruits of his triumph, we pulled back to the southern wall without stopping to reckon the number of men whose deaths in the service of such pointless imperial hubris were demeaned by that retreat.*

He patted Arabus on the shoulder reassuringly, keeping his voice low as he replied.

'In which case we'll leave the spirits of the departed well alone, shall we? Let's move on.'

Leaving the road's course as it ran away to the north, the direction in which the Tungrians had marched earlier that day, the line of men advanced out into the Black River valley's patchy mixture of swamp and firmer ground at a deliberately cautious pace set by Verus. The soldier took slow and deliberate paces, interspersing them with pauses where he probed the path in front of him with his spear, feeling for the firmest footing on which to lead the party forward. Marcus tested the ground to one side of the path during one such pause, finding his boot sinking into the liquid mud so easily that his leg was already immersed to the ankle before he could pull it free. The loud sucking noise made by the swamp as it surrendered its grip on the leather drew a sharp hiss from Arabus, and a stifled laugh from Arminius, who whispered in his ear as the party started forward again.

'A fine example you're setting us, Centurion. Perhaps we might have brought a trumpeter with us just to ensure that the Venicones know where we are?'

Verus stopped at the noise and turned back to address the raiding party, his voice a low hiss that they had to strain to pick out of the wind's soft moan while the desolate landscape loomed around them unseen in the darkness, no less threatening for its invisibility.

'There are thousands of sinkholes like that one on either side of the river, and any one of them can swallow an armoured soldier whole in seconds, with no trace that he ever existed other than a few bubbles. An alert man might manage to call for help before he was sucked under by the weight of his equipment, but even when the paths were well marked and fresh gravel was laid on a regular basis, men would still stumble off into the swamps and never be seen again. Now that the paths have all but sunk from sight this place is ten times as dangerous as it was before, so watch your feet!'

He turned back to resume their slow progress into the swamp, leading the party forward into the impenetrable darkness until at length what little was left of the pathway reached the river's dark expanse. Its black water was riffled into tiny waves by a brisk wind that swirled the marsh grass through which they had made their cautious way down to the wide, slow-flowing stream's bank. Lugos stepped forward, pulling off his heavy outer garment and easing himself into the black water as silently as he could.

'Give me swim rope.'

Marcus handed him one end of a long coil of line that was much thinner than the knotted rope they had used to control their progress, passing the other end to Arminius.

'Tie this to a tree will you?'

Once the slender cable was secure about one of the stunted alders that studded the swamp, the massively built Briton clamped his teeth about the end he was holding and then turned and pushed himself off the riverbank, sliding into the deeper water and breaststroking his way slowly and quietly out across the river's black expanse. The men watching him in the stars' meagre light waited tensely for any sign that an ambush had been laid on the far banks, but after several moments they saw the big Briton's barely distinct form climb wearily out of the water, vanishing into the marsh grass beyond. A moment later the rope went taut, dipping to kiss the river's slow-flowing water in midstream but strong enough to provide a swimmer with the means of supporting his weapons and wet clothing against the stream's pull. Marcus gestured to Arabus, who had unstrung his bow and coiled the string into a tight package of oiled cloth which he held in his mouth. The two men exchanged meaningful glances and then the scout was in the water and crossing quickly and smoothly, pulling himself along the rope quicker than a man could swim against the outgoing current. Climbing from the water on the far side Marcus knew that Arabus's first action would be to restring his bow and nock an arrow to it as they had agreed earlier in the day, ready for any sign that the men who would follow him might seek to betray their presence. The Roman waited a moment more before gesturing for Tarion to cross, then Arminius, followed by the Sarmatae twins.

'You have determined our order of crossing carefully, I see.'

Drest's whispered comment carried an edge of bitterness to Marcus's ears. He shrugged, watching Ram slide into the water in his brother's wake.

'Indeed I have. When I trust your men I will refrain from my precautions, but until then I will ensure that any opportunity for one of them to frustrate our plan, however unlikely that might be, is minimised.'

Drest shrugged in frustration, pointing a finger at The Fang's glowing spot of illumination on the dark summit that had risen into view before them.

'You had better come to that decision quickly, Centurion. Tomorrow night we will be faced with the walls of that fortress looming over us. If ever there was a time for one shout to tear apart your plans then that would be the time, I would imagine?'

He slipped away into the water with a final meaningful stare at the Roman and pulled himself across the river hand over hand. Once he was safe on the far bank Marcus untied the rope from the tree to which Arminius had fastened it and tied it around his waist, walking carefully into the water and signalling to the men on the other bank. The stream was sluggish, but the water itself felt thick, as if it were as much mud as water, and he grimaced with the unpleasant sensation as the silt insinuated itself into his armpits and between his buttocks. A gentle pull on the rope eased him out into deeper water, and a series of further pulls propelled him across the river's width, hands reaching out to help him climb, shivering uncontrollably, out of the water's cold embrace. Looking about him he saw that the raiding party's members were all speckled with the river's mud, their faces indistinct under the fresh coat of dirt. Lugos untied the rope from about his chest and coiled it into a tight circle, handing it to Arabus who stepped in close to speak with the young centurion.

'Another two miles and we will reach the hiding place I described to you.' He glanced up at the stars. 'We have enough time to go slowly and carefully. At least this –' he raised a grimy hand '– will help to disguise any scent we might have been carrying.'

Marcus nodded and gestured to his companions to follow the scout forward into the darkness, watching as each man took up the knotted rope that would both keep their spacing constant and allow any of them to signal an alarm.

'Remember my words earlier. There are hunters roaming on this side of the river, so you must move in silence and stop where you stand at the slightest hint of anyone other than us being out here. Arabus, take us to your hide.' He rubbed at the intaglio bound to his spatha's hilt with fine silver wire, feeling the delicately engraved lines under his calloused fingers as he muttered too quietly for anyone's ears other than his own to detect the words.

'And keep us safe, Lord Mithras, from whatever might step into our path.'

Dawn came to the Tungrians in an eerie silence, the slowly lightening sky untroubled by any hint of wind. The soldiers followed their instructions and built one large fire for every century, adding enough green stuff to the dry wood they had gathered the previous evening to guarantee that sufficient smoke rose into the still air to betray their position, visible for miles around.

'There'll be no hiding from the ink monkeys with this lot to guide them. Doesn't make no sense to me, first we sneak away from the river so's *not* to be found, then we set fires so's we *can* be found.'

'You might try listening when the grown-ups explain what we're doing, eh Horta?' Sanga shook his head in disgust at the soldier who had raised his voice in complaint. 'The finer points of soldiering are a mystery to you, ain't they? Here, Saratos, you're supposed to be nothing better than a poor, dumb barbarian, can you explain to our slow-thinking mate here what we're doing?'

The Sarmatae recruit was yet to fully master Latin, but there was no hiding the raised eyebrow of amusement as he turned to face the man in question.

'We here to bring enemy running. We allow Centurion Marcus to attack Fang.' The soldier looked blank. 'Fang? Big fort on hill?' Saratos shook his head, spitting out a choppy stream of his native language which, to judge from the look on his face, was far from complimentary before making another effort. 'See, today we run away from barbarian, let them chase horses.'

'Why the bloody hell would they chase the cavalry when they could be chasing us? They ain't going to catch no bloody horses, are they?'

Saratos shook his head again, tapping it as he did so.

'Is like Sanga say, up here is thinking, and down there –' he pointed at his booted feet '– and down there is marching. And you, you is *marching.*'

The maligned soldier bristled, clenching a fist and jutting out his chin.

'You taking the piss, horse fucker?'

The Sarmatae smiled back at him, tapping the dagger at his belt.

'You need be careful. I not start fight, but I end fight, and quicker than you like. And was no horse I fuck, was your sister. To be fair, she do *look* like horse . . .'

He turned away, apparently lacking any further interest in the confrontation, but Sanga saw him slide a hand to the side of his body that was shielded from the other man's view, gripping the knife's handle and tensing his body for any attack. Fixing the irate soldier with a steady gaze, the veteran shook his head in a manner he hoped would be discouraging.

'I wouldn't if I were you, Horta old mate, I've seen this one fight and I have to tell you it wasn't pretty. Besides, think of your poor sister . . .'

He puffed his lips out in a passable imitation of a horse snorting, prompting an immediate outbreak of hilarity in the men standing around them and turning their mood from the excited anticipation of a fight into uncontrollable laughter in an instant. Realising that there was no way he could win the argument, the insulted soldier turned away with a muttered curse, pursued by the laughter of the men around him.

'You do realise that you most definitely *didn't* make a friend then, don't you Saratos?'

The Sarmatae shrugged, poking Sanga's armoured chest with a big forefinger.

'He too stupid to argue, and he too soft to fight. And it was *you* tell me to argue him, not true?'

Sanga nodded, conceding the point with a shrug.

'True. Anyhow, you'd best get your kit ready and a handful of breakfast down your neck. I reckon we'll be on the move soon enough now that we've sent out a signal to the ink monkeys to come and get us.'

While the soldiers prepared for their day's march, Scaurus and Julius were appraising the fruits of the previous evening's work by Titus and his axe men. Working swiftly in the last of the day's light they had stripped branches away from the trees beside the Tungrian camp, being careful to take their cuttings on the side facing away from the path down which the Venicone pursuit must inevitably come. Lashing several branches together at a time, they had fashioned fans of foliage eight feet in width, which they were now making doubly secure with more rope. Silus was standing off to one side, discussing the contraptions with his deputy, who was shaking his head in disbelief.

'What do you think, eh Decurion?'

Silus scratched his head with a look of bemusement.

'I'm not really sure, to be honest with you, Tribune. If the horses will stand for it then I suppose these brushes will drag enough of a track in the grass to fool the barbarians, if they're not looking too closely. But how is the trail that we'll leave with those things going to fool anyone? There'll be no bootprints, for a start . . .'

Julius nodded knowingly.

'I asked the same question. Apparently the answer's very simple, once you think about it.'

'And indeed it is.' Scaurus turned back to his first spear with a decisive slap of one hand against the other. 'Muster the cohort please, First Spear, and we'll see how convincing a vanishing act we can do.'

'Make yourselves comfortable, since we're here all day. Keep any talking to a whisper, and move as little as you can. If you need to shit then go into the undergrowth, dig a hole and then bury it. I don't want to be lying here with the ripe smell of yesterday's pork tickling my nostrils, thank you very much, never mind who else might get wind of it.'

Marcus smiled at Arminius's terse, whispered instructions to Drest and his men. Rolling himself in his blanket he allowed himself to drift off into an uneasy sleep, reassured by the looming presence of Lugos sitting cross-legged and apparently asleep next to him. After several hours' uneasy doze, pursued from one brief dream to the next by both his father and the reproachfully silent and bloodstained Lucius Carius Sigilis, he started awake to find the enormous Briton still in the same protective position, his eyes slitted but nevertheless open and alert. Easing himself up into a sitting position Marcus rubbed at his bleary eyes and accepted a swallow of water from the offered skin.

'Have you slept?'

Lugos shook his head, his voice no more than a quiet rumble. 'Was watching . . .'

He tipped his head at Drest and his men. Drest himself was asleep, Tarion was playing a solitary game of knucklebones, and the Sarmatae twins were talking quietly in their own language. The legionary Verus was huddled into his cloak, staring at them with eyes that seemed unfocused.

'Where are the others?'

The big Briton pointed across the clearing.

'Watching for Venicones. War band passed earlier, running east.'

'Get some sleep.'

Suddenly awake, the Roman eased through the small copse's trees in the direction indicated by the tribesman until he found the two men crouched in the cover of a tall oak, gazing out across the sea of grass. Easing himself down beside them, he looked out across the river plain's rippling green carpet, in which nothing was moving other than the vegetation. To their right the slope of the hill on which The Fang stood rose out of the plain at an angle so steep that Marcus found himself wondering just how they would be able to climb it in the darkness. The fortress itself was out of view, hidden by the foliage above their heads.

'Any sign of whatever it was that was hunting out there last night?'

The raiding party's progress after their crossing of the river had been slowed by frequent pauses in their march, responses to the distant but unmistakable sounds of something or someone moving through the marshy plain's long grass. Arminius grunted, looking out across the flood plain.

'Nothing close enough to worry about. But we did see a war band pass on the far side of the river, four thousand men or so. They were running for the eastern hills, hunting for the cohort.'

'Are you sure?'

The German shrugged.

'Nobody else out here for them to be going after. Between the emperor and the Venicones, the legions on the wall are all too scared to move as much as an inch. Besides that, we saw smoke in the hills to the east once the sun was up.'

Arabus spoke with a note of admiration in his voice.

'Clever work. Just enough green stuff to make the smoke visible, not enough to look like an obvious lure. Your tribune has a hunter's cunning.'

Arminius shook his head.

'What my tribune *actually* has are the balls of a fully grown ox. And sometimes, but *only* sometimes, he is also as clever as he imagines himself to be. We must just hope that this is one of those times.'

Calgus looked down from his horse at the trail left by the Tungrian cohort, the once narrow game track now a trampled mess of boot- and hoofprints. One of Brem's scouts put a hand to the ground, touching the edge of an impression left by a hobnailed boot.

'Fresh, my lord King. Less than half a day old. The infantry first, and twenty or so horsemen following them. Most of the bootprints are destroyed, but they are clearly Roman. See the mark of their nailed boots.'

The Venicone king nodded decisively.

'We'll follow them, and look to take them from behind without warning.'

Calgus frowned at the trail, looking down its length until it vanished over a rise.

'Why would they march west? Surely there's nothing out that way but more of the same, trees and hills all the way to the sea?'

Brem snorted.

'It's obvious enough to me. They are attempting to get around our defences and come at The Fang from the north and west, attacking up the easy side of the hill when they believe we will least expect it.'

Calgus wrinkled his nose in disbelief.

'And they built fires whose smoke we could see from miles away? What sort of devious approach march does that sound like?'

The king waved a dismissive hand.

'These are Romans, Calgus, men of no great subtlety who are used to marching and fighting in great strength, and their arrogance has betrayed them. We will hunt them down and fall on them like wild animals, leaving them neither the time nor the space they need to mount their usual defence. Here in the forest they are on our ground, and we will show them the error of their intrusion in the time-honoured manner, with sword and spear. Forward!'

The former Selgovae shrugged, watching in silence as the fastest of the trackers sped away up the path, following the broad trail left by the Tungrians. He found nothing to trouble him in the surrounding trees, but was unable to keep from muttering to himself in a discontented tone pitched low enough that only he would hear it.

'*Perfect* ground for an ambush . . .'

He spurred his mount alongside the king's horse, ignoring the way that Brem's bodyguards fingered their sword hilts as he did so.

'If I might make one small suggestion, my lord King?'

'Your idea seems to have worked, Tribune. I'll admit that when we had the entire cohort messing about walking across those planks two hours ago I was more than a little uncertain about the idea.'

Scaurus peered through the hillside's scattered bushes at the Venicone war band in the valley below, careful to keep his head covered by the cloak that Julius had thrown over them both with its dark-green lining uppermost.

'So it seems. I fear, however, that this is the first and last time that our adversary will be this easily fooled by such an elementary trick.'

They watched in silence as the war band's scouts continued on up the track, the barbarian trackers attending closely to the boot-prints of the men who had been chosen to run in front of the horses and therefore add the necessary footmarks to make the phantom cohort's trail appear authentic. Scaurus frowned down at a group of horsemen who were following the scouts.

'I should have kept Qadir and a few of his archers with us. They could have dropped those horsemen from here with their eyes closed, and if I'm not mistaken that's our old adversary Calgus on the black horse, looking about him as if he expects the Sixth Legion to come storming out of the trees at any moment. Never has the old adage about faeces bobbing to the surface rung more true.' He shook his head ruefully. 'Although I'm not sure that I would have wanted to sell my life quite so cheaply as to pay for Calgus's skin with it. No matter. Those animals will run after Silus and his boys to the west for the rest of the day, either until they reach the end of the trail he's laying or when they see the smoke from tonight's camp. Either way they'll be a good day's march distant from The Fang as Centurion Corvus takes his men up the slope.'

Julius nodded.

'And so it seems that your ruse has succeeded. In which case, Tribune, I find myself wondering why we should take the risk of sending up smoke again this evening? You said yourself that they'll overwhelm us in no time if they catch up with us, and if they realise that they're being lured away from The Fang and turn for home early enough, then they might well be closer to us than we'd like when we start burning the green stuff. Why not just let them sulk their way back home without another clue as to where we are?'

The tribune watched the war band's rear end vanish over the rise before replying, keeping his eyes fixed on the spot where the last warriors had disappeared from sight.

'Because, First Spear, the very last thing we can afford to have happen is for those warriors to be anywhere near The Fang when our men come down that slope and make a run for it across the Dirty River's plain. Evading the pursuit of a few Venicone hunters is one thing, but being forced to find a way past several thousand warriors is entirely another matter. And if that means that we have to take a few risks, I'd say we can console ourselves that it's not all that much compared to the chance that Centurion Corvus and his men are about to roll the dice on.'

He gestured to the north, and the direction that the cohort had taken once they had walked carefully away from the campsite across rough planks which Titus's pioneers had carved from trees felled in the forest the previous evening, thereby avoiding any obvious sign of their departure, the last men away from the camp having taken up the walkway and tossed it into the trees.

'Now, shall we?'

5

Marcus made his way back to the tiny clearing to find that Lugos had wrapped himself in his cloak and huddled into the shade of a tree. Verus seemed less distracted, and greeted the centurion's return with a wry smile.

'If only I'd known this copse was here when I came down that slope, I might have rested a little easier that first night.'

The thief shook his head briskly.

'I doubt it. You'd have been too close to the fortress, and too easy to find. What did you do, when the horns started blowing and you reached the valley floor?'

The soldier looked at Tarion for a moment before answering.

'I ran blindly out into the grass, with the sounds of the hunters closing in behind me to give me wings of fear. And then I fell into a bog, concealed in the darkness by the grass until the ground fell away and I found myself mired in its stinking mud. If I'd been wearing armour I would have sunk without trace, but naked I was light enough to keep my head above the surface.'

The thief smiled darkly.

'You were lucky then. The mud covered your smell, right?'

'Yes. The monster that the hunters were using to follow my scent was unable to find me, huddled in the thick rushes.'

One of the twins interrupted with a look of disbelief.

'*Monster?* You were scared of a *dog?*'

Verus shivered, his face dark with the memory.

'A dog. Yes. But unlike any dog you've ever seen. Bigger than a wolf, with a jaw strong enough to tear lumps out of a man's body and a howl like the spirits of the dead returning for revenge on the living.' He paused for a moment, sneering at the Sarmatae.

'You sit there grinning at me, happy in your ignorance, so let me tell you what happened when I was taken prisoner. I wasn't the only man taken alive, several of my comrades were also captured alongside me, and the man crouched next to me was in a sorry state. I got knocked on the head and woke up with a knife at my throat, but he had tried to run from the barbarians and was taken down by that dog as he ran, or so he told me as we lay shivering under the Venicones' spears. He had a bite on his arm that looked as if he'd put it into a mantrap, and the animal was sitting close by, watching us with a look that promised pain if we tried anything.'

The legionary shook his head in apparent self-disgust.

'I was terrified of the bloody thing, but at least I managed to keep my mouth clamped shut, unlike my comrade. I never knew his name, he was from another century, but I knew him for a coward soon enough. He'd pissed himself at some point, and the dog could smell it and the fear that was coming off him in waves. It kept shuffling closer with its eyes locked on him, and the closer it got the more agitated he became, until the men set to guard him were standing round us and laughing at the state of him, encouraging the beast to have another go at him. And just when I thought it was about as bad as it could get, the dog's mistress came back with a bloody knife in her hand, fresh from whatever she'd been doing to our dead. If the dog was frightening then she was something much worse.' He paused and swallowed, the memory clearly still vivid. 'The bitch was as thin as a whip, all black hair, sinew and tattoos.' He paused for a moment, shivering as he saw the woman again in his mind's eye. 'There were so many tattoos on her face that it was like a death mask, and her eyes were the only thing alive in her stare, if you could call them alive, horrible cold green things, and when she stared at you, well, you just knew she was looking at a corpse in her mind's eye. She had cheekbones like axe blades, and she was festooned with weapons, a long sword on her back, a pair of hunting knives at her hips, shorter broad-bladed iron strapped to both her thighs, and one nasty little skinning blade in particular in a sheath against her spine. I found out later that they call her Morrig, but by then I'd got used to calling her The

Bitch in my head. She took one look at this poor nameless bastard
and I guess she must have known that there was no sport to be
had from him, no resistance to be broken. She hauled him up onto
his feet by his throat, turned him round until he was facing towards
safety and then kicked him in the backside, sending him away
towards the Wall in a staggering run. That boy didn't need telling
twice, he took one disbelieving look back at the rest of us and then
ran like a madman for safety, while the woman just stood and
watched him with a blank stare, as if she was waiting for something.
The guards were laughing and hooting with excitement because
they knew exactly what was coming. Just for a moment I hated
and envied him more than anyone else I'd ever met as he ran for
his freedom, but then she turned to look at the rest of us with eyes
as dead as stone, and I realised just what her purpose was in
releasing him.

'Once he was well out of sight she snapped her fingers and
sent the beast after him, and I swear I've never seen anything
move as quickly. The fucking monster was away like a racehorse,
and it was only a moment later that we heard the man scream as
it overtook him in the darkness beneath the trees and brought
him down. I thought that was it, but then he let out a horrible,
piteous howl, and then another, and another, each one more
frantic than the one before. One of the guards took great pleasure
in explaining it to us later, laughing at us in his broken Latin as
he explained that the animal kills its victims in a leisurely manner,
knocking them to the ground and then rearing back from them
for a moment before sinking its teeth into their thighs, or groin,
or guts. He told us the woman's name for the bastard thing,
something unpronounceable, but then he was kind enough to
translate it to one of the few Latin words he knew, a word I'm
pretty sure he'd heard from other prisoners. He called it
"Monstrum", and from then on I could only ever think of it as
the monster.'

He paused.

'We crouched, shivering with terror and thanking our gods that
it wasn't us out there in the dark while that *fucking* dog killed him

one piece at a time, each scream he gave out more soul rending than the last. When at last he fell silent I muttered a prayer to Mithras for his soul, but more than that, I prayed for my own end at their hands to take any form other than that nightmarish death. After that we expected the monster to return, but its mistress turned away without a second glance, and the guards just kept laughing and making chewing faces at us.'

Marcus frowned as the meaning of the soldier's words sank in.

'It was . . . *eating* him?'

Verus shrugged, his face as devoid of emotion as that of the female warrior he had described a moment before.

'Yes, Centurion. As I'd already realised from the look the woman gave us as she waited to release the beast, our comrade's death was a simple and terrifying way to completely subdue us. When the dog was done with his body the remains were left where they lay for the carrion animals to complete the job that the animal had begun.'

He stared levelly at the two Sarmatae.

'And still you fail to believe my words, I can see it in your eyes. If either of you has half the intelligence with which you came into this world you'll offer up a prayer now that if you should die on that hill tonight then your end will be with an arrow in your chest or a sword blade in your throat, and not with a dog the size of a donkey ripping out your guts while you wail for help that is never going to come.'

Marcus nodded slowly.

'And they used the dog to hunt you, once you had escaped from The Fang?'

'They hunted me for eight days and for all that time the beast was never far away, baying for my blood. Every time I heard that sound I wanted nothing more than for the hunt to be over . . .'

'You considered giving yourself up, if only to put an end to the torture of constant pursuit, right?'

The soldier looked across at Tarion, a calculating look on his face.

'It wasn't the dog that stopped me from surrendering myself.

By the time I'd been in their hands for twenty days I'd have settled for death by his teeth in a heartbeat, given that the Venicones were intent on killing me one tiny piece at a time with sharp blades and hot iron, and worse, intent on hollowing me out until there was nothing left of me but a shambling shell of a man.' He looked across at Marcus as if weighing the Roman's capacity for survival under the same torment. 'There were seven of us taken prisoner, so with the man that The Bitch set her dog on that left six. A couple of the lads were big men in every respect, right hard cases who had gone down fighting under the sheer weight of numbers thrown against them, and from the first chance they got they struggled against our captors, fighting the ropes that bound them and spitting in their faces if they got the chance.' He laughed without any hint of humour, looking up at the branches above them. 'The Venicones broke them in days, of course, degrading them brutally in front of the rest of us in order to show us all what was to come, until both of them were incapable of any resistance, and were begging for release from their torture and humiliation. That taught me the most important lesson in my survival, that fighting back against such inhumanity would only serve to incite our captors to greater ferocity. I learned never to show any signs of resistance or hatred, but to keep that fury bottled up tightly in here . . .'

He tapped his chest.

'After twenty days there were only three of us left alive, and another ten sunrises saw the other two dead in just the same way that each man had died before them, once his spirit was broken so completely that he would go to his death as a willing sacrifice to their gods. The king's priest had them tied down on his high altar and then ritually murdered them with a long knife he wore at all times, tearing open their chests and pulling out their beating hearts while those left alive were forced to watch, our eyes held open to prevent any attempt to avoid the sight.'

The Roman frowned in incomprehension.

'You prayed for a swift death, and yet they kept you alive for another month?'

Verus nodded.

'I can only assume that they knew that they had failed to break my will, and that total submission was the price of what they saw as a merciful death. They could see it in my eyes, I expect, my rage and horror at the bestial tortures to which they submitted me, and my constant promises to myself that the day would come when I was the man with the blade in his hands, and those torturing bastards the ones doing the screaming. I told myself that I would die like a man attempting to escape rather than submit to an animal's death on that slab with my spirit finally broken.'

Tarion, who had listened to the soldier's story with a look of fascination, nodded slowly.

'And so you found yourself hiding in the swamp, torn between the urge to strike out at your pursuers and simply to slip away into the darkness, and for ever escape their attentions.' He met Verus's questioning look with a knowing smile. 'How do I know this? It's simple enough. I have been in the same position more than once. When a man thieves for his livelihood he must sometimes take risks that no sane man would consider acceptable, if he is to eat. I have hidden in a tiny space with my guts growling for days at a time, waiting for the hunt to die down so that I could slip away into the night.'

The soldier grimaced.

'I would not have thought to compare our places in this life with anything other than contempt for the path you chose, at least before those bastards up there taught me that a man cannot always choose his path. So how did you end up as a thief?'

Tarion shrugged.

'How does anyone come to a way of life that they would not have chosen for themselves, had the choice ever been there to make? Ill chance, the wrong people . . .' He paused for a moment, smiling lopsidedly at the men around him. 'Verus is right, it's easy to despise a man like me, isn't it? A man who has chosen to live by stealing the work of others, judged to be the lowest form of life in a *civilised* society. Except, my friends, we do not live in a civilised society, no matter what we tell ourselves about the nobility of the empire. My father died of the plague, brought to our town by soldiers who had travelled in the east, and my mother was left without any means of supporting herself since she refused to whore out her body. And so I found myself a thief, untrained and initially unskilled, but believe me when I tell you that I was a fast learner. The first apple I lifted from a market stall almost saw me caught and doubtless sold into slavery, and I was saved only by the fact that I was light on my feet, but thieves tend to band together and so before long I was part of a gang that made a living by robbing anyone of anything as the opportunity presented itself. My speciality, as it turned out, was the theft of men's personal possessions in the street, especially the contents of their purses.'

He held up his hands.

'Soft hands, you see, and nimble with it. Combine these with a good sharp blade and I could have the bottom sliced out of a purse and the contents in my palm in the space of a breath. It was even easier when one of the pretty girls we knew would saunter by the target with a saucy smile on her face in exchange for a small coin, so that he'd be more interested in the contents of her stola than the man who bumped into him and was gone the next instant. But the day came, as it always does to every thief, when my luck ran out, or my touch deserted me, depending on whether I'm feeling sorry for myself or not. I was caught with my hand on another man's purse, beaten senseless and then put before a magistrate who was eyeing me up for crucifixion before Drest offered to buy me as a slave instead.'

'What about your mother?'

Tarion looked across at Marcus.

'My mother? She died in her sleep the night before I was caught, Centurion, worn out by the hard labour to which she had been reduced by her reduced status when my father died. You might wonder if my capture was partly caused by my being distracted at her death.' He grimaced at the Roman, shaking his head. 'Or you might wonder if her death, and her release from the slavery to which she was subject in all but name, was perfectly timed by the gods to spare her the shame of my capture and likely execution.'

Marcus touched the intaglio on his spatha's hilt in a reflex gesture.

'And yourself, Centurion? How do you end up sitting in the cover of a tree, waiting for night to fall in order that you may climb into the most dangerous place in all of Britannia? Your voice sounds like that of a cultured man to me, the sort of man whose purse I used to lighten without a second worry as to whether he could afford to lose the contents.'

The Roman shrugged at the thief's question, long since used to combining fact and fiction in his answer to any such query.

'Money may serve to relieve a man of the burdens of everyday life, but not every man born into wealth enjoys good fortune. My family was unfortunate, and so I found myself here in Britannia making a home with the Tungrians. You might find it ironic when I relate that I have enjoyed a great deal of good fortune since that day, not least that my brothers in arms have chosen to accept a good deal of personal risk in providing me with shelter. And so when the opportunity to do something as insane as what we plan for tonight arises, I consider myself to be the natural candidate as a meagre means of repaying them for the chance they took in admitting me to their ranks.'

'There's more to it than that, I'd say.'

Marcus turned his head to regard Drest, who had rolled over and was sitting up, rubbing his eyes and then rolling his shoulders.

'You have the air of a man carrying a burden, Centurion, some heavy weight of guilt, or shame. Or perhaps a violent urge for revenge? Whichever it is, you must realise that they are all corrosive emotions, and will pick at your spirit a pinch at a time until one day you discover that you have become an empty vessel, hollowed out by tiny increments but hollow nonetheless.'

The Roman looked back at him levelly.

'I have my faith to protect me. The Lord Mithras watches over me.'

The Thracian shook his head.

'The Lightbringer? Yet another in a pantheon of non-existent deities whose only function is to provide his followers with a prop for their need to explain everything that happens as "the will of the gods".' He turned to the thief. 'And that's enough talk from you, Tarion, get yourself bedded down and sleep for a while. You'll be first over the wall tonight, and for all our sakes we need you to be fresh when the moment comes to put your head over the parapet.'

'Well, we've made it to sunset without seeing any sign of the enemy, so all things considered I'd call that a successful day, wouldn't you?'

Julius didn't answer his tribune for a moment, shading his eyes and staring out from the marching camp to the west, squinting into the sunset.

'Let's hope you're not premature in that statement, Tribune. Unless my tired eyes are deceiving me there are riders coming—'

A sudden chorus of shouts from the sentries watching the western horizon interrupted him, and the camp erupted into the chaos of a stand-to, men grabbing at their spears and shields and running to line the camp's earth walls in the standard response to the approach of unknown cavalry.

'This late in the evening? It can only be Silus and his scouts.' Scaurus shaded his eyes and followed Julius's stare. 'Yes, that's Silus, I can see their dragon standard glinting red in the sunset. He's got a pair of empty saddles too.'

Tribune and first spear walked swiftly to the camp's western gate, greeting the incoming horsemen as the sun dipped to touch the horizon. Silus jumped down from his sweat-soaked mount and passed the reins to another rider, gesturing to the horses. One of the mounts was riderless, while another had a dead man's body draped over its back and held in place by its saddle horns.

'Make sure they're properly wiped down, we don't want them wet when night falls, and give them all an extra half-ration of feed, they've earned it.' He dismissed his men with a wave, turning to salute his superiors with a dejected expression the like of which Julius had never thought to see on his face. 'Evening sir . . . First Spear. Forgive me if I'm a little sweaty myself, but we've had something of a day of it.'

Scaurus turned away, waving a hand for the two men to follow him.

'In that case, Decurion, I expect you'll be needing a cup of wine.'

In the relative security of the command tent, the decurion sipped mechanically at his cup without any sign of tasting the drink, closing his eyes for a moment and rubbing a hand over his weather-beaten face.

'We dragged the lures for fifteen miles or so, as you commanded Tribune, until we were well past the Frying Pan's western rim, then dumped them and made our way along the range that forms the western side. I thought we'd had the perfect result until the archers hit us.'

Julius shot a glance at Scaurus as he spoke.

'Archers?'

'Yes. No more than half a dozen of them, and they were shooting from the hillside that overlooks the path around the northern edge of the range, but either they were the best shots in the tribe or they got luckier than they deserved. I lost two men, the one you saw and another who fell from his horse with an arrow in his back. Cocidius forgive me, I left him to lie there, and whether he was living or dead I have no clue. I knew that if I went back to recover him the archers would probably hit more of us, and I'd end up with more empty saddles . . .'

He sipped the wine again, and Julius spoke quickly, flashing a warning glance to Scaurus.

'That's the reality, Silus, the hard truth of commanding men out here with no one to fall back on. Do the right thing by your lads and suffer the guilt of a missing man, or do the right thing by him and lose more of them to no military purpose. How would you have felt if you'd ridden back with half your squadron shot out from under you?' Silus nodded, his eyes starting to moisten.

'And if you feel like crying, get it over here and now, and don't go out there until you can look your men in the eye and tell them that you did the right thing, no matter how bad it feels. After all, you've got a reputation for being a hard arsed, smart mouthed, couldn't give a shit arsehole to maintain, or had you forgotten?'

The decurion stared at him for a moment, then stuck his jaw out and drained the wine in a single gulp, putting the cup down on the tent's map table with a soft click. He saluted and turned for the tent's doorway, stopping to brace his shoulders before stepping through and back out into the scrutiny of the cohort's men.

'That was harsh, Julius, even if it did seem to put some life back into the man.'

The first spear turned to look at Scaurus with narrowed eyes.

'I agree, Tribune. In truth it should be you and I agonising over a man left for dead, and quite possibly writhing under the ink monkeys' knives even as we speak. But then you and I have long since hardened ourselves to those sorts of dilemmas, haven't we? And now, if you'll forgive me, I'll be away to tell the sentries on the western wall just what I think of the fact that I spotted Silus and his men coming in before they did. After all, I do have a reputation as a tirelessly vindictive bastard whenever I find any sign of weakness in my cohort, don't I?'

He stepped out of the tent, leaving the tribune staring after him. Scaurus refilled his wine and drained it, dropping the empty cup onto the table, watching as it rolled to the edge and fell to the grass floor. From outside the sound of his first spear's enraged shouting reached his ears, and the Roman shook his head with pursed lips.

'Hardened ourselves to those sorts of dilemmas? It feels more like we've both found our own ways of coping with the pain to me. And now for tomorrow's dilemma . . .'

He unrolled the scantily detailed map of the area north of the wall and moved a lamp to illuminate it, leaning his clenched fists on the table and staring down at the lines on the thick paper with a calculating expression.

★   ★   ★

'We have word from the scout party you sent to the north, my lord King!'

Brem stood up from the fire around which he and his bodyguards were warming themselves, turning to face the speaker. Alongside the member of his household who had spoken stood the leader of the half-dozen men he had begrudgingly sent over the northern hills' rim at Calgus's suggestion. The man's heavily tattooed face was forbidding in the firelight, and Brem realised that he was one of the hunters who ordinarily accompanied his hunt master Scar, men with the ability to ghost through the forest without leaving any trace of their passage, and preternaturally skilled with the bow. Beneath the swirls of ink his face was hard, lined and seamed by a lifetime's exposure to the elements, and his eyes were stone-like in the tattooed mask, flat windows on an untroubled spirit.

'You have news of the Romans?'

To the king's relief the scout bowed before speaking, saving him the problem of whether to punish a man who he guessed knew and cared little for such things as failing to show the proper respect. When he spoke the words came out in a low growl, almost inaudible over the fire's roaring crackle.

'Enemy horsemen, King Brem, riding along the northern side of the hills towards the east. We shot two of them from their horses.'

'Did either of them live?'

Calgus was at Brem's shoulder, his body alive with twitching impatience.

'No. The enemy took one body, the other was dead where he fell. I have trophies . . .'

He gestured to a leather bag hanging at his side, but the king raised a hand to forestall any grisly display.

'Good work. Make sure that your prizes are given to the priests when you return to The Fang, and they will be given pride of place in the eagle's shrine. Now go, and eat your fill from the deer your brothers have brought down for us.'

The hunter nodded and stepped back from the fire, his face vanishing into the shadows and leaving Brem and Calgus looking at each other. The Selgovae kept his face neutral, knowing that this was not the time for any display of pleasure at being proved right in his guess as to the Tungrians' dispositions.

'It seems that you were right, Calgus. The enemy are at large between us and The Fang, and we are miles too far to the west as a consequence of following what seemed to be their trail today.'

Calgus bowed deeply.

'A lucky guess, my lord King, and fortunate in that you humoured me sufficiently to send your best men to investigate my wild idea. I am grateful to have been of some little value to you.'

The king stared at him for a moment, until he was convinced by his adviser's apparent show of modesty.

'Indeed. The question is how we should now react to this news? I am minded to run our men to the spot where the scouts intercepted these horsemen, and follow their trail to wherever it is that the Romans camped for the night. I'll wager they won't have gone far by the time we get there.'

Calgus thought hard for a moment, masking his horror at the plan's high likelihood of failure with a calm expression of contemplation.

'In truth, my lord King, while your first reaction is a valid response to this news, I wonder if we might run the risk of your warriors being wearier than would be ideal when we overtake the Romans. And let us not forget, they still have enough horsemen to scout the ground around them well enough that they will doubtless see us coming before we see them. I wouldn't put it past these Tungrians to have a prepared position ready by the time we arrive, and I doubt we have the strength to attack them head on under such circumstances. It might be better to use your men's strengths in a different manner?'

He held his breath, waiting for the king to dismiss his doubts, but the success of the scouting mission he had inspired was enough to stay Brem's hand.

'And how would you suggest I do that?'

The Selgovae lowered his body painfully to squat on the dry earth, waving his fingers at the ground.

'I'll show you – if I might borrow a knife to draw a picture here?'

Brem pulled a dagger from his belt and handed it to him, waving a hand to calm his bodyguards as they reflexively reached for the hilts of their swords.

'Go on.'

The Selgovae drew a circle in the dirt with the knife's point, then sketched in the line of the Dirty River to its north-east.

'This is the ring of hills, here is The Fang, and we are here . . .' He scratched a pair of crosses onto the hard surface, one alongside the river, the other almost directly opposite it beyond the circle to the west. 'Our opponent is here, more or less . . .' He drew another cross to the circle's north. 'On the face of it he has us at a disadvantage, since he is between us and the fortress. But I do not think he plans to attack us there, for he knows that he would be trapped on the wrong side of the river, and therefore facing certain destruction. No, I think he will make another sidestep, expecting us to come after him now that we know where he is, and there is only one way he can move without any risk.'

'South?'

'Yes, my lord King, south. I think he will climb over the hills and dive back into the forests that grow so thickly in their bowl. The only question is whether he will then turn east or west when he reaches the fork in the bowl's centre.'

Brem looked down at him, his face ruddy in the firelight.

'And what would you do, if you were this Roman?'

Calgus didn't hesitate.

'Whatever I thought you might expect the least, my lord King. I think I would turn . . . west, and go as fast as possible while you hopefully searched for me to the east. And this has one more advantage as a strategy.' He waited until the king's silence encouraged him to continue. 'When we finally found his track heading away from The Fang we would be enraged at being sidestepped once more, and would chase him back to the west while whoever it is that he has sent after the eagle makes good their escape.'

He waited, tensed for the inevitable explosion at the mention of the eagle, but to his surprise Brem nodded his head slowly.

'In truth this Roman's behaviour starts to look less like the behaviour of a commander seeking an advantageous position from which to fight and more like that of a little dog which runs yapping around a bull, running the beast around the farmyard to confuse it. We must pin him down and smash him, before he has the chance to escape. So, how would you recommend that we achieve that, Calgus?'

The Selgovae pointed his borrowed knife at the picture he'd scratched into the dirt.

'I have an idea, my lord King, a way that we might trap the Tungrians in the forest if my guess is correct, and yet still hunt them to their destruction if they turn in a different direction. But what of The Fang?'

Brem shook his head.

'You should worry more about succeeding in giving me the heads of these Romans, and less about whatever games they might try to play in the swamps that guard my fortress. Scar and his Vixens will make short work of whatever poor fool they send across the river, you can be assured of that!'

The raiding party waited until the sun was below the horizon before stirring themselves in readiness for the climb to The Fang's walls, chewing on the dried meat handed out by Arminius as Marcus briefed them.

'Verus will lead us up the slope. He's been here before, and he knows what to look for better than the rest of us. I will go next, followed by Arabus, then Drest and his men, then Lugos and Arminius. Any questions?' The men looked back at him in silence in the day's last light. 'Very well. We leave as soon as it's properly dark. Be ready.'

They left the copse's cover once the stars were visible overhead, sliding down the shallow slope and into the long grass in silence. This far from the river the ground that sloped gently towards the hill's steep face was dry, and the plain's quiet was broken only by the susurration of the grass, as a gentle wind rustled the long stalks.

'Do you hear anything?'

Arabus shook his head in response to Marcus's whispered question.

'Nothing at all. If there is anyone out there then they are lying still and waiting for their prey to come to them.'

Both men looked up at the fortress perched high on the hill's summit hundreds of feet above them, seeing the pinpoint flickers of torches that lined its walls.

'This is a dangerous place. You will surely need your god with you this night, Centurion, and I mine.'

The scout reached into his tunic and pulled out his pendant of the goddess Arduenna, riding to hunt on a wild boar, rubbing the figure between finger and thumb before dropping it into his clothing and turning back to the hill. They followed Verus down into the grass, moving slowly and cautiously across the short distance between the copse and the point where the plain's flat expanse suddenly reared up to form the dizzyingly steep slope of the hill on which the Venicone fortress stood. The legionary had already started climbing the slope, his gaze fixed on the hill's black outline high above them, and Marcus followed with Arabus's soft footsteps barely audible behind him. After a climb of roughly one hundred steps Verus paused with his chest heaving, and Marcus stopped beside him feeling a similar burning in his chest as his lungs sucked in the night's cold air, turning to look back across the plain to the flickering dots of light on the Roman wall in the far distance. The soldier pointed, his face distorted by the effort of forcing air into his lungs, whispering softly between gasped breaths.

'Can you imagine . . . Centurion . . . the feelings . . . I experienced . . . as I struggled . . . down this . . . terrifying slope . . . in the darkness? How it felt to look out . . . and see the lights on our wall . . . so very far away . . . while above me the horns . . . of my pursuers . . . screamed at the night?'

Marcus nodded, realising that the other man's grimace was the result of more than his exertions.

'You must have been terrified.'

The soldier turned to him, and in the dim light of the stars the Roman realised that his teeth were bared in a snarl.

'Terrified? Oh *yes . . .*' He breathed in again, more slowly now as his body started to recover from his exertions, the muscles in his arms knotting as his body tensed at the question. 'But more than that, I felt enraged . . . *enraged,* Centurion, incensed to be abandoned so lightly . . . and to have been used so cruelly by the Venicones. That rage was what gave me the strength to survive, to elude my pursuers and crawl from one stinking bog to the next.'

He turned away and resumed his climb, leaving Marcus staring at his back for a moment before he too started up the hill again. The line of men climbed steadily until they reached the point where the slope's near-vertical pitch abruptly started to level out, and Verus flattened himself to the ground, beckoning the Roman alongside him. Waving a hand at the men following him to hold their current positions, Marcus crawled up alongside the legionary and looked out across the hill's summit. Fifty paces or so from the hill's brow The Fang's outer wall rose from the gently rounded hilltop, a ten-foot-high rampart of rough stone blocks that stretched across their field of vision and seemingly encircled most of the hilltop. Inside the wall's perimeter rose another structure, only one third of the size of the outer defences but towering over them to a height that Marcus estimated at forty feet. Torches burned at intervals along the parapet, casting pools of insubstantial yellow light over the ground beneath the walls, and as Marcus watched, a single sentry paced along the chest-high breastwork, the torchlight glinting off the blade of his spear.

'There. That is where I was imprisoned, and from where I made my escape.' Verus pointed at a section of the wall to their left, on the fortress's western side. 'The fortress's only gate is on that side of the hill, and so is their equivalent of what we would call the guardhouse. We need to go round to the right, and climb the wall on the eastern side. The legion's eagle is kept in a shrine on the tower's upper floor. They dragged me before it on several occasions, threatening to kill me in the presence of "my god" as an attempt to break my will before my ritual murder.'

He stared fixedly at the tower for a moment before speaking again, having apparently mastered his anger.

'There are usually three sentries posted on the walls at night. I saw them when I was dragged from my cell for each session with the priest who was my main torturer, one to watch the eastern wall, one the north and a third to the south, the man we can see now. The western wall is watched from the gate. When I saw them, the sentries were always standing between the torches to try to preserve their ability to see in the darkness, but from my time standing guard on our walls I'd bet that they can't see very well into the darkness. When he moves, so should we.'

Marcus nodded agreement, looking back at the men waiting on the slope behind them and beckoning them forward until they formed a tight huddle.

'The next time that man up on the wall turns away to walk his beat, we go, quickly, quietly, and together. Be ready.'

They waited in silence, every man tensed for the order to move. The sentry on the fortress's southern wall put a hand up to rub at his eyes, and the Roman smiled to himself at the memory of nights spent fighting off the need to sleep while standing guard, with nothing happening and nothing likely to happen. Stretching his arms the barbarian turned to his right and paced away down the wall's length towards the main gate. Waving his men forward in a silent command, Marcus led them in a soft-footed rush towards the wall, flattening himself against the stones and listening intently for any sound of the alarm being raised. The silence stretched out until he was convinced that their approach had gone unnoticed, gesturing to his men to follow him as he set off cautiously around the wall towards the eastern side, hugging the rough stones closely until he judged that they would be more or less beneath the spot where the next sentry would be standing. Taking a pair of heavy woollen strips which had been wrapped around his belt, he tied them about his boots, checking with his fingertips to be sure that the heavy hobnails were all covered by the coarse fabric and watching as his companions did the same. With everyone's boots suitably covered, he pointed up at the wall's parapet and gestured to Drest with a finger across his neck, the Thracian in turn waving the Sarmatae twins forward.

The raiders watched in silence as both men put their backs to the stonework and cupped their hands to provide a pair of platforms into which Tarion put first one and then the other of his feet. The twins silently hoisted the thief until his head was just below the wall's edge, and Drest stepped forward to grip his calves, holding him firmly in place against the wall. Sliding a knife from his belt, Tarion flattened himself against the wall and waited in silence until the eastern sentry's footsteps approached them along the curving walkway behind the parapet. As the Venicone walked to within a few feet of them, the thief reached out with his knife and tapped the wall gently with its point to make an almost inaudible sound. Continuing the insistent, almost subliminal rhythm of iron against stone he waited, staring intently up at the rampart's edge with his body flattened against the stonework and his free hand poised with the fingers hooked wide.

A head appeared over the wall, the sentry drawn by the tiny, insistent ping of metal on the wall's rough surface to peer out into the darkness in search of its source. Striking with the same blurring speed that had taken Marcus aback in the Lazy Hill headquarters building, the thief whipped up his open hand, grabbing the sentry's hair and dragging his head down even as he thrust the long knife blade up into the hapless barbarian's exposed throat. A thick spray of blood cascaded down onto the men below, and with his vocal cords and jugular vein severed the sentry struggled in silence for a moment before slumping onto the parapet as he lost consciousness. Tarion pulled the blade loose and gripped the man's clothing at the back of his neck, pulling hard to send his victim's inert body tumbling to the grass below, its thumping impact the only indication of the stealthy attack. He hissed a command down at the blood-flecked Sarmatae who promptly thrust their hands upwards to propel him up and over the wall in a silent, rolling movement. Silhouetted against the stars above them he immediately snatched up the dead sentry's spear from where it leaned against the wall and assumed the pose of a man watching the ground beyond the rampart, providing any of the sentries whose glance should stray in his direction with the image that they would expect.

When there was no outcry from the other men pacing the wall he shrugged off the rope that was coiled around his shoulder, dropping one end down to the waiting raiders and tying the other to the heavy wooden post of a stairway that rose from the courtyard below. Marcus climbed over the wall first, ducking into the parapet's shadows and staring across the fortress's open interior at the indistinct figures of the men standing guard on the south and north walls, less than fifty paces distant. Tarion whispered in the Roman's ear as Verus came silently over the wall.

'They won't notice us unless we give them reason to. They stand here day in, day out without ever seeing anything to excite their interest, so why should tonight be any different?'

Arabus slid over the parapet and into the shadows beside Marcus and Verus with his bow in one hand, the other reflexively reaching for an arrow as he settled into the cover of the deeper darkness. Marcus touched his arm, pointing into the fortress's interior.

'I'm going to find the eagle with Verus and the thief. Don't loose an arrow unless you have to, but if you have to start shooting then put an arrow in any damned thing you see moving. You know the watchword.'

The scout nodded at his centurion, easing down the wall to allow space for Drest who had followed close behind him, leaving Lugos and the Sarmatae twins below to watch their entry point. Marcus tapped Verus on the shoulder, gesturing to the darkened fortress's interior.

'Nothing complicated now, just take us to the eagle's shrine quickly and quietly.'

The legionary led them along the wall's curving parapet and then down a flight of stone steps into The Fang's interior, while Drest took up the thief's role of masquerading as the dead sentry.

With each step that he took down into the darkened stronghold, and as they tiptoed carefully into the fort's gloom, Marcus felt as if he were submerging himself deeper into dark, still water. As Verus stopped and looked cautiously about him at the bottom of the flight of stairs, the Roman tilted his head and listened for any sign that the garrison was awake to their intrusion. The silence was almost palpable, as if time itself had stopped for a moment, and after a while he realised that Verus wasn't going to move without some encouragement. He reached forward and touched the legionary on the shoulder, feeling a tremor that was coursing through the soldier's body through his rough woollen tunic.

Before the Roman could comment, Verus padded away into the darkness, staying in the shadows of the southern wall with Marcus and Tarion close behind him, pacing cautiously forward until they were as close to the doorway of the tower that gave the fortress its name as was possible without crossing the thirty paces of open space that lay between them and it. Backing slowly away from the wall, Verus craned his neck until he was able to see the sentry standing guard on the south wall. The tribesman was leaning against the wall with his head supported by his hands, his spear propped against the parapet's stonework. The legionary waved quickly, beckoning Marcus and Tarion on, then turned and flitted across the open space, his hobnails muffled by the thick rags. Marcus followed with his heart in his mouth, stealing a glance back over his shoulder at the wall to see the sentry still motionless against the parapet, and still apparently staring out over the Dirty River's valley. Tarion whispered in his ear as the two men followed Verus's apparently charmed path to the tower's great wooden door.

'*He's asleep!*'

The soldier's grin had an almost manic intensity as they joined him at the tower's door, his whispering voice harsh with anger in the fortress's slumbering silence.

'*Wait 'til they find out that we've got away with the eagle and he saw nothing! That fucker will be beaten to death in a moment!*'

For all that his voice was lowered almost to the point of in-audibility, Marcus wondered if he detected an edge of hysteria in its slight quaver, but before he had time to do anything more than narrow his eyes in question, Verus was through the noiselessly opened door and into the towering central redoubt. Motioning the thief to follow him, Marcus took one last look around before slipping into the building, easing the dead legatus's gladius from its scabbard in a soft scrape of polished iron over the scabbard's fittings. The tower's ground floor was empty for the most part, a fifty-pace-wide hall lit by torches suspended in heavy iron sconces, and the room was dominated by a massive wooden throne on a raised platform at one end. A wooden staircase wound around the chamber's walls up to the tower's second floor, an open centred platform beneath the tower's heavily beamed roof. Verus was already advancing up the stairs, and whilst he was keeping to one side of the treads to avoid the inevitable creaking that would result from stepping on the central section, Marcus had the uncomfortable feeling that the situation was getting further out of his control with every step the soldier took.

Exchanging glances with Tarion to find the thief's expression mirroring his concerns, the young centurion went up the stairs behind Verus with as much speed as he felt he could risk, given the silence that sat heavily upon the building. The legionary was clearly intent on something above them, and as he looked up and across the hall Marcus realised that he was sweating profusely, his lips moving in a silent babble of words, but even as he increased his pace in an attempt to overtake the other man he realised that Verus too was moving faster than before, his steps no longer silent as the treads creaked beneath his feet. Reaching the top of the stairs the soldier moved with complete confidence to one of the four doorways that beckoned them, his sword raised ready to strike as he lifted the latch and pushed the heavy wooden door aside.

Reaching the doorway close behind the soldier, with Tarion at his heels, Marcus looked over the legionary's shoulder and realised exactly what it was that had drawn him up the stairs with such irresistible power. The room's interior, dimly lit by another pair of torches jutting away from the walls on either side, was a grotesque combination of shrine and torture chamber. The walls were lined with the decapitated heads of dozens of men, all with skin oddly shrunken and distorted around their skulls, and the air was thick with the aroma of burnt wood underlain by a subtle but unmistakable tang of decomposition. Verus turned back to him, his face pale with tension as he whispered his explanation of the bizarre spectacle before them.

'They dry the heads just as you might preserve a fish, burning wood chips and sawdust to make the smoke required to preserve the dead men's flesh.'

Marcus nodded at Verus's whispered words, pushing the wide-eyed soldier into the room and beckoning Tarion in. The thief closed the door noiselessly behind him, turning to look about him with a grim expression, his attention fixed on the far end of the room with the look of a man who had sight of his objective. At the far end, behind a stone altar whose surface was carved with runnels to carry away the blood that was shed on its smooth surface, stood a tall wooden case whose doors were firmly shut. To either side of the altar were racks of iron bars, each one a different length and thickness, and a heavy brazier stood in one corner with a stack of wooden fire logs piled neatly beside it. Marcus stepped forward to pick a torch from its holder, sweeping the brand's light across the wall to examine the rows of heads that had been placed on flat wooden platforms to either side of the altar.

'These men were Roman.'

The heads were unmistakeably those of soldiers, for the most part at least, their hair cut short, some with healed facial scars while others bore fresh and in some cases horrific wounds which had never been granted the time to heal. The young centurion scanned the array of dead men arranged before him, and his gaze was drawn to one man in particular. He reached out and took the head down from its pedestal, looking into the dead eyes of the man he had discovered to be his birth father only after the legatus's death in defence of his legion's eagle.

The thief rounded the altar and stopped before the wooden case that was the room's apparent focus. Reaching out a hand, he flicked away the iron latch holding the case closed and parted its doors, sighing with pleasure as the contents were revealed. Shining dully in the torch light the Sixth Legion's eagle was perched at eye level atop a wooden staff carved with the symbols of the god the Venicone tribe shared with many of the locally recruited men who manned the Roman wall, Cocidius the hunter. The eagle's gilded surface was crudely painted with a rough black covering which seemed to have been slopped across it in random patterns, and whose consistency varied enough to allow flashes of the metal's formerly shining surface to peep out from beneath it. Scratching at the surface he sniffed carefully at the standard, then turned back to Verus with a questioning look.

'Yes. That's the dried blood of those men whose heads bear witness to their sufferings. The Venicone priests bring the eagle out to witness their ceremonies, and spatter it with the hot blood of the men they sacrifice to their god, to subdue the standard's spirit and reinforce their domination of everything it represents.'

Marcus nodded grimly at the soldier's words, replacing the torch in its holder and pacing across to Tarion, lifting the staff on which the eagle stood out of the case and testing how securely it was fastened to the ornately decorated wooden pole.

'It's too firmly fastened for me to get it free, and too noisy to break it off. We'll have to take it as it is.' He peered into the case from which their prize had been removed. 'What's that?'

Tarion reached in with a smile and lifted out a heavy metal bowl, placing it onto the altar with a reverent care. The size of a shield boss, it was made from solid gold and richly decorated with the same ornate patterns that ran up and down the length of the staff on which the eagle perched.

'It's the ceremonial dish they use to collect the blood of the sacrifices, when they've done with putting the legion's standard to shame.' Marcus raised an eyebrow at the soldier, who shrugged with no sign of emotion. 'I was made to witness their rituals. I expect that they believed that seeing our eagle so misused would be enough to break my resolve . . .'

'And the loss of so precious an object will be enough to leave Calgus in a very exposed position indeed.'

He looked pointedly at Tarion, and the thief nodded his under-standing, slipping the bowl inside his cloak and dropping it into a deep pouch sewn into the garment. Seeing that the arrangement left both of the thief's hands free, Marcus reached out and took the eagle's staff from its resting place atop the altar, lifting the legatus's head from its shelf and handing it to the other man.

'That's enough risk, if we want to escape with these prizes. We're leaving.'

As they turned to the doorway the sound of a voice from the landing outside reached them, conversational tones, the speaker apparently on the other side of the door's thick wood. Marcus put a finger to his lips, glaring sharply at Verus as the soldier flattened himself against the wall to one side of the entrance, sinking into the shadows so that only the contours of his body were dimly visible. Marcus and Tarion ducked behind the altar, putting themselves out of sight from the door, and the thief deftly closed the doors on the wooden case, bargaining that the open latch was a small enough detail to avoid casual scrutiny. The door opened, and soft footsteps paced across its threshold and into the room. The Roman waited until the sound of the door closing reached them and then ushered Tarion to his feet, pulling a finger across his throat.

The newcomer's back was turned to them as he fiddled with the door's latch, still muttering quietly to himself in a grumbling tone. An elderly man, his back was stooped and covered in long white hair that had recently been released from a formal plait to judge from its wavy appearance. The thief tensed himself, his right arm cocked to throw the knife that he had plucked from his tunic before his victim turned to see the threat at his back, but as his free hand reached forward to balance the throw, Verus broke the silence with a heart-stopping roar. The sudden scream of rage erupted from him like the pain-crazed bellow of a man undergoing the most savage torture. Springing forward from the shadows with three quick steps, he confronted the old man with his arms spread wide and his face frozen in a rictus of rage, emitting another ear-splitting scream as the terrified priest spun and looked up into his face with an expression of amazement that turned to horror as he realised exactly who the blood-spattered lunatic confronting him was. Raising his hands in a futile gesture of self-defence the priest gabbled something in his own language as the legionary sprang onto him, bearing him to the ground with both hands locked about his throat.

Tarion reacted first, sliding the throwing knife away into its sheath and gesturing to Marcus.

'Time to leave!'

Shaking himself from the amazement that had momentarily frozen him in place, the Roman followed him across the room, both men stepping past the spot where the old man had fallen to the floor under Verus's frenzied attack. The legionary was throttling his victim with one hand, and had levered himself off the feebly struggling priest far enough to be able to frenziedly smash a clenched fist down into his victim's face as he closed the strangling hand about his throat. The priest was emitting a desperate gargling sound, pausing only to grunt every time the berserk soldier smashed a punch into his battered face. Tarion ripped the door open, stepping out onto the broad wooden landing and then recoiled back against Marcus with the shock of what was waiting for him. The Roman pulled him aside with his free hand, thrusting the eagle's staff at him and drawing his long spatha as he advanced out onto the wooden platform.

A massively built warrior was advancing down the landing's length towards him with another man at his heels, a long spear in one hand which he threw at Marcus as the Roman emerged from the doorway. Jerking his head back, he was too slow to avoid the viciously sharp spearhead's blade completely. A cold, stinging sensation drew itself across his nose and cheek as the spear thudded into the door frame beside him, and as the cut went from its initial numbness to the familiar burning pain of severed flesh he snarled out his wounded fury, ducking under the spear's shaft and stepping out to meet the charging warrior blade to blade as the Venicone wrenched his sword from its scabbard. Parrying the onrushing warrior's first vicious thrust with the spatha's angled edge he raised the legatus's gladius high to his left like a scorpion's sting, putting a shoulder hard into the big man's chest to stop him dead and using the impact's circular momentum to spin fast, burying the shorter sword deep into the back of his neck and feeling the snap of his attacker's spine as the sword's stout iron blade cleaved through it and ripped out through his mouth. Leaving the sword buried in the warrior's slumping corpse he took the spatha two-handed, looping the long blade behind his right shoulder and up high into the smoky air before stepping forward to drive it down into the man behind his first victim as the Venicone cringed under the descending line of flickering steel, grunting with the effort as the patterned sword slashed down into the helpless man's body and cut him in two from shoulder to hip. The corpse tottered for a moment and then fell apart in a rush of blood and internal organs, while the Roman stood with one leg pushed forward and the sword held in both hands with its point almost touching the floor and a savage snarl on his blood-speckled face.

'Run!'

Tarion's shout snapped Marcus from his momentary reverie, his gaze following the thief's pointing hand across the tower's open square to the landing's far side where another four men were running from the room opposite them. Wrenching the gladius's blade from his first victim by stamping on the dead man's head and twisting the blade to free it from the severed vertebrae's tight grip, he followed the fleeing thief down the stairs three at a time. Looking back, he saw that Verus had lifted the terrified priest's body over his head and carried him out onto the landing, screaming defiance at the advancing warriors while the old man struggled helplessly in his iron grip. Staggering to the platform's edge, the legionary grunted as he hurled the holy man out into the void, then squealed out a high-pitched laugh that raked the talons of its insanity down the back of the Roman's neck as the soldier drew his sword to fight. The priest flew to the ground below them with a final scream of anguish, his frenzied howl cut off as abruptly as he hit the stone floor with a crunching impact. Tarion shot an amazed glance at Marcus.

'If they're not awake down there then they never will be. *Come on!*'

Bounding down the stairs the two men stormed past the fallen priest, Marcus noting from the corner of his eye that one of the old man's fingers was twitching against the cold stone flags. Looking back up at the platform above them he saw Verus overwhelmed by the men storming in to assault him, one of the warriors burying a spear deep in his side before another thrust a sword up into his jaw as the legionary staggered under the first wound's fearful pain. Turning back to the hall's door the Roman readied his weapons as Tarion pulled the heavy wooden door open, crouching low to peer around the door's thick frame. There were half a dozen or so corpses scattered across the open courtyard, some of them lying still while a pair of men were still writhing, grasping ineffectually at the arrows that protruded from their bodies. As he stared out into the darkened compound an arrow hissed overhead from his left to rattle off the stones of the wall by the main gate.

'We can't stay here!'

The thief was tugging at his shoulder, pointing back at the Venicones hurrying down the stairs behind them, their blades black with Verus's blood. Marcus nodded decisively, taking a deep breath.

'Follow me!'

Ducking round the door frame he ran for the fortress's eastern side with the thief close behind knowing that the archers at the courtyard's other end would be putting arrows to their bows in reaction to the sudden movements below them. With a hissing riffle of feathers and the sigh of iron cleaving the air, an arrow flew past his ear so close that he felt its passage as much as he heard it.

'*Eagle! Friendlies coming in!*'

The answering shout from the darkness beneath the eastern wall was recognisable as Arminius's voice, a note of urgency in his bellowed response.

'*Get down!*'

Marcus dropped to the ground, dragging the thief down with

him, and flinched as a flight of arrows whirred over their heads. Looking back over his shoulder he saw a warrior who had clearly chosen to pursue them into the teeth of the unseen archers' threat stagger backwards clutching at his chest, while another turned tail and hobbled back into the cover of the tower's open doorway with a hand grasping at his wounded thigh.

'*Now! Run for it!*'

Both men leapt to their feet at the command, sprinting across the fortress's courtyard with arrows loosed from the western wall flicking past them and clattering off the stone walls.

'*Here!*'

Marcus recognised Arminius's voice and ran towards it almost blindly, his ability to see in the darkness still compromised by his exposure to the tower's torchlight, dragging Tarion along in his wake. The German took his arm and they climbed the stone stairs that led to the wall's fighting platform.

'We need to go quickly, before they wake up and send a party around the walls to cut us off from our escape route!'

He bundled them along the wall, past the two Sarmatae who were nocking arrows to their bows and shooting into the darkness at the fortress's far end. As the German passed the two men they shot one last arrow apiece and then abandoned their positions, dropping in behind Marcus as he followed Arminius around the wall's curve to the spot where Drest waited for them, huddled in behind his heavy wooden shield from which a pair of arrows protruded, one barely an inch from the rim. Arminius gestured to the wall, and without a word the Thracian tossed his shield over the parapet and then climbed after it, keeping his body low against the stones as he eased himself over the wall. Readying himself for the ten-foot drop on the wall's far side, Marcus moved to follow him only to receive a heavy blow from behind that forced his face into the cold stone of the wall, the eagle falling from his hand onto the walkway's hard surface with a harsh metallic clatter.

6

Turning awkwardly, Marcus pushed the dead weight of a man's body from his back and found himself looking down at Tarion, who had dropped onto his knees and was bent back as if in adoration of the sky above.

'Arrow.' Radu pointed to the thief's back. 'He is dead, even if he is still breathing.'

'Aye.' Arminius's voice was flat with resignation in the young Roman's ear. 'We'll have to leave him.'

Nodding his head in a reluctant decision, Marcus hooked a thumb over his shoulder, gesturing to the two Sarmatae.

'Go.'

The two men squeezed past Arminius, who stepped forward and lifted his shield over Marcus in readiness to thwart any further well aimed or lucky shots. Turning his attention back to the thief, he felt around the dying man's back until he found the arrow's shaft, gripping it and twisting sharply to snap the thin wooden dowel. Tarion shuddered, groaning with pain as the arrow's barbed head moved inside the wound it had carved deep into his body. Grimacing with self-loathing at the act even as he performed it, the Roman stripped away the thief's cloak, feeling the weight of the golden bowl and the dead legatus's head in the garment's hidden pouch as he draped it over his own shoulders. Pulling the dagger from his belt he cut the thief's throat without ceremony to spare him any further pain, then sheathed the weapon and touched the intaglio on the pommel of his spatha.

'I have no coin for you, my friend, but may Our Lord Mithras receive you into the joy of his light in the afterlife as your reward for this noble end.'

He snatched up the eagle and the two men slid over the parapet, dropping to the ground below to find Drest waiting for them, a questioning look on his face as he glanced back up at the wall.

'Tarion?'

Marcus shook his head wearily, raising the eagle's staff to display the shining metal bird.

'He's dead.'

The Thracian made an intricate gesture over his forehead before speaking again. 'Then we must leave. Come.'

Advancing round the wall's curve towards the almost sheer slope they found Arabus and the two Sarmatae with arrows nocked to their bows, all three of them ready to shoot but without any target. Lugos was lurking behind the bowmen, the frustration in his voice at watching other men do the fighting for him obvious as he turned to speak to them.

'Venicones try to attack.'

He indicated the patch of ground before them that was lit by a torch on the wall above, and Marcus saw that there were several more bodies littering the turf. The Briton waved a hand at the carnage.

'They not come again until many more men. Fetch from camp.'

Marcus nodded his understanding in the torch's faint light. At least half of the fortress guard's strength would have been asleep in their camp alongside the fortress when the alarm was raised moments before.

'They'll have enough force to rush us quickly enough . . . ' He looked across the short stretch of ground to the point where the gentle slope abruptly faded away into darkness. 'We need to get away from here now.' Pointing to the Sarmatae pair, he gestured at their escape route. 'Leave your bows and go!'

The two men looked at each other for a moment.

'*Go!*'

At Drest's shouted command they rose as one man and dropped their weapons, shrugging off quivers that contained a few arrows apiece before running to the edge of the drop and picking up their shields, vanishing from sight down into the gloom. Marcus picked up one of the bows and nocked an arrow to it, turning to his companions as Drest did the same with the other weapon.

'Arminius and Lugos, you're next!' The German opened his mouth to protest, but closed it again when he saw the look on Marcus's face. As the two barbarians climbed down over the drop-off Arabus looked back and called out a warning, and the Roman flicked a glance back at the fortress to find a huddle of men approaching them at a cautious run behind a wall of their shields. He loosed the first arrow without thinking, watching it fly into the group of men as he reached for the next.

'Shoot low!'

The three men worked their bows as fast as they could, sending arrow after arrow into the oncoming Venicones whose advance withered under the hail of sharp iron, first one man and then another falling with arrows in their legs. As they drew closer Marcus judged that they were inside the range at which an arrow might penetrate their shields' layered wood, and raised his aim to send his next shot straight into them, rewarded by a yelp of pain and a sudden recoil from the man he had wounded. Drest loosed one more arrow and then threw his bow down, his supply of missiles exhausted.

'We go!'

Dropping his own bow the Roman grabbed the eagle and led them towards the hill's edge, picking up his shield from the spot where he had left it and groping for the drop-off with his booted feet as the slope abruptly fell away beneath him. Looking back over his shoulder he realised that the Venicones were within a dozen paces of them, and drawing back their spears to throw in the single torch's uncertain light.

'Jump!'

Allowing his feet to slip out from beneath him he slid the first few feet of the descent, aware that he was perilously close to the point where the slope went abruptly from steep to precipitous, hearing rather than seeing the spears that arced over their heads and were lost in the darkness. With a frustrated roar one of the tribesmen, whether braver or simply more foolhardy than the men to either side, leapt over the drop-off and raced down the steep slope beside Marcus, reaching out with a big hand to snatch at the eagle's staff as the fleeing Roman fought for balance. Digging in his booted heels to arrest his downward rush, Marcus lowered the eagle and swept it at the warrior's ankles, knocking his feet out from under him. With a wail of realisation that he was helpless to resist his own downward momentum the Venicone slid for a dozen feet, slipping ahead of the Roman until he encountered a bump in the slope's surface that threw him unceremoniously out into thin air, screaming and kicking his legs as he fell out of sight onto the steep slope's waiting boulders.

A spear flashed past Marcus, and he looked back up the slope's almost vertical rise to find a group of warriors silhouetted above them, baying their frustration at having missed the chance to recapture the eagle. An arrow whipped between the Roman and Drest with a whirr, and another glanced off the metal eagle with a clang as the two men's eyes met. Marcus raised his voice to bellow down the slope at the men below.

'*Shields up!*'

He raised the heavy wooden shield which he had grabbed at the slope's edge and cautiously started his descent again, holding it over his head and praying to Mithras for his divine protection. With a numbing blow to his raised arm he felt something hit the shield, and glanced up to find the point of an arrowhead poking through the solid wood. As he looked over at Drest a rock smashed into the Thracian's raised shield, hammering it down onto the other man's head and very nearly knocking him off his feet.

'*Keep moving!*'

Above them Marcus could hear horns blowing distantly off to their right.

'*Hunters!*'

He nodded grimly at Arabus's pronouncement, focusing on keeping his footing on the slope, every step down requiring him to leave one foot planted while the other reached down two or three feet in search of safety. Another arrow clipped the side of his shield and flew off into the darkness below, and then there was silence other than the distant shouts and horn calls of the hunters working their way down the shallow hillside away to the west. Looking up again, wondering at the cessation in their harassment from above, Marcus realised that a handful of the more foolhardy warriors had started down the slope, and were coming down the precipitous hillside above them as fast as they dared, their bodies outlined against the stars above. Looking down again, he saw that against the hill's slope the raiding party would now be invisible, lost in the dark mass of the ground below them.

'Drest, pass me one end of that rope!'

At his whispered command the Thracian carefully made his way across the slope towards his dimly seen outline, handing him the tarred butt-end of the coil of line that was over his shoulder.

'Get as far to your right as you can. When I tug on the rope once, go to ground and pull it taut! When I tug it again, run up the slope as hard as you can!'

He saw the other man bare his teeth in a slash of white and then Drest was gone, crabbing away across the slope as fast as he could. Their pursuers were closer now, and Marcus could hear them calling softly to each other as they skipped nimbly down the steep hillside. He tugged on his end of the rope, then pulled hard to take up the slack and raise the cord a foot or so off the ground. The warrior closest to him caught sight of the Roman in the corner of his eye just as he reached the trap, turning to point with his mouth opening to shout a warning as he tripped and cartwheeled away down the hill, the breath bursting from his body in a loud grunt as if he'd been punched in the gut. Marcus tugged frantically at the rope again and ran back up the slope, his legs pumping as he dragged the rope upwards, praying that Drest was doing the same. Another warrior tripped and was gone without ever seeing the impending threat, and then the rope snagged against something more solid. Making one last titanic effort, Marcus turned his back to the hill and forced himself up another few paces with his thighs aflame from the effort, wrenching the rope upwards to be rewarded by a cacophony of screams as the knot of men who had stopped to listen, alerted by the shout of their comrades as they fell, were pitched into the air to tumble away down the slope. He listened for any other presence on the hill, but could hear nothing other than the wind whispering across the slope. Even the cries of the hunters were now inaudible, although whether that was a good thing or not was beyond his understanding.

Sanga's tent party reported for their spell of guard duty four hourglasses after darkness had fallen, and were directed to their section of the marching camp's perimeter by the ever irascible Quintus, the century's chosen man and its acting centurion in Marcus's absence.

'You know the drill. Keep your mouths shut and your eyes and ears open. If you hear anything more exciting than a hedgehog grunting out a curler then you blow the fuckin' whistle and wait for the rest of the century to reinforce you, right?'

While most of the cohort had the luxury of removing their boots and rolling themselves into their cloaks and blankets, the Fifth were dozing fitfully, fully equipped and with their weapons close to hand, ready to form the first line of resistance to any threat that might materialise out of the night's stygian darkness. Sanga, the unofficial leader of the eight-man group who would be guarding a third of the camp's perimeter, saluted the chosen man and watched him limp away into the camp's interior.

'Poor bastard. Without a centurion to take some of the load he's on his feet every two hours to make sure the incoming guard climb out of their nice warm blankets and take their turn.' He spat on the turf and shook his head. 'I could almost feel sorry for the man. Almost . . .'

At his side Saratos grunted, reaching a hand up into the sleeve of his heavy chain-mail armour to scratch at his armpit.

'Had hard day. His leg hurting a lot, from way he walking.'

Sanga shrugged, the gesture almost invisible in the starlight's dim illumination.

'Like I said, I could almost feel sorry for the bastard. Right then, my lads, just like it always is. Take up fifty-pace spacings down the turf wall, and use the marks chopped into the mud to tell you where your beat starts and stops. Keep walking, keep your eyes and ears open and shout for me if you see or hear anything you don't like. Don't put your helmets or their liners on unless you hear the stand-to being blown, or you won't be able to hear the bluenoses sneaking up on you, and I don't care how cold your delicate little ears get. Anyone I catch leaning on the wall will get a good fucking dig from this –' he held up a scarred fist, and then lowered the hand to tap meaningfully at the hilt of his sword '– and anyone I find asleep won't have to worry about being sentenced to death because I'll already have sent you to meet the ferryman myself, right?'

The knot of men gathered about him nodded dourly and dispersed to their various points along the camp's turf wall, as familiar with the routine of guard duty as they were with Sanga's threats, which were more than idle. Saratos lingered for a moment, watching as the other men trudged away to their posts before turning back to Sanga.

'We march fifteen miles today, north and then east. Tomorrow perhaps we march west back to gap in hills, then south back to yesterday camp, then go back to fort of Lazy Hill. Is a long march. You think Quintus can march so far?'

Sanga laughed softly in the darkness.

'Old Quintus? He's had trouble with that hip of his for years now, and every winter sees it get a little bit worse, but I'll bet you a clipped sestertius to a freshly minted gold aureus he'll go the distance tomorrow just fine. See the thing is, if he doesn't manage to keep up with the blokes he's shouting at he's no more good as a chosen man than a wooden fire poker, at which point he'll get offered his discharge without the option of refusal. And he's got no more idea what to do if he ain't a soldier than most of these dozy sods. Now get about your watch, old son, and don't forget, mates or not, if I catch you leaning, I'll give you a reaming!'

The Sarmatae recruit smiled to himself and turned away, pacing down the turf wall until he reached his allotted stretch of the camp's defences, as far down the four-foot-high rampart as it was possible to march without turning the corner into the next tent party's patrol area. Fighting off the urge to yawn, he started his beat, up and down the mud wall, stopping to stare out into the darkness every few paces, sweeping his adjusted vision across the landscape and cocking his head on one side to listen intently to the night's incessant background noise for any sign of a disturbance that might indicate the presence of an enemy. Other than the wind's gentle hiss through the trees beyond the marching camp's walls there was little enough of any note other than the occasional disconsolate bark of a fox in the distance. Frowning at a tiny sound, almost more imagined than actually heard, he stared out into the darkness for a moment and then turned his head to look up the wall's line to his right, the man patrolling that section of the camp's defences lost in the gloom. As he swung round to look to his left, wondering if the sentry from the next tent party was perhaps enlivening his shift with a little sport, he was hit from behind by a pair of bodies, the wind driven from him by the impact.

Drawing breath to shout a warning, he felt a coarse piece of cloth being thrust into his mouth, reducing his protest to an inaudible murmur, and one of the men crouched over him stabbed a fist down into his temple, momentarily stunning him. Blinking furiously to clear the flashing lights from his vision, the Sarmatae felt himself being dragged across the grass and into the cover of a small tree that had been deemed too much of an effort to uproot from within the camp for the sake of one night. A hard voice whispered in his ear, its tone laden with menace.

'Right, you fuckin' know-all barbarian ballbag, I'm going to teach you what it means to respect the blokes what have been here a lot longer than you, eh, horse fucker?'

Coming to his senses Saratos recognised the harsh whisper as that of Horta, the soldier he had faced down that morning, his eyes narrowing as he recognised the dull silver line of a dagger in the man's hand. Shaking his head again he tried to get his feet beneath him to push his body upright, only to have them kicked away by the knifeman's comrade Sliga, who bent to mutter a warning with one hand squarely planted on the Sarmatae soldier's face, the other brandishing a knife. He hissed a warning, flying spittle flecking Saratos's cheeks.

'*No you fucking don't! You can take your punishment like a good little boy!*'

Taking the opportunity fleetingly presented to him with a feeling of incensed gratitude at the soldier's mistake, Saratos spat out the cloth gag and snaked out his free hand to grab at the neckerchief intended to protect his captor's neck from the edges of his mail's iron rings, dragging the soldier's face close to his own. Before the man could react he found his nose firmly gripped between Saratos's teeth, with a sudden intense pain from which no amount of arm waving would free him. Tensing his arm to strike out with the dagger, he found his fist wrapped in the fingers of the Sarmatae's free hand, pinning the weapon against his body, and after another hideously painful squeeze of the recruit's jaws he found himself unceremoniously kicked away, as Saratos leapt to his feet with his assailant's dagger in his hand.

'*You fucker, what you done to him!?*'

Horta lunged with his knife, all thoughts of dealing out a private punishment lost in his rage as his mate whimpered on the ground, a hand clutching his bloody face. Saratos took the stabbing blow on the blade he'd torn from the other soldier's grasp and pushed it wide, feinted with his free hand to distract the soldier and then stepped in to hammer his knee into his assailant's testicles. Dropping his weapon, the agonised man staggered backwards and then sat down hard, clutching at his bruised manhood with a groan of agony.

'What the *fuck* . . . ?'

Sanga stared aghast at the fallen soldiers, his gaze turning to Saratos as the Sarmatae dropped the dagger next to his first victim.

'They think funny to take me in the dark, cut me to teach me lesson.'

The older man looked at the helpless men with a curled lip.

'You stupid pricks! I fuckin' warned you what would happen

if you tried to get smart with a bloke that grew up as a barbarian warrior while you were still playing knucklebones. Once you're done with your crying I'll take you back to your tent party and let your senior man see what mess he's made of you both. Wouldn't surprise me if he gives you another kicking for being too stupid to do the job properly . . .'

Horta staggered to his feet with both hands on his knees, the dagger still gripped in one of them and with an evil look on his face as he winced from the pain shooting through his groin.

'This ain't done, horse fucker, this ain't finished, not by . . .'

Sanga snorted, then lifted his knee and smashed the hobnailed sole of his boot into the crouching soldier's face. Horta went down as if he'd been hit with an axe handle, his cheek bleeding from the iron studs' tearing impact. Reaching out to grip the fallen man by the ear he dragged him across to where his mate still squatted with both hands clutching his nose. Sanga examined the beaten soldier's face in what little light there was, grimacing at the bloody marks where Saratos's teeth had torn the skin.

'That'll scar up nicely. I suspect you'll be going under the nickname "Nibbles" from now on, mainly because I'm going to make sure that everyone knows how your conk came by that interesting little decoration.' Keeping his grip on the man's ear he dragged him over to his semi-conscious tent mate, taking Horta's ear in a similar grip and dragging their heads together. 'You pair say this isn't over? Well let me tell you something very clear now, it fuckin' well *is*! The next time I catch either of you even looking at my man here funny then I'm going to tell him to do to you what he held back from doing a moment ago.' He stared down at them with a pitying gaze, shaking his head slowly. 'Haven't you worked it out yet, you morons? From what I saw when I got here, Saratos here could've stuck you both and walked away clean, given you was both stupid enough to come out here to attack him, but he was still willing to let you off with no worse than a few marks and a lesson you'd not forget. Only *you* pair of pricks –' he wrenched Horta's ear and pulled his face so close that he could whisper his warning and still be heard '– are too fuckin' stupid to take a hint! So, no more hints. Next time you'll be collecting on your contributions to the burial club, and if he won't do the deed on the pair of you, I *will*! And I think you know what a bad mood I've been in ever since my old mate Scarface got nailed by the bloody barbarians in Dacia.'

He stood up, keeping a grip of both ears and dragging their owners into uncomfortable crouches.

'Right then, let's go and acquaint your senior man with the facts of this little disagreement, shall we? With any luck he'll do the job for me . . .'

Marcus slid the last dozen paces to the slope's foot to find Arminius and Lugos standing over the corpses of the men who had pursued them over the summit's edge, their weapons black with fresh blood. Ram and Radu were behind them, their swords still sheathed.

'Half of them were dead before they hit the ground, and the rest were too stunned to offer any resistance.'

A gleam of gold winked from the neck of one of the corpses, and Marcus bent forward to lift it off the dead man's chest. It was a rope of thick gold links, heavy enough to raise his eyebrows.

'Somebody was important.'

The Roman nodded at Drest's comment, looking around to find the Thracian and Arabus close at hand.

'Probably the leader of the men that were left behind to guard the fortress. I tripped him up there, when he was trying to take the eagle from me, and the mountain did the rest.'

In the distance a dog bayed, and an instant later half a dozen more responded with their own howls, the sound disquietingly alike to that of a wolf pack on the hunt. Gesturing to the scout Marcus pointed out into the darkness towards the river.

'We need to go now, before whoever's coming down the hill the long way gets here. Arabus, lead us away.'

Arabus stepped forward, his expression questioning.

'I fear that if we use the same route by which we approached this place those hunters will beat us to the river. They must know the paths through the swamp better than we do, and they will undoubtedly move faster than us. I recall enough of the map the centurion showed us to take us away from here by a more southerly route, and hopefully avoid their net?'

The young centurion nodded his agreement.

'We're in your hands then. Just let me do one thing before we move on.'

He put the staff on which the eagle was still mounted onto the ground, then flashed out his spatha and hacked at the wooden pole, chopping it in two an inch from the point where the proud standard's metal base met the wood. Sheathing the sword again he unwrapped the heavy wool strips from his boots, winding them around the eagle before dropping it into the cloak's pouch alongside the golden bowl and the legatus's head, then gestured to the tracker to proceed. Arabus uncoiled his rope, waiting until they were all holding on to its rough length before moving off.

'Follow me, and from now no one talks unless necessary. Sound will carry a long way in this place.'

He led them away from the copse at a fast walk, prodding at the ground before him with his unstrung bow. Within moments the path they were following had turned from hard packed gravel to the rotting timber remains of a narrow wooden causeway, and then, with disquieting suddenness, to a carpet of soft waterlogged moss which squelched beneath their booted feet. He turned and whispered to Marcus, who was following him closely.

'This was shown on the map as a patrol route, as I remember. It led to a river crossing point perhaps two miles from here. The Venicones have torn up the causeway to prevent it being used by an attacking force, but the ground ought to be firm enough for the most part.'

The dogs howled again, closer now and away to the raiding party's right, and the sound of raised voices reached them across the swamp's desolate waste. Arabus nodded knowingly.

'You see, they're making for the easy crossing. We would never have reached it before they ran us down.'

'The *easy* crossing?'

'Where we crossed earlier was the Dirty River's narrowest point for miles, and close to The Fang. Where I'm leading us is much farther away, and when we get there the river will be at least twice as wide. We have avoided quick discovery at the cost of a less certain escape.'

The raiding party pushed on into the swamp, the soft mossy ground beneath their feet becoming increasingly liquid with every step until Marcus's boots were sinking up to his ankles in the gelatinous mud. They had barely covered another quarter mile when the sound of shouting tribesmen reached them across the swamp, and the Roman tapped his tracker on the shoulder, whispering in the Tungrian's ear.

'That sounds as if the hunters have reached the river and realised that we were never heading in that direction. Push on Arabus, we've no option but to reach the river or else we'll be trapped here under their spears when the sun rises.'

The party struggled on into the swamp, muffled curses and imprecations marking the spots where boots came loose from feet and had to be dragged from the mud and moss's sticky grip, and all the time the sounds of pursuit gradually moved from the right to their rear. Having barely moved five hundred paces from their last halt, Arabus turned back to face Marcus with a look of dismay.

'I've lost the path, it seems. The legion engineers must have changed direction to get around this morass, and there's probably no safe way through to the river by going forward. We'll have to backtrack . . .'

The Roman cocked his head to listen, then shook it decisively.

'There's no time!' The excited baying of the hunting dogs was drawing closer. 'They have our scent, which isn't surprising given the amount of blood we've shed in the last hour. Besides, we'll never reach the river before dawn at this pace . . .' He mused for a moment on something Verus had told the centurions in the Lazy Hill headquarters before coming to a decision that he'd been pondering since the party had blundered into the swamp. 'No, the answer's not to look for a way back, but to go forward, deeper into the swamp.'

Drest stepped forward, his whisper full of urgency.

'Are you sure, Centurion? It looks like a death trap to me. Even if we don't sink into one of these mud pits we'll surely be seen in no time once it's light.'

Marcus shook his head.

'It's what Verus did to evade pursuit when he was running from these same hunters. We'll have to go as far into the marsh as we dare, and then bury ourselves in the mud as deeply as we can. Hopefully the Venicones won't be able to see us, and their dogs won't be able to fasten onto our scent for the stink of rotting vegetation. It's either that or we make a stand here against whatever it is that's hunting us down. And besides, we have one other edge on them. They know this path intimately, whereas we blundered off it and into this desert of mud and water at the first opportunity.'

Drest frowned wearily at him.

'Eh? Exactly how is that an *advantage*?'

Another shrill cry rang out across the marsh, and an otherworldly note in the hunter's scream raised the hair on the back of their necks.

'There's no time, I'll tell you when we're safe in the mud. *Come on!*'

'More of the same today is it, sir?'

Tribune Scaurus nodded equably and stared out across the grey dawn landscape, too busy chewing a stale piece of bread to answer Julius until he'd managed to swallow the tough mouthful and swill his mouth out with a cupful of water.

'Quite so, First Spear, more of the same indeed. My intention is to sidestep the Venicones as you would a charging bull. Since they already know roughly where we are from their ambush of our cavalrymen, I think it best if we march south the way we came, up through that convenient little defile in the hills and back into the Frying Pan. And then, and this is the bit I really like, once we're back inside the Frying Pan I think we'll turn west and march back towards them.'

'*Towards* them?'

He grinned at Julius's incredulity.

'You heard me. Only we'll be on the southern side of the hills and they'll be marching towards our last known position and therefore on the northern side. We'll head west across the Frying Pan and out over the hills on the far side, and once we're on the far side of the western rim we can head for any one of a dozen forts and get on the protected side of the wall. With a tiny bit of luck they'll never know which way we went until we're safe on the other side.'

His first spear scratched his head and thought for a moment before replying, trying unsuccessfully to suppress a note of evident unhappiness.

'It's not the most devious of ruses, Tribune. What if they work out what's going on and decide not to take the bait? What if we meet the war band coming the other way somewhere in that bloody forest?'

Scaurus nodded, acknowledging the point.

'I think it's time to send Silus and his horsemen forward to scout the route. If the Venicones decide to come back this way down the path they trod yesterday that ought to give us ample warning.'

Julius saluted and went off to gather his centurions, brooding on the potential for disaster entailed in his tribune's plan of action.

'He don't look happy.'

Sanga snorted at the opinion of one of his tent mates, his hands busy packing his kit into his blanket, fashioning a bundle small enough to rest in the crook of his carrying pole.

'Neither would you mate, not if you was responsible for a cohort with a tribune who's determined to dance around in hostile country shouting, "*Come and get me!*" to the bull that wants to stick its horns right up our arse. An' every day we do this little dance we have to get lucky enough to avoid the bluenoses, whereas they only has to get lucky enough to catch us just the once. It'll be another day of double-time marching from the looks of it, so you'd best make sure you've got some bread handy for eating on the move.'

He looked up from his packing to find a pair of eyes locked on him from the next tent party, naked hatred smouldering in a face so badly bruised as to be almost unrecognisable. Horta stared at him for a moment longer before turning away to mutter something to his mate, who turned and regarded Sanga equally coldly, his nose livid with bruises and deep bite marks. The soldier got to his feet and shrugged on his baldric and belt, adjusting the hang of his sword until the weapon's pommel was directly beneath his right armpit. Pulling the dagger from its place on his left hip he examined the blade's edge for a moment before pushing it back into the polished scabbard's tight leather lips, then looked back at the two men to find them still regarding him with jaundiced eyes. Shaking his head in disgust he strode the few paces required to bring them face-to-face, raising a finger in warning.

'You two want a fight, you come and find me once this excitement's done with and I'll put you both under the doctor's care for a month. Try to take me unawares and it'll be the last trick you ever try to pull. You both been warned, right?'

He turned away with a contemptuous sneer, seeing Quintus strolling down the century's line alongside Morban, his eyes roaming his command's ranks in search of anything with which he might take exception.

'Now then lads! Get yourselves on parade before the chosen man has to start shouting! You make me look bad and I'll have to send whatever shit he drops on me down the hill to where it belongs!'

His words were loud enough to carry to Quintus, who smiled wryly at Sanga's blunt way with the men of his tent party even as he drew breath to bellow his first command of the day.

'Right then you apes! Let's have you in nice straight lines and ready to march! The last man in position with all his kit gets a tickle from my little friend here!' He raised the shining brass-bound iron ball on the end of his staff and grinned mirthlessly across the ranks of his century. 'It may not be a vine stick, but I think you'll find I can swing it just as quickly! *Move!*'

The Venicones were making ready to break camp when it happened, men still fighting weariness in the cold of the early morning's thin light, huddling around rekindled fires and chewing on whatever was left of the previous night's food. Brem was briefing the clan leaders as to the day's plan, deliberately kept as simple as possible by Calgus to ensure that there was little to go wrong. The Selgovae had left Brem to perform the briefing alone, knowing that any idea from his mouth would be regarded by the king's men with deep distrust.

'Half our strength will head north-east, around the northern side of the hills, and scout for the Roman camp. When you find it –' Brem nodded to the man to whom he had given command of this half of the advance '– then you must simply follow them at a pace that will reel them in but also leave your men fit to fight. I expect that they will head south, over the hills and into the forest. The other half, which I will command, will march directly east, and set up an ambush in the forest. I expect that this Roman will attempt to bluff us once more, and will march his men west, in the direction we would least expect, and if he does, I will be waiting for him. In the event that his track takes him west, as I expect it will, follow him at your best pace and act as the hammer which will crush these Tungrians flat against our anvil, if we've left any alive for you.'

'And if he turns east, my lord King?'

'Then send messengers to find me, and chase him down before he reaches their wall. This is our chance to put this man's head on my roof beams, and I will not miss the opportunity that our scouts' discovery of yesterday has given me. So, my brothers, go and—'

A man burst into the circle, prostrating himself in apology for his interruption.

'My lord King, the Roman wall!'

Brem frowned down at him.

'What of it, idiot?'

'The wall forts, my lord King. They're—'

'On fire, my lord Brem.' Calgus limped into the circle of men, any concern with his likely reception from the gathered Venicone nobles removed at a stroke by what he had seen on the southern horizon. 'The sentries have spotted three of the wall forts alight, and if three of them have been torched then you can be assured that every one of their stinking little wooden enclosures from the Clut to the estuary of the Dirty River will be aflame. The Romans, my lord King, are retreating from your lands, just as I told you they inevitably would.'

Brem clenched a fist, bellowing his joy at the news.

'Come then, my brothers! Let us go and find this Roman and teach him the meaning of Venicone revenge!'

And then, to the amazement of the men gathered about the king, Calgus stepped forward, putting up a hand to silence him and speaking quietly in the sudden hush.

'My lord king, I suggest that—'

No man among them would ever bring himself to contradict the king, and yet here was the still hated deposed ruler of the Selgovae daring to speak to their leader in just such a way. Half a dozen of them started forward, but to their dismay Brem held up his own hand to forestall them.

'Let him speak.'

Calgus smiled about him with the same knowing expression he had shown them on the day that Naradoc and his younger brother had been murdered at his suggestion, then turned back to face Brem and bowed deeply.

'All I was going to say, my lord King, is that this is a fortuitous turn of fate that no one could have predicted. A turning point in our struggle against these invaders of which many people, including that Roman we're hunting, will still be unaware . . .' He paused, smiling beatifically at Brem in his flush of new-found confidence as the situation played smoothly into his hands in a way he could not have dared to dream. 'Quite simply, my lord King, this changes *everything*.'

★   ★   ★

Dawn came slowly to the swamp, its weak light struggling to penetrate the thick fog which wreathed the Dirty River's valley. The raiding party had taken shelter from view in the cover of the swamp's thin vegetation, pressing their bodies into the sodden moss as the sounds of the hunt around them began to resolve themselves into a clearer pattern. Keeping flat to the waterlogged ground and raising his head with slow, deliberate care, Marcus stared out into the grey murk for any sign of movement, his body liberally coated with the thick, clinging mire that surrounded them on all sides and his head heavy with the layer of camouflaging mud which Arabus had insisted the raiders should all smear into their hair and across their faces. The heavy mist clung to the sodden ground, reducing visibility to no better than a dozen paces and protecting them from the sharp eyes of the hunters whose voices they could hear over to their right. Another one of their stalkers called out in a high-pitched tone edged with frustration, and the Roman fought the urge to shake his head in amazement that the grassy river plain was indeed patrolled by women, while warning himself that they were in no less danger than if the warriors tracking them were male. Having seen the dull glint of razor-sharp iron in the mist a moment before, he was clear that their pursuers were both close at hand and sufficiently well armed to deal with a few tired intruders.

'You see?' Putting his mouth close to Drest's head he muttered in the Thracian's ear. 'We don't know these paths anywhere near as well as they do, so we ended up off track and deep in the swamp. Whereas they do know where the firm ground is, and followed the path around us. And it sounds like their dogs can't smell us either . . .'

Whether the senses of their hunting dogs were being frustrated by the vapour in the air or simply by the rank stink of the mud daubed on the raiders' bodies was beyond his understanding, but it was clear from the querulous tones of the dogs' occasional barks that their quarry seemed to have vanished into thin air. One voice raised itself above the indignant complaints of the searching women, strong and masculine in tone as it issued what sounded like a string of instructions. The volume of the unseen man's commands seemed to strengthen and weaken by the moment, sometimes sounding close and then suddenly distant, a combination of the mist and the fitful breeze blowing across the marsh, Marcus guessed.

Lifting his head slowly and carefully to look through a straggling bush, the Roman managed to catch sight of an indistinct figure advancing slowly across the moss's surface with a spear held ready to strike. The hunter was close enough that, were she to catch sight of him through the mist, her thrown spear would easily have the reach to put iron in his chest. She was stalking across the mossy swamp with slow, careful steps, her left arm held forward for balance and ready to pull sharply back for added power in the event of her finding a target at which to launch the spear, and Marcus nodded minutely in recognition of her apparent skill. The woman looked young, no more than fifteen, but the Roman knew that the danger she posed to the fugitives lay not simply in her fighting abilities but rather in the risk that were she to spot them and raise the alarm the raiders would quickly be mobbed by more spears than they would ever be able to fight off. As he watched, she stopped and lifted her head to stare out across the swamp, her youthful eyes sharp beneath the thick layer of mud with which, like their quarry, the hunting party had daubed themselves as a means of disguising their outlines.

Unwilling to move a muscle under her scrutiny, even though he judged that he was safe enough behind the bush's camouflage if he remained completely still, Marcus raised his eyes in search of the hill fort's brooding presence high above them. He was relieved to find The Fang still invisible in the early morning's shifting banks of fog, although, he noted, the hill's presence was detectable by a darker band low down in the mist to their north. After a long, slow scan across the muddy wasteland the woman turned away and vanished, wraithlike, into the murk. Wondering how long it would be before the sun rose high enough to burn away the layer of vapour that was helping to protect them from discovery, the Roman slowly lowered his head back to the ground before working his way slowly down the line of prostrate men until he found Arabus.

'We can't stay here much longer. Once the mist's gone we'll be caught, unable to move, and once they get sight of us there'll be two or three spears for every one of us.'

The tracker nodded glumly.

'The Dirty River's half a mile or so that way . . .' He tilted his head fractionally to the south. 'As we get close to the water there'll be more vegetation to hide in, but for most of the way we'll only have the moss and grass to hide us, and for all I know there are more rotting pits waiting between us and the water.'

Marcus nodded, putting a hand on his shoulder.

'We need a way out of here, and we need it soon. You go forward to the river and look for something, anything that can help us to escape, and I'll keep these men quiet and still.'

Far out in the mist the sound of urgent fluttering wing beats broke the dawn's quiet as something sent a covey of waterfowl splashing and squawking into the damp air, and with a chorus of shouts the Vixens ran for the spot, water splashing up beneath their bare feet where they sank deep into the moss. Marcus tilted his head fractionally, listening to the dogs baying with excitement as the hunters' net closed around whatever it was that had flushed the birds from their nesting places. The grunt and savage yell of triumph as one of them cast her spear swiftly turned to a groan of disgust, as the high-pitched squeal of an animal in agony sounded across the marsh. After a moment's pause the dogs raised their voices in yelping, snarling flurries as they fought for the meat of whatever hapless creature had crossed the hunters' path, the animal's last screams piteous as it was torn to pieces. Arminius grunted beside Marcus, staring out into the impenetrable mist.

'They must have found an otter or some other water animal. And that's what they'll do to us, if they find us . . .'

Marcus turned back to Arabus, but the tracker had already vanished into the mist.

*   *   *

'You called for us, First Spear?'

The Tungrians had marched south back up through the gap in the Frying Pan's northern wall of hills in silence, alternating between the standard pace and the exhausting double march as Julius sought to put as much distance between them and the unseen Venicones as possible before the tribesmen hopefully discovered that they had been duped for a second time. With the column halted for a brief breather, once the cohort was safely inside the ring of hills and the concealment of the sea of trees that carpeted its broad bowl, Silus had trotted his detachment of horsemen up to the first spear as commanded. One look at the senior centurion's face had persuaded him that this would not be the best time to indulge in their usual banter, and he had simply jumped down from his horse with a businesslike salute to first spear and tribune. Julius stepped forward, saluting in reply.

'It's time to get back on the other side of the wall, Decurion, before we put a foot wrong in this dance with the Venicones and end up getting the chance to see what colour our livers are when they're ripped out.'

Silus nodded, looking about him at the trees that stretched away into the seemingly infinite woodland on either side of the hunter's path.

'And given that we can't see more than fifty paces in this lot, I presume you'd like me to scout ahead and make sure the ground's clear for you, Tribune?'

Julius nodded grimly, stepping closer to the decurion and lowering his voice.

'You've got it. Better to have you find any barbarians than for us to drive the entire cohort into a bloody great ambush.' He raised an eyebrow at Silus. 'But in the event of an attack I want *you* back alive, understood? Send a few men up the path ahead of you and have them send a rider back every now and then; that way you'll get some warning of any nastiness waiting for us without having to stop an arrow yourself.'

Silus pulled a lopsided smile as he saluted again, barking out the army's standard response to an order.

'We will do what is ordered, and at every command we will be ready!'

Julius stared at the decurion for a moment before showing him the rough drawing he and Scaurus had made in his wax-faced tablet.

'Follow this path for another two miles and you'll come to a fork in the road. Follow the right-hand path until it climbs out of the Pan on the south-western rim, then send word back that the road's clear. We'll be following up at a decent pace behind you, so hold there and we'll make the march in to the closest of the wall forts together. And there will be *no* fucking heroics, Decurion. If you see any sign of the Venicones you kick hard this way and we'll head back to the east and get onto safe ground via Lazy Hill. Got it?'

Silus nodded, saluted again and vaulted onto his horse, leading his squadron away at a brisk trot.

'And you honestly think he'll follow the order not to put himself at risk?'

Julius turned back to Scaurus, shaking his head slowly.

'After last night? Not for one moment, Tribune. He's been smarting ever since you ordered them away from the frozen lake in Dacia, having to abandon his men to the Venicone archers will have re-opened that wound, and this is the perfect opportunity for him to show his lads that he still has a pair. His *"we will do what is ordered"* act doesn't fool me for a moment, but at least he's ridden off knowing that I'd rather get him back alive if they do blunder into the shit. Let's hope he doesn't end up having to make the decision whether to fight or run, shall we? In fact, this might be a good moment to have a quiet chat with your man the Lightbringer and ask for his blessing on us all . . .'

The voices of the Vixens slowly faded away to the north, the young female warriors calling to each other as they hunted across the swamp's mossy surface in the obvious hope that a closely spaced line of hunters would stumble over the hidden soldiers in mist which seemed to be getting thicker as the morning progressed.

Marcus and the other men around him were shivering with the cold when Arabus reappeared out of the murk and crawled up to the Roman's side.

'I've found the river, and a way to get to it without being sighted. Follow me.'

He led them across the marsh's claustrophobically fog-bound landscape, confident in his path as he retraced the steps he had taken moments before, weaving around the darker patches of the spongy surface beneath their feet which betrayed the presence of sinkholes waiting to trap the unwary. The raiding party followed him, Marcus waving the others to go before him and backing away from the spot cautiously, dividing his attention between watching the path and straining his eyes to stare out into the wall of mist that hid them from the hunters, looking for any trace of movement which might indicate that their withdrawal to the river had been detected. Starting involuntarily at an eddy in the fog that for an instant looked like a human figure advancing out of the murk, he lost his concentration for one critical moment and strayed a pace or so from the path along which the tracker was leading them. With dismay the Roman felt his foot sink into the moss, his already waterlogged boot flooding to the brim with the swamp's fetid water. Before he had the chance to wrench himself free, the straining layer of vegetation beneath his foot tore and his leg sank into the watery void beneath the ruptured surface. Suddenly and helplessly unbalanced, he lurched uncontrollably into the fetid mixture of water and rotting vegetation that had been concealed by the moss's covering layer with a squelching hiss of displaced gases from below the surface. Wincing at the fetid stink of decay, the Roman found himself up to his waist in the sink hole, and instinctively struggled to climb out for a moment before realising that his efforts to escape were only working him deeper into the mire. The water had now risen to his armpits, and even as he froze into immobility he could feel the weight of his weapons, and the heavy gold cup hidden in the thick woollen cloak's carrying pouch, slowly pulling him deeper into the morass.

Looking around he realised that the raiding party had vanished into the mist to the south without realising what had happened to the last man in their straggling column, and the true depth of his predicament dawned upon him with a simple but chilling logic. He was doomed to drown in the swamp, alone and unnoticed, unless he called for help, but his only means of summoning rescue would almost certainly bring their pursuers down upon them all, and guarantee that every one of them would suffer torment and death of a far more prolonged nature than the relatively painless demise that now beckoned him. His mind raced, and alighted on the two most important things left in his life, his family and his faith, and closing his eyes he muttered a prayer to the deity.

'Lightbringer, I implore you to grant me one last favour . . .'

Moving one arm from the surface of the swamp he reached down into the slurry, feeling his body slip lower into the morass as he shifted position to grip the hilt of his long spatha and slid it from the scabbard. He lifted the weapon through the soupy water, straining to free the blade from the mass of rotting vegeta-tion. Exerting all the strength he had, he forced the sword's blade up out of the swamp, holding it upright in the grey light and staring at the delicately carved intaglio tied to its pommel with silver wire, nodding with a gentle smile at the beneficent figure of the god.

'Thank you, my Lord. If it be your will, allow this fine weapon to be returned to my wife.'

Holding the blade's shining line of finely polished steel above his head he felt the swamp belch beneath him, another pocket of gas bursting as his feet sank into it, the sudden release of gas sucking his body down into the stinking pit so that his nostrils were barely clearing the disgusting water's surface. Instinctively gasping in a deep breath, he barely had time to close his eyes as the morass took him down into its heart, feeling the cold water close over his head. At peace with himself, Marcus waited for the darkness to claim him as he knew it surely would when the effort of holding his last snatched breath became unbearable.

*   *   *

Silus and his men reached the path's fork without seeing any sign of the Venicones, and when they dismounted to listen, the forest was silent apart from the rustle of the trees' canopy as it was stirred by the breeze. The decurion grimaced at the forest about them, shaking his head at the apparent tranquillity.

'Nothing. This place is as innocent as your sister before she discovers the joys of cock.' He spat on the path's verge. 'Of course there could be a whole fucking tribe within bowshot of us and we'd never know it until one of them farted and gave us a clue.' The detachment's men grinned wryly at each other, well accustomed to their leader's colourful turn of phrase. 'So, let's play this just the way that dear old Julius wanted it.' He pointed at four men in succession, the corner of his mouth lifting mirthlessly as each of them winced slightly at their selection. 'You four, ride ahead and scout for any sign of the enemy. *Any* sign, mind you. Worried-looking badgers, shifty squirrels, anything you see or hear that makes you uneasy, you just turn around and you come back this way at just the same pace. No speeding up, or if you've already passed their forward scouts they'll shoot enough arrows into you to put a nasty crimp in your day. Just make it look like you've scouted as far forward as you were told to and now you're on your way back to report there's nothing to be seen. Send a man back to the rest of us every now and then so that we know you're still alive, and when the path starts to climb out of this bastard forest you can stop and wait for us. Off you go.'

He watched as they trotted away to the east, shaking his head again in disgust and commenting to nobody in particular.

'This isn't what I had in mind when I joined up to ride horses for a living, and that's a fact.' Shrugging fatalistically he untied the string of his leggings and turned to the forest, grunting with pleasure as he emptied his bladder onto the bushes beside the path. 'Take the chance while you have it my lads. There's nothing worse than fighting off a barbarian ambush with your legs soaked in cold piss.'

★   ★   ★

Feeling the vestiges of his self-control slipping away from him, as the pain in his chest swelled from a dull ache to the stabbing of a red-hot dagger, and as his pulse thundered in his ears, Marcus sensed the sword's hilt moving gently in his grip as if it had become possessed of a life of its own, the pommel sliding from his grasp to be replaced by the feeling that his hand was being held by another, the fingers as long and powerful as he had always imagined they would be. Smiling beatifically at the obvious message from his god, he surrendered to the urge to take his last fatal breath, his eyes suddenly snapping open as, in the act of filling his lungs with the stinking water, he felt an abrupt sensation of rising up through the swamp's clinging muck. Feeling solid ground beneath him he retched up a gout of filthy swamp water, opening his eyes to see a massive figure looming over him. Spluttering out another mouthful of water he stared helplessly up at his rescuer, sucking air into his lungs before coughing furiously into his hands, seeking to muffle the irresistible need to rid them of the last of the bog's fetid liquid. When he managed to speak his voice was little better than a croak.

'*For a moment there I thought I was dead, and that you were Mithras himself.*'

The answer came in a harsh whisper, the man crouched over him lowering his head to look into Marcus's eyes.

'No, Centurion. Mithras will have to wait for another day. Now cough quietly, unless you want to bring those harpies down on us!'

The Roman stared up in bemusement for a moment, then closed his eyes and shook his head, chuckling quietly.

'Thank you, Arminius, although for a moment there I was actually disappointed not to be in the underworld.'

The German raised an eyebrow.

'It can still be arranged, if you really wish it to be so. But I doubt that our Lord would look as kindly on a man killed by an irritated German as one who had decided to accept drowning in silence in order to save his comrades from detection.'

Marcus struggled into a sitting position, looking about him at the men gathered around the bog and smiling wanly.

'It seemed the right thing to do at the time . . .'

Arminius pulled him to his feet, then stooped to pick up the Roman's sword, slotting it back into the empty scabbard in a gush of water from the soaked leather sheath.

'And the right thing to do now is to get ourselves away from here before the mist lifts. It already seems a little lighter, although that might just be the sun getting higher.' From across the swamp to their north a high-pitched call rang out, answered an instant later by a dozen more voices. 'See, they're still out there hunting for us.'

The Roman nodded, gesturing to Arabus.

'Lead us to the river.'

The scout turned away and headed south once more, picking his steps with delicate care, and Arminius propelled Marcus along behind the Tungrian with a hand on his shoulder.

'And this time, Centurion, watch where you put your feet. I've already repaid my debt of a life to you, so if I have to pull you from another stinking bog you'll be building a debt to me instead.'

7

The deeper the mounted detachment moved into the Frying Pan's heart, the less Silus was able to shrug off the feeling of disquiet that had gripped him since the moment they had ridden away from the cohort. The forest was silent, even the birds' song stilled as if in reaction to the presence of intruders, and the absence of any natural noise other than that of the wind through the trees was more chilling than would have been the case in the presence of a marching cohort of soldiers to fill the silence. A rider cantered easily down the path towards them, reining his horse in with a salute to the decurion.

'Nothing to report sir! The forest is quiet, and we've seen nothing to make us think there's anyone else about.'

Silus nodded, gesturing back up the path.

'Back you go then, and when you reach your mates send another man back.'

The rider saluted again and turned his horse, galloping away back down the path to the east. Silus's Pay and a Half muttered a comment, looking out into the sea of trees with a dour face as the party continued walking their horses down the narrow path.

'Perhaps this place really is deserted. After all, nobody would ever describe them tattoo-boys as being overly blessed with brains, eh? They're probably just running for the place we camped last night.'

The decurion shrugged.

'One of the benefits of having a gentleman like the tribune for a boss is that he does tell an interesting and informative story with a cup of wine in his hand. I was lucky enough to hear him telling the first spear about a German called Arminius the other night, not that big oaf who keeps his boots clean for him, but a tribal chief who led a revolt against the empire in Germania two hundred years ago. Seems this man was a tribal prince, just a boy mind you, and he was taken from his family by our soldiers as part of a peace settlement with his tribe once they'd been given a beating. He was brought up in Rome, see, as a member of the nobility, and they taught him to be civilised. They made him into a Roman gentleman, or as much of one as he was ever going to be given where he came from, and then they put him in the army, as an officer of course. He was a tasty piece of work according to the tribune, a man with a talent for getting stuck into the barbarians and hacking them up in the front rank, rather than posing around on his horse and trying to sound noble and commanding like most of them do.'

The men around him murmured their approval, and more than one of them patted a sword hilt or reached up to rub the iron head of their spear with a silent prayer.

'Anyway, it seems this Arminius was eventually persuaded to betray Rome by his old tribe, and so he led three full legions deep into country just like this, without any room for them to manoeuvre, and then showed his hand. The tribesmen waited until the legions were nicely bottled up in their trap, strung out along a thin forest track just like this one –' he looked around at his men, gesturing to the forest around them '– and then they stormed in from either side and tore into the poor bastards, not allowing them time or space to get into battle formation. They gutted three whole legions and took the rest as slaves it seems, captured their eagles and then sacrificed the senior officers and centurions on altars to their gods, while the ones who weren't dead yet listened to their screams and waited their turn to be murdered. The way the tribune tells it, the emperor banged his head on the wall with rage when he was given the news, all shouting and screaming and cursing the silly aristocratic bastard who led his army into such an obvious ambush, although how *obvious* it was before it happened isn't all that clear to me. Everyone's clever after the event, aren't they?' He paused, looking round at his men questioningly. 'So then, what do we learn from the tribune's story?'

'Not to trust fuckin' barbarians?'

Silus snorted at the man's offering.

'We already knew that, you clodhopper. What about the way the Germans attacked?'

Another of the riders spoke up, his voice edged with reluctance to appear stupid in front of his comrades.

'Is it the way they waited until the legions was all in the trap before attacking?'

Silus nodded.

'Give that man a prize. Exactly. They kept their heads down until the mules had all marched into the killing zone, and it was only then that they gave it the old charge and hack. And that, my lads, is why Julius has sent us forward to scout the path before he brings the cohort down it. So keep your bloody eyes and ears open, and stop dreaming of drink and whores, or you'll end up finding out what really happens once you've been taken prisoner and some big hairy tattooed bastard decides to make you his new girlfriend, won't you?'

The raiding party made it to the Dirty River's bank without any further incident, Arabus leading them to the course of a tributary river whose four-foot-high banks provided them with ample cover for the last half mile of their perilous crossing of the swamp.

'So what do we do now? I can't see the far bank, but as I recall it from the maps the river's too broad for us to swim it here.'

Arabus grinned triumphantly at Marcus's question.

'When I was talking to the scouts at Lazy Hill they told me that the garrison's best men used to be sent to sneak around out here under the cover of darkness, once they'd got to know the marsh as well as the locals. Their job was to fight fire with fire, and put some fear of the dark into the tribesmen's minds by picking off individuals and cutting them up, leaving their mutilated corpses for the Venicones to find come sunrise. Apparently they would come out this way and use boats to cross the river when the mist was in their favour, rather than use the more obvious crossing further up, because they knew the Venicones would have the easier crossing points watched. He told me that there used to be a couple of boats hidden on both sides of the river in those days, their hulls well tarred to keep the damp out and pulled up into the rushes to keep them out of the water, surrounded by enough vegetation that you'd never spot one unless you knew what to look for. There's one a few hundred paces that way –' he pointed south-east down the Dirty River's course '– and it looks solid enough for one last crossing.'

He led the exhausted raiders down the riverbank, the men casting nervous glances at the mist about them which had lightened from dull grey to an ethereal shade of white during their trek across the marsh. The Tungrian tracker set a pace that had them gasping for breath, each step requiring every one of them to physically drag his trailing boot out of the estuary's thick mud only to have it sink inches back into the ooze when he stepped forward, and soon their legs were burning at the effort required to advance along the stream's margin. Marcus was about to call a halt when Arabus motioned to them to stop, darting into the thick reeds that lined the river's bank, and the party gratefully sank into the vegetation heedless of the stinking mud that coated their lower bodies. The Roman rubbed at his thighs, the muscles trembling from the painful slog, wiping away the mud and strands of rotting plant material that had befouled his swords' hilts.

'The boat is here, and as I thought, it looks sound enough for a crossing.'

Marcus stirred himself from his tired reverie and climbed to his feet, crawling into the reeds behind his tracker, Arminius following while the rest of the party collapsed exhausted into the cover of the river's bank. The three men advanced cautiously into the four-foot tall grass until they encountered a small clearing in the thick vegetation, and Arabus pulled a rotting canvas cover away from a humped shape that filled the small gap in the plant cover, revealing the shape of an eight-foot-long boat.

'See, they put a thick layer of planks over the mud to keep the hull from getting too wet and rotting away.'

The Roman leaned forward and prodded the rough platform with a finger, wrinkling his nose at the spongy feel of what had once been sound wood. By contrast the boat's heavily tarred hull was relatively firm to the touch, although it was clear to even a cursory examination that twenty-odd years in the open had taken its toll on the boat's timbers.

'That's not going to hold all of us, not with a Briton the size of a year-old bull aboard.'

Marcus nodded agreement with Arminius's flatly stated opinion.

'We'll have to do it in two trips. Arabus and I will take Drest and his men across first, and then Arabus can bring the boat back for the two of you while we scout the ground on the far side. With luck we'll be away before the fog lifts, and the Venicones will be none the wiser.'

Arminius nodded reluctantly.

'It's logical enough, if you think you can trust those evil little Sarmatae bastards.'

The Roman shrugged.

'They've had enough opportunities to betray us, wouldn't you say?'

The German raised an eyebrow.

'Perhaps. Best if you don't turn your back on them though.'

They shared a look of mutual understanding, and then Arminius gathered the rest of the party to move the boat from its hiding place thirty paces down to the water. The men watched critically as it settled onto the river's surface with Arabus standing thigh-deep in the river to hold it steady, and Marcus leaning into the boat to examine the bottom.

'There's a little water coming in, but not enough to worry about.' He turned to Drest, gesturing him forward. 'We'll go first, with your men, and Arabus will bring the boat back for these two once we're across.'

The Thracian nodded, climbing into the boat and gesturing to Ram and Radu to follow him. They leaned over the skiff's other side to counterbalance the weight of Marcus boarding, then pulled Arabus over the side as Arminius pushed the boat away from the shore. Rowing slowly, careful not to make any loud splashing sounds that might betray their passage across the river, Marcus and Drest paddled the boat across the slow, silent river while the two Sarmatae stared out into the mist to either side, their faces unreadable to the Roman's snatched glances. Within a dozen strokes the river's northern shore was almost invisible, and they rowed on through the mist's densest concentration in silence, each man alone with his thoughts. After a few moments of steady paddling the river's southern bank materialised out of the murk, an expanse of wind-ruffled reeds and marshy ground beyond that mirrored the northern shore, and as the boat grounded on the bank's mud Marcus gingerly climbed out, drawing his patterned spatha and advancing up into the reeds. Tilting his head for a moment to listen, he turned back to the others.

'Nothing. Drest, get your men out of the boat and hold a position here while I scout ahead to make sure there's nobody waiting for us out there. Arabus, you can be on your way back for the others.'

The tracker nodded and turned the boat around, settling into the prow and paddling to either side of the pointed bow with the boat's stern slightly lifted. The boat was swiftly lost in the mist, and Marcus turned back to Drest, shrugging off the thief's cloak and dropping it beside the Thracian.

'Keep an eye on that for me. That way if there are men waiting for us in the mist you've still got the eagle, and a chance of getting it back to Prefect Castus.'

Drest nodded wearily, getting to his feet and putting a hand to his sword's hilt.

'It'll be safe here. Don't go so far into the mist that you lose your bearings and fail to find the way back, eh?' Marcus nodded, turning away and stepping forward into the swamp that bordered the river's bank, and Drest was clearly unable to avoid a further gentle jibe at his expense. 'And don't go falling into any more—'

He grunted in mid-sentence, and Marcus turned back to find

the Thracian standing stock still with a startled expression. A harsh voice sounded from behind him, his pronunciation a little rough-edged but surprisingly fluent by comparison with the Sarmatae twin's previous utterances.

'Enough of your prattle, old man.'

Drest was staring down at his chest with a look of amazement, as if he were trying to work out where the sword point that was thrust out between his ribs had come from. As the Roman watched, Ram, who had moved to stand close behind the Thracian, raised a hand and pushed Drest off the long blade with a lopsided grin, shrugging as his erstwhile master slumped to the sodden ground with blood blossoming from the wounds in his back and chest.

'And now you want to know why, don't you?' Radu stepped around his brother, drawing his own sword and pointing it at Marcus. 'Why didn't we just wait for you to get out of earshot before killing him and taking the eagle?'

The Roman lowered his own sword's point to the ground, shaking his head in response.

'I already know why. You've been paid to retrieve the eagle, and make sure its discovery remains hidden, for whatever purpose, but there's something more that you've been offered money to deliver back to your new master, isn't there?'

Ram stepped over Drest's slumped body to stand beside his brother, his bloodstained weapon levelled at Marcus's face.

'Yes. We've been paid to bring back the eagle, but the price is trebled if we have your head in the bag with it.'

Radu grinned at Marcus in anticipation.

'And it'll be the easiest money we'll ever make.'

The Roman raised his spatha, drawing the eagle-pommelled gladius and putting the shorter weapon's blade alongside it.

'You're forgetting two things.'

The twins edged forward, their interest in the conversation clearly limited to the amount of distraction it would provide for them while they moved slowly apart, seeking to outflank the Roman and attack him from both sides at once.

'And what are those two things, dead meat?'

Marcus grinned mirthlessly at Ram.

'Firstly, I've already had a knife at your throat once, and this time I won't be dropping my swords.'

The Sarmatae snorted derisively, and took another pace to the side.

'And the other thing, before we cut you down and take your head?'

The Roman turned sideways on to the two men, swinging the spatha in a quick, whirring arc that left an eddy in the riverbank's mist-laden air.

'I've already held my god's hand once today. And once was enough.'

'We've ridden the path from here to the rim of the Frying Pan.'

'And seen nothing?'

Silus nodded at Julius's question. The cavalry detachment had met the marching cohort a mile west of the fork in the path, and the first spear had called a rest break while he consulted with his decurion.

'And seen nothing at all. This forest is as quiet as the grave, First Spear, so if this is the path you want to use to get back to the wall then I suggest we get on with it before the ink monkeys stop being quite so accommodating.' Julius nodded decisively, and was turning away to start issuing orders when Silus spoke again. 'One more thought, First Spear?'

The senior centurion turned back to him, one eyebrow raised in sardonic challenge of the unaccustomed formality.

'Decurion?'

'My boys and I were talking through that story the tribune told us the other night, the one about the three legions that were lost to the barbarians in Germania, and one of my brighter lads came up with a decent idea to put the bluenoses on the back foot if they were to spring an ambush on us out here.'

Julius frowned.

'I thought you said the path was clear?'

Silus spread his hands.

'I did. And I also said that the forest was as quiet as the grave. But that's not the same as knowing for sure that the Venicones have all taken the tribune's bait and gone charging off to the north-east, is it?'

The first spear nodded slowly.

'So what was the bright idea then, being ready to run like fuck at the first sign of unpleasant men with sharp iron?'

Silus nodded, his face lighting up with genuine amusement.

'Pretty much, although he did have one small wrinkle to add to that basic tactic.'

Julius listened to the decurion's proposal with a guarded expression, nodding slowly as the point of Silus's suggestion became clear.

'Not bad, even if it is as risky as anything the tribune might have come up with. You'll soon be giving Scaurus a run for his money in coming up with devious schemes that will either work like miracles or get us all killed.' He turned to his chosen man. 'Fetch me the tribune and centurions, will you Pugio? I think this needs a bit of a wider discussion . . .'

The two Sarmatae stepped forward again, both men taking another careful step to either side in order to further spread themselves out, and split the Roman's attention to both sides at once. Ram spoke again, his face creased into a self-satisfied smile.

'Tribune Sorex told us that if we don't bring your head back then we might as well not come back at all. He really doesn't like you, Centurion, although he seemed to have a better opinion of your wife.'

On the Roman's right Radu advanced forward another pace, putting his sword points so close to Marcus's spatha's blade that the slightest of lunges would start the fight.

'Oh yes, he had an eye for her all right. He'll have been up that pretty little thing like a prize stallion at the first chance, in fact he's probably balls-deep right now—'

He snapped the longer of his two swords forward in a powerful lunge, bending his knee to launch the point at Marcus's chest with the other blade held high, ready to either parry or strike. Ram leapt into the fight from the Roman's other side, looking for the opening through which to land a killing blow. Making the snap decision to take the fight to him, the twin he had previously bested, Marcus quickly sidestepped away from Radu's attack, parried Ram's initial strike and feinted with the gladius in his left hand before spinning low between the two men, aiming to slice a deep cut into Ram's thigh with a sweep of his spatha's long blade. The Sarmatae jumped back almost quickly enough to evade the blow, the spatha's blade slicing a gash across his leggings and leaving a thick red line of blood welling from the wound, but as the Roman took guard again a line of cold fire across his left bicep told him that Radu had managed to put iron upon him as he had spun past. The Sarmatae grinned widely at him, pacing around a dark patch in the reeds and raising his swords again, nodding at a drop of blood as it ran down the angled blade of his spatha.

'You're bleeding, Centurion. A few more of those will give you lead boots soon enough.'

Ignoring the jibe Marcus backed away towards the river, knowing that he needed something to provide him with the opportunity to attack one of the brothers without the other taking advantage of his distraction. The Sarmatae warriors followed closely, still split to take him from both sides, and Ram crabbed further round to his right with a slight limp from the flesh wound in his thigh, stepping over Drest's crumpled body with his eyes locked on Marcus's.

'We don't need to bleed him! I'll have his fucking head clean off for cutting me. I'll—'

His face abruptly contorted in pain, as Drest rose white-faced from the reeds and gripped his foot, sinking his teeth deep into the tendon at the back of the Sarmatae's ankle. Ram turned awkwardly to hack his sword down at the stricken Thracian's head, the heavy blade's impact sounding like a cabbage being attacked with a heavy cleaver. Knowing that the opportunity Drest's suicidal attack had won him would be fleeting, Marcus went for Radu with sudden, urgent speed, repeating the trick he had played on Ram on the Arab Town parade ground by parrying the Sarmatae's blades wide and then throwing his own swords aside, stepping in close to grab the other man by the tunic. His opponent grinned in his face, pulling his head back to prevent a snapped butt from the Roman's head and changing his grip on his short sword, angling the blade ready to stab it deep into his opponent's defenceless left side. Marcus roared with anger and effort, hoisting the amazed Sarmatae from the ground and feeling the sting in his wounded bicep as he strained the muscle, then straightened his arms convulsively to throw Radu backwards into the mist with all his power. Not waiting to see the result he spun and sprinted forward at Ram, reaching to his belt for the small knife he'd had forged from the deadly sword blade of a bandit leader he had killed in Tungria the year before. Ram had managed to hack Drest into a state of insensibility, and with a scream of frustration and pain he reached down and levered the dying man's locked jaws from his ankle. As he turned back to face Marcus, the charging Roman hit him hard, smashing him down into the reeds and pinning him with his free hand while he punched out with the knife's evilly sharp blade. Once, twice, three times the rippling steel darted between the Sarmatae's ribs, and with each impact Ram grunted as if in surprise, his eyes snapping wide open as the knife's questing point tore into his body.

Marcus rolled away from his victim, coming up onto his feet in a fighting crouch, but realised that Ram was dying where he lay. Foaming blood was leaking onto his chest with every beat of his heart as he shook his head, eyes unfocused, and attempted in vain to raise the swords that were still gripped in his numb hands.

'Ra . . . Ra-du!'

Marcus looked over to where the other twin had landed, shaking his head at the gurgled entreaty for assistance.

'Radu can't help you, not this time. I would tell you to go and meet your gods, but since your head will shortly be at the bottom of the Dirty River while the rest of you festers here, there doesn't seem to be much point.'

He turned away from the dying man, listening as the sound of frantic paddle strokes grew louder. The boat scudded out of the mist and slapped into the riverbank, disgorging a pair of warriors who stopped in their tracks at the sight of their centurion standing waiting for them, cleaning his swords on Ram's cloak. Lugos shook his head in relief, pointing back across the river.

'We hear iron in mist. Vixens hear it too. We hear them follow.'

The Roman nodded, slotting his spatha into its sodden scabbard.

'It seems that Ram and Radu were just waiting for their chance to strike without you two around to spoil things. I knew I had to flush them out soon, or they would probably have given us up to the Venicones and looked to make their escape in the confusion. They put Drest down with a sword in the back, but they didn't kill him. If he hadn't sunk his teeth into Ram's leg and distracted him for long enough that I could deal with Radu, then the two of you would probably have got here too late to do anything but bury the pair of us.'

As if on cue the Thracian twitched, raising a shaking white hand as he stared sightlessly at the grey sky above him, his lips moving noiselessly. Marcus bent close to him, putting his ear to the dying man's face.

'*Lord . . . Jesus . . . grant . . . me . . . eternal . . .*'

He shuddered and lay still, and the Roman shook his head as he stood up.

'He was a Christian, it seems. I wonder if Prefect Castus had any idea he had taken a religious maniac into his familia.'

Arminius laughed curtly, pointing at the twin whose leg Drest had savaged.

'Christian or not, he saved your life with nothing more than his teeth. If that's Christianity we'll have to be careful of them if they ever manage to get an army together.'

He leaned over the gasping Ram, shaking his head at the ferocity of the chest wounds Marcus had inflicted on him. Putting the blade of his sword to the dying Sarmatae warrior's throat, he casually pushed it down to relieve the dying man of his doomed struggle for life.

'It seems they underestimated just what an animal you can be when you're roused, eh Centurion?'

Marcus nodded tiredly.

'You know how it is. Other men start fights . . .'

Arminius shrugged.

'Where's the other one?'

'He here.'

The German turned to find Lugos looking down at something half a dozen paces away, his head shaking with bemusement. He looked back at Marcus with a raised eyebrow.

'You put him there?'

The Roman shrugged.

'It was a lucky throw.'

Arminius looked down at Radu, whose face was staring back up at them from the centre of a sinkhole, his mouth defiantly shut tight against the water that was lapping over his chin, then played an appraising stare on Marcus for a moment.

'Well you of all people know just how that feels.' He turned back to the doomed Sarmatae. 'Have your feet touched bottom yet, eh Radu?'

The Sarmatae glared back up at them, his eyes hard in a face suddenly pale at the prospect of his impending death, holding his head back to gasp for breath before shouting up at the men watching him.

'Fuck you! Fuck you *all*! I *curse* you! In the name of Targitai the thunder god and by the spirits of my ancestors, I curse you to—'

As he screeched his final defiance at them, Lugos reached out with his hammer, putting the flat side of the massively heavy weapon onto the top of Radu's skull with surprising delicacy. Without waiting to find out what it was the Sarmatae wished them to suffer as payment for his life, he pressed down upon the weapon's shaft until the helpless man's mouth was under water, his eyes bulging with hatred. Lugos laughed down at the Sarmatae, shaking his head.

'Curse not work if I not hear it.'

Radu struggled briefly, the rotten swamp mud covering his nose and coming up to the bottom of his hate-filled eyes, then slid silently under the surface, leaving a trail of greasy bubbles as he sank from view. Marcus lifted the cloak containing the eagle and looked about himself wearily for the path.

'We have to get moving, before the hunters cross the river and come after us. I'm just worried that—'

'No, Centurion, just this once let's not speculate about what else might happen.'

Arminius sheathed his sword, turning away from the rippling surface of the marsh and shaking his head with a grimace.

'A suicidal Christian, a matched pair of murderous barbarians and a whole pack of women with sharp iron all desperate to be the one to cut off my dick and feed it to their hunting dog is enough for one day, it seems to me. If there's any way for this to get any worse you can keep it to yourself, thank you.'

'Halt!'

The Tungrian column shuddered to a stop at Julius's command for the third time in an hour, men leaning on their weapons as their first spear marched forward up the now gently climbing path, his head cocked to listen for any noise other than the wind's passage through the trees and the background sounds of the birds. He stood stock still for a long moment, his head cocked to listen, then shook his head in bemusement.

'Nothing, eh First Spear?'

Scaurus had followed him forward with a hand on the hilt of his gladius, an eyebrow raised at his senior centurion. Julius shook his head.

'Nothing, and yet if there's going to be an ambush on us anywhere, this would be the place, somewhere between here and the rim of the bowl. I wish we had Marcus's Tungrian tracker with us, we could just send him away into the trees and he'd find anything out of the ordinary quickly enough. I—'

'First Spear, Tribune. Might I ask the indulgence of a moment of your time?'

The two men turned back to the column to find a respectful Qadir waiting for them. Away down the path behind him a thin, almost invisible line of smoke was rising from a spot in the middle of the cohort's long column, more or less where his century was positioned in the line of march.

'What is it Centurion?'

The Hamian saluted, taking a tablet from his belt.

'Sirs, when I open this tablet you will see that it contains nothing more than a list of my century's strength from the morning meeting. I am showing this to you in order to allow us to talk without arousing the suspicions of the men that I believe are watching us.'

Scaurus nodded, pursing his lips and pointing a finger to the writing on the tablet.

'So you believe that we have walked into an ambush?'

Qadir nodded, gesturing to the lines of script on the wax.

'I think we are part of the way in, Tribune, and that they are waiting for us to move deeper into their trap before springing their attack. Unless, of course, we show any sign of having realised our predicament.'

Julius put his hands on his hips, forcing himself not to look around for any sign of an impending assault.

'And you know this how, exactly?'

Qadir pointed back down the column.

'A partial bootprint in the mud of this track, First Spear, the heel only, as if the wearer was jumping over the path so as not to leave any trace which might give us reason to suspect their presence but fell just a little short. The impression is crisp, and certainly fresh. One of my men noticed it almost as soon as we stopped, and called it to my attention. I told him to keep it to himself and then took a quick look at the foliage around the print. There are signs of recent passage by more than one man, as if a party of hunters had crossed the path without wishing to leave any obvious sign. I think that there are tribesmen very close.'

He pointed to a line of text in the tablet's soft wax, and Julius nodded decisively.

'Very good, Centurion, in that case we'll just have to go with Silus's idea. You know what to do.'

The Hamian nodded and saluted again, his face still devoid of expression.

'I have taken the appropriate steps. I will pray to the Deasura that we will be successful.'

He turned away and marched briskly back down the column.

'We're actually going to put the decurion's wild imaginings to the test?'

Julius chuckled at his senior officer's bemused tone, turning to him with a broad smile.

'Unless you have a better idea, Tribune? The instant that whoever's out there realises we're not going to take a single step deeper into the trap they've laid out for us they'll do what they always do. Their archers will shower us with a few volleys of arrows and then the warriors will storm in from both sides, looking to chop us up into century-sized groups and then destroy each cluster of men individually. There's probably a good few hundred of them waiting at either end to close the front and back doors and bottle us up, and given that they know our numbers I'd expect whoever sent them to have given their leader at least twice our strength. No, I say we go with Silus's idea in the absence of anything better. You don't have anything better, I presume?'

Scaurus nodded, returning his First Spear's hard grin with a wistful smile, and Julius gestured up the track towards the bowl's rim.

'Let's keep them thinking we're about to move on and make things easier for them. And you, Tribune, can accompany me back to the protection of the first century. I'll feel a lot happier when we're both behind friendly shields.'

The two men walked easily down the path, and Julius's standard bearer and trumpeter got to their feet in readiness for the resumption of the march.

'Sound the stand-to!'

The notes of the command to take position for the march rang out in the forest's silence, and the air was abruptly filled by the sounds of hundreds of soldiers rising and readying themselves to continue up the path. Julius watched them grumbling as they prepared to march again, their preoccupation with the minutiae of their daily lives shining through from every innocent gesture, and prayed that none of the Venicones would be rash enough to betray their ambush prematurely and ruin the plan he had discussed with his centurions less than an hour before. He leaned in close to the trumpeter, shouting in the man's ear.

'Sound it again, and then go straight into the call to form battle line!'

He used the moment while the musician was repeating the first call as an opportunity to tighten the thick leather cord that pulled his helmet's cheek pieces close to his face, then raised his vine stick as the first trumpet call suddenly broke into the urgent notes of the command to form line, already agreed with his officers as the order for them to galvanise their men into action.

'Form line, shields to both sides! Ready spears!'

All along the four-man-wide column shields were being raised, the men closest to the path's edges lifting their boards to either side against the threat of enemy warriors bounding in to attack them with spear and sword, while the men behind them hoisted their shields over their heads to protect themselves and the outer-most soldiers against the volley of arrows that was expected to be the first signal of an ambush. Centurions were bellowing at their men, encouraging their centuries to join up into an unbroken line rather than leave gaps that would enable each of them to be isolated and destroyed piecemeal. In the forest around them Julius could hear shouted commands, and he pulled the tribune deeper into the cover of the shield walls to either side.

'Here it comes!'

The first volley of arrows hammered against the raised boards, some of the missiles rattling off the heavy iron bosses and rims while more thumped into the defence's layered wood and linen to protrude like the spines of a hedgehog. A second volley sighed in the air for an instant before punching into the hastily formed line, the man beside Scaurus stiffening as if a snake had bitten him before slumping to the path with an arrow, which had managed to flit through a narrow gap in the wall of shields, buried deep in his neck.

Julius ripped off the dying man's helmet, tossing it to Scaurus along with the padded liner.

'Put that on! You're going to need it!'

He snatched up the man's shield, putting it back into the hole left by its absence before the gap could become a target for the next volley.

'*Pugio!*'

His shout brought his deputy running up the line in the narrow space between the two banks of raised shields.

'If he's not already dead then put this poor bastard out of his misery! We'll be on the move soon, and any man that can't stay the pace either dies at our hands or theirs!'

The third volley hammered home, but as far as Julius could see the cohort's line was holding firm. With every second that passed without a fourth cascade of arrows he knew the odds increased that the enemy warriors were already on the move. Dropping the shield he raised his head and bellowed the order that would either save them from the ambush or consign them to the horrific death he intended to mete out to their attackers.

'Now Qadir! *Now!*'

From behind the shields that had protected the Hamian's waiting archers a return volley of arrows flicked out into the forest, but as they flew high into the trees it was immediately evident that they were not intended to find human targets. Each of the arrows trailed a thin ribbon of greasy smoke, their iron heads adorned with blazing lumps of wool that had been cut from the archers' cloaks and dipped in oil, ready to be lit from the torch that Qadir's optio had carried from their last rest halt. Each arrow found a mark within fifty paces of the path, slapping into the upper reaches of the fir trees that marched away into the distance to either side in their confused ranks. Within seconds their bright flames had spread into the tree's highly combustible needles, and as the Venicone warriors sprinted from the forest's cover towards the waiting Roman line, their voices raised in a chorus of blood-curdling screams, the trees above them caught fire with a sudden crackle and fizz of burning pine needles. Julius watched with grim satisfaction as his officers bellowed the orders for their men to prepare for the Venicone charge, their soldiers levelling a bristling hedge of spearheads at the oncoming wave of barbarians.

As the warriors charged into the double wall of shields, struggling through the forest's undergrowth onto the cohort's waiting spears, the forest above them bloomed with the light and heat of a rapidly increasing number of burning trees, as the flames that were consuming the archers' original targets quickly spread through the canopy. For a few brief moments the Venicones continued their assault, although more and more of them were looking over their shoulders at the roof of flame that was spreading across the trees behind them, feeling the inferno's searing heat starting to become intolerable. Even behind the protection of a wall of shields Julius could feel the heat increasing by the moment, and he watched in grim fascination as smoke began to rise from the men at the rear of the attacking mob.

With a sudden howl of agony one of the warriors caught light, his clothes and hair flaring up and sending him screaming away from the battle in search of some escape from the intolerable pain, only to run deeper into the seemingly impenetrable wall of flame that was gathering strength about the Tungrians and their attackers. He vanished into the blaze, his screams rising to a crescendo before they were abruptly silenced, and for an instant the tribesmen dithered, staring at each other in consternation as the terrible nature of the trap their would-be victims had sprung on them became clear. With a sudden, apparently collective decision they broke and scattered, each man looking for his own escape as they ran in all directions seeking to get out from beneath the flames that were now licking through the trees above the soldiers. Even with his helmet to protect him Julius could feel the heat of the forest's destruction becoming intolerable, and he realised that if his men didn't move quickly they would share the tribesmen's uncertain fate. Shaking his mesmerised trumpeter by the shoulder, he shouted into the young soldier's face.

'*The retreat! Blow the fucking retreat and start running!*'

As the first notes of the new signal blasted out over the fire's swelling roar the Tungrians stirred from their momentary fixation with the blaze's rippling tendrils of flame, their ranks turning away from the terrified enemy warriors to face back down the path into the heart of the forest.

'Too slow!'

Julius stepped out of his men's protection, putting both hands around his mouth and bellowing a single word down the length of his command.

'*Run!*'

The cohort's column lurched into motion, the soldiers obeying long-ingrained conditioning in the absence of rationality that had fled in the face of the monstrous blaze roaring around them. Goaded and beaten by their officers and chosen men, the rearmost centuries stumbled back down the path up which they had marched moments before. Grateful for his helmet and armour's protection against the fire's heat Julius looked about him as his men started to move, realising that the barbarian war band which had been poised to roll over them in an unstoppable wave had shattered in the face of the fire's awful power. The Venicone tribesmen were still running in all directions in the hope of escaping the conflagration, and as he watched in amazement a tall, heavily built man still holding the axe that he would have been wielding against the Tungrian line sprinted out of the blazing trees with his hair and beard alight, bellowing out his pain and fear. A heavy branch fell from the canopy as the tree above him cracked explosively, the thigh-thick bough smashing the burning man to the ground in a shower of sparks. Julius winced, bellowing a command down the column of men in front of him.

'Run! Run for your fucking lives!'

★   ★   ★

Led once more by Arabus, the remnant of the raiding party stumbled out of the Dirty River's swamp and onto the firmer ground of a gravelled path more by luck than judgement. Arabus knelt to touch the packed stone surface as if to give thanks to the divine providence that had led them onto its firm footing.

'This is the way we came the night before last. The road that leads back to Lazy Hill is half a mile or so to the south, and Gateway Fort is a mile or so further on down the road.'

In the thinning mist behind them the calls of their hunters sounded closer than before, the baying of their dogs echoing across the silent landscape in a chorus of eager howls and yelps. The tracker looked up at his comrades and shook his head.

'The hunters have crossed the river. They're close now, too close for us to outrun the dogs.'

Lugos clenched a fist, raising his hammer defiantly.

'Then we *fight!*'

Marcus shook his head.

'There must be twenty of them, or more. If we make a stand here they'll attack us from all sides and drag us down with the weight of their numbers. The only place we stand any chance of defending against that many people is with walls around us.' He pointed down the gravel track's grey ribbon. 'There's no choice. We either get to Gateway Fort before them or we die here, and everything we've gained is handed back to the Venicones.'

Arminius and Lugos shared a momentary glance and then nodded together, the German holding out a hand to the Roman.

'Very well, we run, but when we reach the fort we find a strong place and make a stand. Now give me the cloak. You've carried that weight for long enough.'

Marcus shrugged, turning to the path.

'I'll carry it a while further yet. My birth father's head and a legion's standard are no burden, and I'd rather have you and Lugos with your hands free to fight.' The long, baying howl of a dog sounded again, closer than before as the animal threaded its way through the marsh's paths on the trail of their bloody scent, and the four men set off into the encircling mist at a loping trot.

Knowing instinctively that his place was at the front of the fleeing cohort, Julius tossed aside the shield he'd taken up a moment before and shouldered past the men to his right, bursting through the ranks of his century into the straggling knee-high vegetation between the path and the encroaching forest, moisture steaming out of the greenery as the fire's blazing heat grew. Freed of the obstruction of his men he ran down the length of the Tungrian column with the scrubby bushes and trailing brambles tugging at his legs, his lungs labouring as the blaze raging about them greedily sucked at the forest's air to feed its swelling conflagration. The Tungrians' rear had escaped from the worst of the inferno for the time being, but the first spear realised with a sinking feeling that their progress was slowing, the soldiers bunching up as their pace reduced from a run to little more than a walk. Catching the leading century he quickly realised the reason for their slow progress, the men behind struggling one at a time to a confused halt as they ran into the rear of the Tenth Century's pioneers, who were battling to fight their way through several dozen Venicone warriors. The enemy fighters had clearly been told to close the path to any Roman attempt to retreat, and they were fighting a stubborn action against the Tungrian column's leading ranks despite the desperate situation unfolding about them. The Tenth's hulking axe men were tearing into the enemy with their fearsome blades, but the forest looming to either side was restricting their frontage to no more than half a dozen men, and the Venicones' stubborn defence was holding firm in the face of their assailants' otherwise overwhelming strength. Behind the line of struggling, screaming combatants the pioneers were hacking at the tangled undergrowth to either side of the path in a bid to outflank the outnumbered barbarians and bring the fight to a swift conclusion, but the impenetrable thickets of thick, springy brambles were soaking up their assaults with little visible sign of progress.

The pioneers' centurion Titus stepped forward to meet Julius as the first spear stopped in momentary calculation, his double-bladed axe held in one hand, and his deep, rumbling voice was barely audible over the blaze's growing roar as he bent close to the other man's ear.

'We will all die here in the fire, unless we can break this resistance very quickly now!'

Julius nodded, his face hardening into a snarl as he felt the familiar, irresistible surge of battle rage whiten his knuckles on the hilt of his sword and raise the hairs on the back of his neck. When he replied his voice was thick, and his nostrils flared.

'You're right, Bear, it's time to earn our vine sticks and show these fucking ink monkeys who the real animals in this fight are!'

Titus nodded, gesturing to a pair of his men and growling a response, smashing a fist against his chest.

'Four of us will be enough to unlock this cage. If you three open the door for me then I will paint this forest red with the blood of these sheep fuckers!'

He took a second axe from one of his soldiers while the two men he had beckoned stepped out of the packed ranks stalled behind the desperate fight with expressions of pride and resolve, both of them putting aside their shields and hefting an axe in both hands in the manner of their tribal ancestors, the heavy iron axe heads twice the size of those usually carried by legion pioneers. In a century of men selected for their physical prowess both stood half a head above their peers and almost as tall as Titus himself, their shoulders bulky with the muscle required to swing their heavy weapons in combat. Julius grinned at Titus and his men and then turned wordlessly to face the enemy, pulling off his helmet and tossing it aside along with his vine stick in readiness for the melee before sheathing his sword and stooping to pick up a shield and an axe dropped by a wounded man, screaming a challenge at the enemy warriors barely a dozen paces distant.

'*Tungria! Tungria and Cocidius!*'

Planting his feet ready to charge, his gaze locked on the short enemy line, he felt the bulk of big men on either side as Titus's selected soldiers settled themselves at his shoulders while their monstrous centurion stepped close in behind the first spear. Their voices echoed his bellowed challenge loudly enough for the enemy warriors to look past their assailants at the small knot of men.

'*TUNGRIA!*'

Baring his teeth in an uncontrollable snarl Julius raised the axe in his clenched right fist and pointed its blade at a face chosen at random from the line of warriors, selecting a man with a long white scar down one side of his jaw and deciding without any conscious thought that the Venicone would be the first victim of his burning need to kill. The tribesman shouted a challenge back at him and raised his spear, his defiance wrenching an involuntary barking laugh from the Tungrian as he lowered the axe and readied himself to attack, sucking in one last deep breath. Raising his shoulders like a sprinter readying himself for the burst of effort required to take him to the winning post, the first spear took one last look at the man he had made his target, then bobbed down into a slight crouch, feeling his thighs tense in readiness before springing forward in an explosion of effort, his scream of unleashed fury piercing the fire's incessant roar and turning all heads towards the charging knot of men. The pioneers in their path stepped hurriedly back to clear a way for them, their eyes hardening at the sight of their first spear and centurion rampaging forward at the enemy, ready to throw themselves back into the fight at their officers' backs.

Bounding towards the man he had selected as his target, and watching as the Venicone stepped back a pace in preparation for the impact, Julius retained sufficient calculation in the last moment before colliding with the warrior's raised shield to sidestep the man's spear thrust, marvelling for a brief instant at the fleet-footed skill with which the big man to his left matched his movement. Without time to consider his next move the Tungrian dipped his shoulder and smashed his shield hard against his enemy's, bursting through the line of tribesmen with a triumphant roar and scattering the warriors to either side in momentary confusion. Knowing that Titus would be a half-pace behind him he spun to the left while the Venicone was still reeling off balance from the impact, allowing the axe's handle to slide through his hand until he held the fearsome weapon by the last few inches of the stave's length. Judging the blade's arc to perfection, Julius buried the brutally sharp blade deeply into the hollow just above his victim's buttocks, snapping the Venicone's head back with the agony of the cold iron's brutal intrusion even as his spine was severed, and wrenching an involuntary wide-eyed howl of triumph from the first spear as his victim arched back over the axe's head before sagging limply to the ground.

Stamping down on the paralysed warrior's spine for leverage, Julius wrenched the weapon free with a fierce pull and then turned in search of another target, swinging the axe high over his head and slamming it down into the head of another Venicone who was in the process of raising his sword to strike at Titus, as the massive centurion carved a path into the warriors around him with both of his axes flying in sprays of blood. The heavy blade carved through the warrior's iron dog cap and hacked deeply into his skull, lodging so firmly that just the feel of the handle told Julius that it would take too long to free from the dying man's body in the chaos of the fight. He released the weapon, allowing the Venicone to stagger away with a long groan, his eyes rolling up as the weight of the axe dragged his head backwards. He tottered for a moment as the first spear watched, then fell headlong with the axe handle pointing incongruously at the forest's canopy, holding the Tungrian's fascinated gaze even as one of Titus's men screamed a warning at him.

'*Look out!*'

Julius barely had time to realise he was under attack before the shield boss hit him hard enough to rattle his teeth, a punching blow to his shoulder that rocked him back on his feet followed by a spear thrust that slithered across his mailed chest rather than punching through it purely by dint of the step back that he had taken to keep his balance. Tearing his sword from its scabbard in the knowledge that he had to step forward and counter-attack rather than wait for the barbarian's next move, he found the Venicone ready and waiting for him with his feet set and shield raised, calm eyes in a hard face watching the Tungrian from behind a levelled spear. Julius's sword thrust was delivered with more speed than finesse, and the enemy warrior easily batted the blade aside in a defensive move designed to leave his opponent wide open for the spear that the warrior held ready for the kill. Julius knew only too well what was coming, as the Venicone raised his front foot to stamp forward and bury the spear's glinting iron head in his throat.

As the long blade thrust towards him the Tungrian desperately sidestepped to his left and swayed away from the attack, allowing the spear to slash past his face only to find himself on his back with the wind driven abruptly out of his lungs as the warrior expertly hooked his leg and upended him, raising his weapon again to drive its iron head down into his helpless enemy. With the polished blade poised momentarily above him, and as the Venicone pivoted forward on his right foot to deliver the killing thrust, the enemy warrior's body suddenly shuddered, his eyes jerking wide open with shock as an axe hammered into his back. The soldier who had charged into the battle on Julius's right tore his blade free from the gaping wound in the reeling barbarian's torso and dropped him to the ground with a vicious kick to his knee, swinging his other axe in a flashing arc to behead the stricken warrior.

The soldier stood over Julius, his chest heaving from the effort of the brief fight as his first spear climbed back to his feet, his armour already running with the blood of the men who had died on the blades of his axes. A growling roar caught both men's attention, and Julius's anger was instantly rekindled at the sight of Titus embattled in the middle of half a dozen enemy warriors, the bodies of several more men at his feet as he fought furiously with his twin axes, the blades' whirring arcs of silver flashing red in the light of the fire. As they watched he hammered one of his weapons down into a hapless warrior's shoulder, cleaving the man's chest down to his right nipple, staggering as another of the men around him slashed at him from behind with a long sword. Both men sprang forward towards their embattled comrade, Julius realising that the Venicone line was crumbling under the renewed attack from the Tenth Century's enraged soldiers who were clearly desperate to rescue their officer from the enemy warriors swarming around him. Before they could reach the surrounded centurion, first one and then another of Titus's assailants sank their iron deep into his unprotected back, his mail's iron rings no defence against the swords' sharp points. He sank to his knees with his face distorted into an animal snarl by the wounds' pain, and with a roar of anger at the sight of their centurion being felled the Tungrians burst forward in a wave of berserk fury to send the remaining Venicones fleeing down the path before them. Julius caught the arm of the century's chosen man as he made to pursue them, pulling him close and shouting in his ear over the combined din of fire and fight.

'The Bear's out of the fight, which means that you're in command! Either carry your wounded or give them the mercy stroke, but get your fucking century moving down that path at the run! Pull yourself together and *do it!*'

The chosen man took a moment to gather his wits before nodding and turning away to shout instructions at the men following up behind those already pursuing the tribesmen away down the path. Julius sheathed his sword and took a deep breath before forcing himself to turn back to the stricken centurion lying motionless beside the path with his two comrades kneeling to either side. The man who had rescued Julius a moment before looked up at the first spear with a look of despair at his centurion's plight.

'I saw that.' The big man's voice was thin and strained, and a trickle of blood ran from his lips as he spoke, his words barely audible. Julius bent over him, putting his ear close to the wounded centurion's mouth. 'I felt the iron in my back, and I can feel it still. Not long left for me, is there Julius? Don't you lie to me, boy . . .'

The first spear shook his head, feeling a presence at his side.

'Lying down on the job *again*, eh Titus?'

A smile cracked their comrade's face as he looked over Julius's shoulder.

'Just too late for the fight *again*, eh Dubnus?' He raised a trembling hand, reaching out to grasp his brother officer's shoulder. 'You missed a good one, little brother, there were enough of the tattoo boys for all of us. Our first spear here fought like a barbarian . . .'

Julius smiled gently.

'And our colleague here fought like a warrior king.' He gestured to the grievously wounded centurion. 'Cocidius himself would have been envious.'

Titus coughed, more blood seeping from between his lips, his voice almost inaudible.

'He'll have the chance to tell me so soon enough. Now, get me standing up. I'll not die here on my arse.'

Julius and Dubnus nodded to each other, gently lifting the man to his feet and then allowing the two men who had accompanied centurion and first spear into battle to take their officer's arms and hold him upright, tears streaking the drying blood that masked both men's faces. The centurion's back was sodden with blood from his wounds, and Dubnus realised that there were half a dozen rents in his armour, wounds inflicted from behind as he had laid about him with his axes. A tear ran down his face as he stared at the ruin of his brother officer's body.

'You threw yourself into them like a bear into a pack of dogs, didn't you?'

Titus stared down at him with eyes struggling to focus, swaying on his feet and only kept upright by the support of his men to either side.

'No man lives forever, Julius.' He coughed again, and this time a gout of blood fell onto his mailed chest. 'Time for us all to be leaving, I'd say. You have to go that way . . .'

He nodded a weary head at the path and the soldiers marching past, many of whom averted their glances as they passed, unable to take the sight of the seemingly indestructible centurion brought so low, while others stared numbly at the sight. The fire's roar was growing around them, and Julius realised that the blood that coated his friend's body was beginning to steam off in the extreme heat.

'We must indeed leave now, before the fire you bade me start consumes us all.' Qadir was standing behind them with a look of

sadness. 'Farewell, Brother Titus. I would have liked more time
in which to know you better, but the gods clearly have another
purpose for you. I will include you in my prayers to my goddess,
the Deasura, and ask her to intercede for you.'

Titus smiled wearily, his eyes closing.

'That's good enough for me, even if you are still an eastern
bum boy.' He was silent for a moment, his body shuddering in
his soldiers' hands, and then he reached a shivering hand to the
amulet that dangled from his other wrist, pulling it off and putting
the charm into Dubnus's hand. 'Take command of my men, little
brother, if you have the balls for it, and ask Cocidius to gather
my soul to him. Now, prop me against a tree and let me burn
with the rest of these corpses. Raise a cup to me and sing the
old marching songs in my memory every now and then, will you?'

His head sagged, and the soldiers holding him up looked at
Julius.

'We could carry him away, but I think it best to do as he asks.
Lean him back against that tree and let's get away from here
before the fire takes us as well as our brother.' He turned to
Dubnus and Qadir. 'Get back to your centuries and get them
moving faster. We've got several miles to run before we reach the
lake. We'll worry about who's commanding what once we're out
from under this fire.'

The two men saluted and headed away down the path in pursuit
of their centuries, and Julius put a hand into his belt pouch for
a small coin which he pushed into the dead centurion's mouth
with a swift prayer to the big man's chosen god. He turned away
from his brother officer's corpse to find Scaurus waiting for him,
and his own First Century jogging past at the column's end. The
tribune shouted above the fire, pointing to the ground nearby
where Julius's helmet and vine stick lay in the long grass.

'I won't ask you what happened, we don't have time, but you
might want to collect your kit and come with the rest of us for
a bit of a run. This is an unhealthy place to be now that some
madman's set light to a million bloody trees!'

8

'Faster . . . they're getting . . . closer.'

The four remaining members of the raiding party half ran and half staggered down the gravel path towards the ruins of Gateway Fort, the baying of the Vixens' hounds seemingly hard on their heels as they paced through the thinning mist towards the illusory safety of the customs post's burned-out shell. Arminius threw a glance back over his shoulder before replying to Marcus's gasped words, his own voice strained with exertion.

'If they . . . catch us . . . you two . . . keep running. Lugos and I . . . can deal . . . with a . . . few dogs.'

The hounds' barking changed abruptly from its previous howling and baying to a chorus of excited yelps, and the runners looked at each other with a shared realisation of what was about to happen. Lugos was still running easily, two of his slow, loping strides covering the same ground as three of the other men's, and his voice was untroubled when he spoke, taking the heavy war hammer down from his shoulder and turning to face back down the path.

'Venicones send dogs to stop our run. Now we have to fight.'

The German turned to join him, and Arabus pulled his bow from its place on his shoulder, stepping off the path to give himself a clear shot past the two barbarians. Pausing to wrap his cloak about his bow arm, he stabbed a handful of arrows into the ground at his feet before putting one to the string, lowering the weapon to point the missile at the ground before him rather than hold up his heavily padded arm and risk tiring the muscles. Marcus dropped the thief's cloak and drew his long spatha, putting his thumb to the intaglio of Mithras and muttering a swift prayer to the Lightbringer.

'I thought . . . we agreed . . .'

The Roman overrode Arminius's protest with a swift shake of his head, taking his place beside the two men on the far side of the path from the tracker as he fought to get his wind back.

'*You* might have agreed . . . but I didn't . . . If there's a fight to be had . . . then my place is here . . . not running for safety . . . while your lives are at risk.'

They waited in silence, staring down the track as the dogs' frantic barking grew louder, the only sound a gentle creak as Arabus drew back the arrow that he had nocked to his bowstring a moment before, bending the weapon until it was all he could do to hold the arrow from flying. In a flurry of movement the first half-dozen dogs charged out of the mist towards them in a rippling carpet of fur and flesh, and the tracker loosed his arrow into the onrushing pack, reaching for another even as the first struck home with a piercing yelp of pain from whichever of the dogs had stopped the missile's heavy iron head, as it tumbled into the gravel. He sent a second arrow after the first with a similar result, but dropped the bow and ripped his long hunting knife from its scabbard rather than attempt a third shot as the remaining four dogs leapt at their waiting swords.

Arminius took a step to his left and cut horizontally with his sword, leaning into the stroke as the leading dog leapt at him. The iron blade severed the animal's front legs just below its chest and dropped it writhing and screaming in agony at his feet. Another pair of hounds jumped at Lugos, who stunned the first with a stab of his hammer's heavy iron head and then pivoted to meet the other with the thick metal-shod staff on which it was mounted, smashing the leaping hound's face with a crack of bone. The last of the dogs went for Arabus, but the tracker was ready with his long hunting knife, holding out the arm he had padded with his cloak. Seizing hold of the presented limb with its powerful jaws the beast made to pull its intended victim to the ground, but the Tungrian was faster to the decisive blow, driving his knife's long blade up under the dog's jaw and cutting its throat with a flick of his wrist before shaking the choking, writhing animal from his arm and finishing it with another quick stroke of the weapon. Sheathing the knife he nocked a pair of arrows to the bow's string and turned the weapon from vertical to horizontal, levelling it down the path with a nod to Marcus, who had watched him slaughter the dog with a raised eyebrow.

'There are wild dog packs in the Arduenna forest, Centurion. My years of hunting taught me that the lure of a padded arm is the best way to bring the animal close enough for my knife to take his life. Dogs can make good eating, if the animal is not too old.'

Looking at his comrades to either side Marcus stepped backwards three long paces, measuring the distance between himself and the other men with a slight nod of his head as he raised the long spatha's dappled blade and angled it to his right in readiness for the first stroke. As he readied himself to fight, another wave of hounds broke from the fog, the slower and heavier animals that had lagged behind their faster pack mates, a massive beast that Marcus realised must be Monstrum at their heart. As they charged fearlessly at the waiting men Arabus loosed his arrows, one sticking cleanly into a leading dog and dropping the animal in wailing agony, while the other flew cleanly over the oncoming pack and was lost in the mist. The remaining beasts bored in to attack despite the piteous yelping of the legless dog still writhing at Arminius's feet, their numbers so great that the men waiting for them unconsciously shuffled closer together.

With a collective, rippling snarl the pack launched itself at them as one animal, the dogs scorning the waiting sword blades and hurling themselves bodily at the men behind them exactly as they had been trained. Arminius managed to behead the first of them to attack him with his sword before another two took him down, one of them darting in low to fasten its jaws on his ankle while the other leapt at his sword arm, catching his wrist in its jaws and pulling him to the ground. The German reached for his dagger with a shout of pain as the dog savaging his legs sank its teeth deep into his calf, but a third animal bit into his hand with a grinding snarl, reducing his attempt to draw the weapon to an impotent struggle. Lugos smashed his first attacker's skull with a crushing sweep of the hammer's heavy beak, but as he lifted the huge weapon to strike again a pair of dogs leapt upon him, the fearsome Monstrum hitting the massive Briton in the chest hard enough to send him sprawling headlong onto the path's gravel surface.

As Marcus watched the ferocious dog sprang forward upon its victim's body, raising its head with the jaws momentarily gaping wide as if it were considering where best to place the bite before lunging bodily at Lugos's vulnerable throat to make a swift kill. As the dog's head darted forward to strike, and before the Roman had the chance to defend his friend, the Briton's spade-like hand closed around the root of the animal's penis and its dangling testicles, his face contorting as he clenched the fingers into a tight fist and wrenched the arm down his body, pulling the beast away from his face. Screaming like a gut-stabbed tribesman the animal snapped at empty air as its head was bodily dragged away from the Briton's neck, and Marcus stepped forward with his spatha only to watch in amazement as the dog tensed its muscles and then defied the Briton's vice-like grip to spring forward again, opening its jaws wide ready to tear into the prostrate giant's head. Turning his face away from the lunging attack, Lugos bellowed in pain as the beast tore away a chunk of his right ear, the muscles of his right arm knotting as he wrenched at the dog's balls, twisting his hand violently to double the animal up with an agonised shriek.

Marcus raised his sword again, poising himself to put the blade through the dog's throat, but before he could strike the beast pivoted on Lugos's chest and ripped itself free from the ravaging pain that he was inflicting upon it, springing away into the fog without a backward glance. Turning away from the big Briton the centurion set about the dogs worrying at Arminius, hacking at their backs with swift, efficient killing blows to leave their bloodied corpses littering the ground about his friend. The German climbed to his feet with a wild-eyed look, picking up the sword he'd dropped during the attack and staring at Marcus as the Roman wiped and sheathed his own weapon.

'No sooner do I free myself from your blood debt and you put me under a fresh one!' He looked over at Lugos as the Briton retrieved his hammer with blood streaming down the side of his head. 'And what the fuck happened to you?'

Lugos put a hand to his bloodied and mangled ear, cursing as his fingers discovered the extent of the damage, the upper third of his ear torn raggedly away.

'Monstrum.'

The German laughed dryly.

'Looks like he won that round.'

Marcus gathered up the cloak, turning away towards the ruined fort.

'We need to go, before the Vixens get here and take us in the open.'

They ran again, Arminius limping on the ankle which had been badly bitten during the attack, hearing the sounds of the Vixens' pursuit behind them as the Venicone hunters fruitlessly called out their dogs' names. They had covered less than five hundred paces when a high-pitched wail keened out through the mist, a woman's voice raised in anguish. Arminius increased his pace, wincing at the pain in his leg and muttering almost inaudibly despite the fact that any chance of concealing their whereabouts was now long dissipated.

'Run . . . faster.'

The ruin of Gateway Fort loomed out of the mist, and the four men slowed from their exhausted jog to walking pace, staring about them at the building's blackened timbers and shattered gates. Marcus looked around him for a moment, glancing back down the path as it disappeared away into the mist, the sounds of their pursuers' progress now so loud that they could be no more than a moment behind the exhausted raiders.

'They'll know that we've taken shelter here, we've left enough of a blood trail that they'll realise we can't run much further. Normally you'd expect them to light torches and come in at the rush, but there's nothing to burn for miles around, and those girls are hunters, not warriors. If I was the bastard leading them I'd send them into the fort in a pack to hunt us down in silence. One on one we're more than a match for them, but if they mob us . . .'

Arminius nodded, striding forward towards the fort.

'So we split up and take a building each. That way we divide them up.'

The others followed, looking about them as they passed through the open gateway. The fort's buildings had all been burned out, but their stone shells were still standing, streaked with the droppings of birds nesting in the ruins' less accessible places, and after a moment the German nodded to his companions and stalked away into the shadow to stand at the entrance of the hospital building with his sword drawn. Arabus pulled a handful of arrows from his quiver and jogged away up the fort's main road until he was lost to view in the gloom beneath the far wall. Lugos shrugged and stalked away into the space between a pair of barrack blocks, leaving Marcus standing alone in the roadway. After a moment's thought he turned and padded silently back to the gate, getting down onto his hands and knees before peering round the rotting, blackened timbers. At first he could see no more than the mist-swathed landscape, but as he watched an indistinct figure materialised out of the swirling curtain of droplets, a tall man with a cowl over his head and a long staff in one hand, his face riven by a long healed but evidently grievous wound. He stopped walking and stared hard at the gate, waving a hand forward and pointing at the fort.

From the mist behind him another figure emerged from the grey to stand at his side, her body taking form as if she had been conjured out of the mist, and as Marcus watched she was flanked by another twenty or so of the female hunters, some equipped with swords and spears, a few armed with bows. The hunt's master spoke again, and the archers ran swiftly away to his left, taking position facing the fort's gateway and stringing their bows with swift, economical movements before nocking arrows to them. Risking the chance that one of them might spot him, Marcus kept his eyes fixed on the remaining hunters, watching as their master turned to face them with a gruff word of command. The women drew their blades, standing stock still for a moment, then paced forward slowly towards him with the first woman at their head, her heavily tattooed face unreadable in the pale grey light.

*   *   *

'You do realise that no one's ever going to believe this story?'

Julius raised his head to look at Dubnus, a wry smile creasing his mask of exhaustion.

'Agreed. And you do realise that I'm never going to give a shit? It's enough for me that we managed to pull ourselves out of the trap that some clever bastard had set for us with the loss of so few men. And that fire will have scattered the Venicones all over the forest, which means that we're safe enough from pursuit for the time being. It's just a shame that Silus and his boys were stuck on the far side of it. The odds of our ever seeing them again can't be all that good.'

His friend nodded solemnly.

'I'll miss him, if he's not managed to fight his way past them. There's nothing like having your own tame cavalryman to bait, rather than having to wait all day for one of them to ride past.' He stretched his back, staring down the line of the cohort's weary soldiers where they sat and lay at the forest's eastern edge. 'So, what do you want to do about the Tenth?'

The first spear shrugged.

'They need a new centurion, that's a certainty. Their Chosen's a good enough man, but he's not officer material. And they're a difficult bunch of bastards to manage, ten years under Titus has them thinking they're a cut above the rest of the cohort. Are you sure you can master them?'

Dubnus raised a pained eyebrow.

'This is me we're talking about, Julius. Have you forgotten all that time when I was your chosen man?'

His friend nodded, remembering the casual brutality the muscular soldier had brought to the role as his deputy, in the days before his promotion to centurion.

'I don't doubt your ability to take a century by the balls and make them do whatever it is you tell them, but there isn't a man in the Tenth that doesn't have half a head's height advantage on you. If you try to cow them into obedience they'll most likely spit you out looking a good deal less pretty than you do now, and since that isn't saying much I'm a good deal more concerned with the impact on discipline that would have than any damage you might sustain.'

Dubnus shrugged, flexing his meaty biceps and turning to look down the cohort's column again.

'I'd say we don't have the luxury of discussion. Those men need someone to take a grip of their balls now, before they get any more time to brood on Titus's death. And it has to be now, or they'll get used to getting away with murder under their chosen and the problem will only be harder to deal with when we do confront it. And besides, what if we have to fight again?'

Julius sighed, holding his hands up in a gesture of surrender.

'Agreed. Just don't say I didn't warn you.'

The big man nodded, turning away and striding off down the column until he reached his own century, calling his chosen man to him. The former legionary stamped to attention and waited for his orders, his eyes widening as he heard what it was that his centurion had to say.

'Well Titus, it's your lucky day. I'm taking over the Tenth, now that the Bear's gone to hunt with Cocidius. You're in command of this shower until this is all over, so you'd better make a good enough job of it that I can recommend you get the crest across your helmet and a nice hard vine stick to beat your men with. Fuck it up and you'll find yourself having to take orders from one of your mates, and I can assure you that that isn't going to feel all that funny, no matter how much this lot will laugh at you behind your back. And don't let them get away with any of that Habitus bullshit.' He grinned broadly at the gaping chosen man, slapping him on the shoulder. 'Time for the truth. That story about old Centurion Habitus? It was just a story, something I dreamed up to make you lot feel guilty, and nothing more. So when the first of your mates that thinks he can use it to get an easier ride from you tries it on, you'd better ram it straight up his arse, or they'll have you under their control rather than the other way around. Good luck!'

Leaving the other man staring at his back, he marched on down the cohort's length until he reached the rearmost century, taking in the sight of the Tenth's hulking axe men lounging in the grass to either side of the road with a disapproving frown.

'Canus, to me!'

The chosen man appeared out of a group of soldiers, presenting himself with a look that told Dubnus everything that he needed to know about the man. He stepped in close to his new deputy and fixed him with a hard stare, couching his words in a matter-of-fact tone that left neither room nor opportunity for disagreement.

'You can lose the attitude for a start. Give me one more look like that and I'll rip your face off and wipe my arse with it! Got that?!' The other man swallowed and nodded, and Dubnus knew in that second that he had the man. 'Yes, I'm your new centurion. The Bear handed me the job, along with these . . .' He raised Titus's axe, allowing the dead centurion's Cocidius amulet to swing on its bracelet of leather cord. 'For some reason we'll never know, he seemed to believe that you lot need the love and care that only a man with my reputation for handling his men softly can provide. So start getting used to it, and while you're doing it gather my boys round and I'll give them the good news.'

Canus turned away with a stony face, calling the century to gather round their new officer while the men of the Ninth Century who were just ahead of them in the cohort's order of march watched curiously. Dubnus waited until they were arrayed about him in a half-circle before speaking.

'How many men did we lose in the ambush, Chosen?'

The chosen man, still smarting from Dubnus's brisk treatment, spoke up at once.

'Five soldiers and the best centurion in the cohort, Centurion!'

The pioneers nodded at his words, their expressions still those of men deep in grief, their eyes for the most part fixed on the ground or the clouds above them, few of them meeting their new centurion's eye. Dubnus stared about him with an undisguised look of disgust.

'Look at you all! You look like men who've just buried a father who died in his sleep, rather than witnessed him being hacked to death by barbarians! There's not one of you that has the look of a man who's ready to shed blood in revenge!'

Every man in the century was glaring at him now, their faces hardening as the insult sank in, and one of the bigger soldiers started to climb to his feet with a look of indignant anger.

'Sit *down!*' The pioneer hesitated for a second at the note of command, and Dubnus stepped towards him with his knuckles white around the shaft of his vine stick, his face contorted with genuine anger that left the soldier nowhere to go other than down onto his backside or up onto his feet. 'Sit the *fuck* down, before I put you on your arse!'

The big man sank slowly back down onto his haunches, and the centurion nodded his head slowly.

'That's *better*. I don't want to be slapping my own men about, not when there are barbarians close to hand. Now, where was I?'

He turned away for a moment, deliberately turning his back on the fuming pioneers, knowing that they were restrained from attacking him only by their deeply ingrained discipline. When he spun on his heel to face them the century gathered around him was still frozen in place, a dangerous animal temporarily restrained from attacking purely by the force of his personality.

'You look like a gathering of women in mourning.' He paused, allowing the further insult to sink in. 'Well I've got news for you, girls. We are soldiers, and soldiers die! When we lose a brother in battle we should rejoice in the manner of his falling, and the number of the enemy he takes with him! If we sit around weeping at our loss we only weaken ourselves for the next time that we face an enemy, and bring the moment of our own death racing towards us! You all worship Cocidius, right?'

He waved the amulet at them, drawing an angry growl of affirmation from several of the men facing him.

'Well Cocidius doesn't want you to piss and whine over Titus. Cocidius has Titus sitting at his feast table right now, with a mug of the good stuff in one hand, a roasted sheep's leg in the other, his chin shining with grease, beer spilled down his best tunic and a pair of busty wenches under the table oiling up his cock and balls!' A few faces creased into sad smiles at the memory of their former leader's legendary ability to enter into the spirit of a celebratory feast. 'And right now, brothers, Cocidius is lavishing the old bastard with praise for the glorious manner of his death! And so am I! The Bear lived like a man and died like a warrior, and if I make an equally glorious exit from this life then I'll be more than content as the ferryman takes me across the river.' The faces staring up at him were more thoughtful than angry now. 'When we get back to civilisation I'll be putting an altar to our fallen brother's memory alongside the one that's been purchased for that leathery old sod Scarface at Fort Habitus, an altar to his glorious death and the honour it did to *our* god!'

He paused again, watching the soldiers nodding their agreement, knowing that he almost had them. *Almost.*

'Now some of you are thinking that I'm not the right man to lead you. Thinking that I'm not big enough . . .' He paused and smiled wryly to be voicing such a sentiment. 'You'll be telling each other that I'm not hard enough to lead the Tenth, the biggest, ugliest men in the cohort. That I'm not fit to carry the Bear's axe.' He looked about him again, jutting out his jaw defiantly and raising the dead centurion's weapon above his head. 'Well tough fucking shit! The Bear himself handed it to me, and his amulet to Cocidius, and told me to lead you to glory in his name! So here's how it is, girls! I'm your centurion, at least until we get back on the other side of the wall and we're not being chased around the landscape by a gang of angry tribesmen. Once we're safe again you can decide whether you want to risk putting me to the challenge, and perhaps we'll find out how many of you it takes to put me on my back. *Perhaps.* But for now, we're at war, so it's wartime rules until that happy day. Which means that any man who wants to challenge my authority can expect to find himself subject to wartime discipline. *My* fucking discipline. And if you think the Bear could be harsh, just try those boots on for size!'

Arabus waited silently in the shadow of the fort's northern wall, close to the burned-out shell of a barrack block with his nostrils

filled with the scent of burnt pitch and timber. As he watched, his
centurion stood and ran back from the southern gateway in a clatter
of hobnails on cobbles, ducking into the ruin of the headquarters
building just as the first of the hunters appeared in the square of
grey light framed by the gate. Raising his waiting bow he leaned
forward to put his lips to the tiny statue of his goddess Arduenna
that he had lashed to its wooden stave, muttering a silent prayer.

'Protector of my homeland, lend your exiled servant the gift
of your keen eye and steady hand.'

He loosed the first shot, his eyes narrowing fractionally as the
woman who had been first through the gateway slumped back
onto the cobbles with an audible grunt. Snatching up a second
arrow he put it to the string with hands that seemed to move
without conscious effort, releasing its feathered tail almost before
the bow was fully drawn. A second of the oncoming hunters
spun back against the wall next to her, a third staggering with
an arrow in her thigh as they scattered to left and right, seeking
shelter from the deadly hail of iron he was sending down the
street's hundred-pace length. For a long moment they were silent,
huddling behind the cover of stone walls while he swept the
ground before him with the fourth arrowhead, waiting for a
target at which to send the missile. A head popped around the
right-hand building at the end of the street, and without
conscious effort the arrow was gone from his string, flashing
past the tiny target with inches to spare. A return shot flicked
past him without his ever having seen it, and without stopping
to think the scout plucked the last two arrows from the ground
before him and scuttled, bent low, across the street's width to
his right. The women shouted to each other as they saw the
movement, and the scout cringed at the realisation of the mistake
he had made in leaving the safety of the shadows in response
to a lucky shot. Another arrow fizzed past his head with a whirr
of flight feathers and bounced back from the wall behind him,
the pock of its iron head on the stone like the ring of hammer
on anvil in the ruined fort's silence, and the scout dived into
the cover of the building just as another pair of arrows whistled

down the street, the barbarian archers snap-shooting at his indistinct figure.

A fierce blow to his right leg tripped the scout, sending his body sprawling across the cobbles with his chin split to the bone by the impact, and as he rolled onto his back, his leg afire with sudden pain, he realised that one of the hastily loosed missiles had spitted the meat of his calf. Staggering back onto his good foot he half staggered and half hopped to the building's first doorway, grimacing at the wound's pain as he slunk inside to find the confined space of the centurion's quarters that topped the run of eight-man rooms which composed most of the barrack block's length. The room was dark and damp despite its lack of a roof, the officer's quarter laid bare by the effects of looting and fire, stinking of burnt and rotting wood and offering no hiding place from the pursuit that would doubtless be surging up the fort's main street. The Tungrian nocked his last two arrows to the bow's string and huddled into the room's furthest corner, levelling their iron heads at the doorway and grimacing at the searing agony in his calf that reignited with every tiny movement. A slight scrape of leather on stone in the otherwise profound silence announced the presence of at least one hunter on the other side of the open doorway, and he pulled the bowstring slowly back until the weapon was two-thirds drawn, listening for any clue that the inevitable assault was upon him.

Arminius watched in silence as Marcus retreated into the fort's silent interior, waiting until the first of the barbarian hunters appeared in the gateway's grey opening before barking a harsh challenge at them and stepping back into the hospital building before they could loose their arrows at his momentary target. Running down the building's long corridor with his sword drawn he blew out a long breath of relief as he found the doctors' office that was a standard feature of fortress hospitals across the empire, a small room halfway up the building's run of four-man wards. In the corner of the office a short brick partition butted out from the wall that divided the office from the corridor, and he moved swiftly across the stone floor to look into the space it created. The heavy wooden doors were gone, as were the shelves that had once held the fort's store of pain-killing drugs, kept safely locked away to prevent temptation overcoming any man with the desire to experience their numb bliss once more. Sliding his bulky body into the narrow hiding place, the German eased the point of his sword to rest on the floor and willed his breathing to slow, closing his eyes and feeling the thudding of his heart gradually decrease its tempo until it seemed that he had become one with the darkness around him.

The faint sound of footsteps came from the corridor, two or three hunters at a guess, and he waited and listened as they approached the office, hearing one of them step into the small room and stop barely three paces from him. The pause stretched out until he tensed himself to leap forward and fight, certain that at any second the unseen searcher would realise that there was a blind spot in the room and take the single step forward that would reveal his presence. A stealthy footstep sounded, but the German stopped himself from springing out of the cupboard's conceal-ment by a hair's breadth as he realised that the hunter had stepped out of the office, rather than further into it. Soft, cautious voices sounded in the corridor, the women clearly advancing further into the building, and Arminius poked his head warily round the cupboard's edge to find the office empty.

Taking a long slow breath he stepped warily into the room and flattened himself against the wall alongside the door, peeking up the corridor's length through its opening. Three women were advancing cautiously up the narrow building's length, and as he watched two of them stepped into the wards to either side of the corridor, leaving the third protecting their backs against any threat from the rooms ahead of them. Without conscious thought he stepped into the corridor behind her, drawing his hunting knife and reaching over her shoulder to ram the blade up into the soft flesh beneath her jaw. The hunter's body stiffened, the sharp iron jammed through her tongue preventing her from making any sound as Arminius dragged her back against him, ripping the knife free and sweeping it across her throat to finish her. Lowering the spasming body to the floor, he put the knife down beside her rather than waste time re-sheathing it, drawing his sword and taking a two-handed grip of its hilt as he advanced back to the doorways through which the other two hunters had stepped a moment before, glancing from one to the other and back with the deadly intent of a predator.

A movement to his left had the blade in motion without the effort of conscious thought, a savage blow that caught the hunter as she stepped out of the ward she had just searched and hacked clean through her neck, burying the sword deep in the sodden wood of the door's frame while the woman's headless corpse tottered and slumped to the floor, her head thudding onto the flagstones. A screech behind him was barely enough warning that the last of the them was upon him, and with the sword still buried in the door's frame he stepped over the headless corpse and into the empty ward behind her to avoid whatever attack was upon him, tearing the blade loose and turning to face the threat. The hunter came through the door behind him with her sword's blade ringing on the stone as she threw it aside and pulled a pair of matched hunting knives from her belt, dropping into a fighting crouch facing the German and staying beyond the reach of his long blade as she weighed him up.

They faced each other in silence for a moment, Arminius easing his sword up to point at her face and sliding his feet a little further apart while the woman, her face a swirl of blue ink in which her green eyes burned angrily, lifted the twin knife blades to match the long blade's threat. Bellowing his challenge the German lunged forward, intent on putting the weapon's point through her throat and ending the fight, but the woman stepped neatly aside and pushed his blade away from her with her right-hand knife while the left flickered out and slashed at his belly, forcing him to step hurriedly backwards. Jumping forward to attack him she advanced two swift paces, keeping the right-hand blade against his sword while she cocked her left to stab sideways at his chest. Stepping into her lunge the German smashed an elbow into her face before she could sink the knife into him, sending her reeling back against the wall, but as he gathered himself to hack the sword into her body in a horizontal cut she came back off the stone with an ear-rending howl, her knives flashing as she cut at his arms and slashed a pair of long cuts into their flesh.

Snarling at the pain, and realising that he was in a fight that would probably end in defeat, given his inability to land a killing blow with the longer blade at such close quarters, the German stepped back a pace before snapping his wrists to throw the sword at his opponent, forcing her to duck away from its lethal arc and allowing him a momentary respite from her assault. Bursting through the ward's door he made to sprint down the corridor with the Vixen at his heels, his toe snagging on the body of the headless woman he had killed a moment before and sending him sprawling full length alongside his first victim. Rolling onto his back he tensed to spring back onto his feet only to see his opponent leap through the doorway, diving onto him with her knives poised to strike like the claws of a pouncing hawk.

Marcus found himself in the shell of the headquarters' first main room, the area where soldiers were allowed to come and go more or less freely with messages or making deliveries. A once proud mosaic of Mars was part hidden by the dank fire debris that was strewn across the floor, hundreds of its thumbnail-sized tiles having been torn up during the fort's destruction in an aimless act of vandalism that he supposed characterised the Venicones' urge to remove all trace of the invaders from the south once the legions had withdrawn from the wall twenty years before. On an impulse he bent and picked up a handful of the ceramic squares, retreating back into the inner sanctum where, when the fort was occupied, only the cohort's centurions and its commander would have been admitted under normal circumstances. On the room's far side were the two strongrooms where the cohort's pay and standards would have been stored, and for a moment he considered hiding in their dark recesses before realising that no concealment was going to be adequate to protect him from the searching Vixens. Easing the heavy cloak to the fog-moistened stone floor he sheathed the spatha and drew his shorter gladius, the blade's length better suited to the room's close confines, tensing himself to fight as the almost inaudible sounds of slow, tentative footsteps reached him through the doorway between the two rooms. When the sounds were so close that he was sure that whoever was stalking him was only feet away, on the other side of the wall against which his back was planted, he tossed a single tile into the corner of the room to his front and right, raising the short sword so that the last few inches of its blade were within a hand's span of his face. In the distorted picture of the doorway that he saw reflected in the mirror finish an indistinct white shape emerged from the gloom behind it, a face, and before it came a gleaming shard of iron, either spearhead or arrow, and both equally deadly if the woman hunting him was allowed to strike first.

Swivelling his eyes to watch the entrance, he tossed another tile onto the wall in front of him, and the sudden rattle drew the hunter into the room in a rush, her spear raised to kill. As she came through the doorway, her attention fixed to her left, he sank the blade deep into the space between her shoulder and neck and then twisted the sword as he wrenched it free. Grunting, the woman staggered, half turned to bring the spear to bear and then pitched forward onto her face and lay still, apart from a slight twitching of her hands and feet. Stepping forward Marcus threw the remaining tiles aside, tossed the sword into his left hand and snatched up the spear, pivoting swiftly as he spun it lengthways in his hand and then stamped forward, stabbing the black iron head forward into the open doorway as another woman came screaming through the opening. The spear's blade sank deep into the Vixen's chest, and as she tottered with the wound's pain and shock Marcus tore it free and slashed the edge across her throat to open the artery beneath the surface, sending a spray of blood across the room. He kicked her back into the outer room, wincing as something moved in the shadows behind the dying woman and spinning away to take up a fresh position to one side of the door with the spear raised ready to strike again. With a scrabble of feet another one of them was through the door, but his savage spear thrust found only empty air, and before he could pull the blade back to strike again his ankle was seized in a powerful grip that upended him, teeth sinking into his calf as the dog Monstrum savaged his leg with a succession of lightning-swift bites. Stabbing out frantically with his spear he saw the iron head go wide of its mark by no more than an inch, the enormous dog snarling and springing forward to clamp its jaws around his swordhand before he could strike with the gladius, a savage bite sinking the brute's teeth deep into its delicate bones and tendons and spilling the sword from his grasp. The beast sprang forward again, and suddenly the Roman was face-to-face with the dog's muzzle, staring up helplessly as Monstrum opened his jaws wide and reared back, ready to tear into his victim's defenceless face.

A shape flitted across the doorway and Arabus loosed his arrows, knowing even as his fingers released them that he had wasted his last attack on a ruse. Their iron heads clattered off the wall behind the open door frame and fell uselessly to the floor, and in the moment of silence that followed he drew his long hunting knife and readied himself for death. A single hunter came through the door in a sinuous motion, her spear raised to strike until she realised that her prey had loosed his last shot. They regarded each other for a moment as two more of them followed her into the room, one armed with a long sword, the other with an arrow strung to her bow. The first woman had features which were virtually undistinguishable beneath the tattoos that swirled across her face, but her eyes were twin oases of brown, surrounded on all sides by angry white as she advanced towards the helpless scout, baring her teeth in a snarl that communicated far more clearly than the choppy flow of her own language that she was spitting down at him. Prodding at him with the spear, she gestured for him to put down the hunting knife that was his only remaining defence, and when he shook his head in refusal she stabbed the blade into his calf close to the arrow that still transfixed his leg, smiling down at him as he convulsed with the pain before kicking the knife from his hand. Grimacing up at her as she pulled the spear free, the Tungrian spat at her feet in the only form of resistance he had left.

'Bitch!'

Grinning broadly, the hunter passed the spear to the bow-armed woman and reached to her belt, a wide strap decorated with lumps of leather that had been sewn onto its surface, pulling a short skinning knife with a broad blade from its sheath and motioning her comrades forward while she sized up her victim. Arabus laughed incredulously, forcing a note of bravado into his voice.

'Trying to work out where to start, are you? I'd send the three of you to meet your gods if I didn't have this arrow through—'

She slapped him, hard enough to put stars in his vision for a moment, and her companions pounced while he was still part stunned, taking an arm apiece and pinning his legs with their own while she knelt between them, his vulnerability filling the scout with sudden dread that death was far from the worst thing he faced. Smiling at him smugly, the hunter reached out and gripped the arrow, snapping off the iron head and then pulling its length from the wound while Arabus grunted at the renewed pain, and while the wound bled freely she tore off his leggings to reveal his naked lower body, putting the skinning knife's wide point against the entry wound.

'No, *don't* . . .'

She smirked, pushing her hand forward to sink the blade into the hole, broadening it from one finger's width to three in an instant and tearing another, longer, teeth-gritted snarl of pain from the tracker, who stared in horror at the wooden handle apparently sprouting from his calf. After a moment the woman reached forward and tore the knife free, putting it to her nose and sniffing at the blood that coated the blade with a sigh of pleasure. Leaning forward, she took his penis between her thumb and forefinger, looking up at him and shaking her head in mock sympathy, waggling the flaccid member and saying something to the women restraining him which had them both laughing, their faces hard as they stared down at the helpless man. She spoke to him again, tapping a finger to one of the belt decorations before pointing to his penis with a savage grin, then put the bloody knife's edge to the organ's root and stretched out the terrified scout's member as if to make the act of severing it easier to achieve while Arabus stared at her aghast, the pain in his leg all but forgotten as he lost control of his bladder. Dropping his penis with a shout of disgust, she slapped his testicles hard enough to wrench a scream of pain from him, allowing one to fall from her hand as she pulled the other clear of his body, staring at it for a moment and then back at the terrified scout, baring her teeth in a rictus of hate as she sliced through his scrotum and cut away the testicle with a single savage swipe of her knife.

Somewhere in the derelict fortress a man screamed in agony, the full-throated howl too lost in pain to even know that he was giving voice to it, and the dog paused for an instant at the sound, cocking an ear at the shriek. Summoning all of his strength, Marcus dropped the spear and clenched his unbitten hand into a fist, smashing it into the animal's jaw hard enough to cut the knuckles on its teeth. With a snarl of rage Monstrum darted his head forward and sank his teeth into the bicep of the arm that was attacking him, stiffening the Roman's body with the pain as the dog worried at the muscle with its powerful jaw. Searching across the stone floor for the hilt of his sword with the other hand, ignoring the pain of the damage the animal had inflicted on it a moment before, he found the thief's cloak beneath his fingers. Thrusting the hand into the garment's folds with a desperate lunge, his fingers found the lip of the heavy gold bowl still hidden in the pocket. Pulling it free he swung his arm to smash the heavy dish into Monstrum's temple with a thud. The dog yelped in surprise and released its grip on his other arm, shaking its head in surprise at the crunching impact. Raising the bowl again the Roman repeated the blow with fresh purpose, turning it in his hand to bring the rim's heavy edge down on the same point of the beast's skull he had struck a moment before, and with as much force as his damaged hand would allow. The animal's skull broke with an audible click, and, as it tottered astride him, Marcus swung the improvised weapon a third time, feeling the rim sink into the dog's shattered temple as he hammered it home in the same spot. Rolling off his body, the dog staggered disjointedly to its feet, allowing the Roman to regain his own footing. Snatching up the spear he punched it through the beast's side, feeling a moment of resistance before the wicked iron head burst through the dog's ribcage and found its heart. Monstrum let out a final baying howl of pain and died, slumping onto the stone floor with its eyes rolled up to show only the whites.

Hearing a footstep in the outer room he stamped on the dead dog's chest and tore the spear free, spinning to face his next attacker, as she charged into the room with a scream of rage, running onto the spear with a gasp of amazed agony. Pivoting to one side, and using the last of his strength to lift the wounded woman off her feet, he heaved her body across the room and down into the gaping hole of the inner sanctum's floor safe, tearing the spear's blade free as she crashed down into the four-foot-deep pit and lay still, her feet and ankles protruding from the hard stone box into which she had been pitched. Her right boot twitched and was still, but as Marcus gathered his wits a movement in the corner of his eye made him spin back to face the door, levelling the spear to confront the next of his attackers. As he lunged forward with the weapon, aiming for the shadowy figure's chest, his opponent smashed the weary attack aside with a sword stroke that tore the iron head from its shaft. Stepping back into the inner chamber the Roman picked up his sword, bellowing a challenge at the hunter lurking on the other side of the empty stone doorway.

'*Come on then! Come and finish me off!*'

As Arabus screamed in anguish and agony, and before his torturer could move from her position crouched between his legs from where she was gloating at his despair with the severed organ held high, a ghostly shadow flickered in his peripheral vision. A heavy footstep behind her creased his torturer's face into the beginnings of a frown, but as she started to turn her head to look behind her it was suddenly, horrifically smashed into a grotesque shape by an impact that flung her corpse sideways from his body. Lugos stepped back from his first victim, looping the hammer high over his head in a blur of iron before smashing its beak down onto the foot of one of the hunters restraining Arabus, pulping flesh and bone into a shapeless mess that arched her body in a silent scream of disbelief and outrage.

The last of them jumped away from their erstwhile victim scrabbling for her knife while the huge Briton raised the hammer again, her voice almost lost in the sudden piercing scream as the woman whose foot had been smashed was hit by a wave of unimaginable pain.

'No . . .'

Lugos had turned the iron handle in his hand as he raised it again and spun through a full turn to strike with a horizontal blow, and it was the rough-bladed crescent of metal on the hammer's reverse that punched through her ineffectually raised hands and into her face, taking the top of her head off as easily as cutting into a boiled egg. Arabus flinched as her half-decapitated body bounced off the wall behind him and fell full length at the Briton's feet, grimacing at the burning pain in his crotch as Lugos knelt beside him, ignoring the crippled woman's continuous hoarse screaming.

'You lucky. Still got cock and one ball. Here . . .'

He cut a strip of wool from the fallen hunter's tunic, rolling her corpse away and revealing the horrific wound the hammer's beak had smashed into her face, tying it around the root of Arabus's penis and tightening it until the flow of blood from his torn scrotum stopped.

'You live. Come with me.'

The scout limped painfully down the fort's main street, unable to do anything more than nod when he realised that Marcus and the German were waiting for them on the steps of the headquarters building, the latter's tunic and legs wet with blood. Lugos pointed to the head hanging from Arminius's left hand by its hair.

'All dead?'

The German nodded.

'Looks that way. Since the centurion seems to have killed the vicious bitch that leads that pack of harpies, I thought we might reunite her with them? He'd have done for me as well if I'd not been quick enough to stop him running me through with a spear.'

Leaving the scout sitting on the steps with a mournful expression, his eyes closed against the incessant pain in his crotch,
Marcus paced cautiously forward towards the gate with Arminius
and Lugos a pace behind him. The hulking Briton pointed to the
cuts on the German's arms, and then frowned at the blood-sodden
left shoulder of his tunic.

'What happen you?'

Arminius pulled a dismissive face and raised the woman's head,
spitting into its distorted features.

'One of the bitches was cutting me to ribbons with her knives,
so I threw my sword at her and faked a run and trip to get my
hands on my own hunting knife. When she jumped on me she
managed to stick one of her blades in here –' he gestured at a
bloody rent in his tunic's shoulder with his swordhand's thumb
'– but she missed the fact that I had my own knife ready for her.
So now she's a headless corpse, and I can still hold a shield.'

He waggled the fingers of his left hand with a grimace, and
Lugos nodded, picking up one of the women's discarded shields
and handing it to him. Marcus spoke quietly over his shoulder
as his pace slowed with their proximity to the gateway.

'Give me the head.'

He reached down to pick up another shield discarded by one
of the hunters slain by Arabus's arrows, gesturing to them to stay
out of sight as he climbed wearily up the stone steps that led to
the fighting platform above the gateway. The hunter's heavily
scarred leader stood thirty paces from the fort with a pair of
archers waiting on either side, and Marcus called out from behind
the shield, his voice ringing out across the short gap.

'You have *failed*! You sent children to fight with men, and we
tore them apart like wolves. Run now, while you still can!'

He tossed the severed head down to land at the warrior's feet,
and the older man regarded it sourly for a moment before raising
his hideously scarred face to the Roman.

'*Run*, thief? I think no! My lord Brem depend on me to hunt
you, take back eagle and revenge murder of his son! And my
Vixen hurt you bad, that I very sure! We follow four tracks here,

two scattered with blood. *You* blood. How many of you still can fight, I wonder? And no escape from fort, Roman, only one gateway, no way escape without rope. You got rope?'

He paused, shaking his head at the Roman.

'No, you got no rope. You tired from night in swamp and morning fighting dog and Vixen. No rescue for you, Roman. Men who march north from you wall all dead in fire we see to west. And you look to south, Roman, you tell me what you see, heh?'

He pointed to the forest behind Marcus, visible now that the day's passage had burned off the mist that had shrouded the trees, and as the centurion turned to follow his hand he realised that a murk was hanging over the distant hills, a thick column of smoke rising from the forest to feed its bulk. Turning to his right he peered over the trees that surrounded the derelict fort on three sides, starting at the sight of several thinner plumes of smoke across the southern horizon. The disfigured hunter spoke again, a note of triumphant glee in his voice.

'Forts that guard wall on fire, thief! You army run, leave Venicone people as masters here! No rescue for you, thief, you friend kill by fire in forest and you army run away to south.' He held out a hand. 'Throw down what you steal and I let you go. You run quick, perhaps you live. Or I keep you trap here, until Brem come and kill you all. He kill you all slow, thief, take many days, make you bleed for kill his son!' Marcus stared down at him from behind the shield, his gaze playing bleakly across the smouldering wall fort and the ground between them and the Venicones before him as the scarred man called out again, pressing his apparent advantage home in a triumphant tone. 'You surrender me, Roman, I give chance to run!'

The young centurion leaned forward over the wall, his harsh voice cutting across the Venicone's threats.

'You were right, Venicone, there *is* a better view to be had from these walls. And yes, I do see smoke to the south, the destruction of our forts which tells me that the legions have indeed been ordered to abandon them, but that is not *all* that I see. Your own doom approaches from the south, carried on swift hoofs that I would imagine you might hear if you could only shut your mouth for long enough to listen.'

The hunter spun to stare towards the burning pyre of Lazy Hill, his head cocked to one side, and after a moment the distant drumbeats of horses on the move reached them. From Marcus's elevated viewpoint he could see a score of horsemen cantering along the forest's edge towards him, and as he watched them a single long horn note rang out across the landscape as the cavalrymen spotted fresh prey. He leaned over the wall and shouted down at the dithering Venicones, pointing to the north.

'Run, Venicone, run now before my brothers ride you down and spit you like the animals you are!'

While the hunters were still staring at the oncoming riders, Arminius and Lugos stormed out of the fort's empty gateway bellowing their challenges from behind shields taken from the dead Vixens, and at the sight of their blood-soaked clothing and weapons the remaining Vixens turned and ran in panic, away from the forest in which they might have taken shelter and into the paths of the oncoming cavalrymen. The scarred warrior stared up at Marcus for a moment before drawing his sword and turning to face the oncoming riders, but if he hoped to take any of them with him into eternity his ambition was short lived. While the rest of his men rode down the fleeing women and speared them swiftly and mercilessly to death, Silus leaned out of his saddle and hacked the heavy blade of his spatha across the hunter's back, felling him to lie lifeless on the wet ground before cantering up to the fort and sheathing his blade at the sight of Marcus atop the gate, shaking his head at the sight of the two barbarians' exhausted bravado.

'Fuck me, and I thought we'd had a rough time of it! You three look like men who've been to the gates of Hades and back! Where's the rest of your party?'

Arminius sheathed his sword with slow, weary movements, looking up at the decurion through eyes slitted with exhaustion.

'Hacked to pieces for the most part, although the big man here did drown one of them to stop him from putting a curse on us.'

Silus cocked his head at Marcus who had climbed down from the wall and walked out to join them.

'They're *all* dead? Only you three made it out?'

Arminius shook his head with a mirthless laugh.

'Arabus still lives, but he's not quite the man he was. A small part of him will always remain here . . .'

Silus looked down at him quizzically, but his enquiry as to the German's meaning was cut off by Marcus's urgent question.

'What about the cohort?'

The decurion shook his head.

'No idea. We were forced to head west by the fire that Julius started when they were ambushed—'

'We started the fire? Whose idea was that?'

'Ours, as it happens, and if they've survived it's probably been the saving of them. We made to ride around the Frying Pan's southern rim only to find ourselves overtaking two thousand angry-looking barbarians who're heading the same way with the evident aim of cutting off any survivors that might have made it through the forest.'

Marcus looked at him with fresh respect.

'You rode back up here, even though there's no way to escape if the Venicones block the road south of the wall?'

Silus shrugged.

'I was struck with an irrational urge to hear that song your mules like to sing about us just one time more before I die.'

Arminius looked up at him, shaking his head in disgust.

'Irrational. That's one word for it, I suppose.'

'Doesn't look like much, does it?'

Tribune Scaurus turned the eagle over, examining the dents and scrapes that it had suffered over the two hundred years of its life. He was standing with Julius at the head of the Tungrian column, although this was little more than a thousand-pace-long row of soldiers lying on both sides of the rough track that bordered the forest this far north of the wall, most of them taking the opportunity to sleep after their exertions of the previous few hours.

'The damage you mean?'

Julius nodded, pointing at a long scratch on the underside of the bird's left wing, revealed by the careful removal of the dried blood that had coated the standard's surface.

'Surely there's no need for something that important to look like something a scrap merchant would turn his nose up at?'

Scaurus shook his head briskly, looking down at the eagle in his hands.

'You're missing the point, First Spear. Of course it would be easy enough to polish out that scratch, but this is not only a symbol of imperial power, but of that power's longevity. We've ruled the lands around the Mediterranean Sea for hundreds of years, and subjugated the greatest powers the world has ever seen. Greece, Egypt, Carthage, the Gauls, the Persians, they've all been ground into the dust under our boots no matter the losses we've taken in the process, and the Sixth Legion's eagle has been witness to over two hundred years of that history. That bird was first blessed by Caesar's nephew Octavian, the man we now call the divine Augustus, and it was present at the battle of Actium that sealed his victory over the usurper Marc Anthony. It looked down on Galba when he was declared emperor in the Sixth's camp in defiance of Nero, much good that did him mind you. It screamed its silent defiance at the Batavians when they revolted on the Rhenus and had to be put down in a welter of blood, and it marched to war in the conquest of Dacia under Trajan. If that battered and scratched bird could talk, First Spear, it would have tales to tell that would leave us both wide-eyed at the glory it has seen and horrified at the shame it has suffered since its capture.'

He looked up at Julius.

'Our duty is to ensure that it remains out of barbarian hands, either by fighting our way through to safety or by hiding it beyond any risk of its being discovered if that proves impossible. Which sounds like the more likely eventuality to me, given the decurion's report.'

Silus had ridden in with what remained of the raiding party

half an hour before, just as the cohort was straggling exhaustedly out of the forest's eastern side, and if their hearts had been momentarily lifted at the safe return of their battered but triumphant companions, the news he'd brought from the south had dashed their hopes in an instant. Julius nodded darkly, spitting on the ground at his feet.

'The wall garrisons will have been away down the road to the south without ever giving us a second thought, and a line of burning forts will have made that painfully clear to the ink monkeys. We're lucky that Silus managed to get around them to provide us with a warning.'

Scaurus set the eagle down on the ground beside him and turned back to his first spear.

'Agreed. So what now, do you think? Do we run, and probably do little more than put off the inevitable, or make a stand and end up as a hill of corpses?'

Julius shook his head.

'Run? Where can we run? There's a war band to the south, a burned-out forest to the west, an impassable swamp to the east and if we run north the Venicones will hunt us down soon enough, given that we're out of supplies and pretty well exhausted. We'd not even make it to The Fang ahead of them, and believe me, I gave that idea some very serious consideration. We'll just have to stand and fight, although with the numbers they've got it'll be a damned short . . .' He frowned at a figure of a centurion advancing up the column towards them with a determined stride. 'Cocidius spare me, that's all I need.'

Scaurus turned to see what he was looking at, a wry smile creasing his tired face.

'There's something in that man's stride that reminds me of the officer he replaced in command of the Tenth Century. Doubtless it won't be long before he takes to calling us all "little brother" and growing his beard . . . if we live that long.'

Julius waited with his hands on his hips until Dubnus reached them, nodding at his officer's salute.

'You've heard the news, and now you've come to offer your

boys as a sacrifice to delay the Venicones while the rest of us make a run for it, right?'

His brother officer shook his head, refusing to take the bait.

'Running's no use, we need to fight. But not here.'

The tribune raised a quizzical eyebrow at him.

'If not here, Centurion, then where exactly would you suggest we *can* make a stand with any chance of success?'

The big man pointed a finger at the forest.

'Back in there, sir.'

Julius shook his head.

'We're better off out here. At least here we can form a line of sorts, whereas in there they'll mob us from all sides and drag us down like a wolf pack falling on a stag.'

He went to turn away, but found Dubnus's hand on his arm.

'You're wrong, Julius. You're forgetting that you've got a century of very pissed off axe men, or most of one at any rate, and they're all looking for a way to get some revenge on the Venicones.'

'And?'

'And I know how we can turn that into a fighting chance to face the bastards down.'

The first spear turned back to him, looking closely at his officer's face.

'You seriously think that we can hold off that many angry headcases without a formed line?'

Dubnus grinned back at him.

'Give me an hour and I'll give you a line in the middle of the forest that'll hold the bastards off for a lot longer than anything we can do out here.'

Julius nodded slowly, turning back to his tribune.

'You were right, sir, he is turning into Titus before our bloody eyes. Very well, Centurion, whatever it is you have in mind you'd better get on with it. We'll be lucky to get an hour for you to work whatever trick it is that you've got in mind.'

9

Calgus stared up at the burning fort, which the leader of Brem's suddenly more respectful bodyguard had informed him had been named the Latin equivalent of 'Lazy Hill' by the Romans, with a mixture of pride and renewed hope. The pride came from the fact that his prediction had been accurate as to the invaders' longer-term ability to stick it out at the very edge of their empire, the hope from allowing himself the faintest glimmer of belief that he might still come out of this whole thing with his dream of evicting the Romans from the province intact. He would advise Brem afresh, he mused, advise him to join forces with the tribes to the north of his land, extending to them the promise of enormous wealth if only they added their muscle to that of the newly ascendant Venicones, the tribe that had sent the Romans running and re-conquered their tribal lands south of the wall without even having to fight. The Caledonii, now there was a people with a thirst for revenge if ever he had seen one, still smarting from their defeat by the Roman Agricola a century and more before, and ready to flood south in huge numbers if the right lever were applied to them. A lever like a Roman legion's captured and defiled eagle might just be enough to tempt them to take the field in over-whelming strength and punch through the southern wall as his own people had done two years before, raising the Brigantes people who lived in captivity behind it in revolt once more. With the entire north aflame the Romans would retreat back to their legion fortresses, unless of course his forces – for by then the rebel army would surely be his once more – managed to isolate and overrun them one at a time and lay the huge riches of the undefended south open to his depredations . . .

Something struck his arm, harder than he would have liked, and the one-time Lord of the Northern Tribes flinched involuntarily, dragging his thoughts back to the present. The king's champion had reined his horse in alongside the mare that Calgus had been given, and pointed wordlessly at the king, who, staring at him through eyes that seemed to burn with anger, gestured to a man standing by his horse, the same hard-faced scout who had managed to ambush the Tungrian horsemen the evening before.

'The time for gazing at a burning Roman fort and dreaming of glory is at an end, adviser, and the time to fight is upon us! My son is *dead*! My scouts found Scar and his Vixens to the north of here, all of them dead save my master of the hunt who was lying helpless with his spine broken. Before they granted him a clean and merciful death he told them that The Fang has been raided by the Romans, the eagle stolen and my son found dead at the hill's foot! My *son*!'

Calgus felt his spirits sink, closing his eyes and slumping back into the mare's saddle.

'They have the eagle?'

Brem snorted furiously.

'Not for long! I'll run those bastards down and put them to the spear! Any that survive will be pegged out for the wolves with their bellies opened! My warriors are seething with anger, mad with the urge to revenge themselves on the men that burned their brothers in the forest, and I'll send them north like a pack of dogs with the smell of blood in their nostrils!'

Calgus fought to stop himself cringing at the mention of the ambush he had suggested setting along the track that ran through the western end of the hills' bowl. Men were still straggling in from the forest's edge, but painfully few of them, and for every warrior who appeared out of the trees ready to fight, another two staggered up to their brothers with such serious burns that many of them appeared unlikely to survive, much less take any active part in any fighting. Few men had escaped the inferno without losing hair and beards, and those warriors who seemed fit to fight stood together in twos and threes, their hollow eyes silent witness to the shock they had suffered when, as it seemed from their stories, the encircled Romans had set fire to the forest and bludgeoned their way out of the trap that had been laid for them, effectively destroying several of the tribe's clans in the process. He forced himself to focus on what the king was saying, a tiny part of his mind still musing on the potential for his dream of leading a coalition of tribes to liberate the province, with himself at its head and Brem's part no more than a line in the great songs that would be sung for Calgus the Red, liberator of the Britons, for generations to come. The king clenched his fist, roaring a challenge at the men gathered around him.

'We must find these men and destroy them before they can escape into the forest and we lose our chance to revenge ourselves upon them!'

The Selgovae's brow furrowed.

'My lord King, surely we can leave them to stew in the cauldron of their own forging? They must by now have exhausted whatever rations they carried with them, and they will have been through the same ordeal by fire that has so horribly burned our own men. Why not simply bottle them up and wait for them to surrender? After all, any chance of their being rescued by the men that were camped along the wall has just marched south . . .'

He stopped talking as the king shook his head, his face set hard. When he spoke his voice was the harsh bark of a man set upon violence.

'Perhaps you can ignore the pain that these invaders have inflicted on me, Calgus, but I *cannot*! They killed my son, cut him down and threw him from the mountain as he fought to defend our fortress! No, they must be made to pay for the havoc they have visited upon my family and my people! I will lead my warriors to victory over them, grind their last scraps of resistance into the dirt and take their heads for my walls. I will prove that I am fit to be king by taking my revenge upon these invaders!' The men around him nodded their agreement, and Brem shook his head at his adviser with a derisive sneer. 'And besides, it is not the way of *my* tribe to shrink from battle when the enemy flaunts his presence on our land!' He stared levelly at him. 'Perhaps it is different for the Selgovae?'

Calgus laughed bitterly.

'No different, my lord King, no different at all. Less than two years ago I stood on the battlefield listening to a man who played much the same role for me that I play for you now tell me just the same thing. My people would not tolerate leaving a single cohort of auxiliaries alive on a battlefield slick with the blood of half a legion, he told me. My warriors would think less of me if I were to do the sensible thing and leave them to stand and stare while we left the field with the legion's eagle, and the head of its leader. And so I sent my men up a hill to take their heads, only to watch as their attack broke that cohort's line like bloody waves upon a beach. And just as my men were finally getting to the point of overrunning that sorry, tattered last cohort, two fresh legions arrived on their flanks and put them to flight in an instant. My acceptance of that advice cost me thousands of warriors, ridden down and trampled as they fled from the legions' bloody revenge, and I learned a bitter lesson, never to attack the Romans when they have time to prepare their defences. And Brem, just in case you doubt my story, it might help to add one more small piece of detail.'

He paused, shaking his head at the irony of the situation.

'That cohort that managed to hold up my tribe's attack until the legions could bring their terrible strength to bear? None other than the same cohort that we have at our mercy now, if only we have the discipline to wait for them to either surrender or make one last futile attempt to break through to the south. The same cohort that will surely kill your warriors in great numbers if you seek to attack them on ground of their own choosing.'

Brem shook his head again, waving a dismissive hand as if to push aside the Selgovae's argument.

'You don't listen well, do you Calgus? I can still muster over two thousand spears even with the losses that we took in the forest, enough men to roll over a few hundred tired and hungry soldiers, I'd say.' He raised his voice, challenging the clan leaders gathered around him. 'We go to fight, my brothers! We'll advance until we find our enemy, use our numbers to pin them down on all sides, and then pull them to pieces at our leisure. Our swords and spears will show these invaders what it means to enrage the Venicone people! Bring me my crown!'

The gathered nobles erupted into a riot of cheering acclaim, their fists punching the air as Brem put the circle of gold upon his head and bellowed orders to his men to follow him, jerking his head at his champion with a curled lip and a glance at Calgus. The grinning warrior took the mare's bridle in his hand and then kicked his own horse forward to join Brem's, pulling Calgus's mount along beside him as the remaining mounted bodyguards closed in around them, knotting the mare's reins to the saddle of the king's massive war horse. Led by the royal party the war band formed into one dense mass and followed closely behind their ruler, their voices raised in the old songs of battle and victory, bellowing their imprecations at the sky as they worked themselves up into a killing frenzy.

Watching the ground before them carefully as he rode behind Brem, Calgus was the first to notice the horsemen cantering towards them when they were still a thousand paces or so distant from the war band. At five hundred paces, as the king's bodyguard were growling to be set loose upon the incoming horsemen, the enemy riders pulled up abruptly, each of them shedding a second man from his beast's back. The dismounted men hurried forward another few paces, forming an orderly line and standing immobile for a moment until a command made almost inaudible by the distance set them into action. Raising their arms they sent a flickering flight of arrows high into the air, the missile's iron heads glittering in the sunlight as they hung for a moment at the highest point of their trajectories before plunging earthwards. Whipping down into the mass of warriors, their impact excited a roar of anger and fear beyond the few casualties inflicted, and the king turned in his saddle to bellow an order for shields to be raised, the men to either side of him having already leaned out of their saddles to put their boards between him and the threat.

Another volley fell, and a few more men were struck down as those that had shields raised them over their heads to protect themselves and those around them close enough to huddle underneath.

'Delaying tactics!' Brem fumed, pointing at the archers and raising his voice to shout over the war band's hubbub. 'Charge them down, my bro—'

He jerked sideways with the impact of an arrow in his left side, and as Calgus's horse shied back a half-step another shot flew past him, close enough that he knew he too had been a target for the men who had waited in the trees to ambush them with such skill. The king slumped over his horse's neck, and Calgus responded the only way he knew, instinctively snapping a command at the closest of the clan leaders gathered behind them and pointing at the forest's edge.

'Send men into the trees! Root out those archers and have them track our progress along the forest edge to prevent any more ambushes!'

The noblemen responded without question, and Calgus urged his horse forward into the protection of the shields that had been raised by the king's bodyguards. Brem had managed to force his body back into an upright position, panting with the pain and shock as he stared at a blood-covered hand.

'Fool . . . to have . . . fallen for that . . . old trick.'

He put the hand back to his side, shut his eyes in anticipation of the pain to come and swiftly snapped off the arrow's shaft where it protruded from his wound. Swaying in the saddle, he would clearly have fallen if not for the strong hands to either side. The Selgovae waited until his eyes opened again, nodding dour respect at the king's resolve.

'Can you continue, my lord King?'

Brem nodded, his face white with shock.

'I have no choice. You men –' he gestured to the bodyguards to either side of his horse '– hold me up. Try not to make it look –' a racking cough shook the king's body, and he coughed a wad of bloody phlegm on the animal's neck '– too obvious.

And march faster. I do not know how long I will be able to stand this pain.'

Their task of distraction complete, the enemy archers re-mounted behind the horsemen who had carried them to their shooting position and cantered away, vanishing into the trees a thousand paces or so further to the north.

'Kind of them to show us the way to wherever it is that they've taken refuge.'

Calgus nodded distractedly at the king's painfully grunted statement.

'Indeed so, my lord King. Although I cannot help wondering why they would choose to face such overwhelming superiority in numbers in the forest, where we will be able to surround them and attack from all sides.'

Brem coughed again, a bubbling, half retch, and spat blood onto the ground to leave his lips flecked with red, and his eyes wide in a face pale with pain.

'I care little. We find them, we crush them, and then I will bear the ordeal of this arrow's removal.'

The path down which the archers had made their way back to their fellows was clear enough, already trampled wide and flat by the passage of hundreds of men, and Brem bent stiffly to look down from his horse with a bitter, painful laugh.

'No deception this time, I see, just . . .'

He fell silent, cocking his head to listen. In the distance, the sound almost inaudible, they could hear the sound of axes striking wood, so many axes that the noise was a continuous hammering. With a creaking tear a tree fell, the noise of its impact with the forest floor lost beneath the continuous racket of chopping, and Calgus smiled to himself at the realisation of what the Tungrians were doing.

'They will use trees as walls.'

Brem spat again, his mouth a sour gash in his face's white mask.

'It makes no difference. We will overwhelm them like hunting wolves. No wall can protect them from my fury –' He coughed again. 'For no wall can be long enough to prevent our washing around it to tear them apart. Onward!'

The warriors surged around them, fanning out on either side of the path with their weapons and shields ready to fight, and all the while they advanced into the forest's dim green light the noise of axes hewing on wood continued, the unmistakable sound of trees falling seeming to reach Calgus's ears with every few steps that his mare took. As the sound of the chopping grew louder the trees began to fall less frequently, until the war band crested a ridge and found the place where their enemies had chosen to make their stand. Calgus stared over the heads of the warriors surging round and past the small knot of horsemen protecting their wounded king with a half-smile. From his position, hunched white-faced over his horse's neck, the king saw the expression flicker into life, and his voice was weak and peevish when he summoned the strength to speak.

'What's so fucking funny, Calgus?'

The Selgovae replied without taking his gaze off the spectacle before him, shaking his head slowly.

'I could never have predicted it, and yet it's just so obvious, my lord King. The enemy have constructed a line that your men will never outflank.'

Before them in the clearing below the Tungrian axe men had formed a great circle, almost two hundred paces across, it seemed, and had then felled every tree around its circumference so that they had fallen into the circle with their tops pointing to its middle. Almost the entire perimeter of their impromptu stockade was refused easy access by the interlocked branches of the fallen trees, and where there were gaps that the axe men had failed to fill the Tungrians were already waiting four and five men deep, their lines formed and ready to fight.

'I have no doubt that we can defeat these tired, hungry men, my lord King, but I also have no doubt that they will make us pay a stiff price for the pleasure. Are you sure that you wouldn't prefer the cheaper option of starving them out over a day or two?'

Brem shook his head, still unable to raise his head into an upright position, his voice even weaker than before.

'Never. Why should I risk the eagle being smuggled away in the night when I can have every man down there dead before the sun sets? Why allow the man who killed my son the chance of escape from my retribution? No! Sound the horns! I will recover that eagle if it is my last act before I go to meet my ancestors.'

'They're coming then.'

Julius nodded, watching the Venicones pour over the lip of the ridge from which he could see the mounted royal party staring down at their improvised defences, the barbarians cheering at each sounding of their horns, shouting insults and threats at the waiting soldiers.

'You didn't expect them to be frightened off by a few trees?'

Scaurus shrugged, looking about the circular space in which his men were preparing to make their stand.

'I had wondered if good sense would prevail. If the positions were reversed I'd be more than happy to wait for them to realise that without food or water they have no choice but to surrender.'

Julius shook his head.

'Not these boys.'

The tribune sighed.

'No. It was always a bit of a false hope. At least Dubnus and his men have allowed us the chance to go down fighting with a little pride, rather than simply being mobbed and ripped apart without much of a chance to let those bastards know they've been in a fight.' He drew his sword. 'I suggest that you take command of the reserve, First Spear, and be ready to hurry them into whichever of the gaps in our defence the tattooed buggers manage to breach first. I'll just wander around and see what good I can be wherever the fighting gets a little warm, if that's all right with you?'

Calgus stared impassively down as the first of the war band's warriors charged into the Tungrians' defences, hundreds of warriors streaming towards a ten-pace-wide gap between two fallen trees at the urging of their clan leaders.

'Good choice.'

'What was that?'

He turned to the king.

'I said *"good choice"*, my lord King. Your men are striking the weakest point in the enemy's defence, throwing themselves into the attack with the ferocity that will be needed if we are to break open this improvised fortress. You can be proud of them Brem, they are spending their lives lavishly in the hope of giving you victory.'

A victory to make your passing a little less sour, he mused, *and to lighten the blow of your having died without an heir. I'll play the role of the disinterested statesman to the hilt, I think, and seek to arbitrate between the various claimants to the throne whilst strength-ening my position with them all to the point where no matter who wins I will be seen as an indispensable adviser. And if the Tungrians managed to take the eagle then presumably they will have put an end to that bloody priest and his predictions of death. The son, the prince and death, indeed? It seems that what he saw was only your death, Brem, as it turned out . . .*

The king suddenly sat up bolt upright, staring down at the battle raging below him. He was sweating profusely, his left side dark and wet with the blood that continued to stream from the arrow wound in his side, but his face was set hard in remorseless lines, as if he had been granted a last moment of lucidity and strength by the gods.

'I see the place where our breakthrough will be made!'

In the gap between two fallen trees Marcus's Fifth Century were fighting for their lives against the mass of barbarians seeking to push them back into the circle, their front rank a dozen men wide, each of them stabbing into the tightly packed Venicones with his sword whenever the opportunity presented itself, their shields scored and notched by enemy blades. Another fifty soldiers were packed in tightly behind them, all of them wielding spears over the front rankers' shoulders to punch the sharp points into the faces and throats of the men facing them. While the Romans' discipline and training enabled them to pull their wounded back through the ranks, the Venicones who fell to their attacks had nowhere to go but down into the foaming blood- and urine-soaked morass beneath the two sides' feet, their attempts to crawl out of the fray adding to the chaos in the war band's ranks as they raged at the Tungrian line. A warrior climbed up onto the tree trunk to the century's right, raising his axe and bellowing a challenge at the men below him, then toppled backwards into the branches with an arrow in his chest, shot by one of the Hamians standing behind the straining century.

'*Push!*'

Quintus had cast his chosen man's staff aside and thrown himself into the struggle with a spear taken from a wounded man, stabbing it repeatedly into the barbarian horde even as he took an involuntary step backwards, his feet sliding through the mud as the Venicones' superior numbers started to tell against the tiring Tungrians.

'A little help seems to be in order here, eh Centurion?'

Marcus turned to find the tribune standing beside him with his sword drawn, but before he could answer Scaurus had swivelled to shout an order at Julius.

'First Spear! Reinforcements are required here!'

Brem pointed down at the circle of trees, and Calgus saw what it was that he was indicating. In the spot that Calgus had seen the tribesmen attack, the Romans were starting to weaken, falling back one step at a time as Brem's warriors pushed them off their ground in the gap between the two trees through simple strength of numbers. A moment before their line had been no more than a dozen paces from the stumps of the trees that formed the battleground's flanks, but now the distance was more like twenty. As the royal party watched, soldiers ran from both sides to reinforce their comrades, sent in groups of six to eight from the centuries that were under less pressure, the officers standing behind the embattled century ordering them into action in support of their men. With a roar that the men on the ridge heard clearly enough they stopped the retreat and started to press the Venicones back. The reinforced Romans seemed to gain fresh purpose, chanting in time as they smashed forward into the war band, battering the warriors backwards with their shields and stepping over the Venicones' dead and wounded, swords and spears stabbing down to finish off the men crawling helplessly in the mud beneath them.

'*No!*'

Brem turned to the leader of his bodyguard.

'Now is the time, my brother, time for me to face the enemy in battle and inspire my people to rip into these invaders until they are no more. Take me to the fight!'

The warrior nodded, looking about him at the rest of the king's guard and jerking his head at the fight below them.

'You heard the king! We fight!'

The mounted men roared their approval, and with a sudden start Calgus realised that his horse's bridle was still tied to the king's saddle.

'But—'

The word was barely out of his mouth before the royal party was in motion, moving down off the ridge and trotting towards the spot that the king had indicated would be the point of decision. Calgus's horse lurched into movement, compelled to accompany Brem's by its tether, and the Selgovae bit his tongue with the first jerk, the sudden pain reducing his protests to a thick mumble. Brem drew his sword, his hand steadied by that of the man riding alongside him, and the guards around him did the same, their weapons gleaming dully in the forest's dim light. The king somehow managed to find the strength to raise himself out of the saddle, lifting the sword high and shouting a battle cry loud enough for the warriors packed into the breach to hear him.

'For Drust! Revenge for King Drust!'

The Venicones responded with a great howl of anger, pushing back against the Tungrian line with a sudden explosive shove that rocked the Romans back by five paces in an instant, and Calgus realised that the king's intervention just might succeed. It was time to play the role that the king had decreed for him, and to remake himself into a credible member of the tribe's nobility once the king was dead.

'You promised me a sword, my lord King!'

Brem nodded at his men, and a heavy length of polished iron with a bright edge was passed to him. Waving the sword in a suitably warlike manner and roaring as if gripped by a ferocious anger, Calgus nudged his mare's sides with his booted feet, urging her up alongside the king to bring him shoulder to shoulder with Brem.

'We fight at your command, my lord King! See, the enemy line is weakening! One more push and they will surely fold!'

In the middle of the Tungrian circle Julius turned to Dubnus and pointed at the Venicone horsemen who were nearing the rear of the crush of men that was threatening to break into the defences.

'I've held you monsters back long enough, it seems. Now's your chance to show Titus's boys what you're made of, I'd say.'

He'd found it hard not to smile when he had joined the Tenth Century in the centre of the circle a few moments before, amused by the way that their new centurion was sitting on a rock in the middle of his men with a small but very clear gap around him on all sides. Where Titus would have been at the very heart of his century's press of men, his growl of a voice inspiring them to the acts of mayhem they would shortly be wreaking upon their enemies, Dubnus was clearly still a man apart. The events of the previous hour had proven that he could command the pioneers, but their attitude towards him was clearly still one of tolerance rather than respect. Dubnus got to his feet, taking a handful of dirt and rubbing it into his hands to dry the fluid that was still leaking from his blisters, the result of taking his turn in the frantic rush to complete the defences that had been his conception.

'Tenth Century, on your feet!'

The pioneers got up from where they were resting after their exertions, a few of them copying their new centurion's manner of drying his hands. Dubnus looked about him, nodding slowly at what he saw.

'That's more like it! Now you look like men who are ready to take their revenge on the bastard who ordered the ambush that led to Titus's death! Who's ready to come with me and kill their king?!'

One of the larger men in the century stepped forward, looking down at his centurion and then across the circle at the heaving press of men that stood between them and the horsemen at the rear of the barbarians.

'I am! But how are we going to get at him, with that lot in the way?'

Dubnus grinned at him, and the pioneer's eyes narrowed at the sudden glint of insanity in his new officer's eyes.

'That's easy enough, if you've got the balls for it!' He raised his voice to a parade-ground bellow, loud enough for every man inside the circle of trees to hear him. 'Tenth Century, if you want revenge for Titus, follow me! If any of you isn't man enough then stay here, and regret missing the chance for the rest of your miserable, snivelling lives! *For Titus!*'

He sprang across the clearing towards the barbarians, and for an instant his men stared after him with sheer amazement before the man he had challenged raised his voice in an equally berserk roar, running after his officer with his axe raised over his head.

'For Titus! Follow the Prince!'

Suddenly the entire century was in furious motion, the soldiers pumping their legs with all their might as they strove to catch up with their centurion, shouts of *'Titus!'* and *'The Prince!'* rending the air. In his place behind the Fifth Century Marcus saw the pioneers flooding towards him with his friend at their head, but as he opened his mouth to welcome them to the fight the big man winked at him and leapt up onto the tree to his right, running up the trunk's inclined surface as quickly as he could. His men followed, more of them climbing onto the tree to the Fifth's left, and the young centurion's faced creased with amazement as he realised exactly where it was that Dubnus was leading his men. Julius had joined him and Scaurus at the rear of the embattled century, and met his tribune's amazed glance with a shrug.

'Surely he isn't going to . . . ?'

The first spear drew his sword, spitting on the churned ground.

'He bloody well is! It'll either end in victory or kill us all, but he's just shown us our one chance to mount a counter-attack! So, shall we join him?'

Calgus didn't realise what was happening until the trees to either side of the frantic pushing match for the gap began to shake, their branches quivering beneath the weight of the heavy axe men as they stormed up the trunks' gentle incline. With a wild yell the first of them, an officer to judge from the crest across his helmet, threw himself from the very end of his tree, his arms and legs flung back as he flew through the air towards the royal party. For an instant the Selgovae's world was reduced to the murderous expression on the leaping man's face, his eyes pinned wide and his teeth bared in a snarl of bestial ferocity. He was still marvelling at the Tungrian's apparent insanity when the big man dropped to the ground a dozen paces from them, rolled once and spun to his left, laying about himself with the big axe in his right hand and smashing tribesmen from his path with the shield's iron boss, another man leaping from the tree behind him and immediately springing to his officer's side. Within a few heartbeats there were ten of the axe-wielding monsters in the very heart of the war band with more of them jumping into the fight with every second, big men, beyond big, hulking giants who seemed set on painting themselves red with Venicone blood and were going about it at a rage-fuelled pace, hacking their way out from their landing places in all directions in a flurry of heavy axe blades that felled one or two men with every blow.

The closest of the king's bodyguards to the fray fell from his horse, and Calgus realised that the animal had been unceremoniously decapitated, the warrior dying in a froth of blood from a huge chest wound while he was still struggling to free himself from beneath the beast's dead weight. The man who had killed him stood for a moment with his legs astride the still-warm corpse, raising the axe's red blade to the sky and howling his triumph as blood rained down on his face and armour. Leaning forward, Calgus cut the mare's reins free of Brem's saddle, quailing as the king turned and raised his sword with an incoherent cry of rage as he realised that the Selgovae meant to flee. Before the blow could land the wounded king lurched back in his saddle with an arrow protruding from his chest, and Calgus realised that there were archers on the trees to either side of the war band, perhaps thirty of them pouring arrows into the packed mass of warriors as fast as they could. He ducked as low as possible, watching as the king toppled stiffly over his horse's side and fell beneath the hoofs of the remaining animals. Unable to reach the dangling remnant of the mare's reins he grabbed its right ear and pulled the graceful head round, trying to turn the beast away from the fight, but the horse was still wedged between the dead king's mount and the men jostling around them.

The axe men were fighting in a more disciplined manner now, and their initial mad charge into the battle's heart had given way to a tight formation organised around the lead of their centurion. Forming a two-sided line they were hewing at both the tribesmen trapped between them and the circle's defenders and those warriors attempting to rescue their comrades, chanting three words over and over as they hacked their way into the battered tribesmen. It took a moment for him to realise exactly what it was that they were shouting, the chant gradually rising in pitch and volume as the other soldiers took it up, bellowing the words as they stormed into the fight.

'*Titus! The Prince! Titus! The Prince!*'

The Selgovae's blood ran cold at the realisation of what it was that he was hearing, and he redoubled his efforts to back his horse away from the crush of men as the Tungrians, further reinforced by a continual stream of men along the two fallen trees, tightened their stranglehold on the trapped and increasingly helpless Venicones, while the axe-wielding giants fought to keep the rush of men seeking to rescue their brothers at bay. With a last frantic effort he persuaded the mare to back away from the embattled king's guard, as they fought for the body of their dead ruler, praying harder than he had ever prayed for them to ignore him as he turned the beast away from the fight and kicked its flanks to spur it up the ridge, and to the safety of the open forest. Looking back he saw a Roman officer with two swords fight his way out of the fray and stare after him, and he grinned as he recognised the dead legatus's son, the man who had so cruelly cut his ankle tendons and left him for dead on the occasion of their last meeting. Turning in his saddle he shouted back at the Roman, his voice shaking with the closeness of his escape.

'Not this time, Centurion! This time I—'

The mare started at the blare of a horn, and Calgus whipped his head round to look up the slope's incline at the men who were staring impassively back down at him, their line stretching across his field of vision in both directions. One of them pointed with his sword, shouting a command at the line of armoured soldiers that left no room for any doubt in Calgus's mind.

'Sixth Legion, *advance!*'

He dragged the mare's head around and kicked its flanks, only to find himself abruptly and shockingly face down on the forest floor, too stunned by the impact of his fall to do anything but lie helpless while his mount kicked and spasmed in its death throes with a spear buried deep in its neck. The wall of advancing legionaries parted to either side of the dying horse, and the helpless Selgovae watched numbly as the vengeful centurion walked easily up the rise to meet them, clasping hands with the officer who had ordered them forward before staring down at the fallen barbarian leader impassively. His face and hands were covered in lacerations and scrapes, a cut which had barely crusted over decorating the line of his cheek and nose.

'Prefect Castus. You've arrived just in time to help us mop up the remnants, it seems.'

The older man laughed, looking out over the bloody battlefield as the embattled tribesmen were herded into an ever-decreasing pocket of space, swords and spears stabbing into them from all sides.

'I don't know how Rutilius Scaurus managed it, but by the

gods below it's nothing less than a miniature Cannae! Only this time it's not Romans being slaughtered!'

The centurion smiled grimly.

'Just this once the tribune had little to do with the outcome. This was mostly the work of a centurion called Titus.'

Castus smiled delightedly.

'That enormous axe-wielding colleague of yours? In that case I'll buy him a flask of wine and drink his health until we both fall off our chairs!'

The centurion put a hand to the hilt of his sword, his fingers caressing something tied onto the weapon with fine silver wire.

'That won't be possible, I'm afraid. He died earlier today, may our Lord for ever watch over him.'

Castus shook his head sadly.

'A shame. He was a proper fighting man from the look of him, and the likes of him get fewer every year, or so it seems to me. We'll drink to him in any case, you and I, and all of your Tungrian officers. Here I was thinking that I was ending my career in a blaze of glory to lead the legion to your rescue, and yet all the time you were putting it to the barbarians in fine style! Mind you, it was lucky that these hairy buggers left a trail from Lazy Hill that my woman could have followed, and luckier still that I was the officer entrusted with the order to pull the legions back from the frontier and back to the southern wall.'

Scaurus walked up the slope, grinning insouciantly at the prone and scowling Calgus.

'Prefect Castus, never has your presence afforded me quite so much pleasure! Pleasure that is in no way lessened by the alarming irregularity of your presence north of the frontier with such a large body of soldiers. I presume you have a good reason for such blatant disregard of your orders?'

The older man grinned, and took his offered arm in a firm clasp.

'I think we'll put this small deviation from the withdrawal timetable down to what I believe our betters would term "the exploitation of a local opportunity". Which is to say that I spotted the opportunity to give the locals one last spanking before we leave them to enjoy their swamps in peace for ever. Presumably I've managed to assist you in rescuing my legion's eagle?'

Scaurus nodded.

'Battered, abused and only recently washed clean of the blood of our captured soldiers, but yes, your pride is restored.'

The prefect smiled knowingly.

'Excellent! In which case you'll be as amused as I was to hear that one of Fulvius Sorex's centurions has already rescued the Sixth's eagle from a hiding place among the Brigantes people, barely a day's march from Yew Grove and unexpectedly close to home. It would appear that the rumours that it was to be found among the Venicones were nothing more than barbarian lies, intended to lure your cohort onto their ground for destruction. Funny how things turn out, isn't it? Now, shall we crucify this man here and now, or take him somewhere a little more public before nailing him up?'

The Tungrians were in surprisingly good spirits when they marched into Yew Grove a week later, considering that once again they had marched south without diverting to their home on the wall built by the emperor Hadrian. Sanga was still nursing a set of bruised knuckles, incurred during a short and painful session on the subject of promise-keeping for the Fort Habitus stone mason who, it was clear by the absence of the altar to his dead friend when the cohort had arrived at the fort's gate, badly needed to be taught a lesson. His purse was bulging with the money that he had paid the mason and a substantial amount more in enforced compensation for there being no sign of any memorial to Scarface, and in the dead of night, when his tent mates were all asleep, he had promised his dead friend's shade that he would erect a bigger and better stone somewhere fitting at the first opportunity.

The cohort had been marched into the fortress to join the Second Tungrian Cohort in the unexpected luxury of an empty stretch of barracks blocks, where they quickly discovered that, much to their disgust, their sister cohort had sat and waited in the German port until only a week before. While the two units reacquainted themselves, drank, bickered, and in a few cases indulged in inconclusive and swiftly punished fist fights over which of them was the better, the harder or simply the luckier of the two, Scaurus made his way to Prefect Castus's house in the vicus in the company of Julius and Marcus. The prefect, who had ridden south before them to prepare the way for the return of four cohorts to the fortress, opened the door and ushered them through the hall and into the dining room while putting a hand on the first spear's chest.

'Not you, First Spear. You, my friend, should turn right, not left.'

Julius looked to his superior, but Scaurus simply smiled enigmatically and extended a hand to indicate the bedroom door. The baffled first spear followed his direction, making his way through the doorway while Marcus and the tribune walked into the dining room as directed. The young centurion had no sooner entered the room than he found himself rocked backwards by the impact of his wife flying into his arms. Opening his mouth to greet her he closed it again when he realised that she was in floods of tears, sobbing incoherently into his chest. Looking about him in puzzlement he found an explanation in Castus's swift interjection.

'Your wife was assaulted by Tribune Sorex while you were away. The bastard's attempt to rape her was frustrated by an old friend . . .' He gestured to a man sitting quietly in a corner of the room, and Marcus's face split in a broad smile as he recognised his former prefect, Legatus Equitius.

'It was lucky that I came along when I did, and that I'd managed to keep my bodyguard despite my being relieved of command. I sent the evil young bastard on his way before he had the chance to do too much damage, but your woman will undoubtedly need as much love and care as you can provide for a while.'

Marcus nodded, wrapping his arms around his wife and shooting Scaurus a glance laden with pure, undiluted murderous intent. The tribune nodded his understanding, but raised a hand to forestall the comment he expected from the younger man.

'I know, you want to take your iron to him, but I think it better if we stay with our original plan. I don't want the way we address the problem of Tribune Sorex to be changed in any way from what we agreed, or our freedom to act will be significantly hampered. Take some time to reassure your wife, Centurion, and we'll make our way to the headquarters once the lamps have been lit for an hour.'

He turned to the door, smiling at the sight of Julius holding his daughter in his arms with the look of a man utterly besotted. Annia was close behind him, her expression one of relieved delight at the sight of her man having accepted the delivery of a girl with such eagerness.

'Well now, First Spear, it seems that you two are now three. Congratulations! Do the two of you have a name for the child?'

Annia opened her mouth, but found herself cut off by her husband's powerful voice.

'My beautiful daughter will be called Victoria, in honour of the legion that's based in the place of her birth. I expect that she'll grow into a strapping young woman, and I will teach her the skills that will enable her never to go in fear of any man.'

Scaurus smiled again, watching with amusement as Annia's eyes narrowed behind her husband's back.

'Excellent! And I'm sure that your most highly esteemed woman will take whatever steps are needed to ensure that Victoria retains her femininity while you're busy trying to turn her into a Tungrian! Mind you, she seems to have adopted one Tungrian trait. You've clearly been too long in the field, First Spear, or you might have more of an appreciation for the delicate aroma that child seems to have created.'

Turning, Julius saw his wife's face and twitched slightly, holding the child to her with alacrity.

'Here, you'd better make a start on the feminising.'

Annia stepped backwards and placed her hands behind her back.

'No you don't, you big lump of cock-brained idiocy! You named her without my help, so you can change her without my help!

Consider it as training that will enable you never to go in fear of any shit-caked child's backside . . .'

Later, sitting together while Scaurus and Castus plotted the route that the Tungrians would take when they marched from Yew Grove the following morning, Marcus held his wife's hands while she described Sorex's attack to him.

'Please forgive me, my love, he gave me no choice. He would have murdered Annia and the baby while they were unable to fight back . . .'

Her husband squeezed her hands and kissed her gently on the cheek.

'There's nothing to forgive. How could I think any less of you for protecting our friend and her baby in the only way that was possible. Besides, from what the legatus said he hadn't got very far before he was interrupted.'

Felicia nodded sadly, her finger tracing the line of the half-healed cut across her husband's face.

'Your poor nose. No, he hadn't got very far with me, but he told me that he'd been raping the prefect's woman more or less since he arrived, threatening her with ending his career if she didn't comply.'

Marcus frowned at her.

'Does Artorius Castus know of this?'

'No, and he *mustn't* find out, Marcus, not if you value him as a friend. It would end their relationship, and they clearly love each other deeply. Besides, he would almost certainly confront the tribune.'

'And?'

'And that doesn't sound like the way Tribune Scaurus plans to deal with him. I can assure you that he feels rather more subtlety is called for than might feel appropriate to you soldiers . . .'

'Congratulations, Fulvius Sorex, on your most fortunate retrieval of the legion's eagle. You must be delighted to have struck gold so close to home, so to speak?'

The tribune grinned triumphantly at Scaurus, dipping his head in an acknowledgement of his colleague's praise so shallow that Marcus wondered if the intent was rather to mock Scaurus's words.

'Thank you, Rutilius Scaurus. It was indeed a most serendipitous discovery, given that my only intention was to keep the local tribesmen on their toes now that the army's back on the Emperor Hadrian's wall for good. But they do say that we make our own luck, I believe, and so it has proven here. Had I not ordered such an aggressive patrol routine we might never have tripped over the Sixth Legion's standard in such a fortunate manner, although of course much of the honour must go to Centurion Gynax for his persistence in searching the village in question.'

Scaurus smiled, and the men around him held their silence as he had instructed them to do in the most robust of terms only moments before, swallowing their indignation at Sorex's failure to comment upon their defeat of the Venicones.

'Tell me colleague, were you fortunate enough to discover Legatus Sollemnis's head alongside the eagle?'

Sorex shook his head with an expression of regret.

'I'm afraid not. Possibly it has rotted away by now? After all, I doubt that simply placing a man's head in cedar oil is sufficient to prevent the natural processes of decomposition for more than a few weeks.'

Scaurus smiled back at him for so long that Sorex's smug expression began to perceptibly slip, only turning to address Julius when the superior expression had entirely vanished from the man's face.

'I'll have that first item please, First Spear.'

The burly centurion reached into the bag that he had carried into the headquarters and pulled out the container in which Sollemnis's head was suspended in oil. Removing the wooden lid, he placed the cask on the table in front of his tribune with a grimace at the smell issuing from the dark oil that slopped about inside the wooden drum. Scaurus rolled up the long right sleeve of his tunic, speaking to a baffled Sorex in conversational tones.

'Forgive the mess, but when Centurion Corvus presented me

with this item it was indeed starting to get a little gamey. As you say, the Venicones' habit of drying the heads of their victims over burning wood chips seems to be a far from perfect means of preservation, and so I took the precaution of enhancing its chances of reaching Rome in a recognisable condition. It's by no means a perfect way to prevent part of the human body from rotting away, but it seems to have worked moderately well in this case.' He reached his right hand into the oil and grasped something within it with an expression of mild distaste, pulling it out of the miniature barrel with a careful flourish and scattering drops of the pungent oil across the office's floor. 'Here we are then, the head of a dead legatus restored to some measure of dignity after all it's been through since his death.'

Sorex goggled at the decapitated head as Legatus Sollemnis stared back at him vacantly with eyes whose whites had been dyed black by the oil.

'How can we be sure . . . ?'

'That it's his? I took the liberty of taking the first spear of your Ninth Cohort aside when we arrived, a man we got to know moderately well while we were operating north of the Emperor Antoninus's wall, and a man who in turn knew the legatus as well as anyone, given his routine attendance of Sollemnis's command meetings. He confirmed that this head belonged to the legatus, and pointed out two distinguishing features that you might like to note.'

He pointed to a mole on the dead man's jaw.

'There's this, for a start, and although I realise that's far from being conclusive proof, there's this as well . . .' He turned the head and moved his finger to indicate a long white scar down the right ear. 'Apparently he sustained the cut a year or so before he was killed, sparring with naked iron as it seems was his habit. The first spear tells me it took the bandage carriers hours to stop the wound bleeding.'

He fell silent and waited for Sorex to respond with his eyebrows raised in amused anticipation. The tribune stared at the horrific sight of the legatus's severed head for a moment longer before stammering out a response.

'W-well then . . . it, it seems that I'm doubly fortunate. I've restored the legion's eagle to its rightful place and saved the Sixth Victorious from the ignominy of being disbanded, and you've given Legatus Sollemnis his dignity back in pursuance of my orders. Congratulations Rutilius Scaurus, you've earned a place in the despatch that I shall be sending to Rome in the morning to explain this gratifying turn of events.'

Scaurus smiled again, easing the severed head back down into the oil's greasy embrace and wiping his hand on a towel offered to him by Julius before taking a heavy cloth-wrapped item from his first spear.

'And I'm sure that Praetorian Prefect Perennis will be more than delighted to have his confidence in you repaid. After all –' he weighed the mysterious parcel in both hands before removing the wrappings and placing the rescued eagle onto the table before him '– you seem to have done a masterly job of suborning a previously honourable centurion into your deceit, don't you?'

Sorex goggled at the statue, lovingly polished to a gleaming shine and in every respect the equal of the counterfeit eagle alongside which it sat.

'But that's . . .'

'Yes, it is a bit of a problem, isn't it? Only a week or so ago the Sixth had no eagle, and was facing the ultimate sanction for a legion in such disgrace, and now it has two of the blessed things. It's something of an embarrassment of riches, you might say.'

Sorex tried again.

'That can only be a fake, cobbled together by the Venicones, or by this man Calgus I sent you to catch. Mine is the real eagle!'

Scaurus acknowledged the point with pursed lips.

'I had the same concern, if I'm honest. After all, there was always bound to be benefit to *someone* in making a fake eagle, and I am forced to admit that yours is really rather authentic in appearance. Indeed it's so very close to the one that Centurion Corvus and his men rescued from The Fang in terms of both its construction and finish that I'm driven to assume that it was cast from the original moulds. Moulds which, as I'm sure you know, reside in Rome.'

He waited in silence for a long moment.

'No answer, Tribune? Doubtless you're now considering whether you should unveil *your* eagle to your men as soon as this somewhat embarrassing meeting is concluded, and put it in the hands of a brand new and delighted eagle bearer who you will promote from the ranks of the best and most dedicated soldiers in the legion. The soldiers will be ecstatic at the removal of the shame that's been hanging over them for the last two years, and nobody will be particularly interested in the claims of an obviously embittered auxiliary tribune to be in possession of the genuine article, not when the one you "rescued" from the Brigantes is so obviously genuine.'

Sorex met his colleague's eye at last, and in his angry gaze Marcus could see confirmation of Scaurus's words. The legion tribune stared back at Scaurus for a long moment before shaking his head and raising both hands before him in an apparent appeal to his colleague's understanding.

'What else am I to do, Rutilius Scaurus? I have no choice. Perennis holds the power of life and death over my family, and any failure to follow his instructions will bring disaster on us all. The eagle . . . *my* eagle . . . will be restored to its rightful place in the heart of the legion.'

Scaurus nodded knowingly.

'Which is no more than I expected. And so when the three new legati arrive to take up their commands, they will find exactly what they were told to expect by their master before they rode north from Rome. Three legions camped along the length of the Emperor Hadrian's wall in a nice compact group and with their grievances at being sent north having been neatly addressed by the pull back to this more southerly line of defence. They will find the Sixth Legion still overjoyed at the recapture of its lost eagle, and of course they will find you, as ordered, waiting for them with enough gold to award a donative of two years' pay to every legionary in the country. Am I right?'

Scaurus looked directly into Sorex's indignant stare for a moment before picking up the eagle that had been rescued from

The Fang and turning it over, scanning the metal carefully for the tiny marks and scratches that two centuries of campaigning had inevitably worn into its surface. Putting it down again, he lifted the fake eagle and considered it equally carefully.

'Quite excellent work, and most realistically aged too.' He held up the metal bird, showing the fine patina of age that closely echoed that of the original. 'So, you carried that eagle with you from Rome, with orders to restore the legion's pride, and then you sent my cohort north on what was always intended to be a fruitless hunt after a prize you expected to have vanished in the northern mists long ago. You sent us to chase a rumour in order to carry out the last of your orders from the praetorian prefect, which was to send Centurion Corvus here to his likely death along with the rest of us, with a pair of paid assassins nice and close to him just in case the Venicones didn't look like doing the job. And you did this because of the consequences that you knew would befall your family if you failed to carry through your orders from Rome.'

Sorex stood in silence, his face red with shame.

'Nothing to say, Sorex? In that case I will share a suspicion with you. When these three new legati arrive to take up their commands, I suspect that it will become clear that the man behind the throne has decided to break with tradition. Where the commander of a legion would usually be from the senatorial class, these three will all be equestrians. *Equestrians*, Tribune, men without access to the highest positions in the imperium, men like me and indeed, as you'll be painfully aware, men like Praetorian Prefect Perennis. I'm told that he's already managed to have one of his sons put in command of the Pannonian legions, the best recruiting ground in the entire empire and so very handy for a quick march on the capital. So it's my bet that the army in Britannia will come under equestrian command very shortly now, handed to three men who will have access to a very large amount of gold indeed, all freshly minted. Gold like this . . .'

He tossed a shining gold coin at the tribune, watching as the other man caught it and looked down at the coin nestling in his palm.

'It's an attractive design, if a little unconventional . . .'

'How did you—'

'How did I get this? Camp Prefect Castus has gathered men of dubious but valuable skills to him for as long as I've known him. And when I discovered that he had a highly skilled thief in his retinue, I prevailed upon him to see if the man could provide me with any evidence of my strong suspicions with regard to the contents of those heavy chests that you were there to meet off the boat at Arab Town. You see it's just not usual for legionary pay chests to come from anywhere but Rome, in my experience. The throne likes to gather all imperial funds to itself before distributing a share to the provinces, as a means of ensuring that the only embezzlement which takes place is that which has been officially sanctioned. And so the sight of so much gold coming into the province in such an unorthodox manner piqued my curiosity. Procurator Avus was momentarily distracted by the sight of Centurion Corvus here dealing rather brutally with a pair of Sarmatae swordsmen who had apparently sought to challenge him to a somewhat more robust sparring session than usual, enough time for the now sadly deceased Tarion to lift a coin from his purse and replace it with another. And you can imagine just how many more questions were raised for me when I actually got to take a good look at one of them, and for the camp prefect for that matter. After all, I may only be an equestrian, but even I can put two and two together.'

Sorex shook his head violently, holding up a hand.

'I was simply told to restore the legion's morale with the new eagle. I really had no idea . . .'

Scaurus's voice was flat, devoid of any emotion, but it cut the young prefect off in mid-flow with the power of a slap.

'Oh, but you really *did*, didn't you, what with a fake eagle for you to "discover", and enough gold to buy the loyalty of three legions with three new legati on their way to take command. And lastly, with orders to send my cohort north to its almost certain destruction? Come on Sorex, you knew only too well that you were playing a dangerous game that was intended to provide the manpower for an equestrian coup against the throne, and the senate for that matter. Commodus had abdicated his power to Perennis, and the praetorian prefect sees no reason not to make the arrangement permanent it seems with his sons' Pannonian legions, which I'd guess he will call south once he has confirmation that the Britannia legions are marching on Rome; there'll be no force capable of retaking the capital other than the army in Germania. But then this gold came to Britannia via Germania, which means that the governors of the German provinces have probably agreed to sit on their hands and watch without intervening. And of course the Praetorians will be happy enough to see their leader take full control of the empire, given that he'll doubtless reward them even more handsomely than the common soldiery. Everyone wins, don't they, Fulvius Sorex? I suppose that even your father can expect to have some part in the new regime, once the senate has been strong-armed into acclaiming Perennis as emperor, presumably with Senator Sorex leading the cheers of assent?'

The tribune spat his reply, his eyes blazing with anger.

'*We have no choice!* If we fail to do as we're ordered then our entire family will be excised from existence. Do you have any idea what a man will do to avoid the threat of having his line extinguished from history? You've been away from the capital for too long, Rutilius Scaurus, and you simply have no idea just how dangerous Rome has become in the last few years . . .'

His voice tailed off as Marcus stepped forward and fixed him with a murderous look.

'You're right, of course . . .' Scaurus kept his tone light. 'I really don't know what it might feel like to see my entire family killed by an all-powerful man fixated on the objective of taking the throne. But Centurion *Corvus* here does. And perhaps on this very rare occasion we can use his real name. This, Fulvius Sorex, as I expect you know all too well, is Marcus Valerius Aquila. You may recall the murder of *his* entire family two years ago. He's the reason why you were ordered to send an entire auxiliary cohort north to meet its doom, as a means of dealing with this fugitive from the praetorian prefect's justice. And it was his wife, I ought to add, that Legatus Equitius caught you in the act of raping, using the threat of murder against a newborn child as your leverage for her complicity.'

Sorex backed away a step, raising his hands as Marcus paced forward to stand stonefaced before him. Scaurus shrugged, picking up the false eagle and examining it closely for a moment.

'This really is a very nicely executed piece of work.' He dropped it back onto the table. 'It's a pity to see such craftsmanship turned to such a shoddy purpose. But then inanimate objects are neither good nor evil in themselves, they are simply wielded by whatever cause possesses them. So it's a good thing that Prefect Castus took the precaution of having all that gold removed from the storeroom and spirited away to a safe place when the opportunity arose.'

Sorex gave the camp prefect an incredulous look.

'You moved the fucking *gold*?!'

The veteran officer nodded equably.

'When it became clear that you weren't to be trusted, Fulvius Sorex, yes I took that precaution. I've had it taken somewhere where it will provide a little less of a temptation for the wrong sort of person.'

'But I gave specific orders for it to be guarded at all times!'

Castus smiled tightly.

'I know. And hurtful though it may be for you to realise it, when an officer with thirty years' service and a dozen scars to bear witness to them requests the assistance of his legion's senior centurions, they tend to take somewhat more notice of him than of a military tribune whose most dangerous exploit seems to have been escorting the emperor's favourite catamite on his daring shopping expeditions into the Subura.' He strolled forward, patting Marcus on the shoulder. 'You see, the Centurionate has an endearing tendency towards the preservation of their legion's honour above all else, and so when I revealed to the first spear that your marvellous rescue of the eagle was in fact a sham, it was all I could do to prevent him from taking his gladius to you, and bugger the consequences. Moving the gold, once I told him that it was intended for use in setting his legion on a path to treachery and possible disaster, was a relatively easy sell.'

Scaurus nodded sagely.

'And after all, it's an integral part of my plan.'

'Your . . . *plan?*'

Scaurus waved a hand at Marcus, and turned his attention back to the captured eagle. The young centurion stepped closer to the terrified tribune, one hand tapping on the hilt of his gladius.

'This sword belonged to the Sixth Legion's legatus. He left it for me when he was killed, hidden beneath the body of the last man to carry that eagle, because he was my birth father. His legion was betrayed by another of Prefect Perennis's sons, which means that both of my fathers were killed as the consequence of the praetorian prefect's plans to take the throne. Now that we have all the proof we'll ever need to see him executed we're going to deliver that evidence to Rome, and alert the emperor to the danger he faces from his right-hand man.'

Sorex shook his head in amazement.

'You can't just march on *Rome*; you'll be stopped before you even reach the south coast of the province. Once the new legati arrive and find out what you've done they'll send the legion cavalry after you with orders for you to return, and if you fail to obey then you'll be hunted down and then put to the sword in very short order.' He shook his head at Castus sadly. 'And you, Prefect, will find yourself on your way home as a civilian if you're *lucky!*'

'You're right, of course . . .' Scaurus shrugged easily. 'If Perennis's placemen find out what we've done then they'll certainly bring the full weight of their authority to bear on us in order to get that gold back. The thing is, Fulvius Sorex, you have to ask yourself one simple question.' He lowered his voice to a whisper, bending close to his colleague. '*Who's going to tell them?*'

The younger man stared up at him for a moment before the realisation of Scaurus's explicit threat hit him, his eyes widening in horror.

'You *don't* mean . . .'

'You have to admit there's an inescapable logic to my question.' Scaurus raised an eyebrow at his colleague. 'There are only a very few people who might alert the legati to what's happened here, when they eventually arrive. The Sixth's first spear is most unlikely to do so. He's already made sure that the men who moved the gold are in no position to tell anyone else where they took it, since he had them marched off up the road to the Wall to strengthen one of the more remote garrisons the moment the job was done. Which leaves you, Fulvius Sorex. And if *you're* not here to tell them that we've taken the gold with us then they'll be none the wiser, will they?'

He stood in silence, waiting for Sorex to respond while the young tribune looked about him as if searching for some way out of the situation.

'But surely . . . I mean . . .'

'Don't panic, colleague, I'm not ready to put a fellow officer to death quite yet, we do have civilised standards of behaviour to maintain after all. But I'm sure you can see my quandary. If I leave you alive you're sure to inform the legati of what I've done, aren't you?'

'Not necessarily.'

'Really?' Scaurus looked at him sceptically. 'What guarantee do I have that you won't renege on whatever we agree just as soon as I'm no longer a threat to you?'

'My word as a Roman gentleman, Rutilius Scaurus!' The younger man jumped to his feet, holding out a hand palm upper-most. 'I'll swear to you now on whichever god you choose that I'll tell the praetorian prefect's men nothing!'

Scaurus nodded, turning to Castus with a questioning look.

'What do you think, Prefect? After all, I've no desire to spill blood in a legion headquarters.'

The older man shrugged.

'I share your reticence to dishonour this place. And it's hardly Fulvius Sorex's fault if he happens to find himself a victim of unhappy circumstance.'

'Very well colleague, we'll let you live. There is, however, the small matter of making your silence on the subject of our whereabouts look convincing. Surely the record of our presence in the headquarters tonight will leave you open to the question as to why you didn't simply call out the guard to take us captive, if you had even the slightest suspicion as to our intentions? No, we have to make this look more convincing . . .'

Castus held up a hand, reaching into a belt pouch for a small bottle.

'One of the curses of thirty years' service is that I tend to be troubled by the ghosts of men long dead. On those infrequent occasions when I find myself unable to sleep, a few drops of this extract of certain medicinal herbs puts me to sleep as quickly as a lamp being snuffed.'

Scaurus turned back to his colleague.

'There you have it, the perfect answer. You will consume enough of the Prefect's draught to put you to sleep for the night, and I'll tell the duty centurion that you're so drunk that I couldn't get any sense out of you. After all, it isn't every day that a man gains the glory of having regained his legion's eagle, is it? You could be forgiven for having taken a cup or two of wine on board, I would have thought?'

Sorex nodded, the relief he was feeling transparent to every man in the room.

'And a good night's sleep thrown into the bargain. Of course, it's an excellent idea.'

He reached for the wine flask, pouring two cups of wine and handing one to Scaurus, then turned and offered the other to Castus with a small bow. The camp prefect carefully tipped his medicine bottle to allow three drops of the dark, oily mixture to drip into the cup, chatting to the tribune as he did so.

'I must warn you, even this diluted the draught is almost revoltingly sweet. The best way to consume the drink is to tip it straight back, or you may find yourself so put off that you're unable to force the rest down your neck. Here's one more drop for good luck, eh? Gods below but you'll sleep well tonight, and I have to warn you that you may have a bit of a headache when you wake up . . .'

Every man in the room started as the sound of a sword being pulled from its scabbard rasped out, and all eyes turned to Marcus as he stepped forward with Legatus Sollemnis's eagle's-head-pommelled sword shining in the lamplight.

'You're going to let him live? The traitor who sent us north to The Fang with the intention of having the Venicones overrun an entire cohort in the hope of killing just one man? The bastard who's been trying every trick at his disposal to put my wife on her back despite knowing her to be an honourable Roman matron?'

He advanced towards the terrified tribune with a look of unbridled fury, raising the gladius until its point was aimed squarely at his face. Scaurus raised a hand to Julius, who was readying himself to leap at his friend from behind, forestalling the attack as he stepped into his centurion's path.

'Centurion Corvus, lower your sword. You know that there is no honour to be gained from revenge taken in this way. And besides, you can console yourself with the knowledge that Fulvius Sorex will have a lifetime to regret the choices he made in this matter.'

He stared at Marcus steadily, watching as the young Roman looked first at Sorex, still rooted to the spot with fear, and then darted a glance at Castus, who simply raised his eyebrows in reply. Nodding slowly in recognition of the tribune's order, he sheathed the sword and stepped back into the shadows alongside Julius, ignoring the glare that the first spear played upon him. Heaving a sigh of relief, Scaurus beckoned the camp prefect forward, and watched as Castus handed the wine cup to the red-faced Sorex with a wink.

'Remember, down in one's the only way to tolerate the sickly taste.'

He watched approvingly as Sorex upended the cup. The tribune shrugged at them, his face baffled at the absence of any unpleasant taste.

'A little fruity, but there's really nothing to it. So, how long will it take to have effect?'

Castus smiled at him, indicating his chair with a hand.

'I'd sit down now, Fulvius Sorex, if I were you. The drug works quickly at that concentration.'

The tribune turned to walk back around his desk, but swayed where he stood as the concoction started to take a grip of him. Scaurus and Castus took an arm apiece and helped him into the chair, and the senior tribune took the replica eagle and fitted it into his hands with a faint smile.

'Here, you can cuddle up to this. It'll look all the more credible if anyone puts their head around the door. I'll look after the fake for you.'

Sorex opened his mouth to speak, but although his mouth moved it made no sound. Castus tousled his hair affectionately.

'Lost your tongue, Sorex? It's no surprise to me, the lady who gave me the draught told me that it often silences its victims, in that short time between ingestion and the onset of the poison's symptoms, and it seems that she was right. So I feel it only fair to tell you that while you were gibbering at Centurion Corvus, the Prefect here added another dozen drops of that rather powerful medicine to your drink.' He smiled down at the tribune's twitch of an eyebrow, his body apparently already paralysed by the drug's powerful dose. 'Yes, you'll be dead very shortly now, and without a single mark to hint at the manner of your death. Sat here cuddling up to your legion's eagle, I don't doubt that the centurions will be quick to deify you as having died of the sheer joy of your success. After all, you didn't seriously think we were going to fall for that "my word as a Roman gentleman" nonsense, did you?'

Sorex started, his tongue protruding from his mouth as he shuddered and fought for breath. Castus lifted his uncomprehending face, his smile hard and cruel as the younger man fought for his life, his breath coming in tiny pants as the poison slowly but surely squeezed the last vestiges of life from his body.

'And now come the shakes, Sorex, the terrifying struggle to breathe and the slide into unconsciousness. Fitting punishment for a man with your delight in forcing others to your will, like my beautiful Desidra and others before her, I don't doubt. She confessed it all to me earlier, Sorex, she told me what you'd forced her to do in defence of the last years of my career, and made me promise not to ruin my life by taking my sword to you. Fortunately your other victim had already provided me with the perfect means of taking my revenge . . .' He stopped talking, realising that the last light had faded from the tribune's eyes. 'I think he's gone now.'

Scaurus put a finger to the tribune's neck.

'Indeed he is. Let's be on our way. You can have this, Centurion, as the reward for restraining that magnificent temper of yours.' He passed Marcus the genuine eagle. 'I think it's best if we keep this for the time being, and I can't think of a man who's better qualified to care for it until the time comes to return it to the right person. And now I think it's time that we were on our way. We've a lot to prepare if we're going to march south at first light, and little enough time in which to do it.'

The legion's senior centurion was waiting for them outside Sorex's office, his pre-arranged presence clearly making the legionaries on guard nervous to judge from the sweat running down their necks, and the camp prefect took him aside with a broad smile.

'It's the best possible news, First Spear; the eagle that the tribune and his men captured yesterday is clearly genuine. You can't fake that level of craftsmanship, and it has all of the secret marks that confirm it was made in Rome at the imperial armouries. Mars be praised, we've restored the legion's good name!' He handed the centurion a tablet bound in ash and secured with a shining brass hook and eye. 'Here's the record of its markings that your last eagle bearer kept which will help you to prove its provenance. I congratulate you upon the return of so important a symbol of imperial power, and the removal of the threat that has hung over this legion since the battle where it was lost.'

The veteran centurion nodded gravely.

'The best possible news indeed, sir. And the tribune, sir?'

Castus winked in reply.

'Tribune Sorex has clearly had a hard few days and, I would guess from the state of him, a few cups of wine. In truth he was half asleep when we arrived, and he fell asleep while we were examining the standard. I put it back in his hands and left him to it, and I suggest we let him sleep, rather than disturbing him. After all, he's more than earned it.'

The senior centurion nodded solemnly, giving no clue of his complicity with the Tungrians' scheme.

'I'll do that, Camp Prefect.'

Castus gestured to Scaurus and his centurions.

'Before I forget, Tribune Sorex did confirm Legatus Equitius's orders for the Tungrian cohorts. It seems that Tribune Scaurus here is to take both of his auxiliary cohorts south and cross the sea to Gaul. The legatus has word from a colleague in Lugdunum that the province is infested with bandits, and is requested to detach some of our strength to help in their suppression. Since the legion is forbidden to leave camp, the legatus deems it appropriate for an auxiliary task force to be sent in our place, and it seems the Tungrians are well experienced at dealing with thieves and robbers.'

Scaurus stepped forward with a respectful nod to the senior centurion.

'We plan to march at dawn, First Spear, but it seems we have too much baggage for our carts. Perhaps you could assist us with the procurement of some additional transport capacity?'

The first spear's answer was delivered straight faced, but there was no mistaking the tone of his voice.

'Indeed Tribune. I'll have the carts that carried Tribune Sorex's cargo from Arab Town made ready. I'd imagine that should be enough to fit your needs?'

IO

'Well now, if it isn't Gaius Rutilius Scaurus! Well met once again, Tribune, even if not in quite the circumstances we might both have expected!'

Scaurus stepped forward to meet the big man standing in the road in front of the halted Tungrian column, his armour tinted orange by the late afternoon sun and the layer of dust that coated the sculpted bronze plate. Senator Albinus was standing at the head of a group of twenty or so muscular-looking followers who to Marcus had the look of veteran soldiers for the most part, men a few years past their prime whose scars and almost sleepily calm demeanour marked them out as having been hardened in battle. Their meeting point had clearly been carefully chosen, hidden from the straggling settlements that littered the roadside at frequent intervals by trees that arched over the road to form a green tunnel, and Marcus smiled to see Julius looking about him with a look of professional discomfort, his eyes searching the greenery for any sign of movement as he addressed the men of his leading century.

'All the way from Britannia and not a sign of anyone trying to stop us? If it's going to happen anywhere then it's going to happen here, before we reach the city, so just keep your fucking wits about you, gentlemen . . .'

The tribune took Albinus's outstretched arm and found himself engulfed in a powerful bear hug, as the senator greeted him with the same slightly disquieting enthusiasm with which they had parted in Dacia the previous year. The last time that Scaurus had seen the big man he'd been outfitted and groomed for his position as an imperial legion's legatus, his hair and beard cut tight to his powerful head and bull neck, but a year in Rome following his triumphant return from Dacia had clearly encouraged him to follow the latest imperial fashion. His glossy and immaculately barbered beard trailed a good four inches from his jaw, and his hair had been allowed to grow out into a tangle of artfully coiffured curls. When Albinus released him from the grip the bemused tribune stepped back with a wry smile and nodded respectfully, wincing at the dust that had transferred itself from his travel-soiled uniform to the senator's pristine toga.

'Forgive me, Decimus Clodius Albinus, something of my experience from the road seems to have rubbed off on you . . .'

An admonishing finger silenced him, and Albinus held his arms wide, his voice raised to carry to his men.

'I told you in Dacia, Tribune, and I'll tell you again at the gates of Rome, you and I are beyond formalities after the terrible things we've seen and done together . . .' Julius and Marcus exchanged glances in their places behind their tribune, the first spear raising a sardonic eyebrow. '. . . and so to you I will always simply be Decimus, your *friend*.' He brushed at the soiled tunic ineffectually, raising a grubby hand with a laugh. 'And besides, what's a little dust when you've marched for three months from the edge of the world to make it possible for us to save the empire from the grasping hands of a usurper?' Stepping closer to Scaurus, he lowered his voice. 'I've arranged for your men to be accommodated in the city's transit barracks, and I'd suggest that my men take the gold on into Rome from here. What do you say, eh?'

The tribune looked back at him levelly, lowering his voice to match the senator's conspiratorial tone.

'Well Decimus, I think if you were to push the question I'd say that I've not marched fifteen hundred miles to abandon my task at the gates of the city. I suggest that your men march into the city alongside enough of mine to carry the chests, to demonstrate the part you've taken in bringing this matter to the emperor's attention?'

Senator Albinus stared back at him for a moment, his face devoid of any expression, and Marcus saw a predator's calculation in his eyes. After a pause just long enough to show that he clearly considered the decision his to make, the big man's face creased in a slow smile.

'As you suggest, Gaius, as you suggest. We're about to carry out an act that the historians will be talking about a thousand years from now, so I see no reason for us not to share the glory of this evening.'

Scaurus returned the stare for an equally deliberate moment before speaking.

'And the risk, Senator? Presumably the praetorian prefect wouldn't be delighted if he were to discover just how close to hand the proof of his duplicity has come. I'd imagine that we'll end up hanging from our scrotums if his men take us before we get the chance to present that evidence. Indeed my first spear here has been as nervous as a good-looking boy on his own at the baths for weeks now.'

The big man inclined his head.

'As you say. Whatever is to come this evening, we will take an equal share of what results.'

Scaurus nodded and then turned back to the centurions standing behind him.

'Stand your men down, First Spear. The senator and I are going to have a good look at the emperor's gold.'

He led Albinus down the line of weary-looking soldiers, saluting in reply as each century snapped to attention at their centurions' shouted commands, and the senator played a discerning eye across both their threadbare equipment and worn boots.

'Their kit may look a little tatty, but by the gods, Gaius, your troops look bloody good for men that have marched all the way across the northern empire.'

Scaurus acknowledged the compliment with a nod.

'Indeed so. And all the way from Britannia to Dacia and back before that. A few weeks enjoying the greatest city in the world is going to do them more good than a year of quiet garrison duty.'

Albinus snorted.

'That won't be cheap. How will your boys get their fill of wine and whores on auxiliary pay?'

Scaurus waved a hand dismissively.

'Money? That won't be a problem.'

The tribune's response was light in tone, although Marcus knew just as well as Scaurus the direction in which the senator's seemingly careless question had been angled. An unspoken question hung in the air between the two men for a moment before Albinus's patience with his protégée's apparent unwillingness to elucidate on his pronouncement reached its breaking point. While his tone remained jocular, and he smiled as he asked the question, the expression completely failed to reach his eyes.

'You've not had your fingers inside those gold chests, have you Gaius?'

The steel beneath his bonhomie was sufficiently apparent that Marcus found his fingers twitching reflexively, eager for the reassuring feel of his swords' hilts. Scaurus turned to smile at the senator with an absence of humour to match that with which the question had been asked, his grey eyes as hard as flint and his tone suddenly harsh.

'Or rather, have I had my fingers inside those chests without sharing the spoils with *you*, Decimus?'

The senator's eyes widened slightly under his relentless gaze, the only sign of his disquiet the younger man's refusal to be cowed.

'You take my meaning perfectly, young man. Well?'

The tribune shook his head, gesturing to the heavy brass-bound wooden chests each of which had been carried south from Britannia on one of the cohorts' equipment wagons.

'Not likely, Senator. Take a look for yourself.'

He nodded to Dubnus, who was waiting alongside the first cart with his axe's head resting on the road's surface by his right foot, and the heavily built centurion barked an order to the hulking pioneers waiting in silence beside each of the carts. The three men stood and watched in silence as the chests were physically manhandled to the ground ready for their inspection. Taking a key from his belt pouch, Marcus squatted down to open the closest of the heavy wooden boxes, lifting the lid to reveal a sea of gold aureii coins that filled the container almost to its brim. Frowning, Albinus reached down and took a coin, staring for a moment at the finely detailed figure of Britannia on the obverse before turning it over to look at the emperor's head.

'Ah.'

Scaurus took out another coin and held it up before him.

'Ah indeed. Every coin in the entire shipment is exactly the same.'

Albinus shrugged.

'So? It may be unspendable, but it'll melt down just as easily as any other gold.'

The tribune tossed his aureus back into the chest.

'Why not keep that coin as a memento of what we're about to do? One aureus won't be missed, but it's my opinion that we'll be in deep trouble if we remove many more.'

The senator frowned.

'Why?'

Scaurus pointed at the chest's interior wall, and at a line scored deeply into the grain on all sides of the deep wooden box level with the top of the mass of coins.

'The line marks the level that the gold in the chest should reach. If we skim any of it out it'll be more than obvious, and we'll all doubtless be interrogated until whoever did the skimming confesses, and then dies in a manner that won't best please their ancestors. I think it best to play this one straight.'

Albinus grinned wolfishly, lowering his voice so that only Scaurus could hear.

'Unlike the last time we laid hands on this gold, you mean?'

The tribune nodded solemnly.

'Indeed. These coins are highly likely to have been minted from the very same metal that we rescued from Gerwulf last year, after he took control of the Alburnus Major mine and stripped it clean. Gold which I delivered to you, at your explicit orders as I recall it, leaving *you* with the sole responsibility for its safe delivery to the imperial treasury.' He paused for a moment before speaking again. 'And, as I noted at the time, the only official record of its quantity and value.' Albinus nodded, having the good grace to look suitably embarrassed. 'It must have been minted into these coins somewhere under the praetorian prefect's control . . .'

He paused for a moment, waiting for the senator to speak. Albinus stared at the gold with undisguised avarice again before sighing and turning back to the tribune.

'Illyricum, most likely. Perennis has managed to put his sons in command of the armies of both Pannonia and Dalmatia, and there are several cities with the right to mint coins in those two provinces.' He paused, chewing thoughtfully on his lower lip for a moment before speaking again. 'So, he must have ordered the gold to be shipped from Dacia to one of his boys, who then oversaw it being minted into these rather interesting coins after which it was sent north to Britannia. I presume that Perennis had someone in place in Eboracum to make sure that it reached the right hands?'

Scaurus nodded.

'A legion tribune. Perennis took advantage of a stupid little mutiny by the Twentieth Legion that was over almost before it began to sack every legatus in the country, and sent his own men to replace them. This man, Fulvius Sorex, was given orders to make sure that the gold was kept safe until the new men arrived. They were clearly going to use it to bribe the Britannia legions into rising up together, so that they could be marched south through Gaul to join up with the Illyricum legions north of Rome.'

'I see. Three legions from Britannia, another four from Pannonia and Dalmatia, plus all of their supporting auxiliaries would make for an army of at least seventy or eighty thousand men, and that's before we get into the army on the Rhenus. With that sort of military muscle to hand a man close to the throne could assassinate the emperor, take the purple and turn to face any challengers from the eastern end of the empire with his confidence high. I expect that the praetorian prefect was only waiting for word from

Britannia that the legions had declared for him before striking at
the imperial family, although he must have been informed of the
gold's mysterious disappearance by now. But why, I wonder, didn't
he simply send a decent-sized army north to intercept you before
you reached Rome?'

Scaurus looked at his fingers in apparent disgust at the dirt
ingrained beneath the nails.

'That's probably down to the fact that we made sure that Fulvius
Sorex wasn't in any condition to tell Perennis's legati anything when
they arrived. When we left Eboracum the Sixth Legion was under
the command of their camp prefect, a man with no love for the
praetorian prefect, and the story that Perennis's men will have
received from Prefect Castus is that Sorex secreted the gold away
for safe keeping whilst keeping the location to himself. Worse than
that, it seems that the century of men he used for the task of hiding
it were apparently all killed in an ambush north of the Antonine
Wall, which means that there's nobody left alive who can identify
the spot where a fortune in gold is supposed to lie hidden. And
without that gold Perennis's legati won't dare to declare a mutiny,
since its presence in the province was hardly kept secret. The
soldiers of the Britannia legions will believe that the legati are
keeping it for themselves, and they're not likely to risk rebelling
against the throne without getting their fair share of the spoils.'

Albinus nodded his head slowly, contemplating the gold coin
in his hand.

'So it seems that you've saved Commodus from an ignominious
death, young man. Mind you, Perennis will doubtless be readying
himself to strike anyway, and gambling on the Pannonian legions
being strong enough to deal with any resistance, and given his
position of power I'd say he's got a decent enough chance of
carrying it off. He's got the praetorians, doubtless he also controls
the Urban Watch, and he'll not let us get within a mile of the
palace with this gold if he gets so much as a sniff that we're inside
the city.'

Scaurus gestured to Marcus to have the chest locked and
replaced on the cart.

'Which, I'll admit, is what's been troubling me all the way from Britannia. There's not much point in our carrying it this far if any attempt to put it in front of the emperor is likely to end up with us all looking down the spears of unhelpful palace guards. So tell me, Decimus, exactly how is it that you think we're going to be able to carry this gold into the imperial palace?'

The smile returned to Albinus's face.

'Ah, well that's a secret that'll have to stay mine and mine alone for just a little bit longer. Let's just say that the praetorian prefect isn't the only man in the emperor's court with ambitions above his station. All will be revealed in good time.'

He turned back to look down the road towards Rome, the city's walls glowing amber in the late afternoon sun's soft glow.

'And now I suggest that we get your boys here into their barracks, and give you and the men who'll carry the gold into the city time to have a wash and a brush-up, and get them into some clean clothes. Armour, muscles and dirt may be good at keeping the bandits at bay, but they're going to look a little out of place to the Watch, wouldn't you say, not to mention Commodus himself?'

'There's another one having his blade confiscated. There are going to be a lot of happy muggers in the Subura later on tonight when all the men that have been disarmed at this gate try to make their way home!'

The leader of Albinus's bodyguard, a bull-necked man with a decidedly military look called Cotta stood up from the crouching position in which he had been peering around the corner of the side street's last house and shook his head in amazement as he looked back down the length of the column of men waiting behind him. The sixty Tungrian soldiers selected to carry the gold chests were flanked on either side by the twenty men of Albinus's body-guard, most of whom had adopted deceptively relaxed postures and were exchanging banter with the local children, who had quickly overcome their wariness and were swarming around them in the hope of begging small coins. Cotta saluted Albinus crisply, pointing back towards the gate.

'There's no way through there, Senator, unless we want to be relieved of our weapons and probably worse . . .'

Marcus nodded at the words, reflexively putting a hand to the dagger buried deep in the folds of his toga. Albinus and Scaurus were similarly armed, and every man in their twenty-strong body-guard had at least one knife concealed about his person in addition to their heavy clubs, mostly strapped to upper arms and thighs beneath their tunics. The Watch standing guard at the Viminal Gate, one of the north-eastern entrances to the city inside the walls, were clearly taking their time processing the queue of humanity wishing to enter Rome, and searching every man, woman and child with equal thoroughness, and a lengthy queue was building up at the arched gateway. Even in the darkness, hours after the sun had set, the traffic into and out of the city via the gate's opening was as busy as if it were midday, and Marcus was grateful for Albinus's bodyguards both for the protection they provided the unarmed Tungrians and the light from their blazing torches. He looked up and down the queue's shadowy length with an expression of irritation.

'I still don't understand why passage inside the walls is being restricted like this. When I left here the gates weren't guarded, and hadn't been in my memory. Who needs to guard the gates of a city that rules every scrap of inhabitable ground for a thousand miles in every direction, and where the city itself has long outgrown the walls that once surrounded it?'

Albinus laughed wryly, clapping a big hand on his shoulder.

'Well now, Centurion, you sound just like a senator whose opinions I used to admire so greatly when he spoke on such matters, before he was murdered by the praetorian prefect, along with his entire family, simply to silence a potential dissenter and take his estate into the imperial treasury.' He looked Marcus up and down in the torchlight as if sizing him up for the first time. 'You may not look very much like him, but in mannerisms and inflection you could be Appius Valerius Aquila's son for all I know.'

For a second Marcus wondered if he was going to make the obvious conclusion, and identify him as the dead senator's only remaining descendant, but instead the big man waved a hand at the gate.

'The answer to your peevish question is simple enough, Centurion, if you consider the politics of the day and our mission tonight. Perennis controls not only the praetorians, but also the Urban Cohorts and the City Watch. And if the former tend to spend most of their time sitting around in barracks waiting for a riot or a gang fight to give them a reason to break some heads, the Watch are more used to mixing with the people, which is why he's using them to control what comes into the city, *if* you take my meaning.'

Scaurus leaned forward, his voice lowered to little more than a murmur.

'You're saying that he has them looking out for *this* . . .'

He rolled his eyes to look at the nearest of the gold chests, standing in the middle of the side street with a half-dozen brawny Tungrians waiting stoically around it, ready to heft its deceptively heavy weight back into the carrying position. Albinus nodded with a knowing grin.

'Indeed I am. And were we to progress to the front of that most unpleasant-smelling queue we could most certainly expect to be ordered to open the chests. At which point, whilst we greatly outnumber the men on guard, we would quickly find ourselves outnumbered by their reinforcements, surrounded, arrested and dragged away to the local Watch station –' he lowered his voice and adopted a solemn expression '– never to be seen again, I expect.'

The tribune raised an eyebrow.

'Unless . . . ?'

Albinus's grin returned.

'Unless, of course, something were to happen to distract the Watch from their important duty. As it happens, one of the men who passed through the gate just now, having been thoroughly searched of course and found to be carrying nothing more threatening than his own cucumber, is even now acting to provide us with just such a distraction.'

He paused for a moment, staring up at the night sky above the looming city walls before speaking again.

'The problem with owning property in the city, of course, is just how prone one's buildings are to the risk of fire. It only takes the slightest hint of a spark in the wrong place to send an entire apartment block up in flames, a cooking stove overturned in a ground-floor tavern, or perhaps a candle catching at a piece of wind-blown fabric. And of course, once one of the blasted things is alight everything around it is at risk. It's a good thing we have the Watch to deal with such emergencies, wouldn't you agree?'

As if on cue, a faint chorus of frenzied shouts sounded over the queue's grumbling murmur and Albinus nodded smugly. After a short wait, during which the shouting from beyond the walls grew steadily louder, a glow became visible above the wall's rampart, and dirty grey smoke started to rise into view, illuminated from below by the fire's flames. The initial signs of the fire quickly strengthened, the grey stain that obscured the stars rapidly thickening as the fire took hold of whatever it was that was burning fiercely beyond the wall.

'Any time about *now*, I'd say, or at least I bloody well hope so . . .' Just as Albinus spoke, the half-dozen men standing guard at the city gate were summoned by a panting runner, and the senator nodded his head sagely, pointing to a mongrel in the act of emptying its bowels in the shadow of the gate. 'Ah, it seems that the fire is stronger than first believed. At a guess the next-door building has gone up in flames too, and I'd bet a gold aureus to the turd that dog's so busily curling out that it'll be another one of my properties. When the gods decide to punish a man they certainly do so thoroughly, don't they?'

With shouts to the queuing citizens to stay where they were, the Watch ran for the fire, leaving the waiting queue looking at each other in bemusement.

'And there's the only real problem with combining the duties of policemen and fire fighters. When fire strikes, who's to watch the city, or in this case, the city's gates? Come along then, let's not keep our date waiting. He's uncommonly bad tempered when he believes he's not getting the respect that he's due!'

The senator led them through the unguarded gate in the wake of the other members of the queue who had been similarly swift to take advantage of the Watch's absence.

'This way, gentlemen, turn right here and we'll head on down the Viminal Hill until we have no choice but to dive into the slums. You'll be earning your corn soon enough, eh Cotta?'

The streets of Rome were still warm three hours after the sun had dropped below the horizon, and Marcus could feel the heat that had been baked into the stones through the leather soles of the sandals that Albinus had procured for them. Like the rest of the clothing he'd been given the shoes were of the best quality, made with buttery-soft leather that moulded to his feet like a second skin. The three officers were all wearing heavy woollen togas, the hems of both Tungrians' garments decorated with the thin purple stripe of the equestrian class, and the once crisp linen tunic beneath Marcus's weighty garment had quickly become damp with his sweat. Scaurus had laughed quietly at his centurion as the younger man had awkwardly donned the toga, unfamiliar with its folds after so long a gap since the last time he'd worn the garment, pointing to the thin equestrian stripe with a sympathetic grimace.

'Not what you were brought up to expect, eh Centurion, not when you were groomed for the thick stripe?'

Marcus had looked down at the dye that marked the garment's pristine white wool with the symbol of his supposed membership of the equestrian class with a shrug.

'Imperial law says I'm an impostor if I wear a stripe of any thickness, given my father's alleged crimes. And besides, Tribune, I'd sacrifice a stripe of any thickness for the chance to get my family out from under the constant threat of death.'

Albinus's men formed a protective cordon around the party as they made their way along the High Road that ran arrow-straight down the Viminal Hill's spine, and as the senator led them down into the tight, filthy streets of the Subura, his men drew in closer, hefting their heavy clubs with meaningful glances at anyone taking an interest in the column of chests. Each apartment block's ground floor was occupied by taverns that ranged in aspect from simply seedy to openly licentious, prostitutes and their pimps prowling between them in competition for paying clients with money-hungry bar staff of both sexes. At Cotta's command a half-dozen men detached themselves from the group as it progressed through the notorious district, moving ahead of the party and checking the streets to either side of their route with a disciplined competence that hinted that they had worked together before. Seeing the young centurion's eyes upon his men, Albinus dropped back to walk alongside him.

'They're all former soldiers, Centurion, men from one of the Pannonian legions. They hire themselves out as a unit, and their main selling point is that they have never yet suffered the loss of a client. I employ them pretty much full-time at the moment.' He waved a hand at the man walking alongside him. 'Cotta here was the man who came up with the bright idea for them to go into business together.'

Marcus inclined his head in recognition of Albinus's explan-ation, meeting the eyes of the man indicated by the senator's hand and finding them coolly alert as the bodyguards' leader ran his eyes over the soldiers sweating beneath their heavy loads.

'They must come highly recommended for you to trust them to escort us through the poorest and most dangerous suburb of the city with such a portable fortune.'

Albinus nodded at Marcus's question with an amused smirk.

'I don't think there's any danger of them betraying us. I served as the legatus of First Italica with Senior Centurion Cotta, and when he got bored with retirement and decided to pull some of his retiring soldiers together to form this nice little business two years ago, he came to me to ask for the money they needed. And of course I agreed.' He bent closer to the young centurion's ear. 'A man in my position needs to ensure that he has the appropriate protection on the streets of Rome these days.'

Scaurus frowned, having overheard their discussion.

'Your *position*, Senator?'

The big man snorted a laugh.

'You really have been away from Rome too long, Gaius. By "a man in my position" I mean a man who might be perceived as presenting a risk to the emperor, a man around whom opposition to Commodus's rule might, shall we say, coalesce? After all, I am something of a war hero, with a recent and crushing victory over the Sarmatae in Dacia to my credit, quite apart from my excellent record in command of an auxiliary cavalry wing and two legions in the German Wars under the last emperor. I come from an ancient and noble family and I am, as you well know, more than rich enough for the men that manage the imperial finances to have their beady eyes well and truly open for any opportunity to cast my loyalty in doubt, order my execution and sequester my estate and fortune.' He shook his head at the tribune with a grim smile. 'An opportunity which I will never allow them, of course, given that I never make any comment either public or private that is in any way critical of Commodus. Quite the opposite, in fact, but there is still always the risk of a politically motivated assassination. And these men are my protection against such an attempt to take my life. Hello, who's this coming up the road? Someone's got balls walking into this cesspit without anyone to back him up.'

They followed his gaze to find a single man sauntering towards them, passing the first of Cotta's men with a nod. To Marcus's surprise their reaction was incongruous, the soldiers nudging each other and pointing at the lone walker's back with grins, and he looked with curiosity at the powerful figure as he passed, receiving a momentary direct gaze in return. Tall and heavily muscled, the man's face was marked by a pair of scars that combined to form a lopsided cross on his right cheekbone, his hair cut close to his skull.

'Damn me, it's Velox!'

Albinus had stopped walking, and was looking at the receding figure with a stare of amazement.

'Who?'

Albinus shook his head.

'Gentlemen, we have stood in the presence of true greatness. That was one half of a gladiatorial pairing the like of which this city has not seen in my lifetime. Velox is the younger of a pair of twins who have ruled supreme in the arena for over a year now. He and his brother Mortiferum are from the land north of the city that used to be ruled by the Etruscans, and they are without doubt the fastest men I've ever seen with a sword, either of them the match of any other three men you could choose from Rome's gladiators. When they fight, which isn't very often these days given just how special they are, they usually take to the sand as a pair, matched against half a dozen opponents at a time. And because they've never lost a fight, either together or fighting solo, they're worshipped by the plebs. Which explains why he's not afraid to walk alone – there's not a man in the Subura that would dare to touch him for fear of being beaten to death by his peers.'

As they watched, the lone gladiator turned off the road and walked into the garden of a mansion that Marcus had noted a moment before, its grounds wedged tightly between a pair of apartment blocks. Albinus laughed quietly, shaking his head in amusement.

'Well now, I wonder if the man of the house is at home. That young man has a well-justified reputation for taking advantage of his exalted status, I hear. Indeed I believe he's cut a swathe through the otherwise respectable female population of the rich and well-to-do like a hot knife through butter. Women and gladiators, eh? What is it, I wonder, that draws them to men who have so degraded themselves by adopting the status of infamia? Mind you, it's rumoured that his twin swings in the other direction, if you take my meaning, so perhaps he's just doing his best to compensate . . .'

Shaking his head in wry amusement he signalled Cotta to resume their march, and the party continued south with increasing caution as they approached the edge of the Subura's cloak of anonymity. Albinus called a halt at a street corner, looking out over the first of the forums that they would have to traverse with an uneasy gaze.

'And now for the time of maximum risk, gentlemen. If Perennis has warned his men on the streets to be on the watch for men carrying heavy burdens then we're going to stand out like tits on a bull.'

He chewed at a fingernail as the scouts headed out into the wide and empty moonlit space, staying within the shadows wherever possible, but there was no sign of either praetorians or the Watch to be seen, and the party's main body followed the scouts across the forum as quickly as the Tungrians carrying the gold could move under its crushing weight. Another few moments of nervous progress brought them within sight of the Senate House at the Forum's western end, and Cotta waved them into the cover of a building a hundred paces or so distant from the official building.

'There'll be guards on the Senate House for certain. You wait here, and I'll signal you when the way's clear.'

He signalled to his men, and a pair of rugged-looking bruisers stepped out of the shadows with their arms linked like old friends holding each other upright after a heavy evening of drinking, one of them pulling the stopper from a leather wine flask and taking a gulp so large that a red stain blossomed across his tunic as the wine leaked from his overflowing mouth. He raised his voice in a drunken shout, the words ringing out across the Forum's open space.

'Come on Luca my old mate, let's show these praetorian *cunts* how real soldiers march, eh?'

His companion grabbed the flask and upended it, wine flowing in equal quantities into his mouth and down the front of his tunic, then hurled it towards the Senate House with an apparently drunken flourish and a below of challenge.

'Yeah, praetorian *cunts*! Come and have a look at some real soldiers, you fuckin' toy-box tunic lifters!'

The pair staggered out into the Forum and broke into song, their words slurred as if from a long day's drinking but still recognisable as a legion favourite from the days when imperial guard cohorts had campaigned alongside the regular army.

'The scorpion is their emblem, the emperor's favoured boys,
They strut about like heroes and make lots of fucking noise.
They're bold and brave when they're on parade and
      danger they dismiss,
But they run for the rear when it's time to fight and
      their boots fill up with piss!'

The men guarding the senate were the first to react, a pair of immaculately turned out soldiers stamping down the steps to confront the drunks who had the temerity to insult them so publicly. The older of the two stepped in close with one hand on the hilt of his sword, and even at fifty paces it was plain to Marcus that his face was dark with anger.

'Get the fuck out of the Forum you pair of pissed-up mules, before my temper gets the better of me and I take the flat of my blade to you.'

The play-acting bodyguards swayed on their feet for a moment before reacting, then burst into peals of mocking laughter, one of them pointing at the guardsman while the other supported himself by leaning on his friend, apparently overcome with hysteria.

'Ha . . . hahahah!' The pointing man wiped at his eye as to remove a tear. 'He's going to take his sword to us!'

His companion shrieked with laughter, losing his grip on the other's shoulder and falling backwards onto the flagstones, raising his voice in a camp falsetto squeal.

'Ooooh! His *pork* sword!?'

The first man's hysterical laughter redoubled as he sank to his knees and then slumped to the ground, and the praetorian shook his head in impotent anger as the two men rolled about at his feet. The other guard joined him, and they glared down at the apparently helpless drunks for a moment before the older man waved a hand at the guards standing duty on the Temple of Vespasian, raising his voice to call them over.

'Here lads, there's a lesson needs teaching to these two idiots!'

Suitably reinforced, the four men took an arm apiece and pulled the drunken soldiers to their feet, prompting a further volley of abuse from their captives.

'Fuck off you arseholes, haven't you got donkeys to be buggering?!'

A swift slap silenced the protest.

'Shut the fuck up, soldier boy. You're just about to find out what happens when you take the piss out of the praetorian guard in our own city!'

Moving swiftly the guardsmen dragged the seemingly helpless drunks into the Senate House's shadows, and silence fell across the Forum. Cotta nodded to Albinus and gestured to the wide street's far side.

'All clear sir. Do you want to go now, or should we wait for our boys?'

Albinus raised an eyebrow.

'That rather depends on how long you think they're likely to be, doesn't it?'

The bodyguards' leader smiled wryly.

'Two lads that were the bare knuckle champions of their cohorts for as long as I was a centurion? Not very long . . .'

As if on cue the two bodyguards walked out of the senate's shadows, one of them waggling his fingers experimentally with a grimace as they re-joined the party.

'That last one had a bloody hard chin. I think I've bust a knuckle.'

The party hurried across the Forum's open expanse, Cotta glancing anxiously about for any sign of more praetorians.

'Looks like we've got lucky. Here, this way, and stay close to the wall so that anyone on top can't see us.'

On the southern side of the Forum the walls of the Palatine Hill loomed over them, defences surrounding the city within a city that was the complex of royal palaces which had been built up over the centuries atop the ancient hill, their sprawling grounds having long since coalesced to form a walled domicile for the imperial family. They rounded a corner at Cotta's direction, and Marcus frowned as an apparently dead-end alley opened up before them, a high wall looming ahead. The retired centurion raised a hand in caution, turning to face his master.

'This is the place, Patronus. Wait here please.'

He took a torch from one of his men and walked down the alley, allowing a heavy wooden club to drop from his sleeve into his right hand while the remaining bodyguards fanned out around the Tungrians carrying the three gold chests. In the torch's flickering light Marcus watched as he reached the far end, an apparently flat wall of heavy stone blocks that rose fifty feet above the street. Stopping within touching distance of the seemingly impassable barrier, Cotta raised his club and tapped it against the stonework in a swift rhythm of three blows, paused for a moment and then repeated the sequence. For a moment silence reigned the night air, but then, with a sudden snap, a cascade of mortar fell to the ground, leaving a crack in the wall's surface that followed the line of the stone blocks up to a height of six feet. With a scraping rasp the crack in the previously smooth surface abruptly sprang open, a wide section of the wall hinging smoothly outwards as a trio of heavily built men pushed it clear of the frame in which it was set. An imposing figure stepped through the doorway and into the sphere of light cast by Cotta's torch, beckoning the party forward with evident urgency as a half-dozen men carrying torches and trowels filed past him into the night, one of them carrying a heavy bucket made of coiled rope painted with tar, full of wet mortar.

'Come on then, let's not keep the second most influential man in the palace waiting.'

Albinus strode forward, the grin on his face telling Marcus that he was enjoying being in control of the situation. At the concealed door he greeted the waiting man with a bow before taking his hand in a firm clasp.

'Aurelius Cleander, how very good it is of you to open this hitherto undisclosed entrance to the palace for us. You are clearly a man for whom the pursuit of justice and the protection of our beloved emperor come above any other consideration.'

Cleander inclined his head in turn, although to Marcus's eye the gesture appeared little more than perfunctory, as if it were expected but hardly heartfelt. He spoke, and his voice was rich in timbre, mellifluous and persuasive, as much a weapon of persuasion as a means of communication.

'Greetings, Clodius Albinus. You are indeed most timely in your arrival, for I fear that our mutual adversary is close to issuing his assassins with the order to strike against our beloved emperor. There is not a moment to be lost.'

He gestured to the passage behind him, the tunnel-like walls lit by lamps placed every few feet in sconces built into the walls.

'Follow my men into the palace with your chests, and I will join you shortly. I must ensure that the workmen who will renew the mortar that conceals this door understand the importance of their task, and what unpleasant fate will befall them if I am able to discern any hint of its presence in the morning.'

Albinus bowed again, dismissing his bodyguard with a nod and a wave of his hand. Cotta bowed in turn to his master and took his men away into the darkness while the senator led the Tungrians into the tunnel behind the man Cleander had set to be their guide. He looked at the staircase that climbed up into the wall and shook his head in evident awe.

'We are privileged, gentlemen, to witness one of the imperial palace's greatest and most closely guarded secrets. This is one of the escape routes built into the palace walls to be used in the event of insurrection, and its presence is completely unsuspected by anyone who is not privy to the secret. For Cleander to be willing to reveal its existence to so many men is a mark of just how seriously he regards the evidence presented by these coins. Not to mention the risk he believes we're running in attempting to put that evidence before the emperor. Come on then, let's go and see what fate awaits us.'

He led them up the stairs, stepping lightly as he climbed, while from behind him Marcus could hear the heavy breathing and muffled curses of the soldiers as they muscled the heavy chests up the steep stone staircase. Reaching the top of the stairs he turned back to find the first of the chests close behind, the faces of the soldiers contorted with the pain of their climb but still set determinedly. Albinus and Scaurus followed them onto the flat stone landing at the stairs' top, stepping round the gasping Tungrians to join Marcus.

'You called him Aurelius Cleander?' Marcus could barely hear Scaurus's whispered question to Albinus. 'He's a freedman?'

'Indeed I am, Rutilius Scaurus.' Cleander had approached them silently up the stairs, his footsteps muffled by soft slippers. He shot Scaurus a sardonic smile, his eyes and teeth gleaming white in the darkness. 'And there's really no need to look so surprised, a man doesn't rise to the heights I've reached without being very sure to understand every situation into which he chooses to place himself. My full name, as you've clearly guessed, is Marcus Aurelius Cleander. I was freed by the last emperor, may the gods grant rest to his departed spirit, and since taking his name in gratitude for my freedom I have continued to give service to his family since his death. I am fortunate to have gained some small measure of responsibility for the running of our divine emperor's household.'

He signalled to his man to open the door ahead of them and put a cautious head around its frame, looking about him intently for a moment before nodding in apparent satisfaction.

'There are no praetorians to be seen, so now seems as good a time as any. Follow me as quickly as you can.'

He led them through the wide doorway and strode swiftly away from the shadow of the wall behind them, making for an imposing building a good hundred paces distant. The Tungrians followed as quickly as the men shuffling under the weight of the gold chests could carry their heavy burdens, Marcus and Scaurus looking about them for any sign that the guardsmen standing sentry on the palace had detected the incongruous sight of their procession, while Albinus hurried ahead of them in the freedman's wake. Reaching the building Cleander knocked on the door to which he had led them, speaking briefly to the doorman before waving the party inside.

'Let's get that door closed . . . good. We're safe from prying eyes here; the praetorians never come to this part of the palace.'

With a sudden jolt Marcus realised where they must be.

'This is the Augustana Palace?'

Cleander fixed him with a narrow-eyed stare.

'Yes. But how would you know that, Centurion, unless you've been here before?'

The young officer shrugged.

'I've heard that the emperor spends most of his time in this building, so it was a natural enough deduction.'

The stare lingered for a moment longer.

'Deduction. I *see* . . .'

He turned away from Marcus, his momentary bafflement seemingly forgotten as he addressed Albinus.

'And there, Senator, is the most difficult part of this thing done, other than the moment when we confront Prefect Perennis with the evidence of his planned treachery. I've sent my man to check that our route to the throne room is clear of anyone that might take exception to our carrying those chests to the door. While we wait for his return perhaps I ought to tell you what to expect once we're in front of Commodus?'

Albinus nodded his head gravely, and the freedman paused for a moment before speaking again.

'The emperor is a young man, and is in consequence . . . how shall I put this . . . a little *impulsive* in his manner. On top of that, he likes to devote his energies to pursuits other than the running of the empire, which has created something of an opportunity for a man like Prefect Perennis to take a good deal more control of imperial matters than might ordinarily be deemed healthy. Within a short space of time the prefect has grown in power to the point where it is he, and not the emperor, who controls both Rome and the wider empire. Be under no illusion gentlemen, when we step into the throne room for our audience with the emperor we are choosing a fight which we must win, for if we fail to open Commodus's eyes to the truth we will find Perennis an implacable and merciless enemy. You told me that you had incontrovertible proof of his plan to usurp the throne and install himself as emperor?'

Albinus gestured to the nearest chest, pulling a gold aureus from his belt pouch..

'Each of these boxes is full to the brim with gold coins just like this one.'

Cleander regarded the coin for a moment before his eyebrows raised in amazement as he realised just what it was that he was looking at.

'Show me.'

Scaurus gestured to Marcus, who unlocked the nearest chest and opened the lid. The freedman pushed his hand deep into the box before pulling out a handful of aureii, looking at them one at a time to confirm what had surprised him so much.

'By Jupiter, but that's brazen even by Perennis's standards! You, the deductive centurion, unlock the other chests. I sense the opportunity for a little theatre . . .'

The slave who had been sent to check that their route to the throne room was clear returned and nodded respectfully to Cleander in confirmation. The freedman took a deep breath with his eyes closed, then turned to the waiting officers with a faint smile.

'The next hour will either see us all dead or basking in the glory of having saved the emperor himself from an ignominious demise. Shall we go and meet with that fate?' He turned away without waiting for them to reply. 'Follow me.'

The freedman led them through the palace by a route calculated to avoid the praetorians set to guard the approaches to the emperor, down ill-lit corridors and through rooms which were clearly not in regular use, lit sparingly by single lamps whose light struggled to penetrate their corners. Halting at length before a closed door, he took a deep breath.

'Beyond this door lies the main access corridor to the emperor's throne room. If any of you are carrying knives, then you *must* leave them here. We will be searched before being allowed into the imperial presence, and the detection of a weapon of any sort will not end well for any of us.' He waited while they pulled out the daggers they had hidden in their togas and placed them in a neat pile. 'Good. Now, the gold must stay here for the time being. What I have in mind will not work unless we are completely innocent of its presence when the guards search us. Senator, you and your companions will accompany me into the throne room while your porters will stay here with my man.' He turned to the household slave. 'Listen carefully, and when you hear me call for the gold don't hesitate, but bring it into the emperor's presence at once.'

He opened the door and beckoned them through into a broad, well-lit corridor whose walls were richly decorated with embroidered hangings and with an exquisitely rendered mosaic underfoot. The passageway broadened out into an anteroom at its far end, and Marcus could see a pair of guards in full ceremonial uniform standing sentry duty in the royal palace, each man armed with spears whose blades and butt-spikes shone like polished silver. Cleander gestured to the door behind the guards with a smile, his words muttered so quietly as to be almost inaudible.

'Follow me, and look confident. These men are trained to look for the signs of fear and nervousness.'

He strode up the corridor and into the anteroom, greeting the guards with the weary patience of a man for whom the approach to the throne was simply a dull routine.

'Good evening, gentlemen, here I am again! I have with me a noble Roman senator and two illustrious officers from one of Caesar's foremost cohorts, distinguished men to whom Caesar has most graciously granted an audience in light of their devoted service in Britannia, Germania and Dacia! Search us please, and allow us admittance so that these officers can receive the thanks of their grateful emperor!'

The older of the two guards frowned.

'We've had no instructions to admit any senators or soldiers, Chamberlain, only yourself.'

The freedman frowned.

'*No* instructions? This audience has been planned for weeks! Are you telling me that I must turn away one of Rome's most exalted senators, a hero of the Dacian war, simply because your superiors have managed to mislay the detail of the evening's proceedings?' Shaking his head, he gestured to the men standing behind him. 'And how many men does Prefect Perennis have inside the throne room, all armed with spear, sword and dagger? A dozen? Twenty? What possible threat can three unarmed men, whose loyalty to the emperor has been proven on the field of battle time after time, present in the face of such an overwhelming strength of the finest soldiers in the empire? Shall I tell the emperor that you refused to permit his honoured guests admittance?'

The guardsman pondered for a moment before reluctantly nodding his acquiescence.

'We'll let your guests in, Chamberlain, and I'll send my colleague here to tell my centurion of the change to what's on the roster.'

He signalled to the other praetorian, who set off down the corridor at a brisk pace, and Cleander bowed graciously, gesturing for his companions to step forward and surrender to the praetorian's brisk but thorough search. Once all four men had been cleared to access the throne room Cleander led them through the door and into a large round chamber whose domed roof towered a full thirty feet above them at its peak. The walls were decorated in the same manner as the anteroom, and the floor was patterned with a mosaic of dazzling quality and meticulous detail depicting a circle of gladiators of all types in combat. In the middle of the chamber stood a single heavily decorated chair on a wide, one-foot-high dais, and eight spear-armed praetorians in full armour stood around the wall's circular sweep. Cleander pointed to a spot midway between door and dais.

'Stand here, one pace forward for you, Senator Albinus, you are the senior man in your party. When the emperor enters you must stand to attention and keep your gaze fixed on the wall before you. Commodus does not like to be challenged by any man, and that includes meeting his gaze unless he has invited you to speak.' He smiled wryly at some memory or other. 'And even then I advise you to meet his eyes *only* when you speak, and to avert your gaze at all other times. Trust me on this, you do not want to provoke Caesar, or like others before you, you may find that he is swift to anger and has *very* little forgiveness in him.'

The soldier closest to the door barked an order for the guards to come to attention, and a small door on the chamber's far side opened to admit a man in his mid-twenties. Despite the chamberlain's warning Marcus found himself unable to turn his gaze away from the emperor, watching through narrowed eyes as Commodus walked across the room and stepped up onto the dais. Where the young centurion was wiry and muscled from years of military conditioning, the emperor was more heavily set, with a wrestler's powerful shoulders. His beard and hair were styled in the same fashion that Albinus sported, and he was dressed in a purple toga of the highest-quality wool, intricate gold embroidery stitched around the hem to complete the traditional garment usually worn by a victorious general. Cleander strode forward across the chamber and bowed deeply to Commodus, holding the position in silence as the emperor sat down on the throne and arranged his ornate garment about him.

'Stand up, Chamberlain, and detail our business this evening. And it would be to your advantage were this meeting a brief one. I have unfinished business elsewhere in the palace, and a damned sight more fragrant than this collection of guardsmen and . . .' He looked at the three soldiers properly for the first time, a frown creasing his brow. 'And whatever it is that we have here. What *do* we have here, Chamberlain?'

Cleander straightened up and stood to attention.

'Hail Caesar Marcus Aurelius Commodus Antoninus Augustus! I bring before you three men of the highest honour and dedication to your glorious imperial family, officers in your illustrious legions who have marched thousands of miles to bring you a gift of treasure captured in the war that has recently concluded in Britannia. With your permission, Caesar, allow me to introduce—'

The door through which they had entered burst open with a bang, as if it had been kicked from the other side, causing the three men to turn and stare, although Marcus noted from the corner of his eye that Cleander remained exactly as he was, with his eyes fixed on the startled emperor. As the doors flew open a grim-faced man in the uniform of a senior guard officer marched through them, a troop of a dozen determined-looking guardsmen at his back. With a shiver that was part exhilaration and part dread, the young centurion realised that the man stalking into the room at their head was the prefect in command of the praetorians, and he shivered at the shock of recognition, the prefect's face and gait instantly recognisable from his own short term of service with the guard.

'*Hold!*'

The statement was no more than a whisper from between Scaurus's barely opened lips, but the tone was harsh in its urgency, the unmistakable command locking Marcus's limbs even as he tensed himself to spring at the man who had ordered his father's murder. Praetorian Prefect Perennis walked swiftly up to Cleander and went face-to-face with the freedman, gesturing for his guardsmen to surround the small party. Marcus stood stock still as a hard-faced soldier levelled a spear at him, guessing that the newcomers had orders to take advantage of the slightest excuse to cut them down where they stood. Turning his head slowly back to Cleander, he saw that the chamberlain had at last deigned to look at the prefect, smiling gently in the face of the older man's bristling anger. When he spoke his voice was even softer than before, his words honeyed as he arched an eyebrow in question.

'Prefect Perennis. I always knew you had a gift for the dramatic, but you appear to have surpassed even *your* most extravagant acts of theatre this evening.'

He returned his gaze to the emperor, who was now sitting up on his throne where previously he had been slumped, his expression quizzical. The praetorian commander shook his head angrily, moving to block the chamberlain's view of Commodus as he barked a harsh challenge, spittle flying unnoticed from his lips.

'What the fuck do you think you're doing, Cleander? You've just lied to my praetorians and brought three complete strangers into the emperor's presence! Explain yourself!'

I I

Perennis flicked a glance across the trio arrayed behind the freedman, a moment of puzzlement crossing his face as his eyes met Marcus's. Cleander raised his hands in a gesture of resignation, and the praetorian's eyes returned to him before the split-second sensation of recognition had time to sink in.

'Forgive me, noble Caesar, for my impetuous decision to bring these men into *your* throne room with me. Knowing of your deep love for the men of *your* imperial army, Senator Albinus and these two loyal officers begged me to allow them to offer you their deepest respects in addition to their quite stupendous gift of booty from distant Britannia. How was I to resist such a heartfelt plea for them to be allowed to prostrate themselves at your feet on behalf of the senate and the legions, especially as I knew that you would be modelling your toga picta this evening? What better sight could there be for devoted officers than their emperor dressed in the very garment that celebrates the martial prowess they exercise in your name?'

Perennis bridled, his face darkening as his anger waxed full.

'You don't talk to the emperor, Chamberlain, you talk to *me*! What *possible* justification could you have for compromising the safety of our beloved Caesar?! These men have no official permission to enter the imperial presence, no good reason for doing so, and any one of them could be an assassin bent on murder!'

Cleander shrugged, waving an arm at the thirty or so armed and armoured men positioned around the chamber. His voice softened slightly, a note of unalloyed praise licking at his listeners' ears.

'Surely not, Prefect? For a start, your guards on the door were most assiduous in their searches of Caesar's guests, and I note that you had more than the regulation number of men on duty even before you burst in with this fresh contingent of guards. I feel safer here and now than I would in the middle of one of Senator Albinus's legions, given the famed loyalty of you and your men to our beloved Caesar.' He paused significantly, allowing Albinus's name to sink in. 'And surely you recall the senator, he was most warmly greeted by the emperor earlier this year on his return from Dacia, having not only put down a Sarmatae rebellion both cruelly and without any danger of it being repeated for a generation or more, but also having saved one of Caesar's most profitable gold mines from an upstart German prefect and his cohort of deserters, if my memory serves me right.'

Albinus bowed slightly to the prefect, his face a study in passivity, and the freedman pressed on, clearly calculating that he could not afford to allow the praetorian back into the conversation.

'And so I entreat you to forgive me this small indulgence, Caesar. The senator and his colleagues, both men who fought alongside him with great distinction and took part in the rescue of the gold mine, represent no more threat to you than the most loyal of your guardsmen. And besides, when I saw the magnificence of the gift they have brought to you from the empire's distant north frontier as a mark of the legions' loyalty and love for their emperor, I knew at once that you would have me struck down as a disloyal cur were I to deny them an audience.'

Perennis opened his mouth to speak, his eyes narrowing as he began to wonder as to the exact nature of Cleander's game, but the emperor spoke first, his voice eager as it cut the prefect off before he had a chance to speak.

'A gift? What is it, Cleander?'

'Gold, my Caesar. A quite *startling* quantity of gold.'

The freedman smiled into Perennis's sudden consternation, smirking as the prefect's face turned an ashen grey. Commodus nodded, although to Marcus he looked a little put out.

'Gold, you say? I suppose an emperor can never have too much gold, although recent confiscations have swelled the imperial coffers quite nicely, eh Prefect? I was hoping for some captured barbarian weapons, and perhaps a few dozen captured slave girls.'

Cleander spoke quickly, recognising the danger in his emperor's lukewarm response.

'Yes, my Caesar, the prefect and his men have indeed made you richer than you might ever have expected through their pursuit and prosecution of those among us whose loyalty has not been to the empire and your pre-eminent position as its ruler. But this gift of which I speak is a *fortune*, Caesar, enough wealth to allow you to indulge yourself in whatever way you choose. Enough money to build you your own gladiatorial arena here within the walls of the Palatine, and to recruit the cream of the empire's gladiators for your private entertainment. Enough to recruit a harem of beauties from every province so that you can take your pleasure with a pair of different women every night for the rest of your life . . .' He paused to allow Commodus's imagination to work on the images he was suggesting before delivering the killer punch. 'Given the apparent weight of the consignment, I estimate that they may have brought you as much as one hundred million sesterces worth of gold.'

The emperor's eyes narrowed as his servant's words sank in, and Perennis stared at the chamberlain in barely disguised horror as Commodus leaned forward and gestured his chamberlain closer.

'*That* much gold? And these men have marched all the way from Britannia to bring me this fortune?'

Cleander smiled slightly, calculating that he had sufficient control of the conversation to allow Albinus to speak.

'Senator? This was after all *your* idea . . .'

Remaining rigidly at attention, the senator spoke quickly, knowing that Perennis was seething with poorly disguised fury at the sudden uncontrollable turn of events.

'Hail Caesar! May it please you Caesar, Tribune Scaurus here was the officer who liberated this prize from the barbarians north of the wall built by the divine Antoninus Pius, utterly destroying our last remaining enemy on the frontier in the process. He brought his discovery to the attention of the imperial Sixth Legion's acting commander . . .' He paused, as if searching his memory for the name. 'Ah yes, Camp Prefect Castus.'

Perennis started again, his eyes betraying his surprise at not hearing Sorex's name.

'But I gave orders for there to be no operations north of the wall! All units were to hold in place until—'

'Yes, Prefect Perennis.' Albinus and Scaurus had considered their story with the greatest of care before leaving the transit barracks, and the senator was swift to cut Perennis off before he could take control of the situation, the urgency of his interjection spurred by the knowledge of what the praetorians would do to him if he failed to get his story out. 'Having taken advantage of a brief opportunity to kill five thousand barbarians, and liberate this startling quantity of gold from them, that most experienced officer Prefect Castus quite correctly deemed it best if Tribune Scaurus marched it south under the guard of his two auxiliary cohorts, rather than have it fall under the control of any single senior officer. The prefect deemed it best to remove the temptation presented by so much wealth, so to speak, enough gold to buy the loyalty of the Britannia legions, and in doing so take the chance to pay homage to your imperial glory, Caesar. Tribune Scaurus and I were colleagues in Dacia, and so he thought it best to bring the gold here to Rome, into my safekeeping. At my suggestion his fifteen hundred spearmen have brought the spoils of war to your palace, Caesar, every man sworn to die in defence of their emperor, every man the veteran of a dozen battles fought in your name to bring you triumph!'

Perennis stared at him for a long moment in the silence that followed, then turned to face the emperor, either rage or a mortal fear for his own life making his right eye quiver minutely.

'Caesar, with your permission, I feel that it would be unwise for us to indulge these fantasies any longer . . . I'll have these men . . .'

'*Us*, Prefect?' Cleander's voice was still soft, but it cut across the praetorian commander with more than sufficient authority to silence him. 'You feel it unwise for *us* to indulge these *fantasies*? Surely it is *Caesar's* place to determine if this gift is a fantasy. Caesar's place, Prefect, and not *yours*. After all, a million aureii should prove difficult to conjure out of thin air, wouldn't you say? It is of course *your* decision, my Caesar . . .'

Commodus spoke quickly, waving aside Perennis's horrified protests, his eyes gleaming with the excitement of the moment.

'Bring in this gift, Cleander, and prove that what you say is true. Prefect Perennis, order your men back to their places.'

The freedman strode back to the doors, ignoring the praetorians who had frozen where they stood at the emperor's command, and flung them open again to reveal the startled guardsmen they had passed moments before. He called out a command in a loud, clear voice at odds with the previous softness of his tone.

'Bring in the gold!'

The door to the room where the Tungrians waited opened in response to his shouted command, and one by one the chests were carried through it and up the wide corridor into the ante-room. Cleander stepped closer to the door guards, and Marcus barely heard his softly spoken words as he muttered a dire warning.

'These chests contain the proof of your prefect's treachery. Make any attempt to block their entry to the throne room and I promise you that you'll die with him. Just not as quickly . . .'

Stepping back into the room, he raised a hand to point to the gold bearers' slow procession as the first of the chests approached the doorway.

'These boxes full of gold are carried by loyal auxiliary soldiers of the First and Second Tungrian Cohorts, Caesar, the men who captured this magnificent prize for you. And note, Perennis, they are unarmed, and represent no threat to our beloved emperor.'

Marcus, his gaze fixed on Perennis, saw the prefect's eyes narrow again at the mention of the Tungrians, his face taking on the slightly puzzled expression of a man who knew that the word should mean more to him than it did, as Cleander continued his address to the emperor.

'These men have proven their loyalty to you on a dozen

battlefields across the northern empire, as you can see from their faces, and now they bring you the spoils of their struggles as homage to your pre-eminence among all Romans.'

As the first chest was carried into the throne room Marcus realised the brutal logic that had underlain Albinus's selection of men to carry the gold through the city. Not only were the soldiers he had chosen among the biggest and strongest men in the two cohorts, but to a man their faces were disfigured by scars inflicted on them by their enemies in the succession of battles that the Tungrians had fought since the beginning of Calgus's rebellion two years before.

'That's close enough!'

Perennis had regained something of his composure in the face of looming disaster, and stepped forward to stop the procession, drawing his sword in a rasp of iron on scabbard fittings. Cleander smiled crookedly at him, shaking his head slightly as the Tungrians lowered their burdens carefully to the throne room's intricate mosaic floor.

'I always thought that being the only member of the imperial court to carry a sword was a purely ceremonial privilege. After all, the days when the emperor Trajan told his prefect to use his *for* him as long as he ruled well, but *against* him if he ruled badly, are long gone, are they not? But to draw your sword in the presence of the emperor, Prefect? Who presents Caesar with the greater threat, I wonder, his loyal servants who have risked their lives to win him a fortune, or any man who dares to unsheathe a blade in his presence, no matter how elevated his position? But no matter, I'm sure Caesar knows best . . .'

He strode across the room and threw back the lid of the closest chest and thrust a fist into the sea of gold coins within, pulling out a handful and nodding to Albinus, who quickly opened the other boxes to reveal the treasure that filled them almost to their brims. Striding past the praetorian prefect he went down on one knee before the emperor, holding out the coins while Perennis looked on white-faced.

'Here, my Caesar, look at these coins, and tell me if Prefect

Perennis's charge of fantasy rings true.' He waited while Commodus stared down at the small heap of gleaming gold coins in his lap, then picked one up and peered more closely at it. 'See how the reverse of the coin is decorated with an image of Britannia, to represent your victory over the barbarians who sought to steal the province from you. It is traditional, I believe, for Britannia to be depicted in chains after such a victory, of course, but you can overlook such an oversight, I'm sure, unless there is some deeper meaning . . .' He looked up at the emperor with his face perfectly straight. 'And now, Caesar, look at the head that adorns these coins.'

Commodus turned the aureus over in his hand, staring down at it for a long moment before his face creased in a frown.

'But this isn't my head.'

Cleander spoke again, his voice subtly changing tone to that of a man reluctantly revealing a distasteful truth.

'Indeed, Caesar, and nor is it your beloved father's. Upon a closer inspection I realised that the profile depicted on these coins seems to be that of your praetorian prefect. But I'm sure there is some rational explanation. What do the words around the coin's rim say?'

The young emperor's voice fell to a whisper.

'*Imperator . . . Fides Exercitum?*'

For a moment the throne room was utterly silent, as Commodus digested the full magnitude of what had been revealed by the three simple words that circled the profile of his closest adviser.

'*Emperor? Loyalty of the soldiers?!*'

The words were bellowed at the top of the emperor's voice as he rose from the throne in a scatter of flashing gold, turning to point an accusatory finger at the recoiling Perennis who raised his hands in helpless defence, his unsheathed sword unwittingly held out before him.

'M-my C-caesar . . .'

'*Emperor?! Fucking EMPEROR?!*' Commodus strode forward, putting a finger in the prefect's face with an apparent disdain for the sword less than a foot from his body. '*You sought to take my throne, and now you raise your sword to me?! Seize him!*'

The praetorians closest to Perennis snapped out of their amazement and stepped forward, gripping the man who until a moment before had been the master of their world. Perennis allowed the sword to fall from his hand, and it clattered loudly onto the mosaic to lie unnoticed at his feet. Cleander stood in silence with a grim smile of satisfaction, watching as Commodus's volcanic temper took hold and burst from him in an angry roar.

'I'll have you beheaded, here and now, you scheming bastard. I'll have your guts ripped out while you're still alive to watch, and then I'll . . .'

'Caesar!'

Every man in the room turned to stare at Scaurus, both Cleander and Albinus gazing in amazement as the tribune stepped forward and snapped to attention. Commodus turned slowly to face him with a blank-eyed scowl of fury, and for an instant Marcus was convinced that the emperor was about to take out his ire on the man with the temerity to interrupt his furious screams of rage.

'Forgive my interjection, my Caesar, but I must bring a matter of great importance to your attention before you pass judgement on this man.'

Falling silent, Scaurus waited with a commendably blank face for Commodus's reaction. Again the entire throne room seemed to hold its breath, and the emperor stared down from his dais at the lone figure standing before him. When he spoke his voice was calm, although it seemed to Marcus as though his grasp on the rage that had boiled through him a moment before was tenuous at best.

'And who are you, that dares to interrupt your emperor? Perhaps I'll have your tongue cut out to teach you to respect the throne a little better?'

Scaurus went down on his knees, lowering his gaze submissively.

'Caesar, I will happily cut out my own tongue if you command it, if only you will hear me out.'

Commodus stepped down from the dais and walked with slow, deliberate footsteps across a tiled representation of a retiarius, the gladiator's net and trident held ready to strike, producing an ornately engraved dagger from within the folds of his toga.

'I carry this with me at all times, and have done ever since that idiot Quintianus tried to knife me on my way home from the theatre one night. My praetorians were too slow in realising that he was among them, and if he had not stopped to shout that the senate had sent him to kill me he'd have put this blade in my guts. Ever since then I've gone everywhere armed with the very knife that would have killed me if he'd not been such a fool.' He paced to a halt before Scaurus with the knife raised. 'So, tell me your story, Tribune, and believe me, if I don't believe it merited your impudence then I'll cut your tongue out myself!'

From his position behind Scaurus and slightly to one side, Marcus could see the emperor's face with the knife's blade held up before it barely inches from that of his tribune, his eyes gleaming with purpose, but Scaurus's voice was as level as ever when he replied, without any hint of the threat hanging over him.

'Caesar, the praetorian prefect sent one of his sons to Britannia in the position of military tribune three years ago. While serving with the Sixth Legion on the frontier the younger Perennis betrayed his legatus to a rebel leader, and sent the legion into an ambush that cost both the legatus's life and the legion's standard. He hoped to profit from the legatus's death by the grant of a field promotion to command what was left of the Sixth.'

'That's a *damned* lie, Caesar, my son would never have . . .'

Commodus spun on his heel, turning to glare at Perennis.

'*One* more word from you, Perennis, and your short remaining span of life will become very much more painful!'

He slowly turned back to face Scaurus, his tone now more questioning than threatening.

'I am aware of the eagle's loss, as I am aware that a tribune of the Sixth appointed by the former praetorian prefect has recently *restored* that legion's honour by recapturing the eagle.'

Scaurus shook his head.

'Not so, Caesar. The eagle that now parades before the Sixth is a replica, carefully fabricated to match the original's exact specification, but no more the genuine article than the man who discovered it. The eagle's "discovery" was planned by the praetorian prefect, and simply intended to undo the damage done by his son, of whose treachery and death he was informed by an anonymous letter written by a senior officer in the army of Britannia.'

Commodus narrowed his eyes, leaning close to Scaurus and speaking softly in his ear.

'And you have *proof* of these accusations?'

Scaurus nodded slowly.

'I do, Caesar. The centurion standing behind me not only witnessed the original act of betrayal, but he also killed the prefect's son as punishment for his treachery. I therefore felt it fitting to send him north of the Antonine Wall when rumours emerged that the eagle was being held in a barbarian fortress, and at the cost of many good men's lives he managed to recover it along with an item which, while somewhat gruesome, provides provenance for the eagle. If I may, Caesar?'

Commodus nodded, and Scaurus turned to gesture to Marcus. Under Albinus's disbelieving eyes the young centurion crossed to the last of the chests, thrusting his arm into the gold and searching for a moment before pulling out the eagle that had been rescued from The Fang. He stepped forward and knelt before Commodus, holding up the battered golden standard in both hands. Distracted, the emperor handed his knife to a guardsman and took the eagle, holding it up to the lamplight.

'It looks genuine enough, even if it's perhaps a bit too battered to be the real thing. But this alone is not proof, it could easily be a fake.'

Scaurus bowed his head momentarily in acknowledgement of the emperor's point.

'Indeed Caesar, on its own this is not enough to prove my case. But as I said, that isn't all that Centurion Corvus here managed to rescue from the barbarians.'

Marcus paced across to the first chest and dug his hands into the coins, pulling a heavy bag from within the treasure's depths.

Reaching into its open neck, he held up the preserved head of his dead birth father.

'This is the head of the Sixth Legion's legatus, Gaius Calidius Sollemnis, Caesar, hacked from his dead body on the same afternoon that the eagle was lost. Senator Albinus can doubtless stand witness that this is indeed his head. Forgive the smell of cedar oil, I had the legatus's head preserved in it until very recently, and it is rather pervasive.'

The senator nodded slowly, unable to take his eyes from the grotesque object before him.

'Indeed I can, Caesar. He was a family friend. Thanks to these men he can now be accorded some measure of peace, and burial in his family's plot.'

Albinus stared at Scaurus for a moment, and Marcus read a hard edge in the glance that had not been there before. The emperor took the head from the young centurion, sniffing with distaste at the aroma rising from it.

'All of which is very touching, but you still haven't proven that this is really the Sixth's standard.'

Scaurus nodded.

'In that case Caesar, allow me to present the definitive proof.'

He reached into his toga. Half a dozen men tensed, hands on the hilts of their swords, only to relax when he pulled out nothing more threatening than a pair of writing tablets.

'Here is the proof, Caesar.' He held up one of the notepads, its exterior battered and discoloured by a dark-brown stain. 'This tablet is a record maintained by the Sixth Legion's standard bearer, a man of great diligence who wrote a painstaking description of his eagle, noting its every little scratch and dent, before he died in battle fighting to his last breath in its defence. You will note that the tablet's exterior is stained with his blood. And this –' he held up the second tablet, its wooden case crisp-edged and without blemish '– this is the sworn testimony of a Sixth Legion centurion, a man who knew the standard bearer better than any other man alive since they were brothers, that this tablet belonged to his sibling, and that the notes inside are an accurate description of the eagle. If I may?'

He reached out a hand towards the eagle, pointing to a deep score on the underside of its left wing, then opened the stained tablet and read from the notes scratched into its wax.

'Scratch, two inches long, incurred in battle against the Batavian traitor cohorts. Vengeance delivered.'

Commodus nodded slowly, passing the eagle to Cleander.

'Well now, it seems that the tribune here has indeed earned the right to interrupt his emperor, at least on *this* occasion. Chamberlain, you are hereby instructed to have this eagle refurbished and returned to the Sixth Legion, and to remove any stain from the legion's records connected with its loss. It seems that Legatus Sollemnis was the victim of yet more of the former praetorian prefect's poisonous ways . . .' He paused, a peculiar smile crossing his face. 'But before you do, I've an idea. You, come here.'

He beckoned a praetorian guardsman standing by the throne-room's door with a spear held upright in his hand. The soldier, long conditioned to instant and unquestioning obedience, strode across the room and snapped to attention, his eyebrows rising as Commodus reached out and took the spear from him. The emperor held out a hand while he considered the weapon's long wooden shaft, staring closely at the point where its iron head was connected to the wood.

'Sword!'

The soldier obeyed promptly, unsheathing his spatha and presenting it to the emperor hilt first. Commodus took the sword and held the spear out in front of him, raising the spatha and hacking down at a point just below the base of the long iron blade to send it clattering to the floor, leaving a clean stump of wood where the spearhead had been attached. He nodded in satisfaction, holding the sword out to its owner.

'Nice and sharp, just like a soldier's sword should be. Dismissed!'

He waved the bemused soldier back to his place by the wall, contemplating the denuded spear shaft for a moment before walking across to Cleander and taking the eagle back from him.

'Knowing how the military does love to make everything with more than one purpose, I'd imagine that this standard fits quite neatly . . .' The emperor slotted the eagle's hollow base down onto the shaft, nodding in satisfaction. 'There, just as I thought, a perfect match. So, Perennis . . .' He walked across to the disgraced prefect with the spear held lightly in one hand. 'All this time I've treated you as a man whose only concern was with his duty, and with the good of the empire, and, in return, all this time you've been plotting to murder me and replace me on the throne. You had a dynasty in mind as well, didn't you, with those two boys of yours in command of the Pannonian legions? A nice quick march down through Italy and you'd have had half a dozen legions to back up your claim alongside your freshly purchased legions from Britannia. I'll have them both killed, of course, and the only pity is that you won't live to see it happen. Cleander?'

The freedman stepped forward, his face expressionless despite the scale of the triumph he had engineered over his rival.

'Caesar?'

'Send parties of fast horsemen to summon this traitor's sons back to Rome, in their father's name mind you. Let them believe that he's taken the throne, and doubtless they'll provide conclusive evidence of his treachery. Once they're detached from their legions, they are to be killed and buried where they'll never be found.' Cleander bowed and turned away to do his master's bidding. 'Oh, and Cleander . . .' The emperor's servant turned back with a knowing look.

'Caesar?'

As Marcus watched, the same strange smile crept back onto the emperor's face.

'Call for the Knives. Have them come to me here.'

'As you wish, Caesar.'

Commodus turned back to the disgraced prefect with a flourish of his improvised standard.

'And so, Perennis, the wheel turns full circle. You recruited my Knives to do the dirty work necessary to maintain the empire, and now I will unleash them upon your family. Your line will be expunged from existence with the same thoroughness you ordered them to use with the Quintili clan, the Aquila brothers and—'

'*Aquila!*' Perennis's eyes were locked on Marcus, wide with sudden recognition. '*It's him! He's Aquila! He's the son, the only survivor. He's different, older, but it's him, I know it!*'

In the depths of his terror at impending death he had latched on to the name of Marcus's family and finally made the connection that had evaded him moments before, belatedly recognising the Tungrian centurion standing before him. Tearing an arm free from his captors he pointed an accusatory finger at Marcus, his voice close to hysteria.

'*He served in the Guard, before his father sent him to Britannia to save him from imperial justice, and he murdered the men I sent to arrest him and return him to Rome.*'

Commodus turned slowly to look at the young centurion, who stared rigidly at the wall behind Perennis.

'*Really?* You're trying to tell me that an equestrian officer serving in the army of Britannia is the son of a senatorial family you liquidated three years ago? Let's put that claim to the test, shall we?' The emperor addressed Marcus, who stiffened his body as a sign of respect. 'So, Centurion, what is your name?'

Marcus spoke without hesitation, knowing that he could end up dying alongside the man who had ordered the deaths of his family if he failed to convince the emperor of his assumed identity.

'*Caesar!* Marcus Tribulus Corvus, Caesar!'

'And where were you born?'

'Here in Rome, Caesar, in the Caelian!'

Commodus pondered.

'I see. And how did you come to be serving in an auxiliary cohort? Wouldn't the son of a member of the equestrian class be better off taking a position with one of the legions?'

Marcus creased his lips to simulate a gentle but uncontrollable amusement, lowering his voice from the harsh bark he had used to answer the emperor's previous questions.

'My father, Caesar, served with the same cohort when he was my age. It was his opinion that it would be more character forming for me to be exposed to the rougher elements of the army.'

Commodus smiled.

'Did he, indeed? Fathers have a habit of wanting what they believe to be for the best for their sons, even if their opinion sometimes runs counter to what their sons might prefer. My own father, may the gods rest his departed spirit, insisted that I study with a succession of tutors when all I really wanted was to learn how best to wield a sword.'

Encouraged by his wistful smile, Marcus chanced one last comment.

'Whereas for myself, Caesar, training with weapons always came before the classroom.'

The emperor nodded absently, turning away even before the young centurion's sentence was complete, gesturing to Marcus with a hand.

'Men like this are what have driven the empire to the successes it has achieved, sons of Rome happy to serve in the most arduous of conditions to secure our frontiers. And you, Perennis, have the temerity to traduce this man's good name by comparison with that of a known traitor!'

Nostrils flaring as he involuntarily sucked in a lungful of air, Marcus fought his instinct to leap upon the emperor, as Commodus unknowingly repeated the false accusation that had seen his entire family slaughtered out of hand. Just as he was about to surrender to the overwhelming urge to snap out a hand and crush the emperor's windpipe, the big man turned away, hefting the improvised legion standard in one hand as he strode back towards Perennis, the anger swelling in his voice as he neared the cringing prisoner.

'I went with my father to Germania ten years ago or so, along with half a dozen legions, and I remember vividly the victory parade after we'd crushed the Marcomanni. There was an eagle bearer out in front of his legion, one arm in a sling, the other holding his eagle held proudly in the air, and my father walked up to him and put a hand on his shoulder, turning back to me with a proud smile. "This is my sort of soldier, Lucius," he said, "a man who will fight to the death for his eagle even when the enemy swarm all round him."'

He paused, turning a circle to show his improvised standard to everyone in the throne room.

'You see, this eagle bearer, despite the fact that his right arm had been broken, fought on and flattened half a dozen of the barbarians with his standard, swinging it to dash their brains one at a time. But that wasn't all he did, was it Perennis? I'm sure you can recall the story?'

The prefect's voice quavered as he answered.

'Caesar?'

'I think you know exactly what I'm referring to, don't you Perennis? That noble standard bearer also made full and savage use of *this*!'

The emperor flipped the standard over, showing them the shaft's shining metal butt-spike, a polished iron cone designed to both prevent the weapon's wooden shaft from splintering and to provide some threat if its bladed head was lost.

'Of course the spike's normally not much use for anything when compared with the blade. The Greeks used to call it a *sauroter*, a lizard sticker, but as that standard bearer proved, you can kill a man with a lizard sticker, if you're sufficiently *brutal*—'

He pivoted and stamped forward with a loud grunt, forcing every last ounce of his strength into the standard's shaft as the iron spike punched into Perennis's lower gut with a wet thump, blood spraying to either side of the praetorian as the spear tore out through his back to transfix him. Perennis gasped reflexively, looking down in horror at the wooden shaft protruding from his body, and his eyes rolled up as he slumped forward. Commodus released his grasp on the standard with a theatrical wave of his bloodied hands, turning away as his disgraced adviser staggered forward a few steps and sprawled full length across a mosaic representation of a secutor's armoured body, in a slowly spreading puddle of his own blood, his voice rising in a high-pitched whimper of distress.

'You've ordered the deaths of enough people, Tigidius Perennis, so the least you can do is meet your own end like a man.' The emperor barked out his last command as he headed for a small door to his private quarters on the far side of the chamber. 'He stays there until he dies. And any man who decides to end his suffering prematurely is to die in exactly the same manner.'

The men left in the chamber stared at each other, their eyes drawn to the praetorian prefect as he lay panting on the tiled floor, his hands fretting at the spear shaft that was skewered through his groin.

'Well now, who could have predicted that this would have gone quite as well as it did?' Cleander turned back to his companions with a broad smile. 'My only serious rival dying with a spear though his guts and me with a hundred million sesterces in gold to play with. That and having had the pleasure of witnessing *you*, Tribune, risking your life quite recklessly in order to restore the honour of a man you never knew. Quite amazing . . .'

He turned back to Perennis, smiling sadly down at the dying man.

'As for you, Tigidius Perennis, I'm afraid that I'm going to have to honour Commodus's orders with regard to your eventual death. Praetorians, clear the chamber!'

The guardsmen standing around the room barely hesitated before their discipline overrode their astonishment, and at a barked command from the centurion commanding the detachment they stamped to attention and filed from the room, leaving the four men standing around the writhing body of the dying Perennis. Cleander tipped his head to the door through which they had entered.

'You too, gentlemen, and you can take your soldiers with you. The gold obviously remains here.'

Scaurus and Albinus exchanged glances, the senator shrugging and turning for the door with a gesture to his companions to follow him. They walked back through the palace in silence behind a praetorian who had been detailed to guide them to the gate, and emerged from the Palatine's vastness onto the steps overlooking the Great Circus, the race track's sand gleaming palely in the moonlight. Cotta and his men were waiting patiently at the foot of the wide marble stairway, and the retired centurion took the steps two at a time as he hurried to join his patron. The guardsman turned away and walked back up the last half-dozen steps, leaving the party standing in momentary silence.

Albinus addressed Scaurus.

'I've a bone to pick with you, Tribune, and I neither require nor appreciate an audience of goggling soldiers.'

Scaurus nodded at the senator's barely restrained fury, then turned to the troops standing around them.

'You, Chosen Man. Take these men to the bottom of the steps and form them up to march. We'll have to make our way back to the barracks the way we came in, and the Subura will be no less lively than it was before.'

Cotta and Marcus eyed each other for a moment, the veteran looking his younger counterpart up and down with a slight smile, as if he were calculating the odds, while Marcus simply spread his arms slightly and opened his hands, tilting his head and raising his eyebrows. Albinus, missing the exchange in his self-righteous anger, put a finger in Scaurus's face and launched into a furious tirade.

'You've betrayed my trust, Rutilius Scaurus! You provoked the anger of an emperor which could have all too easily spilled over and seen me dead alongside you, and as for that fool's trick with the eagle . . .'

The tribune stared back at him with eyes suddenly as hard as flint, and Marcus realised that Albinus was about to get another unpleasant shock.

'Words failing you, Senator? You're speechless with wonder that I might take a risk to rescue the honour of a dead man?' He took a pace closer to the bigger man, his face set in lines of anger equally as hard as those on Albinus's face. 'Take a good look at yourself, *Decimus*, or are you back to being Clodius Albinus now that I've offended your dignity? A man of your class died in Britannia at the start of the rebellion, betrayed and left to take the blame for the loss of his legion's eagle, and if you can't see the honour to be gained in restoring his reputation then I can only pity you.'

Albinus sneered at him, shaking his head in angry bemusement.

'You can just call me *Senator* when we meet in the street, Tribune, and make sure you pay me the appropriate respect if you don't want me to set Cotta and his men on you and pay you out for this disrespect with a good beating. Not that you'll be walking the streets of Rome for long, once the emperor's favourite freedman realises just how much gold you took from those chests to make room for the eagle and Gaius Sollemnis's head.'

Scaurus smiled coldly back at him.

'Is your indignation the product of your loyalty to the throne, or simply piqued pride that I took more gold than you managed to slide into your purse back in Dacia when we recovered the Albinus Major mine from Gerwulf and his Germans?'

Albinus shook his head, a superior smile playing across his lips.

'You've no way of proving that accusation, Tribune!'

The smile faded as Scaurus raised an eyebrow at him.

'Don't I, Senator? Are you sufficiently sure of that to gamble your life on it? When you ordered me to surrender the records of exactly how much gold we'd recovered, did you ever stop to wonder if I might not have guessed what your reaction to that much gold would be?' Albinus stared at him in silence. 'Yes, I kept a copy. In fact what I gave *you* was actually the copy, while the original stayed nice and secure in my campaign chest. It's very proper, marked with the mine's official marks, which I'm sure a man as intelligent as Cleander will have authenticated in next to no time, while what I gave you had some small but important imperfections incorporated. I've a most resourceful standard bearer in my First Cohort, a man with an avarice that's the match of your own, if not quite so highly born, and he has a deft touch when it comes to doctoring the records, whether they be those of his century's burial club or the official documentation of an imperial gold mine.'

He grinned at the senator, nodding his head at the other man's sudden consternation.

'I made sure that the little clues he left were subtle, nothing that would stand out to a cursory inspection, of course, but enough to see you condemned as a thief on a grand scale if ever a hint of your sordid little embezzlement were to reach the wrong ears and prompt a proper review of the paperwork. I'd imagine that it wouldn't take very much to work out how much gold you kept back for yourself by comparison with the original documentation I can provide to the Chamberlain if the need arises. Speaking of whom . . .'

Cleander had appeared at the head of the stone stairs, and stood looking at them quizzically for a moment before stepping lightly down to join them, leaving a pair of spear-armed praetorians staring down at them disapprovingly.

'You seem a little perturbed, Senator? Have the events of the evening not played out to your expectations? I have to say that I'm *very* content with life now that my only rival for control of the palace has been dealt with so harshly. I know this emperor well enough to be sure that he'll be turning to me for guidance in Perennis's absence, guidance I'll be more than happy to turn into the exercise of imperial power once our new relationship has settled down. He does so love to spend his energies on the seduction of maidens and practice with his sword, fondly imagining himself as a notorious gladiator rather than the ruler of the civilised world. By simply being reluctantly willing to shoulder my Caesar's unbearable burden I'll achieve just as much control of the empire as that fool Perennis expected to achieve with all of his manoeuvring and plotting.'

He smiled beatifically down at them.

'And now I think it's time for you to take yourself off home, Senator, secure in the knowledge that you've done your duty to your emperor and averted the threat that was hanging over him as long as the previous praetorian prefect was at his side.'

Albinus nodded with more respect than Marcus had seen in him earlier, gesturing to his companions to accompany him.

'We'll renew this discussion elsewhere. It probably isn't fitting for the steps of an imperial palace in any case.'

'Just you, Senator, and your bodyguard of course. The tribune and I will stay a moment longer before he goes on his way.'

Albinus arched a disbelieving eyebrow, but found something in Cleander's level gaze that stilled any complaint he might have made, and he turned away down the steps with a wave to Cotta. The bodyguard stared for a moment at Marcus and then nodded at him.

'We'll meet again, I expect, Centurion *Corvus*.'

Marcus met his gaze and inclined his head in return.

'Indeed, Centurion Cotta. Perhaps we'll provide each other with some sport, the next time our paths cross.'

Cotta barked a laugh over his shoulder as he followed Albinus down towards the street and his waiting men.

'Oh, I have little doubt of that!'

Cleander smirked at Scaurus.

'You need to keep your attack dog on a shorter rope, Tribune. He seems to be filled with the desire to tear out the throat of anyone and everyone that gets close enough to him.' He stepped closer to Marcus, looking him up and down as if he were examining a finely bred chariot horse. 'You're a fascinating specimen, Centurion . . . Tribulus Corvus, was that what you said your name was?'

Marcus snapped to attention.

'Centurion Marcus Tribulus Corvus, First Tungrian Auxiliary Cohort, Chamberlain!'

Cleander nodded.

'Yes, that was it. Tribulus Corvus . . .' He looked at Scaurus with an amused expression. 'I believe that a tribulus is a military invention scattered in large numbers across ground where a cavalry attack is expected, a neat little device of sharpened iron that presents a spike uppermost to pierce a hoof and instantly render a horse lame. A very military name, and in that case surely one that stretches back a fair way in the city's history, and yet I am told by men who ought to know that there is no record of any such clan title. I watched the centurion closely during that entertaining audience with the emperor, and on two occasions I could swear that I saw him barely restrain himself from leaping first at Perennis, and then at our beloved Caesar, by what appeared to be supreme self-control. So, *are* you simply an attack dog, Centurion, or are you perhaps something infinitely more dangerous?'

He regarded them both for a moment in silence.

'I find it impossible to believe that you, Tribune, would do anything to bring jeopardy to your emperor, and you clearly trust the centurion here, and yet I'm finding it hard to avoid the conclusion that Tigidius Perennis was in fact correct when he pointed the finger at this young man and named him as the outlawed son of a senator who was executed for treason three years ago. And if that's the case –' he raised a hand to Marcus as if to forestall an assault by the stone-faced centurion '– if you really are Marcus Valerius Aquila, then having successfully found a place to hide for the rest of your days on the empire's frontier, what would be a sufficiently strong lure to bring you back to Rome? Revenge?' He raised his hands to the night sky above them. 'If so, then how lucky you are to have had the gods grant you the pleasure of watching the man who sentenced your family to death writhe with a spear through his guts, even if it was wielded by hands other than your own. And having met the emperor, you will now be clear that he had little part in your father's condemnation and murder, or in any other part of running the empire for that matter.'

He waited until Marcus responded, nodding reluctantly.

'Excellent. In which case all is well. Perennis is thwarted, the gold he sought to use for his own ends is restored to the imperial treasury, his demise has doubtless satisfied your desire to see him suffer in return for the suffering he inflicted upon your family, and you two gentlemen can return to your cohort and renew the centurion's anonymity. I'm sufficiently grateful to you for bringing this matter to my attention to keep the truth of your parentage to myself, and to allow you to return to the shadows from which you came. I will even overlook the small matter of exactly where the gold displaced from those chests to accommodate the eagle and Legatus Sollemnis's head might have got to. After all, I'm sure that your journey here wasn't without its expenses.'

Scaurus opened his mouth to respond, but before he could speak the chamberlain raised a hand.

'However, it's clear to me that you both possess some rare qualities that might sit well in the service of the throne, at least while I'm consolidating my grip on the city. Two men such as yourselves, backed up by two cohorts of battle-hardened men with no existing political allegiances? Yes, Tribune, obviously I had you investigated as well. It's an old name, they tell me, and once a proud one, now simply struggling to survive with no ties to any of the major families. All in all, I'd say that your continued presence in Rome might well be the answer to my most fervent prayers. So I won't *hear* of your leaving for Britannia until I've extorted one or two trifling favours from you. And gentlemen, just in case you miss my meaning, I used the word *extort* then in the full sense of its meaning. This really isn't a request in which you have any choice.'

He turned away, calling back over his shoulder.

'I'd return to your barracks if I were you, and take some time to show your men the sights of the city. You'll be earning the corn you consume, *and* the gold you spend . . .' He turned back and winked at Scaurus, who met his gaze unblinkingly. 'Yes, you'll earn them both when I finally decide to which of my many problems you're the best answer.'

Tribune and centurion watched as he walked away up the steps and disappeared back into the palace. After a long thoughtful pause Scaurus spoke, clapping a hand to Marcus's shoulder.

'Well now, Centurion, if you're an attack dog then I'd say it's time to get you back to your kennel. It seems we'll be here a while longer, and after all that excitement you're probably feeling as much in need of a bath and a quiet period of reflection in the Mithraeum as I am. Blood spilled in that fashion has a habit of seeping into the soul as well as the pores.'

Marcus nodded.

'Indeed, Tribune. Although I'll be praying to Our Father to grant me the opportunity to shed the blood of the other men I intend to see dead before I leave the city myself, rather than watch another man spill it for me.'

Scaurus shrugged, turning to walk down the steps to where their men were waiting.

'I don't know. It isn't every man that can say they've had their vengeance delivered by an emperor.'

Marcus stared out over the Circus's massive stadium before replying.

'That's true, sir. But if I'm to find peace from my father's ghost I have to deal with his killers myself, not stand by while other men put them to the sword.'

The tribune turned back and looked quizzically back up the steps at him.

'It's not as if you even know whom you're dealing with, beyond the name under which they do the throne's dirty work.'

The young Roman shrugged.

'I'll know soon enough, Tribune. There are men in this city who know their names, and they'll have one simple choice to make, to either aid me or obstruct me. And if they fear what the "Emperor's Knives" will do to them if their betrayal is discovered, they'll soon enough learn to fear the consequences of refusing me a good deal more. Tomorrow I'll bathe, and make my peace with our god, but once that's done I'll be a servant of another god until this matter is dealt with and my family's honour is avenged.'

He looked out over the sleeping city, clenching a fist and answering Scaurus's questioning look with a single word, his voice harsh with his pent-up fury and eagerness to carve a bloody path through Rome, to hunt down and kill his father's murderers.

'Nemesis.'

THE ANTONINE WALL

For a long time overshadowed by its more famous cousin to the south, the wall constructed at the start of the reign of the emperor Antoninus Pius in AD139–142 is now considered to be just as important from a historical perspective as the comparable frontier defence constructed by the emperor Hadrian across northern Britain only two decades before. It was granted World Heritage Site status in 2008, alongside sites in Germany, Austria, Slovakia, Poland and Hungary as part of the Roman Empire World Heritage Site, which also includes both Hadrian's Wall and the Upper Raetian German frontier defences. From the perspective of a historical fiction author whose work is at least partially set in late second-century Britannia, and at a time when this northernmost line of defence which had been abandoned in the early 160s may have been sporadically reoccupied, it was too good an opportunity to miss.

But, to start at the beginning, why would the Romans have gone to the considerable effort of constructing another frontier defence only a hundred miles north of the first one, and so soon after the completion of Hadrian's perfectly serviceable construction? The most obvious answer is that the move to the Forth-Clyde isthmus allowed a much shorter line of defence than the Tyne-Solway line taken by Hadrian's engineers, but we can see from the records of the units which served on this new frontier that this was in reality of little real benefit. Given that the line of this new wall was guarded by roughly the same number of men as that used on Hadrian's Wall (about seven thousand, only a thousand less), the implication is that the significant reduction in frontage did nothing to reduce the troop strength deemed necessary to hold it.

This may well have been a direct consequence of the forward strategy that the emperor consciously chose on taking power, bringing Roman power toe to toe with hostile tribes who had previously been kept at arm's length by the client kingdoms to the north of Hadrian's Wall. Additionally, the ground to the north of the new frontier was probably harder to police than that to the south of its barrier. This might seem counterintuitive, since it was mainly unsettled wilderness, but in reality settled farmland would have been far less forgiving of armed intruders from the north – due to the farmers' understanding of the likely consequences of assisting Rome's enemies – than the empty land that the army was now faced with. Certainly the greatest concentration of Rome's force on Hadrian's Wall appears to have faced what is now known as the Waste of Spadeadam, an area so desolate that it has been given over to an extensive military weapons testing range, and where there were no native farmers to pose a problem for infiltrating raiders. The sheer difficulty of some of the ground over which the defenders had to operate would also have added to the difficulties involved. But if the move north was not likely to generate any efficiency savings in manpower – and the Roman army will have known that all too well – then what was the point of the move?

The answer appears to have been a depressingly familiar one – imperial prestige. Historians hypothesise that while Antoninus Pius did have some good military reasons to reposition the northern frontier, quite apart from any desire to harden his image as a new and militarily untried emperor, it is nevertheless instructive that he deliberately chose to make Britain the place where he would win his first victory – and that he never felt the need to take the title Imperator again in a lengthy reign and despite successive victories elsewhere in the empire. The advance north is likely have been relatively unopposed, given that the Romans had been that way before in the time of Agricola and had plenty of time to prepare the military and political ground. Once the Roman military juggernaut started its move northwards there was simply no way for the lightly armed and armoured tribesmen to defeat the legions and their supporting auxiliaries in open battle. It would therefore appear that the new emperor was pretty much assured of a victory in northern Britannia, once the decision had been made to annex the buffer zone to the north of Hadrian's frontier, and this clearly made the expansion into Scotland a fairly safe bet as a means of strengthening his image.

With the advance complete the army not only built a wall every bit as imposing as that to the south, but also constructed a road onwards into the north, past the current-day location of Stirling and as far into barbarian territory as Bertha on the river Tay. At least four major forts were positioned along this road, to fulfil the same function as the road north from Hadrian's Wall to Trimontium (modern-day Melrose) in southern Scotland did for Hadrian's Wall. As is the case with Hadrian's Wall, this forward projection of Rome's power beyond the frontier provides us with a clear indication as to the new wall's real purpose.

Rather than being a fighting platform, the Antonine Wall was a clear and unmistakeable delineation of Roman territory from that of the uncivilised peoples to the north. It served to make very clear where the empire's boundaries lay, and was used as a customs barrier to enable trade between the two to be carried out on a controlled (and therefore taxed) basis. The men based along its length who were, we should remember, among the best trained and equipped soldiers on the planet, were in no way condemned to a Maginot Line style of static defence. Apart from power projection into the barbarian hinterland, cowing the locals with visible displays of their formidable equipment and discipline, the forts to the north of the new frontier served the further twin purposes of intelligence gathering and early warning for the main line of defence. Their function, if it came to war with the tribes, was to allow time for the legions and cohorts to deploy forward and strike at any attacking force *en masse* – although there is no evidence that this wall, unlike the one to the south which was overrun more than once, was ever tested in such an overt way. Little more than twenty years after its construction the northern line of defence was abandoned and Roman power was withdrawn south to reoccupy the former frontier. Just as with the advance north twenty years before this change of strategy raises a question. Why, when there seems to have been no compelling military reason, would the army have undertaken what must have seemed an embarrassing retreat?

This decision was almost certainly made by the same emperor who had ordered the move north in the first place, Antoninus Pius, as he approached the end of his reign in the late 150s. Ironically, it is quite possible that one of his advisors (for he is known to have been assiduous in seeking counsel before making the big decisions) may have been Lollicus Urbicus, the man who built the new wall on the Forth-Clyde line for him and who was by now prefect of the city of Rome. It seems from archaeological evidence that the army in Britannia, both legionary and auxiliary, was becoming stretched as men were sent elsewhere in the empire to bolster other frontiers. And the praetorian prefect, a major influence in military affairs, had just retired after twenty years, which in turn may have cleared the way for a thorough and probably long-overdue review of troop commitments.

Given that the initial decision to deploy the army further north had been made mainly for political reasons, it feels likely that the men who formulated Rome's military strategy would have welcomed the decision to move south again, and that after twenty years of existence the revised northern frontier would no longer have represented new and therefore inviolable imperial policy. After all, Antoninus Pius had already enjoyed the acclamation of senate and people for defeating the northern tribes and taking their land, and there was little more to be gained from keeping that ground, given the paucity of any desirable resources such as gold or lead to be exploited. In purely financial terms the balance sheet on the revised northern frontier in Britannia simply did not add up by comparison to the way in which a province like Dacia could be seen to provide financial benefit to the empire through its abundance of precious metals. After so long on the throne, and with no obvious challenge to his rule, Antoninus Pius would probably have been perfectly relaxed about the apparent benefits of shortening the army's lines of supply, and pulling back to a line of defence that, with the benefit of experience, was deemed to be more suitable for the long term.

And so the army destroyed what it could, buried what could not be burned or carted away and conducted a controlled with-drawal to the south, reoccupying Hadrian's Wall and reinstating the previous buffer zone to the old wall's north through its control of the Selgovae and Votadini kingdoms. The Antonine line may have been reoccupied, with the military expedition into Scotland in AD 208–210 as the most likely occasion for some refurbishment (and don't worry, readers, we'll be there with Marcus Valerius Aquila alongside the emperor Septimius Severus and his warring sons in the fullness of time), but there is no definitive evidence for any such re-occupation. The wall was left to a slow deterioration, its forts destroyed but its major features, the turf wall and ditch, left intact to slowly slide into ruin over the course of the next two millennia.

If you want to know more about this under-regarded piece of ancient history on our doorstep, so to speak, I heartily recommend David Breeze's excellent *The Antonine Wall*. As with his work on Hadrian's Wall written with Brian Dobson, he has distilled pretty much everything worth knowing about the subject into an acces-sible and engrossing book which informs the reader without ever patronising.

One last (but, as before with this issue, important) point, that of place naming. Not very much is known about the names that were given to the wall forts along this short-lived imperial frontier, mainly due to the fact that by contrast with Hadrian's Wall, which was manned for almost three hundred years, the Antonine Wall's existence was fleetingly brief. We have two main sources of information in this respect, the *Notitia Dignitatum* (literally a List of the Dignitaries), a record of the empire's official posts and military units at the end of the 4th century, and the *Ravenna Cosmography*, a list of all towns and road stations throughout the Roman empire which was compiled from a variety of maps in about AD 700 by an anonymous monk in Ravenna.

Whilst the former is a contemporaneous review of the empire it was carried out two hundred years after the wall was abandoned for the last time, while the latter relied on cartographic material no less than five hundred years after that final occupation – which makes it unsurprising that neither provide us with very much help as to what the forts were actually called by the Romans.

Given this absence of any meaningful information I have been forced to use my imagination in coming up with two of the three fort names used, while one is more probable than definite in its provenance. 'Broad View Fort', modern day Mumrills, was, it is hypothesised, probably Volitanio, the 'rather broad place'. 'Lazy Hill', modern day Falkirk, is my own invention in the absence of anything more concrete, as is the use of the name 'Gateway Fort' for modern day Camelon. The name felt appropriate for an outpost which, being too close to the wall to offer any significant early warning of an attack from the north, has the look of a customs and border control point.

As usual, any and all errors in these and other historical inter-pretations are all my own work!

By the late second century, the point at which the *Empire* series begins, the Imperial Roman Army had long since evolved into a stable organization with a stable *modus operandi*. Thirty or so **legions** (there's still some debate about the 9th Legion's fate), each with an official strength of 5,500 legionaries, formed the army's 165,000-man heavy infantry backbone, while 360 or so **auxiliary cohorts** (each of them the equivalent of a 600-man infantry battalion) provided another 217,000 soldiers for the empire's defence.

Positioned mainly in the empire's border provinces, these forces performed two main tasks. Whilst ostensibly providing a strong means of defence against external attack, their role was just as much about maintaining Roman rule in the most challenging of the empire's subject territories. It was no coincidence that the troublesome provinces of Britain and Dacia were deemed to require 60 and 44 auxiliary cohorts respectively, almost a quarter of the total available. It should be noted, however, that whilst their overall strategic task was the same, the terms under the two halves of the army served were quite different.

The legions, the primary Roman military unit for conducting warfare at the operational or theatre level, had been in existence since early in the Republic, hundreds of years before. They were composed mainly of close-order heavy infantry, well-drilled and highly motivated, recruited on a professional basis and, critically to an understanding of their place in Roman society, manned by soldiers who were Roman citizens. The jobless poor were thus provided with a route to both citizenship and a valuable trade, since service with the legions was as much about construction

THE CHAIN OF COMMAND
LEGION

LEGATUS — LEGION
CAVALRY
(120 HORSEMEN)

BROAD STRIPE
TRIBUNE

5 'MILITARY'
NARROW
STRIPE
TRIBUNES

CAMP PREFECT

SENIOR CENTURION

10 COHORTS
(ONE OF 5 CENTURIES OF 160 MEN EACH)
(NINE OF 6 CENTURIES OF 80 MEN EACH)

CENTURION

CHOSEN MAN

WATCH OFFICER   STANDARD BEARER

10 TENT PARTIES OF
8 MEN APIECE

THE CHAIN OF COMMAND
AUXILARY
INFANTRY COHORT

LEGATUS

PREFECT

(OR A TRIBUNE FOR A LARGER COHORT SUCH AS
THE FIRST TUNGRIAN)

SENIOR CENTURION

6-10 CENTURIES

CENTURION

CHOSEN MAN

WATCH OFFICER   STANDARD BEARER

10 TENT PARTIES OF
8 MEN APIECE

– fortresses, roads, and even major defensive works such as Hadrian's Wall – as destruction. Vitally for the maintenance of the empire's borders, this attractiveness of service made a large standing field army a possibility, and allowed for both the control and defence of the conquered territories.

By this point in Britannia's history three legions were positioned to control the restive peoples both beyond and behind the province's borders. These were the 2nd, based in South Wales, the 20th, watching North Wales, and the 6th, positioned to the east of the Pennine range and ready to respond to any trouble on the northern frontier. Each of these legions was commanded by a **legatus**, an experienced man of senatorial rank deemed worthy of the responsibility and appointed by the emperor. The command structure beneath the legatus was a delicate balance, combining the requirement for training and advancing Rome's young aristocrats for their future roles with the necessity for the legion to be led into battle by experienced and hardened officers.

Directly beneath the legatus were a half-dozen or so **military tribunes**, one of them a young man of the senatorial class called the **broad stripe tribune** after the broad senatorial stripe on his tunic. This relatively inexperienced man – it would have been his first official position – acted as the legion's second-in-command, despite being a relatively tender age when compared with the men around him. The remainder of the military tribunes were **narrow stripes**, men of the equestrian class who usually already had some command experience under their belts from leading an auxiliary cohort. Intriguingly, since the more experienced narrow-stripe tribunes effectively reported to the broad stripe, such a reversal of the usual military conventions around fitness for command must have made for some interesting man-management situations. The legion's third in command was the camp **prefect**, an older and more experienced soldier, usually a former centurion deemed worthy of one last role in the legion's service before retirement, usually for one year. He would by necessity have been a steady hand, operating as the voice of experience in advising the legion's senior officers as to the realities of warfare and the management of the legion's soldiers.

Reporting into this command structure were ten **cohorts** of soldiers, each one composed of a number of eighty-man **centuries**. Each century was a collection of ten **tent parties** – eight men who literally shared a tent when out in the field. Nine of the cohorts had six centuries, and an establishment strength of 480 men, whilst the prestigious **first cohort**, commanded by the legion's **senior centurion**, was composed of five double-strength centuries and therefore fielded 800 soldiers when fully manned. This organization provided the legion with its cutting edge: 5,000 or so well-trained heavy infantrymen operating in regiment and company sized units, and led by battle-hardened officers, the legion's centurions, men whose position was usually achieved by dint of their demonstrated leadership skills.

The rank of **centurion** was pretty much the peak of achievement for an ambitious soldier, commanding an eighty-man century and paid ten times as much as the men each officer commanded. Whilst the majority of centurions were promoted from the ranks, some were appointed from above as a result of patronage, or as a result of having completed their service in the **Praetorian Guard**, which had a shorter period of service than the legions. That these externally imposed centurions would have undergone their very own 'sink or swim' moment in dealing with their new colleagues is an unavoidable conclusion, for the role was one that by necessity led from the front, and as a result suffered disproportionate casualties. This makes it highly likely that any such appointee felt unlikely to make the grade in action would have received very short shrift from his brother officers.

A small but necessarily effective team reported to the centurion. The **optio**, literally 'best' or **chosen man**, was his second-in-command, and stood behind the century in action with a long brass-knobbed stick, literally pushing the soldiers into the fight should the need arise. This seems to have been a remarkably efficient way of managing a large body of men, given the centurion's place alongside rather than behind his soldiers, and the optio would have been a cool head, paid twice the usual soldier's wage and a candidate for promotion to centurion if he performed well.

The century's third-in-command was the **tesserarius** or **watch officer**, ostensibly charged with ensuring that sentries were posted and that everyone know the watch word for the day, but also likely to have been responsible for the profusion of tasks such as checking the soldiers' weapons and equipment, ensuring the maintenance of discipline and so on, that have occupied the lives of junior non-commissioned officers throughout history in delivering a combat-effective unit to their officer. The last member of the centurion's team was the century's **signifer**, the **standard bearer**, who both provided a rallying point for the soldiers and helped the centurion by transmitting marching orders to them through movements of his standard. Interestingly, he also functioned as the century's banker, dealing with the soldiers' financial affairs. While a soldier caught in the horror of battle might have thought twice about defending his unit's standard, he might well also have felt a stronger attachment to the man who managed his money for him!

At the shop-floor level were the eight soldiers of the tent party who shared a leather tent and messed together, their tent and cooking gear carried on a mule when the legion was on the march. Each tent party would inevitably have established its own pecking order based upon the time-honoured factors of strength, aggression, intelligence – and the rough humour required to survive in such a harsh world. The men that came to dominate their tent parties would have been the century's unofficial backbone, candidates for promotion to watch officer. They would also have been vital to their tent mates' cohesion under battlefield conditions, when the relatively thin leadership team could not always exert sufficient presence to inspire the individual soldier to stand and fight amid the horrific chaos of combat.

The other element of the legion was a small 120-man detachment of **cavalry**, used for scouting and the carrying of messages between units. The regular army depended on auxiliary **cavalry wings**, drawn from those parts of the empire where horsemanship was a way of life, for their mounted combat arm. Which leads us to consider the other side of the army's two-tier system.

The **auxiliary cohorts**, unlike the legions alongside which they fought, were not Roman citizens, although the completion of a twenty-five-year term of service did grant both the soldier and his children citizenship. The original auxiliary cohorts had often served in their homelands, as a means of controlling the threat of large numbers of freshly conquered barbarian warriors, but this changed after the events of the first century AD. The Batavian revolt in particular – when the 5,000-strong Batavian cohorts rebelled and destroyed two Roman legions after suffering intolerable provocation during a recruiting campaign gone wrong – was the spur for the Flavian policy for these cohorts to be posted away from their home provinces. The last thing any Roman general wanted was to find his legions facing an army equipped and trained to fight in the same way. This is why the reader will find the auxiliary cohorts described in the *Empire* series, true to the historical record, representing a variety of other parts of the empire, including Tungria, which is now part of modern-day Belgium.

Auxiliary infantry was equipped and organized in so close a manner to the legions that the casual observer would have been hard put to spot the differences. Often their armour would be mail, rather than plate, sometimes weapons would have minor differences, but in most respects an auxiliary cohort would be the same proposition to an enemy as a legion cohort. Indeed there are hints from history that the auxiliaries may have presented a greater challenge on the battlefield. At the battle of Mons Graupius in Scotland, Tacitus records that four cohorts of Batavians and two of Tungrians were sent in ahead of the legions and managed to defeat the enemy without requiring any significant assistance. Auxiliary cohorts were also often used on the flanks of the battle line, where reliable and well drilled troops are essential to handle attempts to outflank the army. And while the legions contained soldiers who were as much tradesmen as fighting men, the auxiliary cohorts were primarily focused on their fighting skills. By the end of the second century there were significantly more auxiliary troops serving the empire than were available from the legions, and it is clear that Hadrian's Wall would have been invalid as a concept without the mass of infantry and mixed infantry/cavalry cohorts that were stationed along its length.

As for horsemen, the importance of the empire's 75,000 or so **auxiliary cavalrymen**, capable of much faster deployment and manoeuvre than the infantry, and essential for successful scouting, fast communications and the denial of reconnaissance information to the enemy cannot be overstated. Rome simply did not produce anything like the strength in mounted troops needed to avoid being at a serious disadvantage against those nations which by their nature were cavalry-rich. As a result, as each such nation was conquered their mounted forces were swiftly incorporated into the army until, by the early first century BC, the decision was made to disband what native Roman cavalry as there was altogether, in favour of the auxiliary cavalry wings.

Named for their usual place on the battlefield, on the flanks or 'wings' of the line of battle, the cavalry cohorts were commanded by men of the equestrian class with prior experience as legion military tribunes, and were organized around the basic 32-man **turma**, or squadron. Each squadron was commanded by a **decurion**, a position analogous with that of the infantry centurion. This officer was assisted by a pair of junior officers: the **duplicarius** or **double-pay**, equivalent to the role of optio, and the **sesquipilarius** or **pay-and-a-half**, equal in stature to the infantry watch officer. As befitted the cavalry's more important military role, each of these ranks was paid about 40 per cent more than the infantry equivalent.

Taken together, the legions and their auxiliary support presented a standing army of over 400,000 men by the time of the events described in the *Empire* series. Whilst this was sufficient to both hold down and defend the empire's 6.5 million square kilometres for a long period of history, the strains of defending a 5,000-kilometre-long frontier, beset on all sides by hostile tribes, were also beginning to manifest themselves. The prompt move to raise three new legions undertaken by the new emperor Septimius Severus in 197 AD, in readiness for over a decade spent shoring up the empire's crumbling borders, provides clear evidence that there were never enough legions and cohorts for such a monumental task. This is the backdrop for the *Empire* series, which will run from 182 AD well into the early third century, following both the empire's and Marcus Valerius Aquila's travails throughout this fascinatingly brutal period of history.